THEIR

TANGLED FATES

THEIR TANGLED FATES

TANGLED AND TRUE
DUOLOGY: BOOK 1

BRIELLA BREZZO

Developmental editing by Scribbling Crow, Ink, LLC
Line and copy editing by Ash Tree Editing

Book cover art & design by Julia Rohwedder
www.LunaryxDesign.com

ISBN 979-8-9939371-0-6 (paperback)

Published by Briella Brezzo
United States

First Edition 2026

Content Warnings

The *Tangled and True* duology references and portrays multiple forms of ongoing physical and emotional abuse, manipulation, and loss of personal agency. While no sexual violence occurs on page, rape is mentioned, threatened, and imagined.

Both books explore fantasy drug use and addiction. They include blood, violence, offensive/sexual language, and open-door spice.

For my children:

may you be scarred for life if you ever read this.

Prologue

Gethin

My son's screams fill the dining room, piercing my eardrums as the cold northern wind gusts through the windows. He sits red-faced across the table, his young mind lost in a tantrum, momentarily forgetting what his mother can do to him.

If I could, I'd take Taran and run, putting as much space between her and us as possible. But I can't. I'm trapped in place—a prisoner in my own body.

Eating blueberries.

My wife had to willbend me. To force me, with the same magic that bends the people of Aedys to her rule. If it were up to me, I wouldn't eat. As it is, I follow the order at the barest edge of its limits. One at a time, grinding each to a pulp. Silently counting the breaths until her next command.

"Stop it, Taran."

Esyllt's voice is sharp. Demanding. But not a bending. She needs to be careful when we're together like this. If she bends him too many times, she'll risk losing control of me.

I hate myself for wishing she'd make that mistake. He's been through enough.

Taran shuts his mouth, his eyes wide and glistening. His lip quivers as realization flickers across his face—he's still free.

"Leave him be," I say, pushing the words out between chews.

She focuses her glare on me. "Such behavior is unacceptable for a prince."

"He's five."

Her eyes narrow. When she speaks, her voice echoes through my mind. "Keep your opinions to yourself."

My hand wavers against the smooth stone of my plate, no longer compelled to move on its own; she nullified her earlier command. I shove another blueberry in my mouth, praying she doesn't realize her misstep. Not that it matters. Anything I try, she can stop with a single word.

I shift my gaze back to Taran. He looks so much like his mother, with his dark hair and green eyes. *How is it that I can love a child with her face?*

A quiet, claiming touch. My skin crawls as Esyllt runs her fingers along my arm. I pull away, sliding my hand beneath the wooden table while continuing to eat blueberries with the other.

She turns her attention back to our son. "Eat your meat."

"I don't want to."

Her thin brows press together, sharp against her pale skin. "You will eat it on your own, or I will make you eat it."

"No! You eat it!" Taran's voice, shrill with the spark of another tantrum, echoes through the dining room. Through my bones.

A bending.

My stomach drops. Before it hits the floor, my hand collides with Esyllt's as we snatch slices of steak from his plate, cramming them into our mouths. Servants rush to Taran's side, fighting for the remains. He curls up, screaming. Terrified.

He's never bent anyone before. And to compel the entire room... He's stronger than his mother. Much stronger.

Esyllt's eyes widen, nostrils flaring with fury that shudders through me as she frantically chews, unable to speak with her mouth packed with gnashed meat. She scans the table, landing on an obsidian knife, then her eyes flick back to Taran.

Dread fills me, outpaced by a surge of panic.

She seizes the blade, raising it toward my son, lunging for him.

I grab my plate and smash it against her skull.

Time stops as she crumples onto the soft fur rug. The knife falls, its tip splintering as it clatters against the table. The servants stare, unsure what to do next. Taran's eyes tremble as he peeks up, silently meeting mine.

My gaze drops to Esyllt, sprawled on the floor. Her eyelids flutter, and time rushes back into motion. I swallow the rest of the meat, washing it down with a cup of wine.

"Take Taran to his room." *He shouldn't be here for this.*

"Yes, Your Majesty." A servant takes his hand, ushering him away.

I lean over my wife. Death is a mercy she doesn't deserve. She should suffer, trapped in her misery, like she imprisoned me for the last century.

I can't willbend—that's a bloodline ability—and it would be cruel to ask it of Taran. But like all fae, I can curse.

I weave it quickly, pressing my hand against her chest. Her heart thuds beneath my palm.

A curse of exile. Let her rot among the mortals she despises, powerless and alone.

Until my final breath.

Part 1

Entwined

Chapter 1

Ellie

Charcoal scrapes along paper. Crisp gray lines and a gentle curve of laughter, brightening his smile. I hesitate, then blend the soft shadows of his lips with my pinky, heat rising in my cheeks.

I tilt the sketchbook up, eyeing my subject from across the room. A gentleman, likely a few years older than me, sharing breakfast with his love. His fingers entwine with hers, resting on the battered table between plates full of eggs, toast, and boiled tomatoes.

There's a spark in his eye—a joy—that I haven't captured.

Mom taps my elbow. She tilts her head close, caramel curls tucked beneath a stylishly askew, lace-trimmed hat. "You need to eat. There may not be another chance before your placement exams."

Pressing my lips together, I snap the leather-bound pages shut. "I'm not hungry."

"Are you nervous?"

"It's impossible not to be," I mumble, then glance around the inn's chilly breakfast room, resisting the urge to reinvigorate the hearth's dying flames with an incantation. At least it's quiet, with no other guests besides us and the couple; my nerves would likely be screaming otherwise. "Where's Father?"

"Already calling the carriage." She tucks back the rebellious wisps that escaped my hastily twisted bun. "Try not to stress over it—there's not a doubt in my mind you'll do well."

A weight bears down on my shoulder, startling me despite its familiarity. "Of course she will," Father's voice rumbles. He pulls his hand away, unbuttoning his violet tailcoat as he slides into the seat opposite Mom and me. Thankfully, he agreed to forgo his full Order regalia today.

"We should leave soon," he says, glancing at the wall clock. "Exams begin at eighth bell, and at this rate, I doubt we'll make it before midday."

Lovely—I'll be lucky to get a full bell to settle in. Mom nods at my plate, so I scarf down a few forkfuls of egg, despite my lack of appetite, then reach for my glass. Empty.

Curves and angles form a circular pattern in my mind, and I silently run through an incantation, drawing power from beneath the foundations. Crystal-clear water fills the vessel at my fingertips.

"Ellie!" Mom's voice is sharp, as is the shake of her head.

My fingers jerk away from the glass. "Right. Sorry."

While it's not as if a single incantation will ruin the furniture, it *is* illegal outside of Academy grounds and members of the Order— a fact I need to get used to now that I'm leaving home. Father's status has always given me leeway, not that most people ever noticed me doing it. I spent most of my life not realizing it was forbidden, assuming everyone else simply lacked the resources to learn or wished to avoid its negative effects.

My elbows tuck in, shoulders hunching. Father eyes me, then clears his throat. "You needn't concern yourself with that. Your professors will see your skill as proof of your dedication to the fight."

Right. *My* dedication. As if following in his footsteps was *my* choice, and not the only option for the daughter of a noble who won't inherit it herself. To someday serve under him, awaiting the day the fae inevitably invade again. No one knows why their attacks stopped, but two decades of peace is nothing compared to the millennia of war that's plagued our people.

"Come along now," he says, giving Mom his hand as she gets to her feet. "We don't want to be late."

I slather some strawberry jelly on my toast, then hurry after them.

Pausing at the door, I peek back at the happy couple. The spark remains, lighting both their faces as they lean close, whispering. After a moment, the woman glances in my direction, raising her eyebrow. I jump, almost colliding with the doorframe in my rush to escape. My face burns, shame and envy winding tightly around my ribs.

Someday, I tell myself, hoping to relieve the ache. And today is the first step. It may be along my father's path, but it's still my first taste of freedom from a life sequestered in solitary study. A chance to finally connect with others.

I shiver as I step out of the inn, my linen blouse a poor shield against winter's bite. Our two carriages await on the lone dirt road of this small town—simply another stop on the three-day journey to the Arandur Academy of Incantation. Eunice, my mother's maid, holds out my coat. I slide my arms into it while my father helps Mom into our family carriage, then she steps in front of me to help with buttoning.

"How's the journey been for you?" I ask. It seems better than discussing the weather.

"Comfortable enough, Miss."

"Was your room warm? Mine was a bit nippy." I cringe as the words leave my mouth. *So much for steering clear of the temperature.*

She glances at the handsome footman loading the last of our luggage, then turns back to me, a smile tugging at her lips. "Warm enough, Miss."

Lucky her.

A snap pierces the air, and one of the horses tosses its head with an irritated whinny. The trace connecting it to the servants' carriage dangles at its side. It's nothing I can help with—even if incanting weren't outlawed, it can't fix torn leather.

"What a way to start the day," Eunice murmurs. When I can't think of a response, she brushes a speck of lint from my sleeve. "I'm sure they'll resolve it in no time, Miss." Then she steps back, no doubt hoping to avoid any further conversation.

So I stand there, nibbling the remains of my toast while my father exchanges words with the coachman. Just as I'm finishing, he heads over.

"We'll move your bag and go on without them," he says, offering his arm. He leads me to our carriage, where I sit on the bench opposite him and Mom.

A sigh escapes me as I peer out the window. *Only four bells to go.* I lean back, closing my eyes while my parents' voices drone to the sway of the carriage. Before I know it, something presses against my knee.

"We've arrived," Mom says, pulling her fingers away.

Rubbing my eyes, I peek out the window, then at my father. "Can you stay here?" I ask. "Please?"

"Of course not. I'm to speak before the exams."

"You can head over separately, Hiram," Mom says. "She doesn't need everyone to witness her arriving with the High Marshal."

Wrinkles form at the corners of his eyes as he considers me. My mother often speaks of how they sparkled like the sea when she first met him, but all I've ever known is the gray of an impending storm.

His lips tighten beneath his mustache, and he nods. "Very well." But before relief can wash over me, he plants his hand heavily on my shoulder. "I know I don't say it enough, but I'm proud of the woman you've become."

It's the closest he'll get to 'I love you.'

My fingers clench in my lap—I can't sit in this carriage any longer. "I won't let you down," I say, hoping it's enough. Unless the fae renew the wars, the only way I'll be able to secure my place as his successor is through skill and fortitude miles beyond anyone else.

After a torturous moment of searching my face, Father knocks on the carriage door. It pops open, the footman extending his hand.

With a deep exhale, I step out to face my new life.

Beyond the crowd buzzing with excited faces, my gaze lands on the rectangular building looming before me, tracing the sharp edges of bricks whose color has long since faded. It's one of many similarly drab structures in this ocean of dirt that looks more like ash, where not even a single blade of grass can survive the drain of constant incanting. Wooden window frames and decorative tiles form uniform rows on its facade, all in dispiriting shades of gray.

Mom steps out beside me, overdressed in her bright, rose-colored skirt and matching jacket. She exchanges some words with the footman, who hands me my bag—it holds only the bare essentials, save my sketchbook. No one brings any prized possessions here, as their vibrancy would slowly dull to nothing. Leaving my paints behind had gutted me.

With a sharp crack of a whip, wheels creak and the carriage rolls away, taking Father to wherever the exams will occur.

Almost free.

I pull my coat tight, seeking warmth against the cold that might as well be emanating from the building itself. "I knew they started term in the winter to ease the transition, but this…" I meet Mom's gaze. "This is bleak."

She bites her lip. "Perhaps that's why they allow students to visit the village so often," she offers.

The village. Right.

I glance behind me. Just a silhouette of dilapidated shacks against the cloudy sky. Beyond that, a rainbow-painted clock tower rises like a beacon of hope, fighting to outshine the gloom.

Mom rests her hand on my shoulder. "Let's get you checked in."

I'm itching beneath the skin as I follow her through the swarm, people pressing all around me, until we find a table of third-years doling out room assignments. Together, we pass through the massive entry doors—the only spot of color on the entire building. My fingers trail along the violet paint that coats them so thick, you'd hardly know they were wood. It chips away at the edges, revealing gray underneath.

We navigate the teeming hallways to a door on the second floor whose number matches my key. With a deep breath, I turn the knob and let us in.

"This is just dreadful! Why couldn't we get a room facing Haven?" A girl with thick hair flowing past her shoulders throws open the ashen curtains of the sitting room, filling the space with pale sunlight. Half her locks, black as the night sky, are pinned up in intricate braids. Compared to her, I must look like an unkempt mess.

"I'm sure there's someone you can bat your eyelashes at for a better view," says a dark-haired man, probably fifteen years my senior. He lounges on one of the two purple damask armchairs in the center of the room, feet propped up on a slate table between him and the matching settee.

I glance nervously at my mom, whose mahogany eyes practically fell from their sockets at his suggestion.

This is it. My first chance to make a friend.

"Hi, I'm Ellie!" I bite back a wince, hoping that didn't sound too eager.

The girl hops down from the bench she was standing on, playfully smacking the man's head as she bounces over. While she's unbuttoned her blouse low enough to tease her cleavage, the sky-blue scarf wrapped around her neck keeps her within the bounds of modesty. If only I could be so daring.

I raise my hand toward her, but she ignores it, yanking me into an exuberant hug. My luggage slips from my grasp, thudding against the floor.

"I'm Alexis!" she says, still gripping my shoulders. Her green eyes sparkle along with the abundance of silver rings in her ears. "That's my uncle, Arron. Ignore him."

The tension that coiled up at her greeting loosens; I'm not the only one with a parental figure in tow.

She releases me to gesture around the room. "What do you think of our lovely accommodations?"

"What's with all the purple?" Arron interrupts.

"It takes the longest to fade," I say, jumping at the familiar topic. "It's the color least found in nature. The hardest one for plants and animals to make."

"Huh." Alexis shrugs, then points at one of the doors. "Well, there's a bathing chamber and three bedrooms, but only two have windows—would you like a view of dirt or a prison cell?"

My nerves tighten again. "Maybe we should wait for our third to arrive? I don't want to get off on the wrong foot."

Arron's face tugs into a smirk. "You should fight for it. First to yield gets the cell."

He's joking, right? I look to my mom, who's eyeing Arron warily as she shakes Alexis's hand.

"I'm Ellie's mother, Grace," she says. "It's been nice meeting you, but I should find my husband."

Alexis's mouth twists in amusement. Mom lets go of her hand, then pulls me to the door.

"I don't want to be in the way," she whispers, meeting my eyes. "Know that we love you. I'm certain you'll place well, and find something here that brings you joy."

"Mom…" My insides twist between giving her the heartfelt goodbye she deserves and avoiding embarrassing myself in front of Alexis.

"Yes, it's dreary, but the people are certainly colorful." She glances briefly at Alexis, who's busied herself checking for dust on the gray wainscoting. "Try to enjoy yourself."

"I will. I'll work hard, make you proud, and make friends." Two expectations, and one for me. Assuming I'm any good at that. Even when the opportunity arose for me to spend time around people my age, because of my father's position, I was a commoner among the nobility. No one wanted to associate with that.

Mom runs her hand along my hairline. "I'm already proud of you. I *want* you to be happy." A lump forms in my throat as she folds me into a tight embrace. "I love you, Ellie. Remember—don't work too hard. Enjoy your time here."

With one last squeeze of my hand and an awkward wave to the others, she turns and leaves.

I wipe my eyes, unsure if the stinging behind them resulted in any tears but unwilling to take that chance. To avoid interacting with anyone, I peek inside one of the bedroom doors. It's so cramped that even the small bed, writing desk, and wardrobe are suffocating.

This is the room without a window. I'm starting to see some

value in Arron's suggestion.

A door clicks behind me, and a squeal from Alexis signals our third roommate has arrived.

"Hi! I'm Alexis. This is Ellie"—she grabs my arm and tugs me over, my leg bumping against one of the armchairs—"and we're your roommates!"

The girl startles at Alexis's enthusiasm, bringing her bag up in front of her as if to form a barrier. Her pale blond hair looks shoulder-length, but it's tied back in a much neater version of my bun. Wayward strands frame her lightly freckled face, and she tucks some of them behind her ear as she recovers, lowering her bag. She gives a small wave with one hand.

"Hi." Her wave ends abruptly as her grip slips. "Sorry, hi. I'm Sophie."

"Let me help you." Arron crosses the room in a couple of strides and takes her bag. He drops it onto the settee before patting Alexis on the back. "I'm heading out. Have fun, show them what you've got, and don't forget to write." He's halfway to the door by the time he finishes speaking.

"Love you!" Alexis calls after him. He gives a curt wave as he walks out the door without glancing back.

She shrugs at us. "He's not one for long goodbyes."

"He's your uncle?" I ask.

"Yep. Raised me since I was two. My parents died in the last of the Border Wars. He was sixteen when he took me in."

My eyebrows scrunch as I work out the math. Sophie takes the easy route, asking her age—twenty-three—then shares that she's twenty-one, a hint of relief in her expression. They both turn to me, faces expectant.

"Twenty." I keep my voice as neutral as possible. That's the minimum age to attend the Academy, and what's typically expected—incanters wield an impressive amount of power, so they need a certain level of maturity. The last thing I want is for my roommates to feel judged for being older.

"Aw, you're the baby." Alexis squeezes my arm. "Don't worry, I'll make sure you stay safe."

Then she skips to the center of the room, turning with a flourish. "Now then. We each get our own room, but one of them"—she points dramatically to the one I peeked in earlier—"doesn't have a window. I say we go by placement results. We pick in order of who does best."

Sophie frowns. "We don't need any extra pressure."

Alexis waves her hand dismissively. "Placements are practically meaningless—they just decide our starting point. This will give them actual stakes."

"I don't think that's fair," I say, peeking at the door to the room in question, slightly ajar. While I'm confident in my ability, I'd hate for anyone to feel trapped in that darkness. "No one should be stuck with the bad room for the entire term because of a poor performance on the first day."

"Have either of you incanted before?" Sophie asks.

"Of course not," Alexis says. "Even if it weren't illegal, I'm in no rush to have my eyes turn gray."

The other reason for the Academy's age requirement that I'm all too familiar with. Mine used to be as dark as Mom's, and I likely have another five to ten years before they lose their vibrancy.

Still, my stomach tangles into a knot. How can I reveal that I have without sharing my father's identity? Once people know, they won't see me—just the High Marshal's daughter.

But Alexis and Sophie are my best chance at making friends, so shouldn't I be honest?

I glance away, running my fingers along the coarse wool of the nearby armchair. "I have… some experience."

Alexis widens her eyes. "How mysterious. Care to elaborate?"

"Not really."

I'm burning up as she quirks an eyebrow, praying she doesn't ask more. But she only shrugs, turning to Sophie. "Whatever. I'm still fine with this. Are you?"

Sophie presses her lips together, then nods.

With my nerves unwinding, I agree as well, mostly because we're running out of time before the exams. Perhaps I should've clarified my history, but Alexis seems really excited about competing. I can't afford to ruin her fun.

Hopefully this doesn't backfire horribly.

Chapter 2

Ellie

It takes a few minutes of scrounging through each bedroom's wardrobes to determine whose uniforms are whose. We provided our measurements as part of our applications, and each holds various sets for different weather. Since we don't know what the placement exams will entail, we all opt for the flexibility of pants, the only option being boring gray trousers.

For my top, I choose a white, long-sleeved blouse to help against the cold, while Alexis goes with the sleeveless version, surprisingly. The collar buttons to the top of my neck as the rules of modesty decree, while a plum bodice with vertical gray stripes down its right side goes over it. I grab my charcoal-colored wool coat before rushing from the room.

By the time we all gather, our wall clock shows we're minutes from the eighth bell ringing—the second of the afternoon. Twelve bells apiece for both day and night, and this one signals the start of our placement exams. We race down the stairs, where some lingering third-years point us in the proper direction, following a stream of other stragglers rushing along a stone path that cuts through the endless expanse of dirt toward the Great Hall. It takes up the entire northern wing of the Academy's main building, and a boisterous crowd, larger than I've ever seen, gathers outside its entrance. While I've attended the occasional formal event with my parents, the people at those are typically more spread out, their voices light and constrained.

Thankfully, we're still at its edges when an older gentleman with trim dark hair and a full beard, both flecked with white, marches up the steps in front of the Hall's large exterior doors. The roar of the crowd dissipates as he surveys us.

"Welcome, first-years, to The Arandur Academy of Incantation." His bright voice carries clearly through the air. "I am Headmaster Gleese. I'm sure you're impatient to begin, so allow me to introduce the High Marshal of the Order of Incanters—Lord Hiram Detura."

I shrink down as my father steps up to a roar of applause. Once it settles, he speaks, his voice a low rumble.

"Thank you, Headmaster. Today begins your three-year journey into a life of honor, dedicating yourself to the continued defense of our proud nation. So long as you work hard, there will be a place for you in our nation's forces upon graduation, keeping eternal vigilance against fae incursions."

I avoid his gaze, barely listening to phrases I've heard countless times before. Honor. Duty. Fortitude. My fellow first-years cling to his every word—they all chose to join this army of elite, magical fighters, after all—and his speech ends with an eruption of applause. His eyes briefly meet mine before he moves away and Headmaster Gleese takes over.

"During your time here, you will attend most of your classes with peers of similar ability so we can best support the development of your skills. While we'll examine everyone individually, we'll summon you in smaller groups, in order of your family name. Upon completing your examination, you'll be sorted into classes according to your innate ability. May Fortune favor each of you."

He gives a curt nod that's met with some half-hearted claps

while most of the students chatter amongst themselves. He descends the steps as a wiry woman with curly hair—so pale, it's almost white—hurries to take his place.

"I'm Professor Mallory," she shouts, making me flinch. "If your family name begins with 'A,' please come to the front. We'll begin momentarily."

I clutch my fidgeting fingers in front of me as murmuring voices begin coiling around us. Alexis bounces on her toes and looks between me and Sophie. "I'm 'B,' for Bunt. How about you?"

"'D.'" I glimpse Father beyond the crowd, avoiding eager handshakes from overly bold students as he makes his way to where Mom waits at the carriage. In mere minutes, they'll be gone.

"I'm 'L,'" Sophie says. "Guess I'll be waiting a while."

Alexis stretches her arms above her head. "So, how should we pass the time?"

I snap my attention back to my roommates, my mind racing to conjure up some suggestions.

"We could practice," Sophie offers.

Alexis drops her arms. "There's nothing to practice. Unless you're admitting you've incanted before, too?" She raises her brow at Sophie, whose ears turn red.

"I... may have." Sophie glances away at the confession.

My stomach dips on Alexis's behalf: that's not good for her hopes of getting a window. She won't blame me, will she?

Is making friends always this complicated?

Alexis narrows her gaze. "Nothing like being tricked into a bet under false pretenses," she mutters.

Sophie's face slowly puckers, lips pressed tight. "It's honestly more surprising you haven't," she snaps, and my eyes widen at her bite. "You must not care very much."

"I care plenty, I just don't see a reason to break the law so I can have a slight edge for a month until everyone catches up."

Sophie says nothing. Alexis scoffs, then takes my arm, storming away. I almost trip glancing back, catching Sophie's face pressing into a frown before she marches off. I force what I hope is a sympathetic smile, not wanting her to think I'm taking sides, even though I'm inclined to support Alexis. Sophie clearly agreed only because she realized the odds were in her favor.

"Why don't we see if there's anyone here worthy of our attention?" Alexis says, her gaze drifting to a nearby fellow—lanky, with clean-cut blond hair—like a cat evaluating prey.

My eyes follow the cut of his waistcoat before returning to his face, only to meet his, staring back. He shoots over a confident smile, and I turn away, swallowing down the flutter in my heart. It'd be a lie to say that wasn't one of my few hopes for coming here: to experience for myself what I've desperately tried to capture in my sketches of couples in love. But it's foolish to get my hopes up.

Before I think up a response, Professor Mallory calls for everyone's attention, her voice ringing with the first list of names. After a group of six makes its way inside, I spend the next twenty minutes trying to keep my breathing calm as the cacophony of conversations and laughter assaults my senses. Amid the barrage, I do my best to entertain Alexis with my opinions on the various men that catch her eye. Her tastes cover a wide range, from softer, studious types who light a spark within me, to more broody ones who deliver a shiver straight to my core. Eventually, her name is called, and I turn my focus inward, wandering near the edge crowd. It's too loud, too confining within, but I don't want to draw attention by singling myself out.

Back to being alone.

I kick at the dirt as I meander, scuffing my pristine leather boots, and consider what I told my mom: *I'll make friends.* Despite my social inexperience, Alexis seems to like me, so perhaps I'm off to a good start? But I worry that the tension brewing between her and Sophie will end poorly, and can't help feeling it's my fault for not recognizing Sophie's intentions earlier. I've never had friends to fight with before—how can I possibly be the peacemaker?

Eventually, I catch some 'C' names being called, which means my turn's approaching. My stomach twists as I head to the entrance, dreading the moment my name's announced. I'll have been anonymous for barely a bell before everyone decides they know exactly who I am and set their expectations.

Just get through placements. I can worry about what everyone thinks of me after.

I close my eyes, focusing on my inhales and exhales. The murmur of the crowd fades away.

Professor Mallory's voice cuts through the air. I pay no mind to the names she says, but the last one breaks through.

"Eloise Detura."

My eyes open. The crowd quiets around me, save for whispers of my father's name and title slithering against my eardrums. I take a deep breath and carry myself forward.

The Great Hall is a cavernous space of gray wood that could easily hold three times the number of people teeming outside. Today, they've divided it into six spacious sections with waist-high panels, with a desk and pedestal standing at the center of each area. The other students in my group follow their proctors to the desks, one for each of them, their voices and footsteps echoing through the chamber. The stillness calms my heart, a respite from the chaos we left behind.

"The examination consists of twelve individual tests," says my proctor, a short woman with glasses and frizzy brown hair that she valiantly attempted to tame with a braid, but it refused to cooperate. "There are three tests of increasing difficulty for each element. Upon completion of each, I will determine whether we continue with the higher difficulties or move on to the next element. Don't worry if you find yourself struggling—the average first-year only completes the four basic tests."

Is it possible she wasn't paying attention to my name? Or perhaps it's simply the same speech for everyone. Either way, my shoulders relax.

She leads me to the last remaining desk, stopping on the side opposite me. Reaching beneath the desktop, she brings out a candle and centers it on the pedestal. Then she rummages through her pocket until she reveals a red quartz crystal.

"This is a fire focus," she says, handing it to me. "Your goal is to light the candle." She pulls two sheets of paper out of her folio and slides them onto the desk in front of me.

"This"—she pushes the one with a familiar circular pattern toward me—"is called a focal. And this"—she moves the other sheet closer so I can see it—"is the incantation. You'll place the focus at the center of the focal and trace the pattern with your finger while reading the incantation. Upon success, you'll have lit the candle. You have three minutes."

I set the quartz on the desk. It's the least important part of incanting: a crutch for those who haven't learned to draw from the world around them. Even with how much has been drained from the Academy and its surroundings, there's still plenty to pull from deeper underground.

Looking at the candle, I visualize the pattern my father had me memorize when I was six and go through an abridged version of the incantation in my mind; half a second later, a flame ignites on the wick.

The proctor stares at the blaze, then looks at me, the candle, and back again.

Perhaps I should have done it how she'd asked?

"Success," she says, her voice breathier than before. She shakes her head quickly as if waking herself from a daze, then scribbles something in her folio. After blowing out the candle, she replaces it with a small, charred log.

"The second test is to ignite this wood." She flicks through the pages in her folio, then hesitates, looking at me.

The log bursts into flames at my silent command. I can't help the smile tugging free as the proctor jumps back, startled, almost dropping her papers.

"S-s-success!" More scribbles, then she lifts her face back to me. "The final fire test is to lift the flames off the log, then extinguish them."

Two consecutive incantations? I can appreciate why that's the ultimate test. You have to be quick enough to get through the second one before the first falls apart.

"Would you like the focal tracings?" she asks.

"No, thank you."

Hand gestures are entirely unnecessary with incanting, but I find it more enjoyable to do them. I flick my wrist upward as I visualize the lifting incantation, then squeeze my fingers into a fist for the extinguishing one.

"Success." Her voice wavers, and it takes a moment for her to remember to write the results. Despite my swelling pride at having so obviously impressed her, a twinge of apprehension itches beneath it.

How much of an advantage has my upbringing given me?

Five minutes later, I've completed all twelve tests, and my proctor excitedly hands me off to a young woman whose eyes widen as she reads my results. She leads me out the doors and into a wide gray and white hallway that leads to the rest of the building. A couple of rooms have their doors propped open, and I peek into one as we pass. Several students lounge idly within, some speaking with each other while others stare out a window or at the decorative molding. Alexis, mostly identifiable by her braids, has her face buried in her arms on one of the desks, asleep.

"This way," my guide says, so I hurry after her. Up the stairs, down another hallway, to a door with *Genevieve Mallory* etched on a plaque next to it. She gestures me into the office and instructs me to wait there.

Two bells pass and I've already perused all the books on the shelves, most of which we have in our library at home, and have moved on to counting the minuscule tiles decorating the floor and ceiling. Unless I miscounted, they're evenly split amongst the various shades of gray, with the darkest hue having one extra due to a mistake in one corner.

My boredom has me weighing the risks of peeking through Mallory's desk when the doorknob clicks. My guide from earlier holds it open for a young man who thanks her before plopping into the seat next to me, wincing as he hits the stiff cushions.

"It should only be a bit longer," the woman says. As she closes the door, I take stock of my new companion.

His skin's several shades darker than my pale, pinkish complexion, but his hair is a similar chestnut brown; long in the front but cropped in the back. The sort of style that can only look good if you keep up its maintenance, making me painfully aware of my own messy bun that hopefully hides my split ends instead of highlighting them. His uniform—the male version of mine with a purple waistcoat in place of a bodice—fits like it was designed with him in mind. It hugs his body perfectly, with his high collar somehow not as stifling as on most. He smiles at me, oozing confidence in a way that makes me want to touch him, then wipe my hand on something.

I force a smile. "So... where are you in the alphabet?"

"Vero. Reid Vero." He taps his fingers against his armrest.

"Thank Arandur. I've been waiting forever."

Reid chuckles. "Just you and me, huh?"

"Did you complete all the tests, too?"

"Yep. So you've also incanted before?"

My fingers clench in my lap as he gets to his feet. He must not have heard my name called earlier. I take a deep breath—there's no point in trying to hide it anymore.

"I have. Eloise Detura. Pleased to make your acquaintance."

Reid pauses halfway around Mallory's desk. "Detura? As in High Marshal Detura?"

"That's the one."

"Huh." He lowers himself into Mallory's chair. "Guess I'm in good company."

Judging me by my father, of course.

My fingers press into the armrest, a coil winding within me as he opens a random desk drawer and peeks inside. I glance at the door—there's no sign of anyone approaching. "Maybe you should get back over here before Mallory arrives? There can't be that many people after 'V.'"

Reid pushes himself up and wanders to the bookshelf instead. He traces his finger along some of the spines, though he doesn't seem to be reading what they say.

"Did your father teach you incanting without speaking?"

"More like expected me to have done it by the time he returned from his border visit." *Wait a second.* "How'd you know I could do that?"

"Because I can, and I assume that's why we're here. If it was just for completing all the tests, there'd probably be a few more of us. It's not *that* hard to do two incantations in a row."

"We can't be the only ones able to. It simply takes practice." With two of the three people I've met so far having secretly dabbled in incanting, it's clear that plenty of people have before coming here. Its legality can't be *that* heavily enforced, which makes some sense. It'd only be a problem if everyone did it all the time.

Reid laughs. "It's hard to practice that much without getting caught. I only managed because everything around here's already dead. Not that the faculty cares—it's just frowned upon. It doesn't matter to them how much grass you've killed."

"So how'd you learn?"

"Frowns don't stop me," he says, shooting me a grin as he finally returns to the chair beside mine. "And I'm from Haven, just down the road. Plenty of ways to access Academy materials, if you're determined enough."

Before I can ask what those ways entail, the door opens and Professor Mallory strolls in. We both shoot respectfully to our feet, but she waves us to our seats as she crosses the room.

"Sit, sit. I've been standing for bells." Her shoulders sag as she sits, then she pulls some papers out of the folio she carries, quickly skimming through them. When she finishes, she looks us over.

"Eloise Detura," she says, perking up. "Nice to finally meet you." Her gaze shifts. "And Reid Vero." My fingers fidget under her scrutinizing gaze, but Reid looks completely unbothered.

"Not just one, but two of you? How pleasantly unexpected." She pushes her spectacles up the bridge of her nose. "As I'm sure you've surmised, you're both here because you completed the entire examination sans verbalization. That is the ultimate goal for our students to reach before graduation, so it's quite unheard of for incoming first-years to be so accomplished.

"One might think we could simply advance you straight to third year. However, I suspect that would lead to gaps in your knowledge that would be a detriment to your training." She taps her finger against her cheek as she takes a moment to think.

"I can assure you, my father provided me with a well-rounded education," I say, as he'd expect me to.

"Did he? Tell me, for your final fire test—did you visualize the two focals sequentially or combine them into one?"

They can be combined? I glance at Reid, and he shrugs.

"Uh, sequentially."

Professor Mallory raises her brow, then turns to Reid. He nods, confirming he did it that way, too.

"As I said. Gaps in your knowledge."

She proceeds to ask us several other questions about our experiences, tapping her chin as she ponders each of our answers.

"The fact is, I cannot advance you to either the second or third year, because while you are adept in some areas, you lack a strong foundation in others. But if I keep you with the other first-years, you'll waste away without stimulating challenges." She paces around the room as we watch in unspoken agreement that it would be unwise to interrupt her.

My ribs constrict with every passing second. There has to be a place for us.

Finally, she sits back down. "Here's what we'll do. You will attend the foundational classes—History, Geography, Strategy, and Writing—with your fellows. For your elementals, each department will develop an advanced curriculum for you. It will, unfortunately, have to be mostly self-study, as our professors all have a full class load, but based on where you two are at, I'm sure that's familiar territory. At least now, you'll have a partner."

I sink into my seat. All I wanted was to escape self-study, to be around other people for once. Not just one person, even if he *is* nice to look at.

As far as I'm concerned, this is the worst possible outcome.

Chapter 3

With instructions to return before the first morning bell to get our schedules, we file out of Professor Mallory's office into the stale, colorless hallway. Reid walks ahead of me, hands in his pockets, with his coat draped over the crook of his arm. My gaze keeps catching on the lines of his waistcoat, following it down to the gray trousers that fit snugly around his hips.

While a nervous flutter flits through my chest at the thought of spending so much time with Reid, this is not how I wanted things to go. I'd been expecting—*hoping*—to make friends with my classmates: intelligent, like-minded young women who'd get together for study groups, gossip, and emotional support. If most of my time will be spent in self-study with Reid, the odds of that happening are slim.

I descend the stairs to find him waiting, lost in thought.

"I suppose I'll see you tomorrow," I say, pausing as I pass him.

"Wait." He faces me, running his fingers through his chestnut hair. "We should do something together. Get to know each other?" He exhales. "We're gonna be spending a lot of time together, so we should get on good terms, yeah?"

"I suppose that's true..."

"Glad we're in agreement," he says, except I don't *quite* agree.

"We should—"

"No offense." *What's the best way to word this?* "I'm not comfortable going off with you alone. I barely know you."

Reid laughs. "You don't need to worry about that. You have any friends?"

My mouth tightens. "I have roommates."

"Great, let's find them." He tugs his coat on and heads for the exit, leaving me to hurry after him.

A sizable portion of the earlier crowd lingers outside, looking for people they know or conversing with friends. Within seconds of stepping into the brisk, late afternoon air, Alexis plows into me.

"There you are," she exclaims as I recover my balance, pulling out of her spirited hug. Her warmth sticks with me—*perhaps I'm doing better at making friends than I thought?*

"I passed five of the tests!" she says. "They said I might have an affinity for water. How'd you do?"

Reid clears his throat, drawing her attention. She blinks, as if suddenly realizing he was walking *with* me instead of near me. He quickly introduces himself.

Alexis shakes his hand while side-eyeing me. "Your study partner?"

"We both placed advanced," I explain, unable to meet her eyes. Steeling myself for the anger that I hadn't clarified my skill level. "The only two. We're stuck together."

"Really?" She doesn't even attempt subtlety as she looks Reid up and down, but it calms my nerves that she moved on so easily. "You make that sound like that's a bad thing."

"Which is why I'm taking her out to show her otherwise," he says, seemingly unbothered by her stares. "Care to join us?"

"I'd love to!"

I'm about to protest, but Reid cuts me off.

"Great, follow me." He strolls along a path that meets the gravel road leading to Haven. Alexis silently squeals before skipping after him.

My jaw tenses. He isn't *that* good-looking, despite his perfect hair and uniform that seamlessly follows the cut of his body.

Torn between hating how different this is from how I imagined making friends and not wanting to miss out on the opportunity, I hurry to catch up, then ask Alexis about Sophie.

"Haven't seen her," she says, waving her hand aside. "She wasn't in my group, so she must have placed low. She better not be in either of the window rooms when we get back."

A cringe pulls my face tight. If Alexis's suspicions are true, then our roommate relations are likely headed in a rocky direction.

"Hey, Cay! Wait up!" Reid calls.

I almost trip glancing at the student walking ahead of us, his hands in his pockets and his head down. He stops, turning back as Reid jogs over to him, and the universe stutters to a halt.

He's a few inches shorter than Reid and otherwise similar in build, but where Reid's appearance exudes care and precision, he's all casual. The waistcoat of his Academy uniform hangs open, while dark, unkempt hair gently curls away from metallic eyes that tug with a magnetism unlike anything I've ever known.

My gaze drifts to the mother of pearl button at the top of his collar—undone, in complete violation of the rules of propriety. The neck should remain covered in mixed company at all times.

I avert my eyes, tearing them away from the glimpse of skin beneath his chin. But Reid and Alexis don't appear bothered, and I don't want to come off as an uptight prude, so I lock my gaze on his face as he approaches.

His soft yet striking face.

"Ellie, Alexis, this is Caeo. We're basically brothers," Reid says, patting him on the back.

Caeo's half-hearted smile sends a flutter through my stomach, and my palms are sweating as I shake his hand and mutter a quick "Hello."

Alexis drops into a curtsy when introducing herself, her eyes practically salivating as they sweep across him. There's a minor relief that I'm not the only one caught in his gravity, but I wish I had her confidence to hide behind.

Reid turns to Caeo. "How'd your placements go?"

"Terribly. I don't want to talk about it."

"Sounds like you could use a drink."

Caeo shakes his head. "I don't know. I have class in the morning."

"So do we," I say, thankful for an excuse to pull my gaze toward Reid. "And I never agreed to go drinking." My nerves are coiling at the very idea—it'd never even be considered at home. Even special occasions are typically limited to lemonade.

"You never agreed to anything." Reid slaps his hand on Caeo's shoulder. "Do you really wanna be alone and miserable right now?"

Alexis rests her fingers against Caeo's forearm. "That sounds awful."

He eyes her warily, and her mouth curls into a disarming smile. Then he glances at Reid and me, and I attempt to veil my face with an impassive shroud to hide the irritation flickering behind it.

"Fine," he grumbles, his shoulders sinking.

Before I know it, they've all made plans, choosing the Kettle Maker tavern for food with hopes to go somewhere called The Duck after. Alexis never let go of Caeo's arm, and Reid rolls his eyes before wrapping his arm around her shoulders and pulling her away.

A sharp thump pounds in my chest as Caeo's eyes land on me. He tilts his head slightly, as if inviting me to lead the way. My nerves swell, but I force myself to trudge after them.

"So, how did you end up on this outing?" Caeo asks, falling into step beside me.

It's easier to keep my eyes off his jawline while walking, and my heart quickly settles back into its annoyance at this turn of events—everyone else seems so at ease, with me clearly the odd one out.

"It's a bonding exercise," I mutter.

"Bonding?"

"Reid's my study partner. Alexis is my roommate."

"Huh. They didn't give me a study partner."

"That's probably a good thing." I narrow my eyes at the back of Reid's head.

Caeo laughs; a light, uplifting sound. "He's not that bad, he just takes some getting used to. And he's really dedicated to incanting, so you don't have to worry about him holding you back."

I bite back the witty response that pops into my head, worrying it'll seem too judgmental. Other options fly through my mind, but now it feels like I've waited too long, and it'd be more awkward to belatedly respond than to let the conversation die.

I chance a look at him—he doesn't look bothered. Maybe a response wasn't necessary?

His lips curve into a slight smile that sends a slow heat rising to my cheeks. I hurriedly turn away, scouring our surroundings for something, *anything*, of interest.

Unfortunately, there's not much to look at.

We're walking along the road to Haven: a wide stretch of gravel cutting through a sea of packed, gray dirt. My view of the town is exactly as it was at the Academy—colorless slums between us and Haven proper, with its colorful clock tower rising above—but slightly closer since we've been traveling for a few minutes. Small clusters of newfound friends travel both ahead and behind us, filling the chilly air with overlapping conversations and bursts of laughter.

Alexis giggles at something Reid said, drawing my curiosity, but I cringe at the idea of clumsily trying to catch up and walk alongside them. Instead, I glance at Caeo and say the first thing that pops up.

"How far is the Kettle Maker?" *That's me, the queen of riveting conversation.*

Caeo shrugs. "It's a walk. You can get to Haven's outskirts in about ten minutes if you're fast, but everything worth going to is further."

I need to come up with some conversation topics, quick.

"Did you grow up here?" I pull my coat tight around me. The winter sun will set soon, and the air's already turning colder by the minute.

"Basically. I don't remember living anywhere else. I think I was four when we moved here." He glances in my direction, seemingly untroubled by the chill. "Where are you from?"

"Durnam."

"The capital? That's pretty far."

"It was a three-day carriage ride. It was my first time traveling, so it was nice to see the countryside. Until we got *here*." My upper lip curls as I gesture at the empty expanse of dirt that surrounds us.

Caeo's eyebrows tilt up. "What? Is learning to fight fae not your idea of a fun time?"

A sharp laugh slips out of me. "No, definitely not." After an exhale, I drop my gaze to the gravel in front of my feet. "Attending the Academy wasn't my first choice, and it doesn't help that it's completely devoid of life and beauty."

"Good thing you brought some with you."

I stumble, glancing back up at him. A subtle smile graces his features, his gray eyes impossibly bright.

A heat rises in my chest. *Is he... flirting with me?*

"Besides, it's not lifeless here." He gestures ahead at Alexis and Reid. "Just look at how much fun they're having."

"They're excited to go drinking." *I'm reading too much into things. He couldn't have meant it like that.*

Caeo shakes his head. "Nope. Reid's excited because he's been waiting half his life to attend the Academy. If you're his partner, you must be just as good as he is, so he's hoping to finally have someone to challenge him."

A twinge of guilt interrupts my thoughts, my shoulders tightening. *Have I been too shallow in my assessment of Reid?* "There's no way I could've known that. We've only just met."

"Oh? Well, I'd say Alexis is excited because she enjoys living in the moment, so while you just see dirt, she sees endless possibilities."

How can he know that? They've barely exchanged ten words. It does fit with my own observations of her, though.

"She also clearly has her sights set on Reid," he adds. "Which isn't gonna happen, so she'll probably turn her attention to me once she realizes that. Unless someone else wants to claim me first?"

My steps falter as his nickel eyes sparkle, accented by that magnetic smile. I may not have any experience with flirting, but that was far too obvious to brush aside. Absurdly bold, even. My gaze falls to the teasing glimpse of his neck, which somehow stopped being scandalous during our conversation and simply became him.

"Are you asking me to?" I venture. Caeo comes to a stop, his smile widening. That pull I've been trying to ignore aches in my chest, yearning to do just that.

"Only if you want to," he says.

Say yes!

"No." My heart slows, and my mind screams at me an instant later.

Why did you say that?!

Caeo blinks, his jaw dropping slightly. He recovers with a tight smile flashing across his face, then turns back to the road ahead. "Alright. Guess I'm a free man."

My insides crumble as he catches up with the others. I know exactly why I turned him down: this is the longest conversation I've ever had with a man who wasn't my father, a tutor, or household servant. While I may have dreamed of this, there's no way someone like him—an absolutely gorgeous boy with perfect, soulful eyes and flawless features—could ever be interested in me. I can't bear the thought of being made a fool.

I walk the rest of the way in silence.

THE KETTLE MAKER, marked by a hanging sign with a simple etching of a kettle on it, is on the main street in the central part of Haven. It looks like the taverns I've passed in Durnam, its coloring normal thanks to its distance from the Academy. It even has some small yellow flowers in the planter box in front of the window, defiant against the winter chill.

Trying to channel that same resolve, I pull my arms close, my insides quivering as we follow Reid through the crowded interior to a small, circular table wedged between others full of Academy students. The space can't be much larger than my parents' sitting room, and it's all just... pressing in. Two dozen tables, crammed between mismatched chairs and walls draped in shadow, dented from furniture knocking against them. The fire roaring in the oversized hearth smothers us all, the smell of smoke and cooked meat saturating the stuffy air.

I end up sitting across from Alexis, squeezing my legs together to avoid bumping knees with Caeo and Reid as every shout and laugh winds my tendons tighter.

"Are you alright?" Caeo asks, his brow furrowed.

Before I can answer, a barmaid appears at our table, wearing a sleeveless dress with a frilly collar and a window cut beneath, revealing the dip between her pushed-up breasts. Caeo tilts his head aside as she runs her hand through his hair before resting it on his shoulder. My fingers clench.

"Hey, Caeo. Reid." Her voice pricks my eardrums as she speaks loud enough to carry over the babble of our fellow patrons, then smiles at both of them. "How'd yer placements go?"

"Fine." Caeo grimaces as he moves her hand off his arm.

"We'll have three ales, a corn brew, and four bowls of whatever you're serving today," Reid says.

"Comin' up."

The barmaid swings her hip into Caeo's shoulder as she departs. He winces, rubbing the spot she hit. "We have to stop coming here."

Reid relaxes into his chair. "It was your idea, man."

I take a slow breath, pushing my palms against the table as I try to relax my face enough that my teeth stop grinding. If I want to fit in, I need to calm down. Just focus on the people I'm with. Or this off-color spot on the table, barely visible by the candle flickering at its center.

"I was hungry," Caeo says, "and The Duck only serves crackers and nuts. I didn't think I'd be getting molested."

"An old girlfriend?" Alexis asks, her green eyes twinkling.

I scratch at the pale marking, the knot within me twisting as I await his answer.

"Hardly," he says. "It was just one time, and we didn't even—"

I snap my attention to Reid, my tension ready to burst. "So you decided to order for all of us?"

He shrugs. "There aren't many options. It's either ale or something harder, but The Duck has a better selection for that."

The barmaid returns with three tankards and a smaller glass, batting her eyes at Caeo before she leaves again. Itching for any form of relief, I reach for the nearest tankard, but Reid grabs it and moves the small glass in front of me.

"Reid..." Caeo warns.

"This is for you." Reid nudges it closer.

I bite my lip. "What is it?"

"Corn brew."

"Don't drink that," Caeo says.

"It's fine. We're bonding, right?" Reid wraps his arm around me with a shake as he squeezes my shoulder. "Nothing builds friendship like a good drink." He lifts his tankard and looks at me expectantly.

Heart pounding, I look to Alexis for guidance. She gives an uninterested shrug.

Thanks.

My arm twitches as I pick up the glass, and Reid knocks it with his tankard. I take a decently sized swig of the corn brew, everyone's attention pressing into me.

I erupt with coughs as I swallow, barely keeping the burning liquid in. Alexis claps her hands together, looking triumphant as my eyes water.

"Damn," Reid mutters. He takes the glass from me and passes his drink. "Here, wash it down."

I eagerly take it from him, desperate for any flavor to replace that of the corn brew. The ale isn't much better, its bitterness making me grimace.

Reid leans close to my ear. "Maybe Caeo can get the taste out."

Arandur's knickers, is he trying to kill me? I glare at him as I force the ale down. A warmth spreads through me as it settles in my stomach.

"Why would you even suggest that?" I hiss.

"Don't tell me you spent half a bell walking with him and didn't think about it. She certainly did." He nods toward Alexis.

Her gaze rests on Caeo, watching him drink his ale as she nurses hers. Halfway through his sip, he pauses and stares at her, his ink-black hair slightly obscuring his smoky eyes. She gives him a gleaming smile, and I turn back to Reid, ignoring the burgeoning heat rising within me.

"Caeo thinks you're excited to be paired with me."

Reid's eyebrow flicks up. "Does he? I wonder why."

"I don't know. Are you?"

"I'm... cautiously optimistic." He prods the tankard toward me.

"Are you trying to get me drunk?" I scan his face, searching for any trace of his intentions. His brow quirks up, but who knows what that means.

"Afraid of loosening up?" he asks.

"I don't need to loosen up." I immediately flinch at a burst of laughter from the table next to us. Fortune clearly isn't favoring me right now.

"Please. You're the High Marshal's daughter and have obviously been studying incantation every day of your life in preparation to be here. Am I right?"

I curl my lips inward. "Possibly."

"So, relax. You're here, and you've placed higher than anyone in recent memory besides yours truly. You can take a moment to live a little."

Liquid suddenly spews everywhere from Caeo's mouth, barely

missing me.

Reid slams his fist on the table. "Arandur's crooked cock!"

My eyes widen. I've never heard that expression before. Mom would probably die of shock if she heard it, and Father... even 'Arandur's knickers' is too disrespectful in his book.

"Aha! I win!" Alexis exclaims, then points at Reid. "You're paying!"

"What's going on?" I glance between her and Caeo, who's wiping his face with the back of his sleeve, his fair skin now bright red.

"Reid bet that I couldn't get Caeo to spit out his drink," she announces. "I suggested a contest: whoever got one of you to spit out their drink first wins. Loser pays for dinner." A smile stretches across her face.

I glare at Reid. "Is that why you gave me that horrible drink?"

"Stop complaining. You kept it down, and now you get a free meal." He swallows the rest of the corn brew, clinking the glass hard against the table when he finishes.

As if summoned by the talk of payment, the barmaid finally returns with our food—some kind of meat stew with the traditional bread rolls sitting on top. At home, they'd have been served on the side, with each diner bumping theirs with their neighbor's before eating, but this arrangement seems too messy for that. Meanwhile, Caeo dodges another of the barmaid's attempts at physical contact by leaning closer to me while rolling his wet sleeves up.

My eyes drift to the curves of his forearms as they twist with his motions, and my voice sticks as I speak. "I can dry those for you. I know an incantation for that."

"Incanting's prohibited outside of the Academy's grounds." He pushes his hair out of his face. "To protect Haven."

Right. "Guess you'll have to stay wet then. So what did Alexis do to make you spit your drink?"

He leans even closer, mere inches away, his breath warm against my cheek. "Ask me again later."

I bite back a giggle, feeling flushed from his proximity. Spoons drop to the table with a clatter, one of them bouncing into Caeo's lap. He offers it to me, and I take it. As my fingers brush softly against his, a smile forms on his lips. A similar tug pulls at my cheeks.

The barmaid storms off before Reid finishes digging out his coins to pay her.

Chapter 4

Caeo

"Hey, Caeo, can you get that barmaid back? I think she's ignoring me." Alexis's chipper voice easily breaks through the boisterous chatter of the tavern. The Kettle Maker's more crowded than usual tonight, thanks to all the Academy students arriving in town. All eager to get the term started, so they can someday join the elite ranks of the Order of Incanters. Must be nice to have that kind of direction.

"Nope, not happening." I lower my tankard of ale. The last thing I need is Mabel feeling me up again, and Alexis hasn't really gotten me in the mood to whore myself out for her benefit.

"I'm not paying for a second round," Reid says.

"Pleeease," Alexis whines, batting her eyes at me.

I ignore her, focusing instead on the beautiful enigma beside me. I've never had to spend this much effort on a girl—that line about claiming me *was* ridiculous, but that shit's always worked before. In my experience, women rarely care about conversation, always rushing into something more exciting. But Ellie... It's as if she doubts my interest is real, though I can't imagine why. Sure, she's a little awkward, but there's this whole personality peeking out that I'm dying to glimpse.

Like now: she's clearly struggling, but forcing herself to push through anyway. And the fact that she's not throwing herself at me like all the others gives me hope she might actually be someone who sees me for once.

She startles at my attention, probably because I caught her staring at my throat again. I've never been one for propriety, so I'm used to that reaction, but her gaze—so timid, but with this longing slipping through—ignites a spark within me unlike anything else. Her sudden movement splashes the stew from her spoon onto her rosy lips.

"You got some on your face," I say, resisting the urge to wipe it away myself.

"I do?" She reaches for the wrong side of her mouth, and I can't hold back anymore.

"No, here." I brush the mess from the soft skin of her lips with my thumb. Her cheeks redden at my touch, and that single dimple on her left peeks out again, like it has every time she's smiled. It's happened enough that I'm certain she likes me, and my lips curl into a matching grin.

Minus the dimple. I don't have one.

A second later, she's staring at her bowl as she fills another spoonful. Hesitating, again.

"Do you know what kind of meat this is?" she asks.

I sink back in my chair, the heat of the moment dissipating. "They never say. Could be horse for all I know."

Ellie's jaw drops, and her spoon falls into her bowl.

A chuckle breaks free at how adorable she looks. "I'm kidding." Taking a chance, I squeeze her shoulder, and her nose scrunches up as she almost laughs.

She grabs her ale and takes another swig, grimacing as she swallows.

"Clearly, this is your first time with mystery meat and ale." I pass her tankard to Alexis once she sets it down. As much as I'd like to take credit for her perpetually flushed face, she's already had half a pint *and* some corn brew. It's definitely had an effect; she's nowhere near as jittery as she was earlier.

"Is it that obvious?"

"You didn't frequent the taverns in Durnam?"

"No, definitely not. A tavern is hardly the place for a young lady."

My throat catches. A lady? Could that be it? It makes sense—her hair's so glossy it's slipping out of her bun, and her skin has the healthy glow of someone who's never missed a meal. She probably sleeps on a feather bed, while my mattress might as well be a sheet on the floor.

Her parents probably wouldn't have allowed me anywhere near her. Even in Haven, having the top button on my collar undone is barely acceptable. I only get away with it because no one cares what poor people do. *Maybe she'd be more comfortable if I fixed it?*

That'd probably just be weird at this point. It's a stupid rule anyway—suffocating collars for everyone just because the previous king had a hideous birthmark. Besides, she doesn't actually seem to mind, as she's back to staring at my neck.

"Hey, Caeo, you done?" Reid snaps his fingers in my face, startling me. "We wanna get to The Duck before it gets too busy."

"Huh?" I glance down at my bowl. Despite how hungry I was earlier, I've hardly touched my stew. I quickly scarf it down because it's foolish to waste a free meal.

"Can you get Mabel back over here so I can pay?"

"Not a chance. I'll see you outside." I pull my coat off the back of my chair and hand Ellie hers. She wobbles as she stands, and I steady her with a light touch on her shoulder. Reid gives me the finger as Alexis gets her coat on, and the girls follow me out.

A shiver runs through me as I step into the brisk night air, so I pull my coat tighter. This is one of the nicer parts of Haven, but probably still questionable for someone living a life of silver and lace. Not that I should judge—I have no way of knowing what life in Durnam's like. Could smell like shit from all the horse-drawn carriages.

Ellie stumbles out a second later, and I catch her before she falls face-first to the ground, her warmth soaking into me where we touch.

"Are you alright?"

She settles into my arms. "I must have missed a step there."

There is no step.

I move her away from the door so Alexis can join us in the street. She meets my eyes as she warms her hands with her breath, raising her brow.

Ellie didn't pull away after I helped her up. If anything, she's relaxed into my chest, fitting into me like a matching puzzle piece as she sinks into the bend in my arm. Her brown hair tickles my chin as I breathe in the soothing scent of lavender, and I resist the urge to nuzzle into her.

"Remind me never to make a bet with you again," Reid grumbles when he finally emerges. "I can't afford this."

"Where to next?" Alexis asks. "The duck place?"

"The Buttoned-Up Duck," I say.

Ellie giggles. "I need to see that."

Alexis's eyes narrow. "Maybe we should head back, El. We have class tomorrow, and I'd say you're already at risk for a massive headache in the morning."

"What? I'm fine. Let's go!" Cold air sweeps in as Ellie untangles herself from my arms and stumbles with her first step. This has to be her first experience with alcohol. Someone needs to keep it pleasant.

I catch her around the waist, pulling her close as Reid snickers. "How about I walk Ellie back, and you two have fun?"

"But I want to see the duck, too."

"We'll see it another time," I say, shifting to meet her eyes. "Come on, go for a walk with me."

A ridiculously adorable grin breaks out on her face, the kind a sober person's incapable of making, and my heart leaps into my throat. I've never felt this giddy around a girl before. The way she looks at me, without motive or judgment—I want more.

Alexis bites her lip, her uncertainty surprising me.

"Don't worry, Lex." Reid wraps his arm around her shoulder. "She'll be safe. Cay's trustworthy, and Ellie's more than capable of burning him to a crisp if he tries anything."

My arms stiffen. *That... seems excessive.*

Ellie focuses on Alexis. "I'll be fine."

A tense heartbeat later, Alexis nods, still looking unsure but apparently unwilling to argue with Ellie's decision. We say our farewells, with Reid and Alexis heading to The Duck while Ellie struts off in the completely wrong direction. I grab her hand, leading her the correct way to the Academy, and she doesn't let go.

With everyone still in Haven for a fun night out, it's just the two of us on the road back. Once cobblestone transitions to gravel, the streetlamps disappear, leaving us walking hand in hand under the moonlight, our fingers entwined. Just us, dirt, and darkness.

Tipsy Ellie's more talkative than sober Ellie, less worried about saying the wrong thing. She's been curious about my life in Haven, asking more about me than anyone ever has, so I've spent the last twenty minutes sharing some of the more entertaining stories from my childhood.

"We could hear my mother yelling, and there was a trail of blue drips on the road behind us. So Reid had the brilliant idea of climbing up the clock tower. 'Because people never look up,' he said. About ten feet up, I slipped and fell headfirst to the ground."

Ellie's eyes go wide. "You landed on your head?"

"That's what I'm told—I blacked out. Reid says I landed right at my mother's feet, and she started screaming her head off. He just scooted to the other side of the tower, climbed down, and ran for his life."

"How are you alive?"

I shrug. "According to the surgeon, it was Fortune's favor. I was out for two days. Reid burned his blue clothes to get rid of any evidence he'd been with me, so I got all the blame. Got put on wash duty every day for three months, because almost dying wasn't punishment enough."

Ellie puffs her cheeks as she exhales. "I've never done anything like that."

"Really? No near-death experiences?"

"Oh, no. My childhood was very regimented. There was always somewhere I was expected to be, and failing to meet expectations was not an option."

"Sounds miserable."

Ellie laughs, the sound warming the cold air. "It does, doesn't it? But it wasn't all bad. My father gave me a couple of bells every day to paint. He even bought me a small easel that I could take to the gardens with me."

"You enjoy it that much?"

I've never had a hobby I was any good at, that I wanted to spend my time on, unless you count getting girls and climbing trees.

"I do." She closes her eyes, squeezing my hand tighter. "I always thought I could see people better when I was painting them. That spark within them, that gives them life."

Her smile builds a steady heat within me as I imagine what it must feel like to have that kind of passion about anything. She glances at me, the moonlight reflecting off her irises.

"Like how you saw who Alexis was, even though you just met her," she says. "I wish I could do that. I have such a hard time relating to people."

"You're overselling it," I mutter. "Outside of Reid, no one's ever stuck around. Once they realize how terrible I am at everything, they bail."

She shrugs. "Well, I don't know about everything else, but you're good at that."

There's a strange feeling in my chest, something I've never felt before. "Huh." I struggle to find the right words, which is really throwing me off. I never struggle when talking to girls. "Thanks for making me sound... special."

Did I really just say that?

Luckily, Ellie's too tipsy to have standards, because that dimple appears again and my mouth goes dry. She stops, taking my other hand in hers as she gazes into my eyes, her icy fingers tickling the warmth of my palms.

"What do you see when you look at me?"

Oh shit. How am I supposed to answer that? I'm praying she doesn't notice me sweating as I search her eyes, weighing the best response.

"I see... a puzzle. One I'd really, really like to solve." Probably the lamest line I've ever used, but true. I don't know why she's so wrapped up in self-doubt—she's smart *and* beautiful. But this need's swelling in my chest, to somehow show her she shouldn't worry so much.

Her gaze drops to our feet, fingers idly rubbing mine. "A puzzle, huh?"

She lets go of one hand but keeps the other as she starts walking.

Neither of us speaks for a while, but it doesn't feel like we need to. Silence can be good.

I walk at a significantly slower pace than before, trying to draw out the time it takes to get to her dorm, but we still arrive sooner than I'd like. Ellie looks up at the bland brick building, its outside lit by ornate, wrought-iron lanterns hanging from the sides and candlelight pouring out its windows, but she makes no move to go inside.

"You never told me what Alexis did to make you spit out your drink."

"Not sure I should." I lean against the chilly metal railing of the stairs. "I'd hate to cause a problem between the two of you."

"Now you have to tell me."

I close my eyes, inwardly groaning at the memory. "Every time I took a sip, she slid her foot up against my leg."

"Why does it seem like every woman you meet can't keep their hands off you?"

"You tell me." I lift the hand she's been holding ever since leaving the tavern. Her cinnamon eyes glare at me, but her lips purse as they fail to hold back a smile. "Anyway... that last time, she stuck her foot directly into my lap."

"She didn't!" Ellie raises her free hand to brush against her lips. Heat rises from deep within me, imagining that gentle touch.

"She did. I blame you for not claiming me when you had the chance."

Ellie's eyes widen, and her fingers graze her chin as she contemplates me. I swallow, not sure how much longer I can keep up this carefree exterior.

She bites her lip and I almost snap. "Is it too late?"

"To preserve my innocence? Yes. But to prevent future incidents?" I pause, forcing a breath through the tightness in my chest. "No, I don't think it is."

She blushes. I probably did, too, warmth building in my cheeks. Pushing off the railing, I close the gap between us and tilt my head down until her face is only a breath away.

"I want to kiss you..." I whisper, inhaling her floral scent, "but I won't."

Ellie's eyes tremble. "Why not?" She's so close, her mouth slightly parted. Hoping. Waiting. It takes everything I have not to give those lips what they want.

"You're drunk." I move close to her ear. "And I want to make sure you *really* want to."

Dropping her hands, I pull away before she can react, cherishing the stunned look on her face. If I'd kissed her, I wouldn't have gotten to see it.

"Maybe I'll see you in class tomorrow." With a short wave of my hand, I stroll away as my heart hammers against my ribs.

She calls after me. "What if you don't?"

"Then I'll find you!"

I don't look back. If I do, I won't be able to keep myself from going back, and she'll discover exactly how desperate I am to kiss her.

I'M STILL RELIVING the feeling of Ellie's hand in mine, the heat of her breath, when I enter the ramshackle abode that barely qualifies as our house. A healthy blaze crackles in the fireplace, which means Mother's still up. Burying my smile, I force a sigh.

"I'm home."

I stand in our combination kitchen, sitting, and dining room, that's also had my bed shoved into the corner ever since I was old enough to not want to share my mother's. The same lumpy pillow and threadbare blanket's been spread on top of it for fifteen years, its holes no longer big enough to stick my arms through like when I was young.

It'd be nice if I could afford to live on campus like everyone else. It's free to attend the Academy, but not to live there. Unlike Reid, it wasn't a lifelong dream of mine—just my only shot at having a future. While he spent our adolescence working odd jobs to save up money so he could get the full campus experience, I wasted that time with various girlfriends.

Mother's feet scrape along the floor as she hobbles into the room from hers, the only other in our two-room shack. She's been looking better lately, with more color in her skin and energy in her eyes, but she continues to move slowly. The years seem to hit her harder than most, leading people to assume she's much older than she is. Not that she's ever told me her age, claiming it's rude to ask.

Normally by this time, she'd have readied herself for bed, but she still wears her widow's cowl—a simple piece of cotton that encircles her face, covering her hairline as it connects beneath her chin to hide her neck. It's the typical fashion for women who want the world to know they aren't seeking a partner, and she's worn it as long as I can remember. She never talks about my father, and has made it very clear it's not a topic for discussion.

"You're earlier than I expected," she says.

I lean down so she can kiss my cheek before she settles into her chair by the fire. "I was tired." My throat constricts with the lie until I'm forced to swallow.

Mother raises an eyebrow. She noticed, as always.

"You don't have to tell me."

Unfortunately, my throat won't feel normal until I do. "I went out with Reid and some girls from the Academy. One of them had too much to drink, so I walked her back."

Her lips press together. "How sweet of you." Then she widens her pale green eyes, hinting I should continue.

"I'm not talking about her with you."

Plopping down on my bed, I start pulling my shoes off. I've long outgrown the stiff mattress—my feet hang off the edge when I sleep—but we don't have the space or money for anything bigger.

"You like her that much?"

"Stop it."

"Alright, alright." She takes a sip of her tea. "How did your placements go?"

"Fine." I grimace as my throat twists again.

"You're a terrible liar."

Biting back a curse, I chuck my shoe into the corner. "I didn't pass a single test, alright? Nothing happened. Even the proctor was stunned." I close my eyes and lean back against the poorly plastered wall. "She had a big speech about how it's normal for people to fail most of the tests, but I guess they still get something to happen. Not me."

Mother exhales. "I'm not sure why you expected it to go well, but it's only your first day. You'll learn more with time."

As supportive as always. "Well, right now it feels like I shouldn't even bother." Except if I hadn't, I'd never have met Ellie. Someone who finally sees past my incompetence, who actually thinks I'm good at something.

Mother shuffles over and sits beside me, mussing with my hair. "Life won't always be like this. Focus on the good things that happened today, yes? Like that girl you're keeping from me."

I swat her away as I hold back the smile creeping in. There's something special about Ellie, and I won't let my mother threaten that with her usual meddling.

She kisses my forehead, then grunts as she stands back up. "I'm heading to bed. Mind the fire? I doubt you want your poor mother to freeze."

"Sure," I say, just wanting her gone so I can get back to thinking about Ellie.

Her door clicks shut as I sink into the lumpy mattress, a smile lighting my face as I imagine finding Ellie's cinnamon eyes tomorrow. For once, the future actually looks promising.

Chapter 5

Ellie

My heart's still pounding as I shut the door to our drab sitting room and lean against it, closing my eyes.

Deep breaths.

All the measured breathing in the world couldn't rein in the smile taking over my face. That actually happened; the handsome boy I just met wants to kiss me.

Me. Not someone alluring, like Alexis, but *me*. Even with all my social missteps.

How will I ever fall asleep?

Forcing out another exhale, I open my eyes. The door to the windowless bedroom is shut tight, while all the others sit slightly ajar. A pile of uniforms lies strewn across our settee.

Oh, right—Sophie. I'd completely forgotten about her.

I knock gently on the closed door. If she's in there, she doesn't respond, so it would seem Alexis's suspicions were correct. I could peek inside, but with my head still swimming from the ale, it's probably not the best time to try to resolve anything. Besides, any conversation with her would likely dampen my excitement about Caeo.

Instead, I move my things into the room closest to the bathing chamber, then take advantage of ending my night early by taking a long, relaxing bath.

The deep tub can only be filled by incantation—it has three sets of focals and incantations carved into its side: one for filling the tub, one for warming the water, and the final for emptying it. I don't need them, since I've used incantations for such mundane tasks on a daily basis for years, but a pang of pity tugs at my chest for my fellow first-years who'll likely struggle.

Soaking in the water, I let my fingers wander to my more sensitive areas as my thoughts swirl around Caeo. To have a certain face in mind, imagining where his warm, steady fingers could travel... the sensation hits an embarrassingly new level. My release uncoils all the tension I had left, then I close my eyes, relaxing into a mellow bliss.

Once I'm out and dry, I climb into bed and curl up on a mattress that's nowhere near as comfortable as what I'm used to, but the heat flushing through me as I recall the feeling of Caeo's arms around me keeps me cozy until I drift off to sleep.

I WAKE TO SUNLIGHT warming my face, having left the curtains open for that exact purpose—Professor Mallory expects me in her office at first morning bell—but that doesn't mean I'm happy about it. I'm besieged by gray, and a dull headache reminds me of last night's drinks. Thank Fortune for Alexis's wisdom in sending me back. Not only for sparing me an even worse hangover, but also for...

Caeo.

My back arches against the mattress as I savor the memory of our walk together. Never in my wildest dreams did I imagine I'd spend my first night away from home on a romantic stroll with a boy I'd only just met. I still can't believe how close we got—it must have been the ale. Things certainly wouldn't have gone so far if I had any experience drinking.

He said he'd find me today, and that motivates me more than anything to pull myself out of bed and find which uniform configuration I look best in. I'm halfway dressed when Alexis bangs on my door, asking if I can heat the tub. After rushing to get the water to a temperature she's comfortable with—very hot—I hastily finish up. There's no time to straighten the kinks in my hair, so I twist it into a bun, slipping some locks out in the front to hopefully frame my face nicely.

I arrive at the main building's entrance with about ten minutes to spare, then struggle to heave one of its heavy wooden doors open. I've pulled it wide enough that I can move into position to push it when its weight suddenly lets up.

Reid's bracing it with his hand. "Allow me."

I exhale a thanks, and it closes with a thud behind us. He looks as put together as he did yesterday, but the darkness under his eyes reveals he didn't sleep much.

My stomach rumbles as we pass the dining hall, the scent of bacon and pancakes tugging at us the whole way to Mallory's office, every step like walking through a world painted solely in gray. She hands us our schedules, informing us that Professor Beckwith expects us to show up early, so we rush through breakfast before hurrying across campus. This afternoon's history lecture is my best chance to run into Caeo, so I simply have to get through the morning's lessons in one piece.

We arrive, huffing and puffing, at the Farshaw School of Fire, a building barely distinguishable from the dormitories outside of its name being plastered on the side in thick, angular letters. Scrambling through its pale halls, we find Professor Beckwith's classroom with a quarter bell to spare.

He looks about ten years our senior, his red hair trimmed short, and is rummaging through papers on his desk on the far side of the room. About twenty pale wooden desks with chairs fill the space between us, and shelves full of off-white candles and various other flammable objects line the walls. At least a couple have color.

"You must be the advanced students," he says, barely sparing us a glance. He finishes writing something on a sheet of paper, then grabs it and walks toward us. "Follow me."

He leads us to a small classroom whose desks have all been shoved against the walls, creating an open space in the center of the washed-out room. A row of austere windows, their frames weathered and gray, let in the morning light.

"Unfortunately, I didn't have time to develop a lesson plan for today, as I already have a full class to deal with. You will therefore spend the morning doing conditional drills." He hands me the sheet of paper, then moves to a shelf on the left side of the room.

Reid peers over my shoulder as we read the messy scrawl.

1. *20 push ups, light on down, extinguish on up.*
2. *20 sit ups, light on up, extinguish on down.*
3. *30 squats, light on down, extinguish on up.*
4. *40 alternating lunges, light on lunge, extinguish on return.*
5. *Hold plank position until collapse while one tries to light the candle, and the other keeps it extinguished. Switch on repeat.*

"You will run through that sequence until I return, at which point I will evaluate where you are in your studies so I can develop a curriculum for you. If you aren't sufficiently exhausted, you will repeat this sequence next class." He hands each of us a candle. "Questions?"

My breath catches as I steal a glance at Reid. Outside of last night, I've never been left alone with a man before—much less while exercising—but he doesn't seem bothered by the notion at all. Society's rules must not trickle down here.

"I can't do a push-up or sit-up," I say.

"Then do the push-ups on your knees and crunches instead. Anything else?"

We both shake our heads.

"Good. I will return at quarter after third bell." Beckwith leaves the room, the door clicking as it closes behind him.

"Arandur's war-torn ass," Reid mutters. He drops his bag onto one of the desks, and it wobbles on impact.

I focus on rereading our instructions. My studies, mentally rigorous as they were, never included anything like this—Father must have intended to fast-track me along an officer's path and assumed the Academy's physical training would be enough. I can't remember the last time I lunged on purpose.

I glance up to find Reid removing his waistcoat and untucking his shirt.

"What are you doing?"

"I'm not doing all that dressed like this." He finishes undoing his buttons, revealing the undershirt he wears beneath. And skin. So much skin, his neck and the dip between his collarbones completely exposed.

I quickly avert my gaze, looking toward the pile of desks.

"Trust me," he says, "you'll be dying in minutes if you keep all that on."

He's right, and unfortunately, I don't have time to waste arguing with myself—not unless I want to do this all again next class. My fingers fumble as I unlace my bodice, but I can only bring myself to untuck my blouse and undo the top buttons of my collar. Heat pools in my belly as Caeo's teasing throat flashes through my mind.

With a deep breath, I remove my shoes before meeting Reid in the center of the room with my candle, praying my cheeks haven't gone completely red.

He rolls his eyes, then we begin.

Every minute is the longest of my life, my muscles burning like never before, until I collapse hard on the floor only seconds after getting into a plank position. Even with the modifications the professor allowed, I can't complete all the exercises. Reid did, but looking at him lying on the floor as I flop myself over, he might as well be a puddle, too.

"I can't move," I say, panting. My underclothes are completely drenched, and I've long since abandoned my uniform in a pile on the floor. It's hard to care about modesty when you can't breathe. Even looking at Reid, the muscles of his arms and chest glistening in what should have been a scandalous display, I feel nothing but exhaustion.

"Why is he torturing us like this?" I moan. "This is supposed to be fire incanting, not bootcamp."

"They *are* preparing us to join the army," Reid huffs, then pushes himself into a seated position. "But they usually ease people into this during second year. We just gotta hope all our professors didn't come to the same solution for a last-minute lesson plan."

"Don't even joke about that."

"I'm not. I'm rather worried they did."

Closing my eyes, I attempt to slow my breathing. *You can get through this. It's only one class.* Rebuttals flood my mind—this is my future, a taste of what's coming if the war ever reignites—but I shut them away. Then Reid's voice breaks through.

"Looked to me like you and Caeo were getting rather cozy last night."

My eyes pop open, air catching in my throat as possible

responses fly through my head.

"Are you jealous?" *Why did I pick that one?! The attention of one boy doesn't justify being so brazen!*

An abrupt laugh interrupts Reid's breaths. "Definitely not. He's like a brother to me. If you'd seen the things I've seen, you'd never let his honey stick anywhere near your beehive."

My... what? I prop myself up on my elbows to better look at Reid. "I don't think that metaphor works as well as you think."

"Sure it does. He puts his stick in your hive and gets the sweet, sweet honey."

If I weren't already burning up from exertion, I surely would be now. "And then what?" I ask. "He gets mobbed by a swarm of angry bees?"

"That's women for you." He drags himself to his feet, then pushes a window open, letting the brisk air in.

"Clearly, you've only been with the wrong type of women," I mumble.

"None, actually. Not interested. But I've witnessed plenty of men court my mother."

"Wait. What?" I sit up further and quickly review all our earlier interactions. He *was* rather nonchalant with Alexis, and I never did catch him looking at either of us the way Caeo looked at me.

"Which part wasn't clear?" he asks. "That I prefer men, or my mother's promiscuity?"

"I..." *No wonder he was so casual about us stripping out of our uniforms.* "Never mind."

I clamber onto my hands and knees, preparing for the next round of push-ups in an attempt to escape this conversation. It's a perfectly acceptable way to live, but if he makes the connection—

"Wait," he says, eyes narrowing. A second later, a grin breaks across his face as his laughter fills the room. "You thought *I* was jealous of Caeo for getting with *you*?"

Darn it. I lower my chest to the ground and light the stupid candle. My arms scream in protest as I push myself back up and extinguish it.

"Wow, you must feel dumb now."

"Shut up."

By Fortune's favor, upon arriving to our water incanting class as a cramping, disheveled mess, Professor Merriweather, a kindly-looking woman in her mid-fifties with graying hair, decides to test our abilities by having us clean ourselves up as best we can, without any instructions or components.

Thus, we're both clean and well-hydrated when we arrive at the dining hall. Rows of faded wooden tables and benches sit under a gabled ceiling, but at least everyone's uniforms fill the space with splotches of various purple tones. Thankfully, it's significantly tamer than the Kettle Maker was, but my insides still itch regardless. Lunch is served buffet-style, and I fill my plate with a bit of everything, hunger gnawing at me like never before. We eat in silence, then I wilt against the table with my head buried in my arms.

"You two look terrible."

My heart flutters at Caeo's voice. Before I know it, his hand rests on my shoulder, tracing gentle circles with his fingers. Goosebumps dance across my skin as I melt into the tabletop. I should look up, I really should, but my nerves keep me pinned down. *What if he only liked me when I was drunk?*

"Professor Beckwith had us incanting while doing push-ups for the entire period," Reid says. "And then made us stay late to run through a dozen tests to see what we know. I despise that man."

The bench shifts as Caeo sits next to me, pulling his hand away and leaving a cold emptiness behind. It's an effort not to slump in disappointment, but I keep my head down, dreading a knowing look from Reid after our moment earlier. Their conversation wafts over me, and by the time Alexis chimes in, I'm drifting away, lulled by the dulcet tones of Caeo's voice. The next thing I know, a hand's gently shaking my shoulder.

"Wake up," Caeo whispers, close to my face. "It's time for History."

I lift my head, blinking. His gray eyes have specks of blue in them that I hadn't noticed before, like a warm sky peeking through heavy fog.

"History…" I say breathlessly, completely lost in those clouds.

"I told you I'd find you." He brushes my hair out of my face, his fingers lightly grazing my skin.

He did. A heat unfurls within me, remembering that moment.

"We should go, or we'll be late," he adds.

My pulse quickens as I shove all thoughts of kissing him out of mind, then gather my things. Reid and Alexis must have gone ahead; it's the only class that all the first-years have together, so most of the students filing out of the dining hall are heading there. My leg muscles burn with a dull ache as we follow, and while it isn't far, I still make a fool of myself by attempting small talk.

"Reid told me he's interested in men, not women."

Caeo raises an eyebrow. "Are you looking for confirmation? I don't have any firsthand experience, but that matches everything I know." He pauses. "Were you disappointed…?"

"No! No, I was only—Do you think Alexis knows?" I'd hate for her to feel led on, especially when I'm the only reason she met him.

"Oh." Understanding washes over Caeo's face. "Yeah, she definitely knows."

I sigh with relief. "Good."

He squeezes my hand, and my nerves settle. Something about him... I should be embarrassed, but I'm not. There's no urge to disappear, to hide from my awkwardness. Just a warm glow in my chest.

The lecture hall's not as spacious as the Great Hall, but large enough to hold all the students in our year, somewhere between eighty and a hundred people. The lower side of the room has a desk, podium, and a large chalkboard—a bold swath of black amid all the gray—and ascending away from it are multiple levels of long desks. They stretch across their entire lengths with benches for the students to sit on, most of which are already full.

My skin's already prickling from all the people packed around us when I spot Sophie in the front row, rifling through her things. I glance away, hoping she doesn't notice me—I should've tried to fix things with her last night. The longer I wait, the more awkward it's likely to become. I glimpse Alexis and Reid further up, but there's no room for us to squeeze in with them.

Caeo leads me to an empty spot on a bench near the back, next to a girl who smiles brightly at him. He completely ignores her, his attention focused entirely on me.

There's plenty of room for both of us to sit comfortably, but he's close enough that the warmth of his leg presses against mine. My inner voice yells that I'm here for class, so I pull my bag up to get some paper, ink, and a pen to take notes, then realize he's still holding my other hand.

I force myself to let go of it.

Our professor arrives, and though his voice echoes through the chamber as he welcomes us to class, I'm straining to decipher his words. In the future, I'll have to make sure to arrive earlier to get a seat up front.

Caeo doesn't bother getting anything out to write with. Instead, he leans his elbow on the desk, chin resting in his hand, watching me. It should make me nervous, but it doesn't, stoking a different kind of blaze within me as I write the title for today's lecture: *The Founding of the Order of Incanters by Gareth Arandur.*

While I generally know the story from my lessons at home, no doubt the professor will get into specific details he'll expect us to memorize. But if Caeo keeps this up, I won't be able to focus at all.

"Stop staring," I whisper. "You should pay attention."

"But you're beautiful. He's not."

A tightness coils between my thighs, and I resist squirming in my seat as I note the details of Arandur's birth. "How are you so bold?" I hiss.

Caeo leans in, close enough that the heat radiating off his skin warms my already sweltering cheek, his breath brushing against my ear. "Because I know you want that kiss."

Ink spots my paper as I mess up the word I was writing. My face is red, I know it, and I can't bring myself to look at him. I bite my lip, forcing myself to focus on the professor's words instead.

"Arandur discovered the connection between the fae's magic and their realm by studying how it diminished the more time they spent in ours. It led him to theorize that their power came from their land itself, and that perhaps there was a way for us to tap into something similar." And as everyone knows, that advancement saved us—without it, the fae would have claimed all our land by now.

The professor turns away, drawing some rudimentary focals on the board. He clearly expects us to copy them down.

Keeping my eyes locked on my paper, I whisper back to Caeo, "Well, if *you* want to kiss *me*, you need to stop being so distracting and wait until class is over."

When he doesn't respond, I chance a quick peek in his direction. He's no longer staring at me, but off into the distance, seemingly daydreaming... his lips curled into a slight smile.

I shake my head, returning to my notes. Another bell of focus, then the rest of the afternoon is him.

Chapter 6

Caeo

Class ends, and bumps and thuds echo through the auditorium as everyone packs their things. Except me. I didn't take any notes, and I barely heard anything the professor said. Why should I care about the wars with the fae? They ended before I was born. Sure, they lasted for thousands of years, but no one's heard a peep from the border in two decades.

It's an odd sentiment for someone at a school whose sole purpose is to train people to fight fae, but most of the students here grew up with family members lost or disabled in battle, with tales of fae stealing poorly behaved children. My mother almost made that seem like a good thing.

Besides, my attempts at incanting in this morning's classes went so poorly that paying attention doesn't seem worth the effort. Especially when I could spend that time watching Ellie instead.

The afternoon sun pouring in from the windows warms her skin, reflecting gold light off her brown hair as she slides her notes into her bag. I wrap my fingers around her hand, stopping her from standing.

"Wait."

She slowly settles back onto the gray bench, pressing her lips together before they twitch into a small smile. Sweat collects in my palms, her nerves somehow bleeding into me; she's not drunk, and there's no more class to distract her. I can't mess this up.

"Do you have another class to get to?" I ask.

Ellie swallows. "No."

"Would you go for a walk with me? I can show you around Haven. The parts with color."

Her dimple peeks out as she nods. "I'd like that."

I can feel myself smiling like an idiot, so I break our gaze and scan the half-empty auditorium. Reid and Alexis seem to have left already. Good—I don't want them tagging along, competing for our attention. I need Ellie to keep seeing *me*.

We head down the stairs, and she winces on the last step, massaging her right thigh just above the knee.

"Are you alright?"

"I'm a little sore. It'll probably be fine once I get moving."

"We can do something else." I scratch the back of my head as I rack my brain over what we could possibly do on campus. "Something with less walking."

Ellie adjusts her bag on her shoulder. "No, I want to go. I'll be fine."

She was not fine.

Five minutes down the road to Haven, and she's already limping.

"Maybe you should stop and stretch? Lean against me and hold your leg like this." I demonstrate, standing on one foot and pulling my ankle up behind me.

"How could this possibly help?" Ellie wobbles as she grips my arm for balance, her nails digging into me, making me instantly aware of all the places she isn't touching like that.

I force my voice to stay casual. "I don't know, it just does—but you have to hold it awhile."

She bites her lip. "I think this is an excuse to get me touching you."

"I don't need an excuse. You can't resist doing that all on your own." And it's not like there's anything else to hold onto—there's nothing but dirt till we reach the outskirts.

Her face flushes a bright pink, and I steady her as she tilts too far to one side.

"You should switch legs now." I keep my fingers gently pressed against her, helping her balance, then weigh our options. Even if her legs feel better, it'd be stupid to have her walk all the way to town. But I don't want to take her back to her dorm; she has roommates, and I doubt she has the nerve to invite me to her bedroom.

"I could carry you?"

Ellie's fingers dig deeper into my arm. "You're not carrying me."

"Why not? This isn't Durnam—no one will care."

"It'd be humiliating! And you'd be in just as bad shape when we got there!"

That's definitely not true, but I doubt she'd appreciate me pointing that out. Luckily, another idea pops into my head. "What if I carry you somewhere closer? Just a few minutes away."

Her eyes narrow. "Where?"

I UNHOOK MY ARMS from under Ellie's legs so she can slide off my back, and her arms unwrap from around my shoulders as her feet hit the ground. I fish out my key to unlock the door, and after fumbling with it for a moment—it often sticks—I push it open and lead her inside.

She stands there, taking in my meager abode. From the beat-up walls to the mismatched furniture, until her gaze settles on me. "This is where you live?"

Maybe this wasn't the best idea. She probably never imagined a house could be this small.

"Why don't you sit?" I offer, my pulse quickening. "I'll heat the kettle."

She grabs my hand before I take a step. "I didn't mean to come off that way. It's nice. Cozy."

An overwhelming urge to kiss her surges through me, but I resist. It's neither of those things, but the fact that she cares enough to say that means everything. Most girls preferred finding a private alley over coming here.

"Thanks." I squeeze her hand before she lets go, then I dig the kettle out from behind a mess on the counter. "My mother has this tea she uses to help with her aches and pains."

"Do you expect her back soon?"

"Nah. She's usually at the shop till dinner."

I fill the kettle with some water from a barrel, then cross the room in a few strides to hang it above the fireplace. After a minute of fiddling with some flint and steel—normally I do this much faster—a decent blaze is going.

When I finally finish, Ellie's lying on my bed in the corner, eyes closed, with soft shadows filling the curves of her face. Heat stirs in my chest. She's certainly not the first to be there, but fuck, she's the first one to make me sweat like this.

I sit next to her, the flimsy mattress shifting under my weight. "I thought it'd take longer to get you into my bed."

Her eyes snap open, and she shoots upright. "I didn't realize. My legs hurt, and there wasn't much else, and—"

"Don't worry, it's just a joke. But that reminds me..." I tuck a lock of her hair back behind her ear. "I still owe you a kiss. If you want it, that is."

My heart pounds as I look into her eyes, my body tensing with every stifled breath. This isn't what I imagined, what I intended. I wanted to get to know her better. But it feels right.

Ellie swallows, trembling with the smallest of nods. "I do."

I bring my hand to her cheek, slowly closing the distance between us. Her lips part, her eyes close...

My mouth brushes gently over her soft skin, my lower lip catching on hers. The warmth of her exhale sends heat rushing through me as I press closer.

I pull back just enough to meet her eyes. "Is this alright?"

She nods, almost a tremor.

My heart's on the verge of exploding, but I'm terrified of scaring her away by going too fast. I gently bring my mouth to hers as my hand slides into her hair, this time teasing her lips open with mine. Once they do, I sweep my tongue in and savor the taste of her.

She gasps, but lets me in, her tongue bumping against mine. A laugh tumbles out of me and into her—she's clearly never kissed anyone like this before. I slow my movements, giving her a chance to figure out what she's doing, heat flowing through me as our kiss continues and her fingers curl softly against my arm. Then she takes a breath, her big brown eyes sparkling, and the dam breaks.

I push my tongue deeper into her mouth, swallowing her muffled squeak as I tug her closer, into my lap. Ellie matches my intensity, pressing my back against the wall. Her fingers rake through my hair as she devours me with desperate, forceful kisses.

The string that held her back has clearly snapped, her hesitation gone. Fire rushes through my veins, urging me to show her how much further we can go. My collar's smothering me, far too tight. I can hardly breathe.

I force my unwilling hands to let go of her and fumble with my top buttons. Ellie catches my bottom lip with her teeth just as I free my neck and inhale the lavender scent of her hair.

Holding her back, I catch my breath as I meet her eyes. "Hungry, aren't you?"

Ellie's lips are swollen and wet, her face flushed with a breathless smile. She traces her fingers along my throat, and a groan escapes me as she sends an aching heat down to my cock.

"I suppose I've claimed you now," she says.

"I'm yours." My voice is thick, lips clamoring for hers, but she pulls away.

Her hesitation's back, her eyes bleeding vulnerability as they search mine. "You won't break my heart?"

How could she possibly think I would? Even considering it sends a splinter digging into my chest.

"Never."

I pull her gently to me, sliding my fingers through the soft locks of hair tumbling out of her bun, and wrap her in a deep but tender kiss. It's less desperate than before, but I hope it conveys exactly how much I need her. Adore her.

The door creaks. My eyes open, peeking past Ellie.

My mother's standing there. And she's not leaving.

Realization hits Ellie that we're no longer alone, and she pushes herself off me, wincing as her legs untangle from my lap. She stumbles to her feet, straightening her clothes and hair.

I fall back against the wall with a thud, then stare at the ceiling. *Fuck.*

"I didn't mean to interrupt," Mother says, followed by a thump as she sets something on the counter. "I've been looking for you—I need to make a delivery, but I'm simply not up to it today."

"I should go," Ellie says, and my gaze drops to her.

She's glancing around the room with all the nerves of a scared bunny, her elbows tucked in as she wrings her hands together. This is the worst possible turn of events. I didn't even keep her from my mother for an entire day.

Mother waves her off. "No, no. Stay. Have some tea. It looks like you already have the kettle going." She walks stiffly over to the fireplace, removing the kettle with a metal poker.

Ellie takes a quick step forward. "Let me help you."

"No need." Mother shuffles back to the kitchen and rummages through a cabinet, looking for tea leaves. "Just a moment."

As she hobbles into the other room, Ellie looks to me for guidance. My instinct is to take her by the hand and get her the fuck out of here, but I'm not quite ready to walk around in public yet. I haul myself off the bed, attempting subtlety as I rearrange myself, then pull out a chair at the table for her. She slowly lowers herself into it while I slump into the other one, buttoning my collar back up.

A moment later, Mother returns, humming nonsense words as she pours hot water into two teacups and a mug, then sprinkles in various tea leaves. "So, tell me about yourself. How did you two meet?"

"I already told you," I mutter, running my hand through my hair.

Ellie's eyes widen, and she brings her hand to her face to hide an emerging smile. My heart flutters, but gets squashed the instant my mother speaks again.

"Yes, you did, but I was asking about her perspective." She looks back at Ellie. "Do you have any classes together?"

"Only one."

Mother gives us each a teacup before sitting with her mug in the well-worn armchair near the fire, where she spends most of her time at home. "Let me know if you need any sugar."

Ellie lifts her teacup, her pinky sticking out to the side, and takes a delicate sip. "This is lovely. I've never had this flavor before."

"This is something I mix up myself to ease my aches and pains," Mother replies, holding up her mug.

I gulp down my tea. It burns, but my body's finally calming down and I just want this over with. The more time Ellie spends around my mother, the more likely she'll be scared off. That was fine with all the others, but not her.

"Caeo was telling me about that," she says. "I had a rough morning, and he thought it might help." She takes another sip.

Mother smiles, but it lacks any genuine warmth. Ellie probably can't tell, but I've seen it enough to know.

"You said you needed help with a delivery?" I ask.

"Yes." Mother sets her mug on the floor. "I finished the alterations on Farmer Crowley's daughter's wedding dress. I haven't had to do such intricate stitching in a long time. He's certainly spending a small fortune on it. He must love her dearly." She focuses her gaze on me. "They're expecting it today, so you had best get going."

Shit. Crowley's is a good six miles away. This will take forever.

"You're lucky I didn't have a second class this afternoon," I mutter. "Come on, Ellie, I'll walk you back first."

She gulps the rest of her tea and grabs her things. "It was nice meeting you."

"Have a lovely day," Mother calls as we leave. I take Ellie's hand and let the door slam behind us.

"Your mom seems nice."

'Seems' being the key word. She can be, when it's just the two of us and I haven't messed something up, but she's never given any of my girlfriends a chance. Some kind of weird jealousy, like she's afraid I'll abandon her. If she were a normal person, she could've given us a moment and come back later, but she chose to make things as awkward as possible.

"Sure, when she's not completely ruining my day," I say, pulling Ellie along the road back to the Academy. I slow down as she grimaces with her steps, but this isn't the best part of town to linger in.

"You don't get along?"

"She has... expectations. When I don't meet them, which is most of the time, things get... tense."

That's an understatement, but I don't need to ruin the moment any more by detailing my childhood beatings. Or making her realize how terrible I am at everything.

Ellie nods. "My father's like that, too. My whole life has been striving to meet the bar he set."

I glance over at her, my chest a little lighter. She understood, when no one else had. They've always just blamed me. Called me weak. But we're both still here, carrying on.

"It sounded like she's a seamstress?" she asks.

"Yep."

"Do you often make deliveries for her?"

"Unfortunately. Most days, she can hardly make it to the shop. But people pay extra for delivery, and we need all the money we can get."

Ellie's steps slow, and a worry burns in my throat that she finally realized how below her station I actually am.

"Maybe I could go with you?" she asks.

Relief washes through me, but it's swallowed by the disappointment of knowing it won't work. "No, you barely made it here. Farmer Crowley's six miles away."

"Oh." She sounds the way I feel, at least. "Well, you should probably get going—you have far enough to go already. I can get back on my own."

The last thing I want is to leave her, but I push that thought aside. It won't help anything, so the best I can do is make sure this final moment together is perfect. I guide her hands to my chest as I step closer, then wrap my arms around her while her thumb caresses me with slow, gentle circles.

Losing myself in the warmth of her eyes, all other thoughts drift away. No one's ever looked at me like this, with genuine care instead of just lust.

"Should I find you at lunch tomorrow?" I ask.

Ellie lifts herself up on her toes, bringing her lips to mine. I breathe in her kiss, holding onto it for as long as my lungs allow.

"I'm counting on it." Her fingers find my hand, lingering in my grasp as she steps away, until I finally let her go. I stand there, waiting for her to look back.

She never does.

Chapter 7

Ellie

I take an extended soak in the tub when I return to my dormitory, longing to ease my aching muscles in the warm water. My next fire incanting class with Professor Beckwith is in two days; hopefully my body will recover in time.

After drying off, I change into a clean uniform and return to our sitting room with my sketchbook, planning to pass the time until dinner drawing. I've just turned to a fresh page when I notice Sophie's door is ajar—she must have returned while I was bathing.

For all my hopes of making friends, I've so far failed at forming much of a connection with either of my roommates. If I can fix their fight, that could go a long way in doing so. After a moment's hesitation, I knock on her door.

"Sophie, can we talk? I haven't seen you since placements."

Peeking into the shadows of her room, I find her at her desk, writing by lantern light, and a potent sandalwood scent overwhelms my nostrils. Her straight blond hair hangs down today, shorter than my brown locks, the sharp edges grazing her shoulders.

She drops her pen and turns to me, her mouth scrunched. "You should've told us who you were, and how much experience you had incanting."

The words I had planned to say next disappear into the darkness—this isn't just about Alexis, but me. I swallow, then my voice comes out dry. "You heard?"

"Everyone's talking about it. Detura's daughter's in our year, and two people placed so high they have their own special class. It wasn't hard to figure out."

I glance around her room, my throat twisting. It's as cramped and bare as the others, but the darkness and flickering orange light offer an unexpected coziness, unlike the pale gray skies that highlight the lack of color in mine.

"I'm sorry. I wanted people to see me, not my father. And I hadn't fully grasped just how far ahead of everyone else I was."

Perhaps that was naive of me, to think others would be motivated to practice in secret—after all, since I'm not my father, I was breaking the law, too—but Reid proves I wasn't horribly wrong in that assumption.

Sophie raises a doubtful brow. "You thought it was normal to incant non-verbally?"

"I didn't really think about it. It was simply what was expected of me." I lean against the doorframe, dropping my gaze. Memories surface of sitting on my bedroom floor for days, struggling to make a flower bloom without a word. Seeking that nod of approval as if it were my only source of air. "My father—my entire childhood, the only other children I saw were the ones I glimpsed in the streets when I looked out my window."

"Are you trying to make me feel sorry for you?"

The edge in her voice snaps me back. "No! I-I wanted you to understand." My chest tightens with worry that I've only made things worse. "I'm sorry."

Sophie's expression is unreadable by the dim light. A moment later, she shakes her head with a scoff. "Little Miss Privilege. Of course the High Marshal's daughter would grow up thinking incanting is normal."

I straighten, my muscles tensing. That wasn't the reaction I'd been hoping for; I must have worded it wrong. "I didn't mean—"

"You have no idea what it's like for the rest of us, do you? I *had* practiced, despite it being outlawed. I wanted to be here, and I wanted to do well. That's why I delayed for a year. I wanted to make sure I was ready."

My brow furrows. "Then why—"

She cuts me off again, pressing her hands against her desk. "You don't even want to be here, do you?"

"It wasn't really my choice, but—"

"My father gave everything to the war. He lost his leg. Yet here you are, acting like you deserve sympathy for having everything handed to you?"

My surprise boils into anger. This wasn't even supposed to be about me to begin with—she's the one who tried to trick Alexis. But she has no right to judge me, no idea what it's like to grow up under the weight of never-ending expectations.

"If you care so much, then why are you stuck in the remedial classes?" The words blurt out before I can stop myself, and I'm immediately flooded with regret.

Sophie's chair squeaks as she pushes to her feet, eyes narrowing. "I choked. Something someone like you wouldn't understand."

I swallow, trying to recover. "You think I don't know what it's like to be under pressure? My father's the High Marshal. That's my entire life."

"Poor you." She crosses her arms, glaring at me through the dark shadows carving into her face. "Now, if you don't mind, some of us have some studying to get back to." She returns to her paper, the tip of her pen scraping against it as she continues writing.

Possible responses fly through my head, from biting retorts to pacifying words, but they evaporate before I can form them. They won't change the fact that I failed to reach her, and every passing second has me wishing I could disappear into the darkness.

THE NEXT MORNING, Alexis and I wrap our coats tight against the cold as we walk the stone pathways that cut through the sea of dirt to Professor Dewey's wind incanting class. I keep my mouth shut about Sophie, worried that the details of our spat could turn Alexis against me, too, despite her not seeming to care about my past. She lost her parents to the war—she could just as easily take my lack of enthusiasm the wrong way.

Reid's waiting in the back when we arrive, so I join him while Alexis finds a seat among the other students. The classroom's similar to all the rest, but with everything placed with precision and care, every desk aligned at perfect ninety-degree angles.

Shortly after our arrival, Professor Dewey strides in, a toadish man with a bald spot and tortoiseshell spectacles. He tells Reid and me to take some empty seats in the back, saying he'll deal with us after he addresses the rest of the class.

After a brief introduction, he makes it abundantly clear that he's a perfectionist with an eye for detail and expects nothing less from us. He draws three focals on the chalkboard, emphasizing the exact degrees of their angles and the percentage of the circles' circumferences and diameters that each line should take up, without using any measuring tools. After directing the rest of the students to copy them, he approaches Reid and me.

Our task is to draw every wind focal we know. He'll review them at the end of the period to assess their accuracy.

Reid curses under his breath after the professor leaves to check on the others' progress. "I haven't actually drawn any of these in years."

At least we're in the same boat.

We leave with pages so marked up, you'd think a cat attacked them, with the expectation of submitting our revisions in two days. It briefly crosses my mind to slide them under Sophie's door as proof that I'm not as perfect as she seems to think, but she'd probably take it the wrong way.

Basics of Earth Incanting is next, taking place outside in the dirt. Professor Thornton at least came up with a creative way to evaluate our skills—we're to recreate all the earth-based focals we know, using the incantation itself to do so: ones that grow flowers should be made of flowers, ones that create stone, made of stone. The most difficult by far is the one that cleaves the ground in two; making a circle out of jagged cracks proves to be quite arduous.

By the end of the period, Reid has seventeen intricate circles of various natural materials while I have nineteen. He doesn't wait for me to walk to the dining hall with him.

One more person irritated by my ability. Not in the mood to risk making things worse, I skip lunch, heading to the library to get started on Dewey's corrections.

THE NEXT DAY'S back to fire and water incanting classes in the morning. As expected, Beckwith has prepared another set of conditioning exercises for us to do in the same small classroom, just the two of us. But this time, he warns he'll return shortly to go over "forms" with us. On the one hand, it's a relief to know we won't be spending an entire bell destroying ourselves again, but it also means we can't strip down to our small clothes this time. I make a mental note to check if there's any special uniforms better suited for this kind of training.

"You're not still upset with me, are you?" I ask, drumming up the courage after Beckwith leaves.

"Huh?" Reid pauses in the middle of stretching his arm across his chest. "What are you talking about?"

"Yesterday, after earth incanting. You left without speaking to me."

His brow furrows. "Oh. No, I was mad at myself. Messed up my circle of vines. If I hadn't, I probably would've gotten one more than you."

Relief washes over me. "Doubtful. I was two ahead, remember?" And just like that, my nerves go taut again. *I shouldn't have rubbed it in. I should've said something encouraging, something—*

"Yeah, but you went the easy route. It's quicker to fix mistakes made of grass and flowers." A smirk flashes across his face as he lowers himself to the floor, preparing for sit-ups.

A warm glow blooms within—my retort didn't make things worse—but my solace is short-lived. Reid and I are a sweat-drenched mess when Beckwith returns, handing each of us a wooden practice sword.

"The sword is the perfect tool to develop and focus an incanter's skill with fire, especially for those who can incant as quickly as the two of you." Unlike us, Beckwith wields a gleaming saber—the standard weapon for the Order, outside of incanting. "It requires precise control of your mind and body, but you'll find the results to be devastating on the battlefield."

To illustrate his point, he ignites the blade without a word, flames surging from hilt to tip in half a heartbeat. Pointing the weapon away from us, he demonstrates a forward thrust that sends the blaze rushing off the tip into a fireball that shoots another two feet before dissipating. The saber instantly reignites with a horizontal swing that leaves flames burning the air behind it.

My jaw drops. It never occurred to me to use incanting this way, always imagining it better suited for ranged combat. The idea of fighting in close quarters makes swallowing difficult.

"Obviously, you won't be attempting any of this with those wooden swords. You'll begin by practicing proper form and basic footwork, and I'll return at the end of the lesson to review your progress."

Professor Beckwith shows us the basic stance: his back foot pointed to the side and his front foot forward, with a slight bend in his knees. We imitate him, and to my relief, he makes corrections to both of us.

"Remember—perfecting your form can mean the difference between life and death."

With those foreboding words as our motivation, we spend the rest of the period taking small steps forward and backward across the room while trying to maintain the proper stance, with the occasional forward lunge to break the monotony of it. The wooden sword grows heavy within minutes, and by the end, I can barely hold my arm up. Luckily, Beckwith returns earlier than expected and is satisfied with our demonstration, so there's time to take a quick soak in my dorm before my next lesson.

Beckwith's the only professor who doesn't overload us with assignments, but at least it's not limited to Reid and me. Alexis often joins us, drawing focals and memorizing incantations late into the night, barely finishing everything before exhaustion overtakes us.

After several days of barely leaving Reid's company except for sleep, I'm in dire need of some alone time. Following a *Basics of Strategy* lesson focused on fae curses—a subject not worth worrying about during the heat of battle but can be incredibly dangerous during prolonged encounters—I decline his invitation to get a head start on our assignment in the library. Instead, I relax into one of the large, cushy armchairs scattered about the Tactical Wing's antechamber and pull out my sketchbook. Like most of the Academy, the ashen space is sparsely decorated, relying mostly on the purple upholstery with floral motifs to give it any semblance of life. A gray carpet muffles the sound of footsteps as it leads up the wide staircase to the classrooms above.

Two girls sit on the far side of the room, speaking animatedly to one another. I sketch several quick gestures of them, hoping to capture their mirth as they gossip about our fellow students.

I've barely found time to draw since arriving here, and my stress rinses away with each stroke of charcoal along the page. A few weeks into term, and life's settled into a routine not much different from home. I haven't spoken to Sophie since our squabble, and while I'm getting along with Alexis well enough, the connections I've longed for still feel out of reach. Despite spending all my time with Reid, I simply don't have the same rapport with him that Alexis does. Incanting seems to be all I have going for me, which means I'll be spending my life praying the wars have truly ended so I never have to fight for real.

"Ellie?"

"Hmm?" I'm so intent on getting this nose right that I don't look up until a hand lands on my shoulder, fingers tracing back and forth along its dips and curves.

Heat blooms through my chest as my heart quickens. It's him.

"Caeo." A smile lights up his face as he squeezes into my seat. It's a large chair, but still meant for one, so we're blissfully cramped together. Butterflies dance in the warmth where his body presses against mine.

He tucks his arm around me. "It's been a while."

It has, hasn't it? Between my roommate drama, heavy workload, and Beckwith-induced exhaustion, I've hardly had a moment to think of him. Realizing how long it's been, my nerves spike with worry that his feelings have changed.

"You didn't find me," I say.

He scratches the back of his head, his brow crinkling. "I guess not. But I did now."

A smile wipes away his concern, and my fears retreat. Last time I saw him, he had to walk six miles to make a delivery for his mother—he's likely even busier than I am.

His gaze drifts from my face down to my sketchbook. "Hey, those are really good."

"Thanks."

I glance down at my drawing, then back to his face, tracing his tender lines with my eyes. My fingers twitch, torn between conflicting urges: to draw him or run through his hair as I kiss his invitingly soft lips.

My mind squeals at the latter. *What has he done to me?*

He looks toward the staircase. "I can't really stay—I'm already late for class. Do you think you'll still be here after?"

"I can wait." My core tingles in anticipation, already imagining the warmth of his body pressed against mine, the taste of his tongue.

Caeo brushes his fingers through my hair. "Then I'll see you later." His touch lingers on my chin as he stands.

I nod, biting my lip, then he hurries toward the stairs.

I turn back to my drawing, smiling to myself. The two girls I was sketching have seemingly disappeared, so I flip to a new page, planning to draw whatever comes to mind.

Nothing does.

But my stomach's grumbling, so I pack up my sketchbook, heading to dinner early.

Chapter 8

Caeo

I slowly exhale, smoke clouding my view of the afternoon sky.

A series of thumps and rustles announces someone climbing over the edge of the roof, and sure enough, Reid grunts as he settles next to me on the slate shingles that have been digging uncomfortably into my back.

Of course he found me here. The blacksmith's roof was a popular escape during our childhood, with a near-constant stream of hot air flowing from its chimney. It was a lifesaver for us poor kids from the outskirts during Haven's frigid winters. All we had to do was sneak in through the neighboring lumberyard, stack some wood against the back wall, and climb up. One time, the carpenter dismantled our climbing structure, stranding us for twelve bells—an entire day— until another kid built a new way up.

I offer Reid my pipe of speckled long leaf.

He eyes the bowl as he takes it. "What color?"

"Red."

"Life's that bad?"

That's a matter of perspective: yellow isn't strong enough to do anything for me anymore, and the giddiness of orange is a waste when you're alone. Which I was, until he showed up. Explaining all that isn't worth the effort, though, so I close my eyes rather than answer.

"I haven't seen you around these last few weeks." Reid nudges my arm, and I open my eyes, taking the pipe back as he exhales smoke. "Thought I'd at least see you at mealtimes."

"I'm not living in the dorms, so food costs extra. I can't afford it."

Thick, puffy clouds roll in from the west. The arrival of spring means the rains will begin soon. While that's good for the farms surrounding Haven, it'll make this rooftop far too slippery to keep using as an escape.

"I'm sure Ellie'd cover it if you asked."

"Hmm?" I squint at a cloud that vaguely resembles a duck wearing a bonnet.

"Did something happen between you two? I would've bet good money you'd be inseparable by now, but she doesn't even mention you."

I blink my eyes, unsure what Reid just said. The long leaf must already be kicking in. "What are you talking about?"

"Never mind," Reid mutters. "Last thing I need is to get in the middle of it."

I take another puff from my pipe. It tastes like ass, but its effects are worth pushing through the flavor. I offer it back to Reid, but he waves it away.

"What's so bad that you managed to scrounge up some red?" he asks.

"You know my mother."

Maternal frustrations were one of the things Reid and I bonded over as kids, with mine bouncing between overbearing affection and beatings while his forgot he existed. Which is probably worse. At least mine still loved me when I wasn't disappointing her, and the hitting stopped once I got bigger. Now she's just a pain in the ass sometimes.

Reid sighs. "Let me guess—playing the victim? Guilt tripping?"

"Both. Every time I leave for class, she's reminding me to come to the shop right after to make a delivery or lift something for her. I barely have time to practice incanting, though at this point I don't know why I even bother."

I gesture to the various foci lying abandoned nearby: a hodgepodge of stones, surrounded by scattered papers covered with circular focals.

"What happened to not incanting in Haven?" Reid teases.

Growing up, I always gave him a hard time about that. He wanted to practice all the time, while I just wanted to get through my days without risking incarceration.

"I'll worry about that once I actually incant something. They can't punish me for tracing lines around pretty rocks while spouting nonsense." I tilt my head as I consider a particularly robust cloud, seeing if any shapes form. It could be a pig's snout.

"Let me help," Reid says, as expected. "There's gotta be something you're doing wrong. I can help figure it out."

This is why I haven't put much effort into crossing his path lately. I know in my gut that there's nothing to figure out—it's just one more thing I've failed at, and I'm running out of time to improve. Having Reid confirm that would only make it harder to pretend I have a future outside of helping my mother at the shop.

"Not now."

After a few more hits of long leaf, I close my eyes, letting myself float away to peaceful oblivion.

I SILENTLY CURSE MY MOTHER as I pull open the door to the lecture hall, cutting off Professor Tillman mid-sentence. Late again, all because she made me wait around for a delivery that never showed.

A hundred sets of eyes focus on me. I quickly squeeze onto the nearest bench next to a red-haired girl who barely scoots over to make room.

Tillman's gaze narrows at me before he continues.

"As I was saying, until recently, the Border Wars were a constant threat against our nation. The sun rose in the east, set in the west, and the fae pushed against our borders, claiming our land as their own. The common man believed the wars occurred simply between us and the fae, but it's important to realize they are not a singular enemy."

As he turns his back to us and draws a map on the chalkboard, the redhead eyes me intently, her lips curling into a smile as she bites the end of her pen.

Wonderful. I force a smile, then fix my gaze on Tillman's map as if I actually care about it.

At best, it's a wobbly oval divided into four sections. The smallest is on the left side, stretching narrowly from the top to the bottom.

"If you've ever looked at a map before in your life, you'll recognize this as Landore, our home."

Tillman taps the smallest area with his chalk. He moves to the other sections of the oval—one covers the top center, another the bottom center, with the third mirroring Landore on the other side, though much wider.

"The faelands comprise three different realms. Thanks to our prisoners of war, we know the northern realm as Aedys, the southern as Ystyr, and the eastern as Llynos." He writes the names on the board as he says them, the chalk squeaking with every stroke. "The Border Wars were fought against Aedys and Ystyr, and this discovery was a turning point in the war—it allowed us to tailor our strategies to each battle's opponents."

Fascinating stuff. Truly. I'm sure it'll affect my life someday.

Warmth presses into the side of my thigh, the red-haired pen-eater having pinned her leg against mine, her eyes locked on me. If I scoot any farther away, I'll fall flat on my ass off the side of the bench.

I really don't need this right now. Attention like this used to be the one thing that made me feel good about myself. And dragging me into their beds—who wouldn't enjoy that? But I'm getting tired of just being a fun piece of meat. There's more to me, and I wish people would see that.

Experience has taught me that rebuffing her advances will risk causing a scene—it's better to give her what she wants, then run as soon as I get the chance. So I put my hand on her leg and give a quick squeeze. Her eyes widen, and I shoot her a smile, praying it'll be enough to keep her hopefully daydreaming till the end of class. Then I lean forward on the desk, prop my chin against my hand and stare at Professor Tillman like he is the most interesting man alive.

He's not. His voice drones on:

"When the Border Wars ended twenty-one years ago, it was because the northern fae, those from Aedys, suddenly ceased hostilities. The last battle occurred a few days later in the village of Oakhurst. The Ystyr fae attacked in force, and it seemed inevitable they would win the day as hundreds of civilians were forced to flee for their lives. But when the Order's reinforcements arrived, they found the village abandoned and the fae border no closer than previously recorded..."

Class ends an excruciating bell later, and I practically leap from the bench into the crowd to escape my would-be companion. I cringe as someone tugs on my sleeve, bracing for the worst as I turn around.

Relief washes over me at the sight of beautiful cinnamon eyes.

"Ellie."

I quickly scan the students filing out behind her for red hair. Catching a glimpse heading our way, I take Ellie's hand and lead her down the hall, around a corner, to an empty corridor that catches the echoes of everyone's departure. Candlelight flickers from the wall sconces, bathing us in a surprisingly sensual light for a lifeless hallway, despite the greasy tallow smell. The warm glow clings to Ellie's skin, making me very aware that my lips could be doing that, too.

"Hiding from someone?" she asks as I check if anyone followed us.

"The girl sitting next to me made it very clear she had intentions for me."

"Did she?" Ellie peeks back, too. "Too bad you belong to me." Her eyes meet mine, and despite the boldness of her words, doubt shadows her face.

It makes my heart ache that she'd question that at all. I know I have a reputation, and by most people's standards, we haven't been taking things slow, but I want things to be different with her.

"I do." Sliding my hands around her waist, I bring her close as I lean against the wall. She lights up with a smile that chases away the darkness, melting me with its radiance.

"Really?" she asks. "I wouldn't know it based on how little I've seen you."

She wraps her hands behind my neck, fingers twisting the curls of my hair, her confidence returning to her touch. Irritation at my mother for keeping me so busy bubbles up, but I pop it, keeping my focus entirely on Ellie.

"Trust me, I'm yours." I bring my lips to hers, giving in to a kiss that pulls every ounce of tension out of me until there's only her.

She smiles as we part, far too soon. "Do you have time now?"

A jab in my chest disrupts the cozy heat within. "I wish—I promised my mother I'd help at the shop." Ellie's hips relax into me as I adjust my grip on her waist. "The equinox is coming up. It's one of the busiest times of the year for her, and she can't sort through all the deliveries on her own. The money from all the new dresses for the ball keeps us fed for most of the year."

"What ball?"

"The Equinox Ball. It's one of the few times a year they actually make this place look fancy. You'll love it." I hesitate, my pulse quickening. "You should go with me."

Ellie's eyes practically glow. "I'd love to."

It's more than I can bear. I lift her onto her toes, peppering her with kisses until she lets me in. She tightens her grip in my hair, twisting as she pulls me closer.

My hands slide down her hips, ready to wrap around her ass and hoist her up, pulling her legs around me so I can push her against the opposite wall. But the instant they curl around her backside, she jerks back, breathless.

"What are you doing?"

"Uh... kissing you?"

Her face burns bright pink. "Someone could walk down this hallway any second."

"Sounds like their problem." But I let go of her, holding my hands up in surrender. I may not care, but the last thing I want is to make her uncomfortable.

She straightens her blouse. "You said you had work to do? Anything I can help with?"

None of my girlfriends have ever offered that before. While nothing would make me happier, if Mother's around, she could ruin everything. "You can," I say slowly, "but if my mother's there, it might be best if you head back."

Ellie's face falls. "Does she not like me?"

"She doesn't like anybody. I just don't want her making you uncomfortable."

Ellie idly strokes my arm as she considers. "Alright. But if she's there, I'm at least saying hello. She needs to get used to me." She presses closer, giving me a quick kiss on the lips. "Because you're mine, and I'm not letting anyone scare me away."

There it is. The spark I've only glimpsed before, breaking free.

I need more.

Chapter 9

Ellie

I'm not going to kiss him. I'm here to help. To get to know him better.

I repeat those words to myself as Caeo leads me to his mother's shop. It's on the way to the Kettle Maker, just past where the gray shambles of the outskirts turn into a bustling town of red brick and brown cobblestone, the squat building pressed between its much larger, gabled neighbors. According to Caeo, his mother inherited it from her previous employer, an elderly woman who still lives in the second-story flat. Horizontal bands of weathered wood mark each level.

He turns the doorknob, but it's locked.

"That's a good sign," he mutters, dropping my hand to dig out his key.

A bell jingles as he pushes the door open, and a whiff of grease hits me as I follow him inside, likely from the cast-iron sewing machine bolted to one of the nearby worktables. A large window fills the cramped room with afternoon light, illuminating cubbies and shelves full of colorful fabric bolts and bundles of thread. Racks of dresses hang to the side, squeezed in wherever they can fit.

Two large wooden crates take up most of the walking space.

"Is that the delivery?" I ask, setting my bag on one of the tables.

Caeo snaps his head back to me. "Hmm? Oh, yeah. They must

have dropped it off during class. I just need to find the crowbar..." His words drift off as he turns to the shelves. Once he finds it, he joins me at the crates. "You wanna do the honors?"

"I've never used a crowbar before."

"It's easy. Here." He wraps his arms around me from behind as he threads it between my fingers. His clove scent and body heat pressed against me has the metal feeling slick in my palms. As we wedge it into the seam at the top, he says, "Rock it a bit for some more space, then push."

The friction of his arms rubbing against me stokes a blaze with every brush. I'd never have guessed something as simple as opening a crate could be so sensual. Not kissing him will be harder than I thought.

I force myself to focus, ignoring how his breath grazes my ear. I grunt, pushing down. The nails squeak as they pop out of the wood.

Caeo pats my hip as he steps away, his fingers running along the lid. "You wanna get the other one while I finish here?"

"Sure." I tear my gaze away from his hand and its imagined touch. It lands on a large crate made from slats of unfinished pine.

A loud crack startles me, and I turn just in time to catch Caeo prying the lid the rest of the way off the first crate, releasing the scent of woodchips into the air. His rolled-up sleeves show off the flexing muscles of his forearms, tightening and twisting with every motion.

He glances my way, then blinks. "Are you just gonna watch?" A smirk stretches across his face.

My lips twist as I hold back a smile. Somehow, I don't feel embarrassed.

"I am helping."

To prove it, I line the flat edge of the crowbar to the thin gap beneath the lid of the crate in front of me. Uncertainty flickers in my mind as my palms slide along the cool metal.

What was I—

I almost jump as Caeo's hand lands on mine. "Move it here for better leverage." He keeps it there as I push down. At this point, I don't know if he thinks I'm helpless or is just looking for an excuse to touch me.

"I could've done it on my own," I say, meeting his eyes.

"I know. But you don't have to."

A twinge of annoyance peeks through the warmth of his sentiment. "What if I wanted to?"

He pulls his hand away, holding it up in surrender. "Then have at it. You can even keep the crowbar. I'll never open another crate without you."

After a second's hesitation, I chance answering that flirt with one of my own. "I think I'd rather watch you do the rest."

He laughs, then has me scoot aside as he wrestles the lid the rest of the way off. He leans it against the wall before resting his hands on the edge of the crate, eyeing its contents.

I set the crowbar down on the table with a clank. Caeo jolts, glancing up at me.

"What's next?" I ask.

"Um... we check for damage, then sort by color. Store them in the cubbies."

"You don't sound sure about that."

He huffs a sigh, then runs his hand through his dark hair. "Sorry, I guess I'm distracted."

My throat tightens. "Is it me? I can go—I don't want to be a problem."

"What? No." He steps closer, taking my hands as he leans against the crate. "Why do you always doubt yourself so much?"

Do I? My gaze drops to his fingers, rubbing softly against mine.

"I... I suppose I don't have much experience doing things on my own. It's always been following whatever my father said. I'm worried I'll make a mistake."

"What's so bad about that? It happens to everyone."

I shrug, still avoiding his eyes. "But what if people don't forgive them? I messed up, trying to fix things with Sophie. I think she hates me."

Caeo brings his hand to my face, tilting my chin up. "I don't know who that is, but anyone who makes you feel bad about yourself isn't worth your time."

"I can tell myself that all I want, but it still hurts."

He runs his fingers along my hairline, tucking a stray lock behind my ear. "I know. But you're a good person. You're kind, and you care. They'll see that. You just have to get more comfortable dealing with people. I can help."

All those words... Tears well in my eyes. No one, outside of my mom, has ever said anything like that before. To see more in me than simply being my father's successor. To want to help me be *more*.

He leans closer, his lips tracking toward mine. The moment's perfect, his tender words pulling me to him. His breath warms my skin, and I tilt my mouth up to meet him...

Against everything, I pull back, my breath snagging in my throat. "No."

Caeo blinks, retreating slightly. "No?"

"I promised myself I wouldn't kiss you. I'm here to help."

"That's not fair," he says, despite the smile breaking through. "I didn't agree to that."

The words fall out before I think. "Sounds like your problem."

Caeo winces. "Ouch. Ellie's got sass." My lungs compress beneath a worry I overstepped, but he brings my fingers to his lips, planting a kiss on them. "I like it."

My heart swells, then he pulls me with him over to the crate.

Our legs press together as he shows me how to unroll about a couple feet of each bolt, checking for damage—the very first one has a brownish stain along its edge, and he has me set it aside. The next one passes inspection, so he rolls it back up and puts it on the floor, explaining that once we have them sorted by color, we'll move them into the cubbies.

He lifts a bolt of periwinkle cotton, examining its edges, and the swash of coral pink beneath it catches my eye. I pull it out, running my fingers along its soft edges as I check for fraying.

"That's a good color for you," Caeo says, bringing the end up to my face. "Matches your blushes."

My cheeks burn as I pull it free from his hands.

Ching.

A bell rings with the scraping of the door behind us. Caeo's body tenses where he presses into my side, spiking my nerves.

It's his mom. Her lips press together before curling into a smile.

"Oh, hello," she says, slipping her coat off. "Ellie, right? I wasn't expecting you here." She hobbles over to a hook on the wall to hang it from.

Determined to follow through on my earlier claim, I'm about to step over to greet her when Caeo cuts me off.

"She was just leaving." He drops the bolt he was holding back into the crate and grabs my hand.

"But..." I swipe my bag from the table as he pulls me toward the door. Glancing back, I get a flash of his mother watching us, lips pursed, before finding myself outside on the street.

"What was that about?" I ask, tugging my hand free as Caeo turns back to me. He rests his hand on my back, guiding me away from the window to the wood-paneled building next door. "I wanted to say hello."

"Well, she did. That's enough, right?"

"Are you really that worried she'll scare me away?" He can't think so little of me, not after everything he said.

He sighs, taking my hands. "No, she's just... not a part of my life I want you around." My face must have fallen, because he quickly stutters, "I-It's nothing against you. Just her. She'll try to make you feel bad about yourself."

The creases etched in his face reveal an insecurity I haven't seen in him before—he must be speaking from experience. While Father never intentionally made me feel unworthy, I'm well acquainted with how it feels to struggle with a parent's expectations. My heart melts as a deep, protective instinct burns in my chest.

I squeeze his fingers. "I understand. But don't let her do that to you, either."

He presses tightly back, then lifts his hand to tuck a lock of my hair behind my ear. "I'll try."

With a sigh, I glance down the road, back toward the Academy. A long walk awaits me, but it's early enough that I should make it back before it gets too cold.

"Promise me I'll see you before the ball?" I ask, turning back to him.

"How about tomorrow after class? I can take you to dinner?"

A smile stretches across my face, and he lights up. He moves closer, kissing right where my dimple crimps my cheek. Over and over again.

Laughter falls out of me, and I step back. "Stop it! I'll see you tomorrow. The steps of my dormitory at twelfth bell?"

"Sounds good." He gives me one last kiss before releasing my fingers, opening the door to the shop, and disappearing from sight.

Chapter 10

Caeo

I've been chugging through the last few days with barely a moment to breathe between class, studying, and heavy lifting for my mother. It's as if everyone decided it's time to make my life as miserable as possible, except for Reid, who showed up at my door insisting we go to The Buttoned-Up Duck and "meet the girls." I don't want to meet any girls, and I'm not sure why he does, either. But he promised to buy me a drink, which saves me from going through more of my long leaf, so here I am.

Warm candlelight spatters the green walls between columns of decorative lace stapled to them. Mismatched buttons line each strip, randomly placed as they climb toward the ceiling and meet a decorative border of ducks marching around the room. Meanwhile, whittled mallards sit at the center of every table and the corners of the bar, some painted, some left bare.

I have no idea what the owner was thinking.

Reid slams a tankard in front of me, then slides into the other side of our semicircular booth. A greenish liquid spills onto the table, and I eye it suspiciously. While The Duck offers an adventurous selection, we usually stick with ale.

"What's this?" I ask.

"It's new from Kestel. Made of something called a melon, I think."

I take a sip and almost spit it out. "Shit, that's sweet." I cough. "Is there even any alcohol in there?"

"They said there was." Reid takes a swig of his drink and relaxes against the wooden back of the booth.

I pull over his tankard. "Give me that." Regular ale sloshes inside as it catches on the uneven planks of the tabletop. "Why do you get ale and I get this poison?"

Reid swipes it back. "Someone recommended it."

I follow his gaze to a man eyeing him from across the crowded bar, who gives me a smile and wink when he notices my attention. It's not particularly well-lit here, but he's got a good-looking face, narrow eyes, and sandy-blond hair pulled back in a knot.

"If you want to get in his pants so bad, you should be the one drinking this swill." I reach for Reid's ale.

My hand jerks back at a blaze of heat, flames igniting at my fingertips.

"Dammit, Reid! That fucking hurt!" I shove my singed fingers into my mouth. I should've expected that; it's not the first time he's used that trick.

"What's he doing now?" Alexis's chipper voice says as she drops into the booth next to Reid.

"Torturing me so he can impress some guy with terrible taste in drinks," I mutter, checking for burns. Just slightly pink.

"Oh?" She searches the room. "Which guy?"

Reid nods toward the bar.

Alexis's eyes widen, her rings clinking as her fingers splay across the table. "No! I danced with him the last time I was here."

"You came here without me?"

Someone taps my shoulder, and the rest of their conversation vanishes into nothing.

"You want to make some room?" Ellie asks, bringing her hand

back to clutch it tightly with her other.

She's wearing her hair in a thick braid today, twisted up behind her head. My fingers itch for the day I finally see it down and they can run through those chestnut locks.

'The girls.' Of course. Reid meant Ellie and Alexis.

"Yes. I mean, yeah."

My heart's already skipping as I scoot deeper into the booth. She sits next to me, her leg brushing against mine under the table, and smiles nervously. A warm tingle fills my chest—I adore watching her push through her vulnerability, revealing her inner strength.

"What happened to your fingers?"

The pain flares up as my attention shifts. "Reid burned them."

"Reid." Ellie glares at him.

"What? He tried to steal my drink."

Ellie rolls her eyes, then turns back to me. "Let me see."

I give her my hand, my fingertips throbbing with my pulse. With a gentle touch, frost crystallizes over her fingers, and a soothing cold chases away the burning heat.

"Let me know if it's too much."

"You're committing a crime right now, you know." My gaze moves from her frozen fingers to her eyes.

She leans in, lowering our hands from sight. "Then I suppose we'll have to be discreet."

There she is, peeking out of her shell.

Despite the chill against my fingers, my chest burns with the memory of the last time we were this close. I tilt my head closer to hers, breathing in her scent, and the ruckus of the busy tavern fades away.

Her light dims as her smile flickers. "I stood you up for dinner, didn't I? I don't know what happened—it completely slipped my mind. I meant to meet you."

"Don't worry about it. I forgot, too."

Ellie's eyes widen. "You did?"

Shit. I probably shouldn't have admitted that so easily, but I'm not even sure how it happened. I must've gotten roped into helping Mother again. "I remember *now*. But I didn't then. It's alright, though—we're both here."

Her face relaxes, her smile returning. "We are."

"And you're good with kissing me today?"

The sweetest laugh puffs her cheeks. "You'll have to find out."

My head sinks closer until she's only inches away, our eyes locked. Her lips slowly part, calling to me. I move to close the gap, breathing in her breath…

"I'm here, too," Reid interrupts.

Ellie blushes, dropping my hand and retreating.

Really? What'd I do to deserve that? I shoot Reid a quick glare, then take Ellie's hand back. "Ignore him."

"Please don't," he says.

I give him the finger while keeping my eyes on Ellie. She bites her lip as if holding back a giggle, and the urge to bite that lip myself has me straining against my pants.

BANG.

Reid's fist hits the table, rattling the tankards. We startle apart.

"Fuck no, this isn't happening." He pushes himself out of the booth.

Confused, I lean past Ellie to see where he's going. Alexis has draped herself over the shoulders of the guy with shitty taste in drinks, laughing at something he said. Reid slides onto the stool next to them and waves down the bartender.

"He's certainly popular," Ellie notes.

"He has horrible taste." I sit back in the booth, begrudgingly accepting that we've lost the moment. I push my tankard toward her. "Reid got me this at his recommendation."

Ellie sniffs it, and her eyebrows shoot up. "Fruity." She takes a cautious sip. "Wow. That is... I've never tasted anything like that." She takes another. "It's not terrible."

"You're kidding." I grab it back and taste it again. "Nope, still bad."

Ellie laughs as I grimace. "Then I'll have this, and you can get yourself something else. Oh, and snacks!"

"Fine, but you better pace yourself. Or don't. That could be fun." I slide out the other side of the booth and give her hand a quick squeeze before weaving through the crowd toward the bar.

I press in beside Reid, claiming some space with my elbows. Waving down the bartender, I order an ale when I finally get his attention. It's painfully loud over here; I could probably make out what Reid and Alexis are saying, but I'm not that interested. One of them must have made a joke, because the guy they're talking to tosses his head back, laughing.

This is gonna be a long night.

The bartender slides a drink toward me. I fish out some money to pay him, then take a swig before hunching over it.

A moment later, I get the uncomfortable feeling of someone's gaze weighing on me. Reid and Alexis's companion is staring at me, a curious look in his eyes.

"Another friend of theirs?" he asks, raising his voice over the noise of the tavern. His tongue flicks between his teeth as he smiles. "You can call me Emmrich."

Reid bumps my arm with his elbow. "What are you doing here?" he hisses, leaning close.

Emmrich's gaze stays fixed on me, despite Alexis attempting a conversation, her fingers trailing along his arm.

Wonderful. The last thing I need is to get dragged into some horribly unbalanced foursome. That'd just open me up to twice as many headaches.

I meet Reid's eyes. "Just getting a drink. I might head home soon."

"Did something happen? I thought I was doing you a favor."

"What are you talking about?"

I jump as someone's hand touches my shoulder.

"What's taking so long?" Ellie leans in on my other side. "Where's the food?"

"Shit." *Why do I keep forgetting things? I haven't been hitting the leaf that hard.* After mumbling an apology, I wave the bartender over again and order some honey chips.

"I'm going back before someone steals our booth." Ellie squeezes my arm before slipping away.

The bartender pushes a bowl of honey chips toward me. I glance at Reid and Alexis, but they're busy fawning all over Emmrich.

Who's *still* watching me, but not in the same way others do. More... contemplative.

"Don't worry, I got that." He flashes a smile before digging through his pocket, then tosses a coin to the bartender.

Reid spins around, his jaw tight. "What are you doing?" He grabs the bowl of chips, forces it into my hands, and turns me away from the bar.

"Go back to Ellie." He shoves me toward the booth where she sits, waiting for me.

Chapter 11

Ellie

Caeo slides into the booth next to me, sweeping the tousled locks of his raven hair out of his face, and puts a bowl of honey chips between us. I take one, munching politely as its sweet flavor fills my mouth, with only the slightest hint of salt. The tavern's still uncomfortably loud, but the buzz of activity's grown more tolerable in the weeks since I left home.

"Sorry that took so long," he says. "My brain doesn't seem to be working right. Must be that melon drink."

I try a joke, hoping to get things back on track. "My brain's still working, so it must be you."

"Wonderful." But his tone conflicts with the sentiment.

Should I try again? He said he liked my sass. "It's alright. I didn't like you for your brains, anyway."

Instead of the laugh I hoped for, Caeo wilts. No smile, no witty retort. Is it possible to ruin everything with a single sentence?

"I'm sorry—I didn't mean it that way." I reach for his hand, praying he'll squeeze it back.

He does, and my throat unclenches. "It's fine, really. I'm only going to the Academy because I grew up here, and that's what everyone does if they have nothing better to do. I'm not like Reid. He actually cares about it."

A warmth spreads through my chest; I'm not the only one unenthusiastic about being here. *And* he gave me an easy way to change the subject, as if he knew I needed it.

"He *is* pretty dedicated," I say, shifting closer to him.

Caeo slides his arm around me, and it's as if my blunders never happened. "We saw one of the recruitment shows the Order does when we were kids. Once he saw what those incanters could do, that was all he wanted in life. Said it called to him. Lucky bastard."

"Lucky?"

"He knows what he wants, and he's actually good at it. Whereas Beckwith and Dewey have already threatened to fail me out before the end of the term."

My stomach sinks. I barely see him already; it'll be worse if he's on campus even less. "It's going that badly?"

Caeo rummages through his pocket and pulls out an aquamarine, placing it on the table. He traces an elementary focal around it with his finger while reciting one of the simplest water incantations I know—one my father had me mastering at six years old.

Nothing happens.

That's impossible.

"What? How did that not...?" I pick up the stone as Caeo slumps back. The table's completely dry, not even a drop of water. That should've been like emptying a bucket onto the table.

"But you said everything perfectly, and the focal was correct."

"It's like that every time. All it does is give me a massive headache. There's no way I'll make it through the semester."

"I didn't know it was possible to be this bad at incanting." I rub the inexplicably dry spot on the table. "I was always told everyone could do it. That it simply took practice."

"That's not really helping my ego."

My entire body grimaces. "That came out wrong. I'm sorry."

He huffs as he returns the aquamarine to his pocket, then takes my hand. "You are so bad at conversations sometimes."

My fingers flinch. "What?"

A smile tugs at his face as he rubs my thumb with his. "It's like, you either plow ahead without thinking at all, or you try too hard. Nothing in between."

"That's not... I just..." I pull my hand away, but his grip tightens.

"Hey." He tilts his head, trying to pull me back to his eyes. "It's fine. I'm not one to talk. I'm terrible at most things."

"Because you don't try." I didn't mean to say it, but it's true. Not once have I witnessed him paying any attention in History.

Caeo's mouth falls open, and the fear that I'm ruining everything rushes back. I stutter an apology, but he cuts me off.

"No, you're right. I don't." He sighs, then runs his hand through his hair. "I guess at some point, I decided it didn't matter how much effort I put in, so why bother?"

"But then you'll never succeed at anything."

He rubs his brow, then looks back at me. "Alright. I'll work on trying harder, and you just... relax. Take a beat, but don't overthink things. And stop feeling like you have to fix everything. Deal?"

A smile blooms across my face. "Deal. And you can start by letting me tutor you."

"Did you already forget the part about not fixing everything?"

"I'm not fixing you—I'm trying to support you."

Caeo's eyes narrow as he holds back a smirk, then he exhales. "Reid's already tried—like you said, I did everything right. It just doesn't work for me."

"Still. You should join us when we study. Your foundational assignments are the same, and we can make sure your incanting work shows an understanding of the material. Maybe that'll be enough for them to let you stay?"

"Yeah, maybe." He rubs my fingers for a moment before grabbing a chip. "But what about you? It doesn't seem like incanting calls to you, either."

It's my turn to sigh, my gaze landing on the silly wooden duck at the center of the table. "Not at all. I'm here entirely because of my father. High Marshal Detura, if you've heard of him."

"*He's* your father? The High Marshal of the Order of Incanters?" Caeo pushes himself a respectable distance away from me. "You should've told me that before I stuck my tongue in your mouth. I'm a dead man."

"Relax, it's not like I'll tell him about that."

"You don't have to. He'll know. Fathers always know."

"Anyway"—I pull Caeo back to me—"while he's a viscount, he earned his title through service, which means I won't inherit it. That limits my marriage prospects, so it's always been expected I'd follow in his footsteps. Coming here wasn't a matter of choice."

His fingers brush against my side. "And if you'd had the option?"

"Then I wouldn't be here. I suppose you'll have to thank him for that."

"Right before he murders me," Caeo mutters, then winces.

I flick his arm playfully. "He's not going to murder you."

"Uh huh." Caeo tucks a stray lock of hair behind my ear. "But seriously—what would you do if you weren't here?"

My heart catches. *No one's ever asked me that.* "I don't know... I doubt I would've had any interest in incanting if it weren't for my father, but it's taken up so much of my life that it's all I am. There was never a chance to find a purpose of my own." Even my tutors' lessons, while well-rounded, all led back to something I'd need to know as an officer in the Order.

"Not even painting?"

He remembered. Warmth spreads from my smile to my toes, and I wrap my arm around his, snuggling into him. "I enjoy it, but it's not really a purpose. Just something that makes life more bearable."

"I get it. Sometimes I feel like I'm a square block being shoved into a circular hole."

And in that moment, he sees me more than anyone else has. Like sunlight thawing my skin on a cloudy day.

He brings his finger to my chin, tilting my face to meet his smoky eyes. "You know what makes my life more bearable?"

He's so close that his clove scent fills my lungs, a heat curling deep within me.

"What?"

His face tugs into a smile. "You."

My breath hitches as my lips part, anticipating his kiss. I lean close, closing my eyes...

Instead, he touches his forehead to mine and whispers, "Come with me."

He threads our fingers and pulls me out of the booth, weaving us through the crowded tavern and out into the chilly night, only a few bells past sunset.

"Where are we going?" I ask breathlessly, then Caeo sweeps me into his arms with a kiss that lifts me to my toes. Three chimes from the clock tower ring before he releases me, my arms still wrapped around his neck as he brings his lips to my ear, his warm breath brushing my skin.

"I have an idea."

He pulls me toward the center of town, my mind barely keeping up with my feet as they stumble along the cobblestone street. Paper lanterns, glowing a warm peachy pink, light our path as we pass villagers and Academy students, chatting excitedly about their night out.

Moments later, we stand at the brick wall surrounding the base of Haven's clock tower, which rises multiple stories over the surrounding buildings. Supposedly it's open during the day to climb to the top, but the wrought-iron gate's currently locked.

"They built this wall after I fell and cracked my head." Caeo glances around before leaning close. "Are you willing to commit a few more crimes tonight?"

My eyes widen. "What are you thinking?"

"We need to get over the wall."

I look it up and down. It's about eight feet tall.

"I think I can do that."

After ensuring no one else is around, I focus my incantation on where the wall meets the earth. Thick vines sprout up, slithering along the clay bricks before curling over the top. Caeo tugs on them to test their strength—they don't budge. He briefly releases my hand as he scales the wall ahead of me, waiting at the top for me to join him. Our fingers entwine as I summon wind to cushion our landing on the other side, then destroy all evidence of our passing by crumbling the vines to dust. I can't tell in the darkness if three incantations were enough to make the bricks fade, but at least no one else would, either.

Caeo leads me across the yard to the tower, constructed mostly of wood and stone. While I know someone decorated every inch of the exposed wood with floral designs in every color imaginable, it's too dark to appreciate their work. As we climb the interior stairs, I run my fingers along the walls, noting they've also been painted, but I can't make out the details.

"You see this flower?" Caeo asks, pausing to point at a spot in the inky blackness. "I added the face when I was twelve."

I can't see anything, so I just say, "It's nice."

"Nice?" He laughs. "You can be honest. It's pretty gruesome."

"You'll have to bring me back sometime when it's light out."

"It's a date." He gives me a tug, and we continue our ascent. While I keep clipping my feet on the steps, he's nowhere near as clumsy; his soft footfalls barely make the wood creak. We finally reach the highest level, where the tower's copper bells, each larger than a person, hang another twenty feet above our heads. The night sky spills in through a balcony, and Caeo gently guides me toward it.

I gasp as we step into the brisk air—I've never been so high up. If it were daytime, I'm certain I'd see the far-off forests and mountains.

Firelight flickers in paper lanterns lining the streets below, and warm light pours out of open doors and windows. Couples walk the streets, holding hands, and a sense of connection pulses between us as my fingers trace Caeo's arm at my waist.

I lift my gaze up to the stars.

No moon hangs in the sky, only an endless ocean of twinkling lights. As if nothing exists outside of us and the starlight.

"It's beautiful," I whisper.

"It's nothing compared to you."

I turn away from the view, winding my arms around his shoulders. My fingers twist through the midnight curls at the nape of his neck.

"Thank you for bringing me here."

"I'm glad you like it." He pulls me tighter against him. "Though I have to admit, I had another motive other than just the stars." Through the darkness, the hunger in his eyes burns into me, the heat rushing between my legs.

Is he hoping to...?

My mouth goes dry, and the truth trembles out. "I'm not sure I'm ready."

His face inches closer to mine, nuzzling my cheek with his nose. "Tell me to stop and I will," he whispers, his breath melting against my skin. Then he kisses me, and my fears fade away.

He's gentle, his lips brushing mine with only the vaguest tease of his tongue. They graze against my cheek, tender pecks along the curve of my jaw, a warmth blooming with every one. My head tilts up, bending to his touch as an ache builds in my core. I'd read stories of kisses unraveling someone, felt it with my own touch, but didn't know, didn't understand what it truly meant until now.

His fingers trail up my body until they're twisting the buttons of my collar. It falls open, undone all the way down to the dip between my breasts. He tugs me closer, chasing away the cold with hot, hungry kisses that devour my neck, tracing its length until he claims the curve of my collarbone.

A sigh escapes me, followed by heavy, desperate breaths as I lift my face up to the stars. This isn't fair—I can't kiss him like this, and the urge to bring my lips to his skin threatens to consume me.

My fingers weave through his hair, tightening their grip. "Caeo, stop."

He pulls back, his gray eyes glimmering as he catches his breath. "Already? Is something—"

I shove him against the exterior wall, my lips crashing against his. He laughs into my kiss, slipping his hands around my waist, then pulls me with him as he sinks down.

I yelp as I lose balance, tumbling into him as he hits the wood floor with a grunt and thud.

"Easy there."

"Are you alright?" I push myself up, my hands pressing into his chest.

"Never better."

His fingernails rake along my scalp, catching in my braid as he pulls my mouth to his. I'm in his lap, straddling him. Absorbing the sweet taste of his tongue, his lips, as his fingers tousle my hair. The hunger within me builds, and I scramble blindly for the buttons of his collar, my hands shaking as I tear them open.

Am I really doing this? The thought vanishes, blown away by the desire to be as close to him as physically possible.

Caeo fumbles with his waistcoat, finally escaping it as I tug open more of his buttons. My mouth desperately claims the smooth skin of his neck, and his clove scent sends my head rushing as my fingers run along his chest, catching on his necklace as they follow the lines of his pectorals.

His hands slide down my sides, along my hips, tightening the aching knot within. They slip further down, his fingers wrapping around my backside, and I gasp as the knot ignites, its blaze sizzling through me.

"Ellie." His rasping groan melts me into him as my lips explore every dip along his skin. My legs spread as he pulls me tight against his pelvis, and a firm length presses between my thighs.

My eyelids snap open, and I freeze, my body begging me to rock my hips as my heart twists around itself in panic.

Breathing heavily, Caeo's eyes flutter open, soft and gray as a rain cloud, searching my face.

"I..." My exhales match his, and I try to form words, but nothing comes out.

His eyes drift shut, and he nods. "Yeah... alright." He doesn't sound frustrated, his touch tender as he pulls me from his lap. I collapse against the wall next to him, and we both sit there, catching our breath.

I don't know what to say. What to think.

Why did I stop? My body yearns to keep going, aching painfully from being left unsatisfied. But my heart... What's this tension curling within? Why does it hesitate to trust what the rest of me wants?

This has all been so fast. Too fast to be real? Or maybe I'm scared. Of baring myself so completely.

No, that's not it. He sees me—more than anyone—and appreciates the person I've kept locked away for all these years, fearing she wouldn't meet expectations. But this is different. The one way I can still disappoint him.

Stop overthinking.

Caeo tucks his arm around me, and I lean into his shoulder, my heart pounding. "It's fine, Ellie. We can wait till you're ready."

A lump forms in my throat. "I'm sorry."

"Don't be."

The tension inside me won't release, and it won't as long as I keep my fears buried inside. If he really cares, then I shouldn't be afraid.

With a deep breath, I force myself to speak. "You've been with other girls before, haven't you?"

Caeo rubs his thumb against my hip. "There's been... more than a few."

I swallow. I can't really blame him. He's gorgeous, and if I'd lived a different life, I'd have liked to be more experienced, too. But my worry lingers. "What if I'm not as good as them?"

He brings his hand to my face, his gentle touch tilting my head until I meet his eyes. "Don't worry about that. You're not like those women."

"Because I stopped?"

"No—I mean, yes, that's true." A soft smile blooms across his face. "But I didn't care about them like I care about you. I told you: I'm yours. I'll never break your heart."

Words escape me, floating just out of reach. Tears threaten to fall as I search his face.

There's nothing but devotion in his eyes.

Bringing my lips to his, I kiss him softly, tenderly. When we part, my own heart's reflected in his gaze. It's unclear what the future holds, but in this moment, with him, it doesn't worry me for once. I curl into his chest, closing my eyes as the steady rhythm of his heart echoes through me.

Chapter 12

Ellie

"Hey, Reid, is this right?" From my spot on the cold, gray sitting room floor, I spin my paper toward him. Normally, a man wouldn't be allowed in the women's dorms, but as he said the day we met, "Frowns don't stop him." So far, he hasn't been caught.

He drops his pen on the table, skimming the page as he leans back in the purple armchair. "No, it's not. That would adjust the temperature, not the pressure." He grabs a spare sheet and quickly sketches a focal. "That's what you're looking for. See the difference?"

I scan the drawing, searching for differences from what I described in my essay. They seem insignificant, but I trust he's right. It's become clear over the last few weeks that he has a better understanding of the theory behind incantation than I ever will. It makes sense—he taught himself all on his own, while I had my father's guidance and countless tutors. Not that I'll ever admit that to him.

With a sigh, I pull out a new piece of paper. Professor Dewey won't accept any mistakes in our penmanship, and unfortunately, no incantation can erase ink. Evaporation still leaves the pigment behind.

A slam of the door startles me, messing up the word I was

writing. I bite my lip in frustration, then let out a deep breath. By Fortune's favor, I was only a couple sentences into my second attempt.

"Arandur's sagging crack!" Reid throws his pen onto the table. His paper, almost entirely full, is marred by a shaky stray line right at the end. "Why are you slamming doors like that? Now I have to start this whole page all over."

He sits back in his chair, crosses his arms, and glowers at Sophie. She stands at the door with her bag halfway falling out of her arms.

"You're not supposed to be here." She adjusts her grip on her bag, frowning at Reid.

"You're one to talk. How are those remedial classes treating you?"

My throat tightens. Reid's spent enough time with Alexis and me to be aware of the situation with Sophie, but I never expected him to actually say something. I should speak up before things get out of hand.

"Don't be a jerk," I say, tapping the table near Reid's knee in warning, but all it accomplishes is drawing Sophie's glare.

"I don't need you pretending to stick up for me," she says.

It's like a thread snaps. "And I don't need you making me feel bad for being who I am." *Where did that come from?* But the words are out, bursting free like a thought I never dared speak out loud. "You're not worth my time."

Instead of regret, a reassuring glow warms my heart.

Reid whistles. "Damn, Ellie."

Sophie's nostrils flare, her grip on her bag tightening.

My paper erupts in flames.

I throw myself back as Reid yells a curse. In an instant, water floods the table as we both use the same incantation to extinguish the blaze. Smoke singes my nostrils, the tabletop marred black beneath the soggy remains of our work.

Arandur's knickers. My eyes verge on popping out of my skull as I turn to Sophie. "Since when can you incant without speaking?"

She lifts her chin, straightening up. "Looks like you're not so special after all." With a sharp turn, she struts to her room, the door slamming behind her.

Not worth my time. My breathing settles, and we spend the next few minutes grumbling through some evaporation incantations until everything's dry. Despite that, I'm feeling taller than ever. I may have made our relationship worse, but I stood up to her. And Reid seemed impressed.

He sits back down, pulling out a new page. I have no desire to start my wind incanting assignment for the third time in less than half a bell, so I switch to writing a paper for my tactics class: *The Dangers of Fae Interrogation.*

It's a subject similar to curses in that it's not something we're ever likely to encounter, unless they invade again and we start taking prisoners. Even then, it's a job for specialists. The most important points are how incredibly alluring fae are, which can lead to lapses in judgment from their interrogators, and that fae can't lie, but excel at twisting the truth.

A bell later, Reid and I are stretching our fingers when Alexis arrives, giving us an excuse to take a break. I wouldn't consider us particularly good friends yet, with her mostly focusing on Reid when we're together, but her easygoing nature sometimes makes it feel like we are. I shift my position on the floor as she lounges on the settee, gesturing animatedly while chatting about her day.

"And did you hear they found some fae sneaking around the border?" She sits up, her elbow digging into the armrest. "Everyone's talking about it."

My stomach tightens. "What? Were they attacking? Is the

Order—"

"Relax, hun," Alexis says, glancing briefly at me as she waves her hand. "The rumors are all over the place. No one agrees on if they were coming or going, if they escaped, were killed, or taken prisoner."

"But... it could mean war's coming."

While many of our fellows, Alexis and Sophie included, have dreamed of vengeance for family members killed or disabled in battle, none of us truly understand living under the shadow of never-ending bloodshed. The fae may never stop being the enemy, but I'd rather they stay on their side of the border, never to be seen again.

"No one ever expected this peace to last," Alexis says, relaxing into the settee's cushions. "And it'd be a letdown to have spent all this time studying incanting and never actually fight."

Reid scratches at the embroidery on his armrest. "I was kind of hoping we wouldn't have to. I just liked the challenge of it—being able to do something no one else could."

"Well that's silly. You may be advanced now, but by the time we're in the Order, the rest of us will have caught up."

Unlikely. If that were true, my father wouldn't have had reason to make me practice so hard.

Reid presses his lips together, focusing on a thread he pulled loose. I'd never have guessed he didn't actually want to fight, that I wasn't the only one with doubts. If only there was something I could say to let him know he's not alone. Something not too sentimental, something—

"Oh!" Alexis exclaims, jolting me out of my thoughts. "You'll never guess what! Oliver, the one with the dimples I was telling you about, he pulled me aside after class and asked if I'd go to the ball with him!" She squeals excitedly.

My brows knit together. "What ball?" Something tells me I should know what this is, but I don't.

"Oh, honey, you need to spend less time studying. The Equinox Ball, of course!"

I glance at Reid.

"They do it every year. It's a big celebration." He twirls his finger in a lazy gesture. "The third years have a competition to decorate the grounds—everyone in Haven comes to see it. But only Academy students and their guests get to attend the ball."

Alexis leans closer, nudging my shoulder. "You should see if Caeo will take you."

"Hmm?" I didn't catch what she said.

But instead of clarifying, she claps her hands on her thighs. "And we can go buy new dresses! It'll be so nice to wear something other than these drab uniforms for once."

My palms grow clammy at the thought of an outing with only her. Without Reid around, I'll have to keep up with conversation all by myself. So I give the first excuse to come to mind. "It seems wasteful to buy a new dress only for one night."

"Oh, it is," Reid says. "That's why they make them quickly and sell them for cheap. Which is great for when everyone rips them off in the throes of passion when they get back to their rooms."

"What?" My eyes widen as my stomach drops.

"Don't act so scandalized. What'd you expect after a night of drinking and dancing, in a school packed with young people? This isn't high society with its arranged marriages and debutante balls."

Alexis leans toward me conspiratorially. "They say the effect incanting has that drains all the color also drains any life from our wombs. So we have nothing to worry about!"

That's disturbing. Though, now that I think of it, that could be why I don't have any siblings, knowing how much my father incants. And it's not the sort of topic my tutors would've brought up.

But they should have. I always hoped to have children of my own someday; I like to think I wouldn't struggle so much to connect with them. If incanting might hinder that... I shake away the worry as my stomach flutters. That's a future problem. Until then, there's always a chance I could enjoy that side effect. Maybe even tomorrow.

"I hope you have fun with that," I say, blushing furiously as I pack my things into my bag.

Alexis grabs my wrist. "Come dress shopping with me. Please? It'll be fun. There's so much we could do with you."

"I don't know..."

"Don't you want to wear something with color? Just for one night?"

It's like she knew exactly which thread to pull. She squeals with delight when I finally agree.

A RAINBOW OF DRESSES hangs from racks haphazardly shoved into the crowded dress shop. The floral perfume of oil lamps saturates the air—it's surprisingly well lit, considering the deep orange sky soaking through windows draped with heavy, cream-colored curtains. The high-pitched gossip of our fellow female students skitters against my eardrums, and watching them confidently try on various gowns already has my nerves tightening.

A coral-pink dress catches my eye. I pull it from the rack, its soft fabric gliding between my fingers.

"You would look stunning in that," Alexis says, peeking over my shoulder.

"It's very... bright. I don't like being the center of attention."

"Everyone will be wearing bright colors, trust me."

She's still wrapped in the dress she picked out for herself: a bright blue ensemble that clings to her waist before puffing into a flowing skirt. It covers her neck, as expected, but a window cuts seductively close to her collarbones and dips down to reveal her cleavage. All the dresses she's shown me, while simply made, have had a similar revealing feature. I lift the pink dress up, letting its full length tumble down so I can determine what its is.

"Besides," she continues, "if you're the center of attention, it'll be because you're with Caeo. I haven't seen that boy enter a room without drawing the eye of half the girls in it. And some boys, too."

My jaw drops as I turn the dress around. "This doesn't have a back."

"Stop acting like a prude." Alexis grabs my arm and pulls me behind a curtain. "Try it on."

Moments later, I'm staring at myself in the mirror, feeling more exposed than I have in my entire life. I've accompanied my parents to a handful of balls, but I've never seen anyone wear anything like this.

It's a simple dress, its only ornamentation being braids of the same coral fabric that trace its edges. It wraps tightly around my neck, then drapes down my front, connecting into a skirt at the small of my back that cascades down to the floor.

Alexis stands beside me, twisting my chestnut locks behind my head. "We'll put your hair up like this, and he won't be able to keep his hands off of you."

My face burns, almost matching the gown's color. The soft fabric clearly reveals the curves of my breasts, and the cold air tickles my bare back, making them peak.

"I don't think I'm brave enough for this."

"You are. You're gorgeous—own it. You won't be young forever, and you don't want to get old and regret never looking this good."

I can't deny the wisdom of that, and beneath my doubt, it *does* make me feel beautiful. So I push through my twisting nerves and buy the dress.

Half a bell later, we're walking amid dusk's lengthening shadows toward the Academy, gowns in hand. We spot Caeo and Reid as we near the outskirts, their voices carrying on the chilly breeze as they approach.

Alexis jumps in front of me. "Don't let him see the dress!"

Caeo jogs over with a smile that quickly gives way to confusion as Alexis continually moves to block the dress folded over my arms, and therefore me, from his view.

He frowns. "What are you doing?"

"You do *not* get to see her dress. You have to wait until the ball." She pulls me around and forces me to continue walking, keeping herself between me and Caeo the entire time.

"But—"

I press closer to her back, imagining his face when he sees me wearing it. She's right—I don't want to spoil the surprise. "Tomorrow," I say, just as I'm forced to look where I'm going to avoid tripping.

Reid slows down as he nears us. "We're heading to The Duck. You should come."

"We have to get our dresses home safely first," Alexis says, then pauses. "You think Emmrich will be there?"

"That's the hope."

Her mouth twists into a smile. "Then I suppose we will. Can't let you have him all to yourself."

Reid rolls his eyes. "See you then." He strolls past us with his hands in his pockets. A few seconds later, his voice drifts from further away. "Come on, man. She'll be back soon."

Curious, I glance behind me to see him looping his arm around

Caeo, pulling him along. A smile blooms across my face before I continue on my way.

SOPHIE'S CURLED UP on our settee, reading a book, when Alexis barges into our sitting room with me in tow, excitedly detailing her plans with Oliver for the next day. Since night has fallen, firelight blooms from the lanterns hanging on each wall, a hint of brown coloring the gray smoke stains above their flames.

"—and after we tour the gardens, I'm coming back to get ready for the ball. You need to be here, too, so I can do your hair."

I rub my eyes. Keeping up with Alexis's energy is exhausting. "I can do my own hair."

"No, honey. No. This dress deserves better than a messy bun. Now go hang it up before it gets wrinkled." She pushes me toward my room.

I shut the door behind me, then take a moment to collect myself. Sitting on my bed, I slide the dress's soft fabric between my fingers. *Can I really be brave enough to wear this?*

Something coils within me, either nerves or anticipation; I'm not sure which. My lungs sink with a heavy sigh, then I steal a hanger from my coat and shove the dress into my wardrobe.

When I return to our sitting room, Alexis is leaning arms-crossed against the wall, watching Sophie gather herself up. She tucks her book under her arm and grumbles, "I can't believe you actually have dates."

As frustrating as she can be, I sense an opportunity to smooth things over. To prove I'm not as conceited as she seems to think.

"I don't," I say, sitting against the back of an armchair.

Alexis snaps her head toward me. "What are you talking about? Aren't you going with Caeo?"

"Caeo?" Sophie asks.

"Reid's friend. You know, he's probably in some of your classes. Black hair, kind of messy. Probably has girls fighting each other to sit by him."

"Him?" Sophie looks to me, her brow arched.

I blink, unsure of what she's talking about. "I don't—"

Alexis steps away from the wall, closer to Sophie. "So you *do* know him?"

"Not really. He sits in the back of a few of my classes. Doesn't seem to be very good at anything." She shoots a smug glare in my direction. "A good choice for someone who needs to feel superior to everyone else."

I haven't the faintest idea why she's looking at me that way; it's unusual for me to lose focus on a conversation like this. When I don't respond, she huffs, then stomps the rest of the way to her room.

The door clicks shut, and Alexis's gaze lingers on it as she approaches. "Rude." Then she turns to me, resting her fingers on my arm. "Don't let her get to you. Some people just thrive on misery."

I close my eyes, rubbing circles into my temple. "I think I'll head to bed. I'm having a hard time keeping up."

"Are you sure?" A frown crinkles her face. "We told Reid we'd go by The Duck."

"You can go. I feel like staying in tonight."

She eyes me for a moment, then shrugs. "If you're sure. Guess I should start getting ready."

There's a tug in my chest as I watch her disappear into her room—a nagging feeling that I'll be missing out if I stay. But my head hurts, and a warm bath calls to me.

I can go to The Duck another night.

Chapter 13

Caeo

Reid and I sit at the corner of the bar in The Buttoned-Up Duck, sipping our drinks. It's fairly empty, thanks to the ball tomorrow. The third-year Academy students start decorating the grounds well before dawn, so they're all trying to get what little sleep they can, and everyone else wants to avoid hangovers for the festivities. I've *technically* gone the last three years, but ended up spending most of my time in my dates' dorms. Now that I'm allowed to attend on my own, it'll be nice to see what the fuss is all about.

But tonight's about Reid. These past few weeks, he's been kind-of-sort-of seeing Emmrich—the guy with shitty taste in drinks—as part of some weird competition with Alexis. He's hoping to invite him to the ball, and asked me along for moral support. So here we are, waiting around in a quiet, poorly lit tavern that smells like nobody's cleaned the floor in ages.

Emmrich announces his arrival by sliding his fingers along Reid's back, making him cough as he chokes on his ale.

"If it isn't one of my favorite people in all of Haven," he says, plopping onto the stool beside Reid. He's got a roguish sort of charm, but isn't the type I'd have ever expected to catch Reid's eye. Even with his blond hair tied in a knot, it's obviously far longer than socially acceptable, and his loose shirt hangs open in the front, his neck only covered by a carelessly wrapped scarf. The total opposite of Reid's well-maintained appearance.

Meanwhile, Reid seems to have missed the opening Emmrich very clearly set up, so I take it for him.

"If that's true, you should join him at the ball tomorrow." *There we go. Easy.*

Reid burns me with a glare. I shrug it off and take another sip of ale. That's what he wanted.

Emmrich winces, tapping the bar. "Tempting, but I unfortunately must decline."

I almost breathe down my drink.

Well, fuck. Guess I messed that up. Could've sworn he was interested.

Reid exhales, closing his eyes as his palm hits his face. I'm definitely getting an earful about this later.

But then Emmrich squeezes his shoulder. "Nothing against you. I just have no desire to go anywhere near that much incanting. However..." He leans close, whispering some rather salacious suggestions into Reid's ear. Reid bolts upright, his face flushing bright pink.

I stop listening as he hisses something back, satisfied that I was right after all. The ball may not have worked out like he'd hoped, but based on their proximity as they trade barbs back and forth, I'd say the odds are pretty good Reid won't be spending the night alone.

That excuse was pretty weird, though. Sure, it's a lot of incanting, but they're usually done by the time people show up. There's no reason to worry about your clothes fading.

Not wanting to be a third wheel, I hurry to finish my ale. Despite my rush, by the time I swallow the last dregs, not one but two girls have approached, inviting me to the ball while demonstrating incredibly liberal views on what's considered acceptable physical contact between strangers. The second makes eyes at Emmrich as she leaves, drawing Reid's attention.

"They're getting bold, aren't they?" he says, and Emmrich chuckles in response.

My tankard clanks as I slam it down. "I can't wait until this stupid ball is over so everyone and their mother will stop asking me to take them."

"Just tell them to get lost—you're already taken."

"It's not that easy." My throat always twists painfully when I lie, and people notice.

"Whatever, man."

Yeah, I know, poor me. With a sigh, I slump against the bar. "I think I'm gonna head home."

Reid jerks his head in my direction. "What? Why? Alexis said she'd meet us later with Ellie."

"So?" *Why should I care about Alexis?*

"So... Ellie. Here."

My mind feels cloudy, as if from speckled long leaf, but I haven't smoked any today. It must be the ale, which is surprising—I didn't drink *that* much.

"I'm not sure what you're saying."

Reid rolls his eyes, then turns back to Emmrich.

Whose gaze is on me, his brow furrowed in thought. For someone supposedly interested in Reid, he sure spends a lot of time staring at me. He better not be hoping for a threesome. That'd be weird. Reid's practically my brother.

"Perhaps you should pay closer attention to your friend," he says, nudging Reid. He answers with a frustrated sigh before turning back to me.

"What's going on, Cay? I'm with Ellie at least ten bells a day, and she never mentions you. You practically jumped on her on the way here, but now you won't even bring yourself to wait for her?"

I blink a few times, trying to clear the fog. "I don't know what you're talking about."

"I'm talking about Ellie."

"Who?"

Reid spins on his stool to face me head-on. "Arandur's clapping cheeks, stop fucking with me. *Ellie.* You met her on the first day of term and were all over each other. We saw her not even a bell ago."

I throw my hands up in the air. "I don't know what you're talking about!"

Reid startles back, wide-eyed. "Stop messing with me."

Exasperation boils within me, ready to explode. "I'm not. You know me—I can't lie to save my life."

There's a pause as his eyes narrow, searching my face. "Yeah, I know." He turns to Emmrich, placing his hand on his shoulder. "I'm sorry, I need to look into something."

Emmrich takes a sip from his tankard. "That's a shame. I was looking forward to some fun tonight. Didn't you say Alexis was coming?"

Reid glances at me.

I shrug. "Do what you want. I'm going home."

Reid's face contorts, his hands clenching into fists, then he forces out an exhale.

"I'll come back, I promise." He squeezes Emmrich's shoulder, then grabs my arm and drags me out of the tavern.

"Why are we in the girl's dormitory?" I ask. "We passed Alexis on our way here, remember?" Scuffed white walls and beat-up doors surround us—this hallway's just as bland as the rest of campus.

Since we left the tavern, the last half bell's been a fog. I kept asking Reid to explain where he was taking me, but he never answered, his frustration mounting as he barked at me to follow. He even resorted to herding me with incanted fire when I tried to turn back.

He comes to a halt, banging on a random door. "Don't act like I'm the one with memory problems."

"Are we even allowed to be here?" Not that I haven't been here plenty of times, but I was always snuck in by someone who actually lived here.

The door cracks open.

"Quiet down, I don't need you waking Sophie," a girl's voice says.

"We need to talk." Reid pushes the door open and pulls me inside.

Ellie stands there, startled, wearing nothing but a towel. She turns completely red as she meets my eyes.

"Ellie," I say. "Hi." My eyes won't stop wandering all over her exposed skin. Perfectly smooth, just begging to be touched. *Why was I trying so hard not to come here?*

"Oh, *now* you remember," Reid mutters, running his hand through his hair.

"What are you doing here?" Ellie pulls her towel tightly around herself, which only reveals more of her legs. Just a little higher and...

"Something's wrong with Caeo," Reid says sharply.

"Not this again," I mumble. *What's gotten into him?*

Worry flashes across Ellie's face. "Let me get dressed." She hurries into one of the other rooms, closing the door behind her.

Reid plops down on a purple settee, and I glance around—the room's lit by several lanterns hanging from wainscoted walls, with five pale wooden doors, all closed. Two fancy armchairs, also purple, and a low table covers most of the floor.

I don't recognize this place at all. "Where are we?"

Reid's eyes widen. "Do you remember coming here?"

Do I? "It's kind of fuzzy…"

He groans. "Just sit down and wait."

Despite my growing unease, I join him on the settee, forcing a relaxed posture. A few minutes pass, with the tapping of Reid's foot growing increasingly antsy as the hands on the wall clock tick by. I almost jump when his tension finally bursts, pushing him to his feet, and he bangs on one of the doors.

"What's taking so long, Ellie?"

It opens a few seconds later.

"Reid? I was getting ready for bed."

Who said that?

"Arandur's fiery mud hole, get out here!" Reid yanks Ellie into the room. She's wearing a loose chemise that doesn't hang much longer than her towel did, and she still hasn't brushed the tangles out of her wet hair.

I bump the tea table as I rush over, the sight of his fingers digging into Ellie's arm lighting a fire within me. "Stop it, Reid. Don't touch her like that."

Ellie's hands come to rest on my arm, a smile flashing across her face as she looks up at me. It fades when she glances back at Reid, her eyebrows pressing together. "You said something was wrong?"

He curses. "Yeah, something's definitely wrong." Then he pinches the bridge of his nose before letting out a heavy exhale. "Just to confirm, you two know each other, right?"

"Of course I know him. What's going on?"

Reid holds up his finger, looking at me.

I sigh. "Yes, I know her."

"Don't move." He grabs Ellie by the shoulders and turns her around, her back facing me.

"What are you doing? Let go of me!" She pulls at his hands, but he keeps them firmly in place.

"Ellie, do you know Caeo?"

I've had enough. "Let go of her."

He shoots me a glare. "Let her answer the question. Do you know anyone named Caeo?"

"No, I don't, now let go of me!"

...What?

My knees buckle as my insides plummet to the floor.

Reid releases her shoulders, and she tugs at the fabric of her chemise, straightening it out. His gaze shifts to me, his face softening.

"No..." I stagger forward, grasping for Ellie's hand. "No. No, no, no!" My hands shake as I pull her back to me. She startles as I cup her face in my palms, frantically searching her eyes for any sign of recognition.

"Ellie? Please tell me you know me."

"Caeo? What's wrong? I..."

A heavy breath slows my pounding heart. "You said you didn't know me."

"I did?" Her eyebrows compress, then her beautiful face contorts as confusion bursts into panic. "Arandur's knickers, I did. I forgot you existed." Her fingernails dig through my shirt as her grip tightens. "How? Why?"

I wrap my arms around her, pulling her close. Her touch calms the anxiety ricocheting inside me, and I breathe in her lavender scent. "I don't know."

Reid groans, sinking into an armchair as he rubs his face with his hand. I lead Ellie to the tea table, facing him.

"What's going on?" I demand.

"Fuck if I know."

"You figured it out, so tell us what you know."

"You were there. I asked you about Ellie, and you said you didn't know her. I brought you here to make sure I wasn't going crazy."

My focus turns back to Ellie as she chews her lip. It seems impossible that I could've forgotten her face. The warmth of her in my arms. I should be dreaming of her every night.

Reid's voice cuts through my thoughts. "You remember that conversation, don't you?"

I search my memory, my brow furrowing.

"We were at The Duck?" he presses. "Less than a bell ago?"

An image of the tavern forms in my mind, and I grasp at the details. Reid and Emmrich were there... Some girls had asked me to the ball... I wanted to leave...

There. Reid had asked why I wasn't waiting for Ellie.

But the memory's already slipping.

"It's there," I say, "but it's like something's fighting me, pulling it away."

Ellie nods. "That's how I felt, too."

"Well, that's great." Reid's hands drop to his lap. "Not only do you not remember any of your time together, but you can barely recall anyone ever talking about her."

I shake my head. "No, that's not right. I remember every moment." Every smile, every kiss, every touch. I brush my fingers along her skin as a lump forms in my throat.

"But then you forget when you're not looking at her." Reid presses his lips together. "That never seemed weird to you? It didn't occur to you to wonder why you never thought about her when you were apart?"

"It did," I mutter, "but it didn't feel important." Even now, it's hard to hold on to the panic.

Ellie rubs her thumb against my arm. "How did this even happen? We haven't been forgetting each other this whole time, have we?"

"You definitely talked to me about Caeo during our first class with Beckwith." Reid snorts a laugh. "I remember that conversation."

Ellie turns bright red, then swallows. "Yes, I recall that as well."

What conversation was this? I tilt my head at her, raising an eyebrow.

She shakes her head. "So it happened after that. But when?" Her face crinkles in thought.

My memory's so fuzzy, I can't imagine how we'll possibly solve this. I fold Ellie into a tight embrace, resting my chin against her hair. Now that I know how easily I can lose her, I never want to let her go.

"Maybe we should go to the headmaster," I suggest. Not that I really want to, but the gravity of the situation kind of calls for it.

Ellie stiffens. "No, we can't. My father..." She takes a breath, collecting herself. "We should try to sort this out on our own first. We don't need my father—the Order—studying our relationship."

Yeah... I can agree with that. She may not be noble herself, but she's still a viscount's daughter. A viscount who's also the most powerful incanter alive. I'm not in any rush to find out where he falls on propriety's spectrum.

Then again, potential brain damage isn't something we can just ignore.

"Well, it's not related to incanting, right?" I look between Ellie and Reid. "It has nothing to do with the elements. And that's how fae fight, too? Something similar, at least?"

I really need to pay better attention in class.

Good thing Reid and Ellie are the top students in our year. "Have either of you heard of anything like this?"

They exchange glances.

Reid shrugs. "I can't think of anything offhand."

"Me neither."

Perfect. I rub my face with my hand. "Alright. So let's figure this out. If we know what causes us to forget, that could lead us to the source."

Reid sighs, then pushes himself to his feet. "Fine, but you'll need to let go of each other."

That's the last thing I want to do, but I reluctantly drop my arms and step back, still keeping a tight hold on Ellie's hand. The smile she gives me twitches with uncertainty before she turns her attention to Reid.

"Now then—Ellie forgot about you when she couldn't see you, so let's see what happens if you hold hands while not looking at each other."

We do as he said, and to our great relief, nothing happens.

"Great," he grumbles. "Because you needed another reason to be all over each other. Now what else can we try...?"

A bell later, I find myself praising Fortune that I have a friend like Reid. Despite his complaints and near-constant snide commentary, he tests the limits of our memory in ways I never would've considered. I watch as he has Ellie face the wall, repeatedly trying to tell her about me to see what sticks. Nothing does. Even the vaguest mentions—saying she has a boyfriend, or Reid just calling me his friend—slip away as the conversation continues.

Our memory loss seems based entirely around sight and touch— if I only hear Ellie, I don't recognize her voice, but if she touches my arm while she speaks, I do, even if I can't see her. In one particularly disheartening test, we discovered just how long it takes for us to lose one another by having me repeat Ellie's name while turning around.

I forgot what I was saying the second she left my sight.

He checks whether our sense of touch keeps us linked if we're both in contact with the same object. It works through clothing, probably because we can feel each other's warmth and pressure, but when he incants a stick and has us hold opposite ends of it, we lose everything once our gazes turn away.

"Wait," I say as the stick crumbles to dust. "What if Ellie makes it?"

She gives me a doubtful look before a pair of vines twist out of her hand, hardening into a short branch. We repeat the test...

"It worked!" It's not much, but my chest still feels lighter.

"Great." Reid collapses onto the settee. "She can leash you with vines and solve all your problems."

The shadows from the dim light emphasize the worry in Ellie's face. "That's not a solution. It can keep us from losing each other, but we won't remember to get together in the first place."

"And we still don't have any idea what's causing this," I add, despite feeling calmer now that we have a better understanding of things.

"Yeah? So go to the library and do some research," Reid says, rubbing his temple. "Or to the headmaster." He glances at Ellie. "And it's not like you're sad about it when you're apart."

"Come on, man," I say. "We won't remember to do any of that on our own. And you've seen how miserable my life's been lately."

He shakes his head, mumbling one of his ridiculous curses under his breath. "Look, I'll get her to you, alright? We have all our classes together, and I know all the places you go."

A spark of hope lights within me.

"Thank you, Reid," Ellie says, her fingers catching on my shirt as her grip tightens.

"I better be hearing that twenty times a day from now on. You two have it easy—I'm the one who'll be suffering here."

I roll my eyes. "It won't be that bad."

"How much do you remember of me dragging your sorry ass here tonight? You fought me the entire way."

My jaw clenches—hardly any of it. Just flashes of him pulling me behind him or pushing me along the road. He must have kept mentioning Ellie.

The thought makes my stomach cave in on itself. Reid's been my best friend for as long as I can remember, but now my future with Ellie rests on his shoulders: we won't accomplish anything without his help. And if we can't figure this out soon, we'll have to involve Ellie's dad. It'd be stupid to risk permanent damage just to avoid that.

And with how tonight's gone, I'd say we're already at risk of getting on Reid's nerves.

"Thank you, Reid. I really appreciate it."

"You're welcome. Now, if you'll excuse me, I have someone waiting for me." He pauses at the door. "I'll make sure you get here tomorrow, and we should probably explain everything to Alexis. She can help, too."

The door clicks shut behind him, leaving Ellie and me alone, wrapped in one another's arms.

Chapter 14

Ellie

Sharp shadows creep along the edges of our sitting room, its lanterns burning low. Cold and gray, countered only by the warmth of Caeo's arms tightening around my waist, my hands resting on his chest. We haven't moved since Reid left. Trapped in stillness, uncertain what to do next.

"Are you sure we shouldn't go to the faculty?" Caeo asks. "This could be some kind of fae magic, right?"

That doesn't seem likely—why would an enemy who hasn't attacked in twenty years randomly decide to toy with the minds of two students? It's so absurd that my mind dismisses the suggestion without a second thought.

"If we can't figure it out on our own, we will."

An echo of my earlier panic clenches my chest, but I force myself to breathe. To focus on the warmth of his touch. I need to believe we'll find the answer; we've already figured out the bounds of whatever this is, and we have Reid's help. This is simply a test of our relationship. We can get through it.

"I'd really prefer it if my father doesn't get involved," I add, reassuring him with a squeeze of my fingers.

That's what will happen the second he hears about it, which would immediately follow any visit with the headmaster. While my mom likely suspected I was hoping to find someone here, I had avoided any discussion of the matter. All the rules and expectations... thinking about them made it hard to breathe. Even if we've managed to stay within their standards of decency, it's unlikely someone with Caeo's reputation—from the slums and on the verge of failing out—is their ideal future son-in-law.

His eyebrows knit together. "But if it's fae magic, shouldn't they know as soon as possible?"

Why is he so caught up on fae involvement? Does he know something I don't?

But no—that doesn't make any sense. So I bring my hand to his cheek, hoping to ease his worries. "We'll figure it out, I promise. *After* the ball."

Despite everything, butterflies tickle in my belly. *The ball.* My reflection from earlier, draped in that sultry dress, flashes through my mind. Caeo's face when he sees me in it. The hunger in his eyes. How his fingers will dance across my skin.

The corners of his lips tug into a smile. "Something on your mind?"

My mouth tightens. "Nothing. Just thinking about tomorrow."

It's suddenly sweltering in here. I glance at the wall clock—already past midnight.

Caeo follows my gaze. "It's getting late. Should I go? Or...?" His brow raises as the word hangs.

Or what? Stay the night?

I didn't think my heart could beat any faster, but I was clearly wrong.

Staying the night doesn't necessarily mean... *Does it?*

But I want it to. I want *us* to.

Don't I?

Twin aches ripple through my heart and my core, insisting I do, but the moment doesn't feel right. Forced, even. I'm tired, exhausted from the night's revelations. The air has a staleness to it, devoid of the romance I've always dreamt of for my first time.

I circle my fingers against Caeo's chest, and they catch on a lump beneath his shirt. "What's this?" I pinch at the form. It's like a pouch, overstuffed with something rough and pokey.

Caeo rests his hand on mine. "A necklace my mother gave me. Said my father would've wanted me to wear it." With it pressed between his palm and his chest, a sharp, steady beat pulses through my fingers.

"You haven't mentioned your father before."

"I never met him. Out of the picture before I was born."

I sigh, my thoughts returning to the issue at hand. Tomorrow is better. Reid promised he'd bring Caeo to me, and Alexis would never let me miss going to the ball with him. We should be safe.

And then my first time can be after a beautiful night, wearing a beautiful dress, with tonight's worries far from our minds. We deserve that. A night to cherish one another before burying ourselves in the mystery coiling around us, threatening to tear us apart. I simply have to believe it'll work out. We've defied the odds so far.

"You should go. I won't get any sleep if you stay, and I want to be well-rested for the ball." I swallow. "And what comes after."

Caeo's eyes widen, and the yearning deep within me twists tighter. "And what's that, I wonder?"

"You'll have to make sure you show up and find out."

His smile falters. "That's really not up to me, is it?"

My heart sinks, threatening to drown if I let it. "We have to trust Reid. It's impractical for us to stay together at all times."

"I know. I just hate the idea of leaving, not knowing if I'll ever see you again."

"That's always the case—it's impossible to know what the future will bring." After all, I never imagined *this* would be my life. "Now, we just won't know what we've lost."

"I don't find that particularly comforting," Caeo mumbles, but he pulls me to the door with him nonetheless. He turns back to me, his gray eyes scouring my face, then brings his lips to mine.

It's a slow, tender kiss, and he pours himself into me, feeding the fire within. Heat stirs between my legs, aching for me to pull him deeper.

No. Not tonight.

Our lips part, and we linger, our breath entwining as I gaze into the smoky depths of his eyes.

"I'll see you tomorrow."

Caeo nods, a subtle twitch of his head. "I'll find you."

He keeps hold of my fingers as he leaves, but they drift out of his grasp as he steps into the hallway.

My chest pounds as I ease the door shut, keeping him in my sight as long as possible while praying I'm not making a horrible mistake.

SUNLIGHT WARMS MY FACE through the window, like it has every morning since my arrival at the Academy. But the world outside is entirely different.

Third-year students, toiling away since before dawn, have transformed the barren wasteland that surrounds the Academy into a lush paradise, with not a speck of dirt visible beneath the trees, ferns, and shrubs blanketing the landscape. Each student tends their own garden, and visitors will stroll through this afternoon, casting their votes for the most impressive displays. They'll announce the winner at tonight's ball, but it'll be a miracle if the incanted flora lasts that long.

Whoever's working beneath my window has an obvious love of pink and green. A stone path with small, rosy flowers filling its cracks meanders through a field of clovers. Boulders of various sizes stand throughout, impeccably placed, with various flowers clumped around them—tulips, camellias, and lilies being the gardener's clear favorites. She's currently focused on sprouting spindly cherry trees whose branches dance gracefully out from their trunks, speeding them through their natural cycles to fill their limbs with delicate pink blossoms.

Minutes pass as I lean against my window, mesmerized by her work. Not even the palace gardens in Durnam have so much color.

I should draw this.

Not her creations, beautiful as they are, but the moment her face transforms from intense focus into the elation of success. I need to capture that.

Time flows by as I sketch, doing quick studies whenever she completes a task. Her eyes, the tug of her smile, how her mouth parts as a tired breath escapes her. Later, I'll use these to build a more complete, polished picture.

Once she moves beyond my line of sight, I reluctantly close my sketchbook and prepare for the day, turning my options over in my mind. Tagging along with Alexis and Oliver would likely be awkward, and I've never actually had to look for Reid before, always meeting up in class. I'm not sure I have the gall to search the men's dorms.

I'm dressed, but still uncertain what to do when someone bangs loudly on the door.

"Reid?" *What are the chances?* "What are you doing here?"

He rolls his eyes. "You don't remember. Of course." He leans closer, peering past me. "Is Alexis here? I never found her last night."

It was too much to hope he was here for me. I let him in, and he goes straight to Alexis's door, pounding on it. A groan sounds from within. A minute later, Alexis emerges wearing the same clothes as yesterday, her hair sticking out at odd angles.

She yawns. "What's going on?"

I lean against the wall, hoping that if I stick around, they'll invite me to whatever they have going on. "Late night?" I ask.

Alexis nods, smoothing the kinks out of her dark braids.

Reid's brow furrows. "But you weren't at The Duck when I got there."

Her eyes pop open, focusing on him. "You actually came back?"

"I said I would."

"Yeah, but we waited forever. We eventually gave up, figured you weren't coming."

"*We?*"

"Emmrich and me." Her face brightens. "We went to his place. The third-years had already started gardening by the time I got back."

Reid's eyes narrow, and I slowly back away from the conversation.

This won't end well.

Alexis shrugs. "He assumed you weren't interested."

Reid's palm flies open in a gesture of disbelief. "Why would he think that? I said I'd come back."

"But you didn't."

I do *not* want to get pulled into this, not after what happened when I tried to smooth things over with Sophie. I creep toward the hallway door.

Reid's eyes shoot daggers at Alexis. "So instead of wondering if I was alright, you just fucked him instead?"

Oh boy.

Alexis pulls herself to her full height, glaring at Reid. "You know what? I did. Twice!"

I rush out before Reid responds.

AFTER A HEARTY BREAKFAST by myself, I head to the library, idly roaming the stacks of dusty books until the gardens open to the public. I pick one from the literature section, a chaste romance being the most interesting thing they offered, but find myself unable to focus as I curl up in a stiff armchair to read. I hope Reid and Alexis can work things out on their own, but fear the worst. The last thing I want is to pick sides, but Reid's talked about Emmrich enough that his interest was clear, while Alexis was already set with Oliver. That should've been enough.

At the same time, it's hard not to envy how she's both confident and desirable enough to be with multiple men. If I were her, I'd want to enjoy that, too.

Once the six noon bells chime, I make my way to the Academy grounds. I may be alone, but that doesn't mean I can't enjoy the festivities. It could even provide a chance to meet people outside my frustratingly small circle.

A sizeable crowd of both students and Havenites trickles through the newly formed paths of the transformed landscape, their awed voices less abrasive than I'd expected for such a gathering. It's a cornucopia of artistic expression, each garden more beautiful than the last, and I wander for several bells, taking in the sights. Despite my attachment to the pink oasis whose creation I witnessed from my window, I eventually discover the clear winner.

This gardener covered their entire area with a shallow pool of smooth obsidian. Perhaps six inches of water fills it, dotted with lily pads and floating flowers, reflecting my face back as I walk along the raised stone pathway that crests the surface. Succulents of various shapes and colors surround the pool, with waterfalls flowing between them.

The path circles the centerpiece—two trees, one with white bark and blood-red leaves, the other dark ebony with leaves of gold, growing beside one another. They bend closer and closer as their trunks entwine, twisting until they merge into one, reaching up to the sky. Water trickles from its highest branches like tears, unending.

A yearning fills me—an ache to have what these trees represent: a love powerful enough to unite two into one.

"Pretty, isn't it?"

I jump at the voice, then find myself face-to-face with the blond boy who caught me eyeing him at the placement exams. He apologizes for startling me, then introduces himself as Theodore.

"It's beautiful," I say, nervously glancing between him and the trees. *Is he hoping to ask me to the ball? Why else would he be talking to me?* "I never would've thought of making something like that."

"Have you seen the one with black and red flowers just down the way?" he asks. I haven't, so he takes my hand and pulls me along the path.

My palm's sweating against his; normally, this would be completely inappropriate, but that's the theme of the day. So I let him lead me, heart pounding as I pretend I'm Alexis and capable of living a life like hers.

By the time she finds us, the late afternoon sun paints the gardens with a golden light. She doesn't care an ounce about the sights; she simply needs me to return to the dormitory so she can do my hair for the ball.

"Who was that?" she asks as we step into our sitting room. Sophie's door is closed tight.

"His name's Theodore. He said he'd look for me at the ball." My face burns at the admission, both from what that might mean for my night and anxiety over Alexis's opinion. But there's something beneath, too. A tightness in my chest, as if something's not quite right.

She raises her brow, then shrugs. "Who am I to judge? Now get dressed—we don't have any time to waste."

Once I'm in my room, I carefully slip my dress on, its soft fabric sliding along my skin. After clasping its collar around my neck, I glance down to where it catches on the peaks of my breasts, sending goosebumps tickling along my spine. I can't wear anything underneath to prevent that, not with my back so completely exposed, and heat rushes to my face as I imagine Theodore's warm fingers grazing my skin if he asks me to dance.

I push the heat back down, warning myself not to get my hopes up.

It takes a significant amount of time for Alexis to style both of our hair, with me awkwardly holding her braids up as she pins them in place. She curls my individual locks into one larger twist, which she affixes to the back of my head. With precise fingers, she weaves pink flowers throughout.

She hands me a small mirror, and my mouth goes dry as I take in my reflection—she was right to style my hair this way. The elegant style highlights my bare shoulders, drawing the eye down the length of my back.

My pulse quickens with nerves. Tonight could fulfill my every fantasy—or utterly humiliate me.

Just breathe.

My innards are completely tangled by the time we reach the Great Hall, just as the first nighttime bell chimes. The gardens have already wilted, incapable of surviving a single day. Workers, likely from Haven, move somberly through the decay, gathering the dead foliage while a crowd of students lingers outside the entry doors, babbling with excitement as they await their partners.

"There's Oliver!" Alexis adjusts her dress before bouncing into the masses.

She disappears from sight just as someone's fingers wrap around my hand.

Chapter 15

Ellie

The crowd fades away as my eyes meet Caeo's gray ones, and the light shining from their blue speckles fills me with a radiant glow. He's as handsome as ever, the waves of his black hair effortlessly framing his eyes. Despite the occasion, he still wears his Academy uniform, but it doesn't matter. I couldn't imagine him in a more formal suit.

He pulls me close. "I found you."

He did.

Caeo smiles through the kiss he plants on my lips, and it unravels all the nerves twisting tight within me.

When we break apart, he brings his hand up between us, perpendicular to our faces. I do the same, laughter slipping out as we say, "Good Fortune," while wiggling our fingers as if pulling invisible marionette strings. The words are important: without them, people often use the gesture to wish bad luck upon others. It all ties back to the monarchy, favored by Fortune to rule.

Our hands drop, and Caeo takes in all of me. "You look beautiful."

Goosebumps spread across my skin as he traces his hand along my bare back.

"I like the dress."

A rush of heat, straight to my core. "I'm glad."

His eyes catch my every curve, his fingers grazing my skin. My entire body must be blushing at this point. I exhale, hoping to cool the desire burning within me. *We'll get to that later, after the ball.*

"We don't need to worry about getting separated," he says. "I won't be able to keep my hands off you."

I curl my lips into what I hope is a playful smile. "We shouldn't leave that to chance."

Clasping his hand tight, I run through a quick incantation in my mind. Vines twist from my shoulder down to my wrist, where they drop about a foot before looping back up to wind around Caeo.

He's bound to me, with two feet of leeway in case either of us loses our grip.

But I don't plan to.

Caeo eyes my creation before entwining our fingers. "A bold choice."

I lean in, kissing his lips. "You're mine. Everyone should know."

He kisses me back, and a warm smile graces his lips as we pull apart. He squeezes my hand, then leads me beyond the massive, propped-open doors of the Great Hall.

While the third-year students handled the gardens outside, the faculty decorated the hall. Shimmering light fills the cavernous space from flames floating above our heads, with glistening ice sculptures decorating every table, reflecting the golden hues. Between the windows, waterfalls pour out of the air itself, fading into nothing instead of splattering against the floor. Flowers blanket every inch of the walls with a rainbow of color.

My breath hitches at the sight, and my next inhale fills my lungs with the bright, floral scent wafting through the air. Who'd have thought this once-hollow cavern could teem with so much life? It's practically bursting with the buzz of excited voices alongside the crisp, soaring notes of the string quintet, set up on a small stage beyond the dance floor.

My gaze lands on Theodore, frowning at us. Shame spikes within me, and I quickly turn back to Caeo.

A boyish grin lights up his face.

"What?" I ask, my voice barely carrying over the hum of the hall.

He leans close. "Your face. I've never seen anyone so enraptured."

My cheeks burn with my smile, and Caeo brings his lips to my ear.

"Dance with me."

I glance toward the center of the room, where couples spin in rhythm with one another, following the music with perfectly timed motions.

"I wouldn't have thought you'd know the steps."

Caeo frowns. "The steps?"

"It's the Grace." I raise my voice even though he's inches away. "One of the most popular dances in high society." Father always joked that it was named after Mom.

"Ah." He glances at the dancers. "Well, I don't know that, but my mother taught me to dance. I think we'll be fine."

With that, he sweeps me onto the dance floor.

He keeps my vine-bound hand clasped in his and slides the other around my waist, his fingers pressing against the small of my back. He glides smoothly between steps, not once looking at our feet. His eyes stay locked on mine.

My heart swells as our bodies sway in time to the music—I never imagined he'd be such a wonderful dancer. While I'd attended the occasional formal party with my parents, learning all the required dances, I've never been so comfortable with anyone else. It hardly matters that I don't know the steps.

I'm practically yelling so he can hear. "What's this called?"

Caeo winces, then shrugs. "No idea. She never told me the name."

It's similar enough to the Grace that we don't conflict with the couples dancing around us, though he keeps surprising me with a sudden shift in the pattern. I give in, letting him lead me where he will, my eyes only leaving his when he spins me around, laughter tumbling from my lips.

A few songs later, sweat is condensing on my skin, especially where Caeo's hands press against me. When the music fades beneath the murmur of the crowd, I lift myself to my toes, close to his ear.

"Let's take a break."

Caeo sneaks in a kiss before I pull away, then guides me off the dance floor. But as we approach the refreshment tables, an uncomfortable weight hovers over my shoulders.

I peek at the crowd. Multiple sets of eyes are fixed on us, none of them friendly. Narrowed, burning glares. Judgmental brows tilting up with whispered words.

My grip on Caeo's hand tightens.

"What's wrong?" he asks.

"Why's everyone staring?" From everything I've heard about tonight, we haven't done anything they should consider improper.

Caeo scans the room. Almost all the offenders are women, many with dates of their own, seeking their attention.

He sighs, running his hand through his hair. "Ignore them. They're just jealous."

I glance between them and Caeo. As handsome as he is, no one's good-looking enough to merit this kind of vitriol. It doesn't make any sense.

But he sees only me. He barely touches any of the food, only taking a few sips of lemonade as he watches me eat, his eyes devouring my every bite. The tips of his fingers, cold from holding his icy beverage, tickle my side as they trace along the edge of my dress.

He really doesn't care about anyone else.

Unfortunately, I can't ignore them as easily. The weight of their stares presses against me, as if I'm at the edge of a cliff.

I ground myself, focusing on Caeo's touch. "Should we dance again?"

He pulls me closer. "Whatever you want."

What is that, really? Do I want to dance, or move on to something else? Something with only us.

I bite my lip as my pulse quickens, outpacing the tapping of dancing feet. "I want..."

Deep breath.

"I want you to take me to my room."

Caeo dips his head, his eyes fixed on mine. "You're sure?"

I answer with a kiss, wrapping my unbound hand around his neck and gliding my fingers through his soft, raven locks.

"Absolutely."

With a grin, he pulls me to the doors, weaving through the crowd. Seconds later, we burst out of the Great Hall and into the chilly night air. He envelops me with another kiss, smothering me with his warmth.

I gasp as I break for air. "There's still people around."

He doesn't spare a glance at our fellow students lingering nearby. "I don't care."

I press my fingers to his lips as he comes in for another kiss. "But I do."

His mouth twists beneath my touch, then he steps back. "Fine. But be warned—I'm gonna have you coming so loudly that the entire dorm will know what I've done to you."

My lungs forget to breathe as blood rushes to my core.

"I…"

I have no words. No response. Just a thundering in my chest as an ache curls between my thighs.

"Is that what you want?" Caeo's gaze pierces through my uncertainty.

Yes, my body says. *Desperately.*

My chin dips, then trembles into the smallest of nods.

A mischievous smile races across Caeo's face, then he interlaces his fingers with mine, pulling me down the steps, across the campus, and toward the dorms.

MY HANDS SHAKE as I fumble with my key, failing to slide it into the keyhole. Caeo wraps his fingers around mine, warm and steady, and guides it in.

The lock clicks open, and he takes both my hands, gently pulling me inside. Dark shadows blanket our sitting room, lit only by moonlight trickling in through the window.

"You're nervous," Caeo says. "You sure you're ready?"

I swallow as doubts creep up, but I banish them all—except one.

"Alexis said I couldn't get pregnant on Academy grounds?"

Caeo shuts the door behind me, then steps closer. "As far as I know, that's true." He cups my cheek with his hand, his face only a breath away from mine. "If you're sure… I'll go slow. Just tell me what you like."

I nod, my nerves twisting my throat so tight I can't speak.

But I want this. I feel safe with him. Seen. So I squeeze his hand and lead him into my room.

With a quick incantation, I ignite the candles on my desk, filling the darkness with a warm, gentle glow as Caeo takes me in his arms. My hands come to rest against his chest, and the vines that bind us unravel, crumbling to dust.

The candlelight dances in his stormy eyes, reflecting a hunger so intense it burns into me, sending my heart simmering with anticipation. He brushes his lips against mine, teasing them open with his tongue. I let him in, melting against his heat.

His hands twist against me as he fumbles with his buttons. Our kiss breaks when he shrugs off his jacket, and I pull open his shirt, revealing the toned muscles of his chest, bare save for his corded necklace. I'd seen some of it before, in the clock tower, but now... his pale skin glows in the moonlight pouring through the window, and I want nothing more than to touch every inch of it.

He shivers as I trace my fingers along his firm abdomen. My other hand toys with the necklace; it seems to be an embroidered pouch, sewn shut, with something inside it. *Perhaps dried leaves?*

"Do you always wear this?"

"Pretty much." Caeo pulls his shirt the rest of the way off, his muscles rippling with the motion. He brings his hands to the back of my neck, fingers pinching the fabric of my collar.

He raises an eyebrow. "Your turn?"

I take a deep breath, then nod.

Caeo releases the clasp, and the top of my dress tumbles down, cool air kissing my breasts. His gaze drops, fingers tickling my skin, then he scoops them in his hands, brushing my nipples with his thumbs. I gasp as they harden at his touch, a spike of pleasure surging between my legs.

"You like that?" He pinches my nipple between his fingers, then flicks them away with a sharp tug. My knees buckle as a sound I've never made before bursts from my lips.

A mischievous grin stretches across his face. "I'll definitely have you screaming by the end of this."

Just like that, my body runs out of patience. Carnal desire floods me, drowning whatever inklings of hesitation my mind had left.

"Then what are you waiting for?"

I tug my dress down, revealing all of me. My breath trembles, worried I've already been too brazen, but one look at Caeo tells me I didn't make a fool of myself for once.

He steps back, his gaze so heavy as it trails along my body that its weight presses against my skin. He swallows, and his voice comes out thick.

"Get on the bed."

With anticipation coiling within me, a twist away from snapping, I lie down on the stiff sheets, surrendering myself to him. He's on me before my next inhale, his lips colliding with mine.

His fingers trail up my body until they're tugging at my nipple, teasing it, sending a jolt racing from my breast to the spot between my thighs with every pull. I break free of his kiss, unable to contain the gasps tumbling out of me. I flush with embarrassment, but the need pulsing within me shatters all thoughts of shame. My legs part, aching for him. It's unbearable.

"I need you to touch me."

He laughs, then releases my nipple, leaving it tingling as he tiptoes his fingers along my belly.

"Like this?"

His eyes stay locked on mine as his hand glides between my slick folds. He brushes his fingers against the spot that sends a shudder through my whole body, elevated by the intensity of his gaze.

"Ohhhh." The sound quivers out as his eyes pierce into me. Until this moment, intimacy was a foreign concept, but now I understand. I'm laid bare before him, completely defenseless, but without fear.

And I need more.

"Is this the spot?" His thumb flicks, and I cry out, eyes widening.

"Yes," I gasp.

Caeo slips from my grasp, and I reach for him, protesting the loss of his warmth. He runs his hand through his raven hair, pushing it out of his eyes, then presses my legs apart.

The heat of his breath against my bud of nerves sends me trembling, and then his tongue flicks against me and my body shakes, a loud wail rippling out of me.

With each sweep of his tongue, more and more pressure builds. My legs buck and kick, but he holds them down. My fingers clench around the bedsheets as my back arches, each stroke pulling noises from deep within me I didn't know I could make.

An overwhelming need awakens—to be filled, utterly, completely, by him. I grasp frantically at his hair as he sends wave after euphoric wave crashing through me.

"Caeo, stop."

My fingers tighten, twisting among his raven locks. He relents, my core throbbing as he meets my eyes.

"You really want me to stop right now?"

I catch my breath as heat radiates through me. This is it—the moment I've dreamed of, that I never imagined I'd be bold enough to claim before knowing him.

"I want *you* in me."

Something flickers in his eyes—admiration, or dare I believe something more—and then he releases me, tugging at his pants. The cold air tickles my flesh as he takes far too long to remove them, but then he's free, and my eyes trail down his abdomen to his thick, erect form.

Every inch of me tightens in anticipation.

Then he climbs on top of me, shifting my legs apart.

"Relax." His voice is soft, and the scent of me on his skin sends my mind reeling over the abyss.

I shake out a nod, my lips clamoring for his. For a moment, all he does is kiss me, and I melt beneath his weight as his tongue slips into my mouth, tasting myself on his lips. My legs spread, my hips pressing against him, begging to be filled. Caeo's hand slides down my pelvis, adjusting its angle, then his firm tip strokes against my entrance.

He eases himself in.

I cry out as I stretch around him, a bite of pain stinging through me, and my fingers claw deep into his back. But it's everything I need.

"Are you alright?" he asks.

I nod frantically. "Keep going."

His forehead presses against mine, our eyes locked, and he slowly thrusts into me, deeper and deeper every time.

"Move with me," he says, the words heavy with his breath.

It takes a few tries to match his rhythm, but once I do, pleasure surges through me with every rock of our hips. I cling to him as our breaths unite, accelerating with his every thrust.

All traces of pain subside, his momentum rolling through me, drawing cry after cry from my lips, and he breathes in each one. I can't get enough of him, my fingers clutching so fiercely they hurt.

This is everything I never knew I wanted. This ecstasy, this feeling of oneness. With him.

With a sharp, sudden thrust, Caeo stops, his eyes sparking with a matching grin.

"Ready to scream for me?"

My core tightens. "What?"

He hooks his arms under my knees, pushing my legs toward my chest. I see stars with his next thrust, tears forming in my eyes as he drives into me, so hard, so deep, picking up his pace. I'm wailing between ragged breaths as pleasure builds to a crescendo, twisting tighter and tighter and tighter.

Just as it becomes too much to bear, everything shatters in a blinding rush. A final cry rips out of me as my body spasms, then I turn into jelly as pure relief washes over me.

Caeo continues thrusting until a shudder ripples through him, and he cries out as he spills himself within me. He collapses, and my core throbs as he pants against my neck, still buried inside me. It's impossible to know where he ends and I begin.

I bring my hand to his face, toying with his sweaty hair as the candlelight flickers in his exhausted eyes. Something flutters in my heart. An awakening, a closeness I've never felt before. The steady warmth floods my entire body, crashing through me like a wave, and the words spill out before I can stop them.

"I love you."

My chest tightens, suddenly unsure—*is that really what this is, or just what I want it to be?* It feels too soon. Almost unnaturally so. But then Caeo's eyes gleam as he breathes out a smile.

"I love you, too."

An almost magical tingle spreads through me. "I could stay like this forever."

"Your legs might start to hurt."

As if that were their cue, my thighs tremble, aching where they meet my pelvis. I groan, and Caeo laughs, kissing me again before rolling away with a matching grumble. Scooting against the wall to make room for him, I rest my head on his shoulder and my hand on his chest, watching it move up and down as his breathing slows.

"I don't want to forget this."

Caeo rests his hand on mine and gives it a tight squeeze.

"Then I'll stay, for as long as you'll let me."

Chapter 16

Caeo

"Caeo, it's time to wake up." Ellie's voice is gentle, as are the fingers stroking my cock.

My eyes snap open to her beautiful face, tousled brown hair catching the sunlight from the open window, with golden strands glowing among the crumpled flowers of last night's hairdo. Memories flood me, glimmering with a steady heat.

She loves me. Ellie loves me, and nothing could diminish the happiness filling every ounce of my body.

My cock twitches beneath her touch, and her lips tighten in a sheepish grin.

"You were already a little... stiff when I woke up." She's wrapped in a sheet, propped on one elbow, still completely naked underneath.

I flick my gaze down, then back to her eyes. "It happens. Seems like you might have something in mind?"

She blushes. "I kind of want to... put my mouth on it?"

My eyes widen. With how inexperienced she is, she probably didn't realize that's a thing people do. *Or is she still getting used to going for what she wants?* Either way, I like this boldness.

"Go for it."

Ellie smiles coyly, then scooches lower. A few seconds later, her fingers brush gently along my shaft while her lips wrap around the tip.

Pleasure tingles through me, my balls tightening as I mumble something, not really sure what, and she giggles in response. But a minute later, it's clear she has no clue what she's doing, so we have to stop so I can enlighten her. Then, for efficiency's sake, I suggest she sits on my face while we both go to town on one another, her pussy grinding against me as she takes my cock down her throat.

What have I done to her?

Despite our best efforts at multitasking, we still end up out of breath and a quarter bell late to her fire incanting class, almost colliding with Professor Beckwith as Ellie throws open the door.

"You're late." His eyes narrow as he notices me standing behind Ellie, squeezing her hand, then they shift back to her. "Reid can fill you in on your instructions for today."

Ellie nods quickly, flustered. "I'm sorry, Professor. It won't happen again." She hurries inside, dragging me behind her.

It's a smallish classroom, mostly empty except for a bunch of desks crammed against the wall, lit by the dull sunlight coming through an open window. Reid's digging through his bag on one of the desks, and I plop down on the one next to him, keeping my eyes on Ellie.

He glances up at me. "Don't you have somewhere to be?"

"I have a free period."

"Great," he mutters, unbuttoning his waistcoat. He turns to Ellie, pulling off her coat nearby. "We're to practice sequences seven and eight today, full fire, for his review at the end."

Wait a second...

They're both stripping down to their underclothes.

I jump to my feet. "What are you doing?"

"Relax, man. You know she's not my type."

"It's a matter of practicality." Ellie's thin white chemisette leaves nothing to the imagination, her arms and legs completely bare. "It's impossible to go through these in full uniform without dying."

I begrudgingly settle back down on the desk, annoyed that Reid has apparently gotten to spend the last several weeks seeing more of her flesh than I did. "You'd think they'd provide special uniforms for this," I mumble under my breath.

"They do," Ellie says, "but they're still rather suffocating. Since it's only the two of us, this is far more comfortable."

They both grab a sword from the shelf and stand side-by-side in the center of the room with about six feet of distance between them. They nod to each other, then move forward and backward, slicing their blades through the air at invisible enemies, completely synchronized with one another.

With fire. Lots and lots of fire, pouring off the gleaming metal, bursting into the air.

It's mesmerizing to watch, and with the heat of the flames filling the room, my temperature rises as I follow Ellie's graceful movements—how the muscles in her arms and legs flex and release, sweat dripping down her skin as she gasps for breath...

"That's it, you're leaving." Reid grabs my shirt and drags me to the door. "I'm not spending the entire period trapped in here while you fuck Ellie with your eyes." He shoves me into the hall.

"I'll bring her to you at lunch. Goodbye!"

A door slams shut, and I'm in a hallway, completely clueless about how I ended up here.

Is this the fire school? I shove my hands in my pockets and start searching for the exit.

THE ACADEMY LIBRARY takes up two entire floors, but despite the space, leather-bound books cram the shelves as Ellie and I meander between the stacks, our path lit by silver lanterns hanging overhead. The air smells of old paper and dust, and Ellie's once again bound my arm with vines to hers, to keep us from losing each other as we skim the spines, searching for anything related to memory.

My gut tells me we won't find anything. She's given up on the incantation section and moved on to medical papers, but for some reason she's convinced our problems have nothing to do with fae, despite that being the only thing that makes sense to me. There's clearly some kind of magic involved, and the only magic outside of incanting is fae magic.

But every time I suggest it, she brushes the notion aside, claiming it's impossible. Who am I to argue? She's a model student, and I'm seconds away from failing out. So we stick to topics she thinks will have better leads, since we have little enough time for research as is.

True to his word, Reid's been bringing Ellie to see me almost every day, but it hasn't been easy on him. Despite promising he'd bring her to me at lunch the day after the ball, I had no reason to go to the dining hall—no money, no food. Instead, I made the unfortunate decision to head home, where my mother bombarded me with questions about why I never returned the night before.

When I couldn't remember anything about my whereabouts, she ended up convincing me I'd blacked out somewhere from too much long leaf, at least until Reid showed up at my door with Ellie after dinner. We haven't spent an entire night together since, because the last thing I need is to spend our time apart worrying I'm overdoing the leaf.

If anyone's suffering from addiction, it's Ellie. Our night together has transformed her into a queen with an unquenchable thirst for my body as tribute. I love it—watching her conquer her vulnerabilities as she claims her pleasure is the most satisfying thing in the world. It's amazing we've been in the library as long as we have; I half expected her to drag me into a closet and have her way with me. But she gets kind of loud, and libraries are supposed to be quiet, so maybe that's why she didn't.

Sure enough, seconds after she flips her latest book closed, she meets my gaze. Her eyes sparkle, telling me she's tired of research and wants to move on to something more stimulating.

The instant we get to her room, she shoves me onto her bed, my head snapping forward as my back bangs against the wall.

"Ow."

"Sorry." Her voice is breathless as she strips her top off.

"Doesn't seem like you are." I catch her with my hands on her sides as she mounts me, completely naked, holding her back from whatever she had planned next. "Slow down, Ellie. Give me a chance to worship you."

Her lips quirk into a dimpled smile as I bring my hands to her breasts, the perfect weight against my palms, and pull one to my mouth as I knead the other. I tease her nipple with my teeth, exactly how she likes, and she lets out a moan that has me hard against my pants.

"That's it," I breathe. "Come for me."

She grinds against my cock, and my groan ends up muffled by her chest. I've gotten her there before, just like this, and it's so fucking worth it. Her eyelids fluttering, her lips parting with gasps and moans as the tension builds within her...

Her voice carries louder and louder until I can't bear it anymore. My pants are drenched from how wet she is, and I'm gonna burst inside them if this goes on any longer.

"Pants," I gasp. "Now."

Ellie presses her hands against my shoulders, pushing my back against the wall as she lifts herself up, and her lavender scent fills my lungs as her hair falls around me. I pull myself free, my cock pressing hard against her pussy.

She lets out a guttural moan as she slowly slides down, stretching around me—so warm and so, *so* wet.

"Fuck... that's good," I groan.

Her head tilts back as she slides up and down my shaft, excruciatingly slowly. My vision blurs at the edges as her back arches, my name rolling off her lips between her gasping breaths.

I slide my hands along her perfectly smooth skin until they reach her hips, then wrap my fingers tight around her, pulling her down to meet a balls-deep thrust. She cries out, the timbre of her voice almost enough to send me over the edge.

Our pleasure pulses through me, our bodies in sync, her voice ringing wildly through the air as she reaches the crest of her orgasm. Her fingernails dig into my shoulders as her body spasms and bucks, and I force her downward one last time. A throaty grunt bursts out of me with sweet release as my entire body shudders, emptying everything within her. Ellie's muscles clench around me, her final cry hanging in the air before she collapses.

I slump against the wall, panting. "That was... incredible."

It takes a few seconds for her eyes to focus on me, and a satisfied smile tugs at her lips between her breaths. She nods as she melts against me, her soft hair tickling my cheek as she keeps me buried within her. In some ways, this is better than sex—our bodies merging, hearts beating as one.

I caress her back with my fingers, my eyes sinking shut as her warmth presses into me. I wish this could last forever.

After a few minutes soaking in our love, breathing her breaths, my stomach rumbles and thoughts start dribbling through my mind. The dining hall will open for dinner soon, and knowing Ellie, she'll want to head over for something to eat, then come back here for another round.

I can't believe I'm saying it, but she's a little too focused on this side of our relationship now. She spends so much time with me that I don't see how she's keeping up on her studies, and if she falls behind, I'm sure her father will hear about it. Considering the whole reason she wants to keep our memory condition a secret is to avoid his intrusion in her life, it'd be ironic if it happened anyway because she was too busy fucking me to study.

And it's eating into our time to figure the whole thing out.

I should take her on a proper date. We haven't really had one outside of the Equinox Ball, and spending time away from the Academy—where there's an actual risk of her getting pregnant— might cool her down enough that she can get by with only ravishing me once a day.

"Let me plan a date for us. I still haven't shown you around Haven."

Ellie lifts her head, her warm, cinnamon eyes meeting mine. "How? You won't remember to make any plans."

"I'll figure it out when we're together. We just need to leave Reid a note."

She groans as she pulls herself off me, and my lap is completely soaked—she'll have to incant my pants clean before I can go anywhere. It'd be nice if I could do it on my own, but I can tell she likes taking care of me. I do, too.

I drag her with me to her desk, holding her hand while I find a piece of paper and scribble a message to Reid, telling him to bring her to my place after their last class this week. Folding it up, I write *To Reid, From Caeo* on the front and pin it to Ellie's bag where he'll easily notice it next time he sees her. After she removed and threw away many such notes in the past, we discovered that if I put my name on the outside, it'll slip from her mind as soon as she reads it, leaving it be.

When I finish, Ellie pulls me back to bed, a lustful glint returning to her eyes.

So much for this being it until dinner. She's gonna destroy me at this rate.

"I'm not ready to go again just yet."

She pushes me down and brings her lips to mine.

"Then I'll just have to get you there."

This is all my fault. I did this to her, and I couldn't be happier.

Chapter 17

Caeo

My key clicks and the door squeaks as I push it open. It catches, forcing me to shoulder it the rest of the way. The wood's probably warped from all the rain lately.

"I'm home," I call, shoving the door shut behind me. My bag hits the ground with a thud, then I sit on one of our beat-up chairs and kick my shoes off.

Another delivery done. I stretch out my exhausted limbs.

Despite how overworked I've been, I haven't felt the need for long leaf lately—I'm tired, but things don't feel quite as heavy as they used to. I *am* significantly hungrier than normal, but unfortunately, the kitchen's pretty sparse right now.

I suppose I could get started on my tactics paper: *Fae Curses*. Could be interesting.

My ability with incanting hasn't improved in the slightest, so getting decent marks in the more mundane subjects is my best chance at not failing out. It surprised me when I realized I cared about that recently. There's even an ache in my chest when I think about dropping out, like I'd miss out on belonging to something bigger than myself. But more than that, there's this urge to be better than I am. Like I actually could, for once.

I've just opened my textbook when my mother hobbles in. She

kisses my forehead before sitting next to me, resting her hand on mine. "Thank you for making that delivery. I'm not overworking you, am I?"

Ever since the night of the ball when I blacked out from long leaf, she's been extra concerned about my well-being. "I'm fine. Life's been better lately."

She brings her hand to my collar, and I flinch away. "You're missing a button," she says.

"Yeah, not sure when that happened." I'll have to get it fixed before I wear this shirt again. Stupid rules of propriety.

Mother smiles, though it doesn't quite reach her eyes. "I wanted to talk to you about something."

That can't be good. I drop my pen and give her more of my attention.

"I think it's time we moved on from Haven," she says.

That gets my full attention. "What? Why?"

Her mouth quirks. "We're here partly because Haven always has work for seamstresses, and because the Academy could provide opportunities for your future. We wouldn't have been able to afford your room and board if we'd lived anywhere else."

"And I'm going there now. So why leave?"

Her face wrinkles as she tilts her head and gives me half a smile. "Do you honestly think you'll make it to your second year?"

Ouch. She's not mincing words today, is she?

My jaw tightens, not wanting to give her the satisfaction of an answer. But it doesn't matter; she knows she's right.

She sighs. "Perhaps a fresh start somewhere else would be good for you."

Something nags at the back of my mind—a reason to stay—but I can't form what it is. The only thing I can think of is Reid, but he's flourishing at the Academy. Leaving me behind.

But with my mother's eyes boring into me, I don't want to admit I have nothing.

She squeezes my hand. "Think about it. You don't have to decide today, but I truly believe leaving would be for the best. A new life, far away from here, where you can find who you're meant to be."

That could be nice. I never did feel like I fit in around here, and it's not like we'd end up anywhere worse than a shack that's slowly losing all its color.

I pick up my pen with significantly less motivation to write my paper.

THE SECOND BELL CHIMES as I sprint to my water incanting class. Late again. To my surprise, Reid leans outside the classroom door, arms folded with a scowl on his face.

"You had to be late," he grumbles. "Now I'm late, too."

I catch my breath before answering. "What's going on?"

"Just meet me for lunch. I'll pay." He pushes off the wall, then storms off.

What was that about?

Bells later, I arrive at the dining hall, starving and thankful Reid's buying. He isn't in the food line, so I scan the tables. There he is—with Ellie, drawing in her sketchbook while Reid scarfs down his meal.

My hunger disappears.

"Thanks, man." I pat Reid's shoulder before sliding onto the bench across from him, next to Ellie. She looks up, lighting the room with her perfect smile.

"Uh huh." Reid takes a gulp from his drink before standing. "Later."

He's clearly in a mood. I'll have to find a way to make all this up to him soon.

I kiss Ellie's hand. "What are you drawing?" I angle my head to get a better look at her sketches.

It's me.

Heat floods my chest as she blushes.

"How did you... Did you remember me?"

She bites her lip. "Unfortunately, no. I wasn't really paying attention to what I was drawing. Just a face. I didn't know it was yours until you sat down."

"It's good, though. It means part of you remembers." I squeeze her hand, and she leans into me, flipping through the sketchbook's pages. My face looks back at me from nearly every one.

"I think part of me remembers, too," I say. "Life's felt better lately, even though everything's still horrible..."

My stomach falls to the floor.

Ellie notices, stiffening as she searches my face. "What's wrong?"

"Last time I talked to my mother, she wanted us to leave."

"What?"

I take both of her hands. "To leave Haven. I was about to agree."

"What? No." She shakes her head. "You can't leave. Why would you leave?"

"Because my life's terrible and there's nothing for me here except for you, but I can't remember that."

"We need to find Reid," Ellie says, shoving her things into her bag.

Still holding her hand, I push to my feet, almost colliding with Professor Mallory. I fumble an apology, but she holds up her hand, silencing me.

"Mister Evers, I require a word."

Ellie squeezes my fingers, clinging to my arm.

"Can it wait?" I ask weakly. I frantically scan behind her for Reid but find nothing.

"It cannot." She looks at Ellie, and her eyes soften. "Miss Detura, if you would."

Ellie slowly releases my arm. I tighten my grip on her other hand.

Professor Mallory indicates I should start walking. I glance back at Ellie, whose knuckles are turning white as she clutches the strap of her bag.

Everything will be fine. I'll see her again soon. A knot in my stomach constricts with such force that my knees almost give way.

"I don't have all day, Mister Evers," Mallory says.

With a final look at Ellie, I let go of her hand and follow the professor.

Our footsteps echo along the barren halls until we reach her office. I don't know what's going on, but this can't be good; I'm not in any of her classes, and she seems to be the one Headmaster Gleese delegates everything bothersome to.

I take the seat across from Mallory at her desk—its surface is relatively clear, with an open folio in front of her. A messy hand scrawled my name on the topmost page.

"I'll try to keep this short," she says, adjusting her spectacles. "I'm sure it's no surprise for you to hear that your performance has been far from satisfactory. In reviewing your assessments, I struggle to recall another student who has ever been so universally agreed upon to completely lack any ability for incantation."

Ouch.

"Perhaps if you had shown dedication to the rest of your studies, this conversation could have gone differently. But by all reports, you're constantly late, barely pay attention, and put forth the minimum effort required for your assignments, even after receiving warnings from all your professors. I am thereby forced to terminate your enrollment at the Academy, effective immediately."

A lump forms in my throat. I swallow, only for it to catch on the coil tightening in my chest. *It's fine. I knew this would happen eventually. Just one less thing to worry about.*

I swallow again, forcing it down despite the effort making my eyes sting, and my head jerks with a nod.

"I understand."

The tension in Mallory's face eases. "I'll give you the afternoon to say your goodbyes, but unfortunately you won't be allowed back on Academy grounds after today, unless you've registered as a guest of a currently enrolled student."

What does it matter if I can't come back? Reid will still visit me. *Only if I stay in Haven.*

An unexpected emptiness fills me. I didn't think being expelled would bother me, but here I am.

Mallory continues speaking, but I pay little attention, wandering out of her office as soon as she dismisses me. I make my way down the stairs, out the doors, and begin the short walk home.

Maybe a fresh start would be nice.

Chapter 18

Ellie

As Reid and I enter the dining hall for our midday break, I search the room for Alexis. Every bench is full, but less chatter fills the air than normal. The arrival of spring heralds our impending examinations, and everyone's exhausted from their increasing workloads. It seems to weigh especially hard on Reid, surprisingly.

He's been growing more and more frazzled with every passing day—late to class, snippy in conversation, and constantly insisting I go to town with him when we really need to study. Yesterday, we had an exceptionally frustrating interaction where, instead of letting me eat lunch with Alexis, he insisted I sit alone for an entire bell while he disappeared, occasionally popping back just to snap at me. He hasn't spoken to Alexis in the almost three weeks since they fought, and despite not wanting to get involved, it's clear I have no choice if I want Reid to calm down and return to normal.

I find her at a table with Oliver, her date to the Equinox Ball. A yawn slips out of my mouth as I step toward them, and I cover it with the back of my hand. Despite all my stress, I've been in surprisingly good spirits lately. Back home, painting helped me relax, but that's impossible here. Instead, I find myself dozing off, missing chunks of my days outside of class and studying. But it's working, keeping me strangely energized and more confident than ever.

I press that courage into my grip as I snag Reid's hand and drag him directly to Alexis, skipping the food line to dodge between crowded tables.

"What are you—Stop it, let go of me!" He curses as he bumps the edge of a bench.

"No. We're fixing whatever's going on between you and Alexis. Now."

He groans as I settle across from Alexis and Oliver, sitting hand-in-hand, whispering to one another. They glance over, and Alexis's smile compresses into an icy glare the second she spots Reid. He drops onto the bench, arms crossed, looking away.

"What are you doing here?" Alexis demands, eyeing Reid.

I turn to Oliver, whose wide eyes would suggest we caught him doing something inappropriate. *How can someone this timid last long with Alexis?* "Sorry, could you give us a minute?"

He looks to her for guidance, and her face scrunches before she nods. He gives her a quick peck on the cheek before rushing away.

Here we go. "Now, as best I can tell, the two of you are fighting over Emmrich. Which makes no sense, because you're with Oliver now. So make up already so Reid can stop being angry all the time." I hold my breath, awaiting their responses.

Reid shifts his weight. "That's not why I'm angry all the time."

"Oh?" *Did I misinterpret things?* "Then why?"

His jaw clenches, then he rubs his brow. "Fine," he mutters, shaking his head before dropping his hand to the table. "I *am* still annoyed with Alexis for sleeping with Emmrich."

"Because I won?" Alexis folds her arms.

"No! It wasn't a competition. I mean, it started out that way, but it wasn't anymore."

Her face softens. "Wait, you actually *like* him?"

Reid turns red, then he looks away.

"I thought... Then why did you want me there at all? I thought it was all just for fun."

Reid stares at a spot on the table while rubbing it with his fingers. After a deep breath through his nostrils, he speaks. "Just because I act confident doesn't mean I always am. It seemed easier if you were there. If it didn't work out, I could blame you."

It's as if he stepped into a new light—I never would've imagined he wasn't as confident as he seemed. It's reassuring that I'm not the only one who worries about what others think.

"Reid..." I lift my hand, debating the best place to give a supportive touch, but Alexis beats me to it.

"Oh, honey." She takes his hand with both of hers. "I'm so sorry. If I had known... You could've told me."

"Yeah, whatever." He pulls free, but meets her gaze. "He obviously wasn't that invested. I'll get over it."

Alexis tilts her head, her lips pursed, then nods.

I let out a sigh of relief—I didn't make things worse. And hopefully, Reid will be in a better mood now.

"We should get some food before our next class." I grab my things, nudging him to get moving. I'd like to avoid things turning tense again because we're grumpy from hunger.

"Wait," he says. "There's something else I need to talk to you about. It's important."

Alexis tilts her brow up. "Alright?"

"I can come by tonight. It'll take a while to explain."

"Sure. I'll be there."

We say our goodbyes, then Reid and I head for the food line. I grab a plate and peek ahead at today's offerings. "What was that about?"

Reid sighs. "Caeo. It's about you and Caeo."

Who?

I'm about to ask Reid for clarification when my gaze lands on the dessert section, and whatever he said slips from my mind. "Oh look, they have pie today." A cozy warmth fills me as I breathe in the aroma of clove and jam wafting through the air.

Reid trails his hand down his face as he groans. "That's it. I'm eating alone. I'll see you in class." He skips ahead, cutting off some people in line ahead of us.

What's his problem now?

I CONTEMPLATE THE WARPED WOODEN DOOR, its bottom half splotchy and stained, with swollen edges where it soaks in the puddle at its base. "What are we doing here?"

Classes have ended for the week, and we stand at the entrance to a run-down hovel with gray, peeling siding. Reid's banging so hard the door creaks with every hit.

"You said we were going somewhere I'd love." This is the sort of place I actively avoid.

"Arandur's stinking cheese." Reid rubs his temple. "In a minute you'll be thanking me profusely, going on and on about how I'm such a good friend. And I am, because you have no idea how difficult you've made my life. I'm seconds away from telling Mallory everything just so I don't have to deal with this anymore."

"Telling Mallory what? What's going on?"

It took a lot of convincing on his part for me to join him on this outing, and I'm beginning to regret giving in. Obviously, there's something else bothering him, something beyond his fight with Alexis, but he won't explain what it is.

He bangs on the door again. "Come on, open up."

I take a nervous step back. "I think I'm going to go."

"No, just give him a minute." Another bang. "Cay, you home?"

"Who are you talking to?"

Reid groans. "He told me to bring you here. I confirmed it the other day." Kicking the door, he drags his hand along his face. His fingers have raked through his hair so many times it's edging into unkempt—he barely looks like himself.

"Great," he mumbles. "Let's go." He shoves his hands in his coat pockets and storms down the street, grumbling to himself.

I take a step, intending to follow, but a tug of curiosity compels me to look back at the door. An uneasy feeling simmers in my chest; there's something familiar about this place, but I can't place it.

Peeking through the small window, there's not much to see: a cramped living space with a single door leading to another room, the mess of someone's life covering the table and counters. If they were home, they would undoubtedly have heard all that banging.

My hand finds its way into my pocket, fingers slipping against a small, smooth circle. A mother of pearl button I found tangled in my sheets as I made my bed this morning. I checked all my blouses, but none were missing any, then shoved it into my pocket before rushing to class. Something about it... it feels important.

I catch up with Reid, passing similar decrepit shacks along the way. "Are you going to explain what that was all about?"

"I could, but it'd be a waste of breath." He stops at the gravel intersection. "Where the fuck could he be?"

A flicker of irritation bubbles within me. "Who?"

"It doesn't matter," he murmurs, not even sparing me a glance.

"It does matter." I grab his arm and force him to look at me. "You dragged me all the way out here and won't tell me anything. Who are you looking for?"

"Cay. Caeo."

I blink, unsure what he said. "What?"

Reid's face tightens, wound up like a kettle on the verge of screaming. "Your boyfriend!"

My... what? My heart stutters. "I don't have a boyfriend."

"Yes, you do. You met him the same day you met me." Reid yanks my bag from my shoulder and starts digging through it.

"What are you doing?" This is beyond acceptable. I reach for my bag, and Reid shoves it into my arms as he pulls out my sketchbook and starts flipping through it.

"Stop that!"

He does, holding it up to me. A page full of sketches—drawings I did when I was bored. All of the same face.

"Him." He forces the book into my hands. "That's him. Caeo. Your boyfriend."

I take the book, running my fingers along the drawings. They're surprisingly detailed compared to most of my work. A fire blooms in my chest as my eyes linger on the lines of his face. I swallow down the drought forming in my mouth.

"This is nobody. A face I drew when I was bored. He's not a real person."

"Caeo is real. I've known him my whole life, and that was his house. He's your boyfriend, and for some reason we haven't figured out yet, you don't remember each other."

My eyes locked on the drawings, I try to form some words in response, but nothing comes out. It doesn't seem like Reid's playing a prank on me, his frustration palpable. But the things he's saying make little sense.

Heat blossoms within me as I take in the face. He looks like someone I could imagine being with, with his messy hair and warm smile. I flip through the pages. He appears multiple times, in varying levels of detail. There's even a drawing of a single eye I know is his.

I glance back at Reid. He's eyeing me expectantly, but I haven't a clue why.

He sighs. "I need a drink."

I slide my sketchbook back into my bag and hurry after him as he marches further into Haven.

Reid's seething aura keeps us walking in silence, interrupted only by the sounds of our feet kicking gravel. The air turns chillier as the sun sets, and soon after the road transitions to cobblestone, I spot the ridiculous sign for The Buttoned-Up Duck: a mallard wearing nothing but a high, frilly collar around its long neck.

"I'm surprised Alexis didn't join us," I say.

"I hadn't planned on coming here. I was gonna drop you off and meet her after."

"Drop me off where?"

"Arandur's flaming oven." Reid halts a few steps away from the tavern's entrance and faces me. "You lost the entire conversation?"

"What conversation?"

He clenches his fists, then bursts into a stream of expletives while kicking the wall of the building.

Has he lost it?

I'm about to ask what's wrong when the door to The Duck swings open. Two men stride out, cutting their conversation short when they notice Reid brutalizing the wooden siding.

"Reid?" the blond one asks.

His face is handsome, with a mischievous glint in his golden—yes, golden—eyes. He's tied his hair in a knot behind his head, and rather than a traditional collared shirt, a burgundy scarf wraps loosely around his neck.

There's something familiar about him. I'm certain I've seen him around the tavern before.

His friend is new. Taller than the rest of us, wrapped up in a dark gray coat that hides most of his clothes. His hood's up, shrouding his face in shadow, but dark, chin-length hair frames his sharp jaw and high cheekbones.

A powerful magnetism emanates from both of them, pulling my gaze despite the heat creeping up my neck, flushing my face. I can't look away.

Reid glances at the speaker. "Oh, fuck everything." He slumps with his back against the building, scowling at the sky as if asking why it hates him.

"Hello, Emmrich." His voice rings with feigned politeness. "Nice to see you."

This is Emmrich? Interesting.

Emmrich eyes his hooded friend, who gives him a curt nod. "It's been a while. Can we talk?"

"Sorry, you must be confusing me with my friend with tits," Reid says, making me cringe. "If you haven't noticed, I don't have those."

"What are you talking about?" Emmrich's brow furrows.

"I know you slept with her, asshole. Get lost."

Emmrich's gaze shifts to me. I shrug—I've involved myself in Reid's relationships enough for one day.

He turns back to Reid. "Give me a chance to explain. Please?"

Reid exhales and pushes himself off the wall. "Five minutes. But that's it."

Emmrich glances between me and his friend.

Does he expect us to go somewhere?

A second later, he grabs Reid's wrist and drags him around the corner of the building, with Reid mumbling another curse before disappearing from sight. I force a smile at Emmrich's friend, hoping this is as awkward for him as it is for me. I step back as a couple passes between us to enter The Duck.

"Perhaps we should move." My new companion gestures across

the street, his voice low.

I nod. "Of course. Don't want to be in anyone's way."

We move to the opposite building, and he leans against its worn-down brick wall. Forcing myself to stop gawking at him, I lean nearby, following his gaze to Emmrich and Reid, now visible from this side of the mostly empty street. They appear to be arguing, but I can't make out anything they're saying.

This is getting uncomfortable.

"So, your friend's Emmrich? I'm Ellie."

"Taran." He offers nothing else, but keeps his eyes fixed on Reid and Emmrich.

Taran? That's an unusual name. "I haven't seen you around before."

"I'm visiting."

After a few seconds of silence, it's clear he won't be elaborating. "From where?"

Nothing.

Lovely. Someone worse at small talk than me.

Giving up, I settle for watching the others argue. Their voices don't carry over to us so it's not that interesting. Perhaps Taran's *also* involved with Emmrich, and that's why he's so invested?

As if he could hear my thoughts, Emmrich glances over at us.

No—at Taran.

He nods, then Emmrich moves further into the alley, out of sight, pulling Reid with him.

What was that about? My body tenses with the realization that I'm now alone with a strange man.

He turns to face me. For the first time, I notice his eyes. A swirling, infinite green, clearer than polished emerald. My heart pounds against my ribs, pulled toward him like a tide.

"Come with me." He holds out his hand, his voice echoing

through my mind.
I find myself taking it.

Part 2

Entangled

Chapter 19

Reid

I cross my arms, avoiding both Emmrich's gaze and touching anything in this dank alley next to The Duck he's dragged me into. "I'm listening. Five minutes, hurry it up."

He's the last person I want to be talking to right now. A fire burns in my chest, full of rage. Nothing but rage.

That's not true. I'm not angry. Except I am. I spent weeks flirting with him, and it finally seemed like we'd take the next step, but he couldn't bother waiting for me. He *knew* I needed to help Caeo, but left anyway. Just dropped me and went off with Alexis instead.

It's not like I don't want him to have a good excuse. To apologize. To shove me against the wall and show me what I missed. But this is the worst possible time.

Which maybe makes it the best time. Ellie doesn't even remember the last twenty minutes, so I could forget about them, too. After all, the entire reason my relationship with Emmrich plummeted into nothingness was because of her and Caeo's stupid memory problems.

Heat flares within me as my eyes meet Emmrich's—such a peculiar shade, like honey. Strands of his sandy-blond hair frame his face, the rest of it tied in a knot behind his head. I shove aside the urge to rake my fingers through it and discover how long his hair really is.

He folds his arms, matching me. "I waited. Didn't seem like you were coming back."

"But I did."

I distinctly remember it. Running through town, catching my breath outside so I didn't appear overeager, approaching the bar... and he was gone.

"Really? When?" His lips curl slightly as he leans against the wall, waiting for my response.

"Seventh bell. I heard it on the way."

Emmrich throws his hand to the side. "You expected me to wait three fucking bells?"

"It wasn't three bells!" *It wasn't. No way.*

"Yes, it was. You left right before the fourth nighttime bell. I waited. Alexis showed up around fifth bell. We waited. At midnight, we decided you weren't coming, so we went on without you."

"Without me? So you *were* planning on fucking us both."

"Yes," he sighs. "Was that not obvious?"

A blaze of indignation scorches my ribs. "What if I didn't want to share?"

"Then you got your wish."

"That's not what I—Look, I meant to come back. I did. But Caeo... Something was wrong, and I had to help." My anger diminishes as I peel away from the wall, and I hope I don't look as pathetic as I sound. "I came back as soon as I could."

"So you could fuck me."

I blink, my brain confirming what he just said.

"Um... yes? I mean, yes."

My face burns, filling me with a sudden, desperate urge to crawl into a hole. Emmrich's eyes mercifully flick away, looking past my shoulder. I follow his gaze to his friend and Ellie waiting across the street.

Emmrich slams me against the wall further into the alley.

On instinct, I throw flames up between us. They extinguish almost instantly, but he still jumps back. A sly smile curls on his face.

"I'm gonna pretend that didn't just happen."

Then his tongue slips between my lips, conquering my mouth before I even realize I've been invaded. Lighting me up as he traces and teases, claiming me over and over again.

I finally break free. "Is this actually happening?"

"Just kiss me."

Yes, sir.

I grab his shirt, pulling him closer as his tongue sweeps through my mouth. I catch his lower lip with my teeth, and he lets out a groan that makes it impossible to ignore how hard I am. He tears open my collar, ripping the buttons, sucking and biting at my neck while his hands travel down my chest.

My mind can't keep up. "What are you doing?"

He lets out a short laugh and bites my ear, sending a sizzle down my spine, just as his fingers tug at my belt.

"No, stop. Stop." If my brain had hands, it would've smacked me.

Emmrich pauses, his features warping in confusion. "What?"

I pull his hands off me and force myself away, fumbling to redo my remaining buttons. "Call me a romantic, but I'd rather not get fucked in an alley with my friend right around the corner."

His expression's unreadable. Catching his breath? Disappointment, maybe? I peek back at the main road to check on Ellie.

She's gone.

So is Emmrich's friend.

"Wait, where'd they go?" I turn back to Emmrich.

And... he's running down the alley and not looking back.

Where's he going?

Puzzle pieces snap together. I left Ellie with his friend. They're gone. Emmrich's running.

Arandur's cock sucking maw.

I bolt after him.

Emmrich leaps over the fence at the end of the alley with impressive grace, hopping off the side wall before grabbing the top and effortlessly pulling himself over.

I definitely can't do that.

But summoning wind is easy—I've done it a thousand times in the last two months. The gust lifts me over the wall with a bounding leap. Landing lightly on the ground, I sprint toward the intersection, giving myself a boost with a blast of air. Even with tension gnawing at my stomach, it's exhilarating to finally experience the fruits of my endless practice.

By the dusk light and paper lanterns lining the road, I spot Emmrich. Down the road to my right, sprinting past a mom dragging her screaming children behind her. I shift the wind and launch myself toward him.

Catching him from behind, I wrap my arms around his midsection and fly forward. He arcs back with my momentum, letting out a strangled yelp.

I rip a wall of earth up from beneath the cobblestones, then swing my legs around, planting them against it. I push off, slamming back into Emmrich. He collapses beneath me, the force of the impact leaving him gasping for air. Incanted roots erupt from the dusty road as I grapple his arms down by his sides, wrapping around his wrists.

"Where are you going?" I straddle him, my legs pressing firmly against his pelvis. "I thought this was what you wanted."

"Get these things off me!" His face contorts as he squirms against the roots, trying to shake me off.

It isn't the busiest street, but a small, murmuring crowd's forming. The Wardens of Fortune will probably show up soon, as I just very publicly broke several laws about incanting outside of the Academy. As the king's militia, they backed the Order during the war, but mostly keep the peace. Just regular people, though there's usually an incanter assigned to them for moments like this.

I lean close to Emmrich's ear. "I'm gonna let you up, then you're gonna tell me why you ran and where Ellie is."

"How should I know?" The mischievous spark in his eyes is gone.

I scowl at him, and he matches my glare with one sharp enough to make my racing heart stumble.

Focus.

Ellie's just as good at incanting as I am. There's no way his friend could've taken her against her will, especially without me noticing, no matter how distracted I was. For all I know, they just went to The Duck to give us privacy.

But why did Emmrich run?

It must have been his job to distract me. Maybe his friend knocked Ellie out before she could react? He wouldn't have been able to get far, so Emmrich running in the opposite direction would've given him more time to flee. But why would they want to kidnap Ellie? Because of her father?

Caeo's missing, too.

Well, he isn't home, at least. That's hardly missing. But I haven't seen him in almost a week, when he met us for lunch after making me late for class.

"You know, and you're gonna tell me." I seize Emmrich's arm as my roots release him. "Or I'll fuck you up in ways you can't imagine." I hoist him to his feet and bind him with thick, thorny vines, ensnaring his entire torso in seconds.

"You'll find I have quite the imagination."

His smile's back. *Dammit.* I shove him down the street.

The sun hasn't even set, and this night can't get any worse.

I SLOWLY OPEN the door to my mom's house, peeking inside while keeping a tight grip on Emmrich's arm, lest the bastard try to run off again. It was the best place I could think to bring him since my mom's usually out this time of night.

Sure enough, the place is empty—except for George, her latest benefactor, snoring loudly in his chair. If not for his nasal thundering, I wouldn't have seen him. He's just as plain and gray as everything else.

I shove Emmrich inside, forcing him into a smaller room off the main one. Mine.

Candles burst to life as we enter. I don't even have to look; it's instinct at this point. It's almost completely bare in here, just battered old furniture shoved into a clamshell of a space. There's nowhere to sit other than the bed, so I push Emmrich toward it before leaning against the wall, facing him.

I'm barely holding on. Life was bad enough having to wrangle Caeo and Ellie's relationship, and now this? I should just mind my own business and let all their problems float away. But Caeo's the only real family I've got. We met when he stole the only girlfriend I ever had—sure, I was five—but she disappeared and he stuck around. Despite all the headaches he's brought me, he's always been there—the only person I can count on.

I can't ignore this.

"Time to talk. Where's Ellie and your friend?"

Sitting on the bed, Emmrich leans his back against the wall, as if it's comfortable. It's not—the bed's too deep. There were pillows for that very reason, but I'd taken them with me to the dorms, along with everything else I cared about. I hadn't planned on ever coming back here.

"Why should I tell you anything?"

"Because I can do *this*." With a thought, the vines constrict, creaking as they dig into his ribs.

Emmrich stiffens, but keeps his face casual except for a slight twitch in his lips. "If you kill me, you'll learn nothing, and you don't have it in you to torture me."

I raise my hand as flames form around it. "You think so?"

"I know so."

Dammit. He's right. As much as I enjoy incanting, I'd always hoped I'd make it through life in the Order without ever seeing an actual battle.

He bends his right leg, resting his ankle on his left knee. "Perhaps you could fuck me for information. Not sure that would get me to talk, but if you can get me begging for your cock in my mouth, maybe I would."

My brain freezes.

"What the fuck is wrong with you?!"

"Careful. Do you really wanna wake your father and explain why I'm tied up in your bed?"

"He's not my father," I mutter as I rub at my brow. "And he won't wake up—he sleeps like he's dead."

Emmrich just chuckles. I should punch him in the face. But it's a nice face. At any other time, I could see myself doing a lot of things to that face. The thought sends heat burning up my collar into my cheeks, and I pray they haven't turned red.

His smile tells me they did.

I groan, burying my face in my hands. He's in control, and he knows it. There has to be a way to turn this around, but I'm running out of time. In my desperation, only one idea comes to mind.

"Please."

"Hmm?" Emmrich's brow arches up.

"Please," I repeat, slumping away from the wall. "None of this makes any sense to me, but my gut tells me my friends are gone, and you know why."

"What doesn't make sense?"

"You wouldn't believe me."

He just eyes me, waiting, so I briefly explain Caeo and Ellie's memory problems.

"Sounds like a fae curse," he says.

... What?

I must have blacked out for a second because the world flipped right-side-up and I have no idea how I'm still standing.

"A fae curse?"

"Yep. Not even a terribly creative one, for that matter."

Oh, fuck.

"I'm so stupid." Top of my class, and I couldn't see a fae curse right in front of me. *Shit.*

"You're not. Caeo wears a necklace that prevents mortals from thinking of anything fae related to him. Though it seems to crack if someone pokes at it enough."

My thoughts stutter to a halt.

What did he just say?

"How in the name of Arandur's wrinkly sack would you know that?"

Emmrich cocks his head to the side and raises his eyebrows.

"Because I'm fae."

...

WHAT?

I don't even know what obscenities tumble out of my mouth. Pain sears my foot as I kick the bed. A ball of ice shatters against the wall that I must have thrown.

I almost fucked a fae. The enemy. Who have been warring with us for thousands of years.

FUCK.

And he has the nerve to watch my outburst like he's evaluating one of Ellie's drawings. I hate this man—this fae. *I hate this fae!*

After releasing a final stream of curses that make little sense, even to me, I collapse on the thin mattress next to him, cradling my throbbing foot. Then I slam my fist against the wall because I don't learn from my mistakes.

Fuck. That hurt.

"He really does sleep like the dead," Emmrich notes.

Deep breaths.

Turning to him, I scour the details of his face as I try to calm down, searching for any signs I could've missed, like glowing eyes. They seem normal, other than the color.

"Your ear..." I reach out, brushing the tip of the one closest to me. Despite looking like it rounds at the top, a pointy tip slides beneath my fingers. My eyes widen.

"A glamour," Emmrich says.

"A what?" I bend his ear back and forth to see if anything changes in my vision. Nothing.

"A glamour. We can use our gifts to change our appearance."

What the fuck...

I release his ear like it's a hot pan and scoot away. "Fae can look human?"

"Don't stop. I was enjoying that."

I glare at him. "Answer the question."

He sighs. "Yes, we can, but don't get all paranoid about it. Most of us have no desire to come here."

My eyes narrow. *He's being awfully forthcoming.*

"And you're just spilling your people's biggest secrets? Why?"

He tilts his head, his eyes darting across my face. After a second, he speaks. "From what I've come to know about you, that seems to be my best option right now."

Is that some roundabout way of saying he trusts me? My stomach flutters, but I squash the feeling down.

"If you really are fae, how did I catch you so easily?"

"Our gifts fade the longer we're in your realm, and I've been here a long time. I let my guard down—I hadn't expected to fight you, and got stuck relying solely on my physical prowess against your foul incantations. Of course you win." He tenses against his constraints, and there's a clear venom behind his words as he eyes the vines.

As much as my brain warns me not to trust a word he says, the rest of me wants to believe he's telling the truth. It's probably a terrible idea, but I loosen his restraints. They wilt, crumbling into dust within seconds.

Surprise flashes in Emmrich's eyes, then he rolls his shoulders, savoring the freedom of his arms.

"Don't make me regret that," I grumble. "I can tie you back up faster than you can blink."

He presses his shoulder into mine and locks eyes with me, the gold within them sparkling.

"I know."

That was definitely a bad idea. But I can't back down. I've made progress, and Arandur help me, I am not losing control now.

"If you can't do magic, how are you glamouring your ears?" I flick one of them to make my point.

"I drink a small amount of water from home every day—just

enough to maintain it."

Alright. Now for the big one.

"And your friend? Did he take Ellie?"

Emmrich's eyes narrow, but he doesn't say anything.

"If you're really fae, you can't lie," I press. "You said you didn't know where she was."

"No, I asked you how I should know where she was."

"So you *do* know."

Our stare-down continues for another moment. A not-insignificant, traitorous part of me hopes he'll break it by kissing me again.

But he doesn't.

Instead, he pushes to his feet. "I know where I'm supposed to meet him. If you'd like, you can come, too. It'd be nice to have someone to keep me warm at night."

Chapter 20

Ellie

Taran leads me to the northern edge of town, my hand firmly grasped in his. He matches my shorter stride, never tugging uncomfortably on my arm.

It's as if I'm wandering through a fog. If I let go of him, I'll get lost, and that would be bad. Everything else blurs at the edges as we pass, nausea swelling within me if I focus on anything but him.

He asks if I've ever ridden a horse, and I tell him I haven't—while we own some, Mom and I have only used them for carriage rides.

Now I'm standing still, engulfed in the stink of manure. There's an itch at the back of my mind... Something about this... it isn't right. But the harder I grasp at the thought, the further it slips away.

Taran lets go of my hand as he helps me into a saddle. The world slowly sharpens, but just as my vision clears, the horse beneath me erupts into a gallop. I throw myself forward, clinging to its mane for dear life.

After a few terrifying minutes of not falling, my heart thundering harder than the hooves hit the ground, I peek my eyes open. The sun's nearly set, and my horse follows behind one galloping through the fields ahead of me. I can't make out the rider, but it must be Taran.

Every incantation I know flashes through my mind. *How do I get out of this?* Fire? Ice? But anything like that would frighten the horse, and I'd get thrown. I can barely stay in the saddle as it is.

Frustration and shame boil within me. All my skills, rendered useless by a horse.

After what feels like several bells, we slow to a trot. The moon hangs high in the sky as Taran dismounts at the edge of a forest, his silhouette approaching in the darkness. He offers me his hand, and I accept it, only because I need to be off the horse before I can attack. But the second I pull away, my legs give out as pain sears through my muscles.

"Let go of me!" I snap when he catches me. He doesn't, so I ignite his arm with a burst of flames.

He yells a curse I don't recognize and drops me, tearing his coat off and throwing it away from the horses. I hit the ground right as my horse rears, screaming in terror. Taran's arms grab me roughly around my midsection, hauling me clear of the kicking hooves.

I land hard on my backside a few yards away. Taran speaks soft words I can't understand, slowly approaching the horse until he rests his hand gently on its side.

My heart rate slows as his calm permeates the air. His coat lies discarded on the ground nearby, still burning; with a thought, it extinguishes, leaving only the moon to offer its faint light. I collapse backward and stare up at it, pain from the saddle radiating through my body.

"Who are you?" I demand. *I need him to talk. Get information. Then figure out my escape.*

"I told you already. My name's Taran."

"Why have you taken me?"

No answer. I push myself up to see him better, the long grass brushing my hands—he's busy untacking the horses.

"Is it because of my father?"

A scoff. "I couldn't care less who your father is."

That's a first. Perhaps we could've been friends if he weren't in the middle of abducting me.

"Then tell me why you've taken me, or I'll—"

"You'll what? You're no killer. Besides, you have no idea where you are or how to ride a horse."

"I'm sure I could find my way in the morning," I say, ignoring his first point.

"So you can go back to learning how to fight and kill an enemy you can't even recognize?"

Finishing his task, he comes over and crouches before me. Even in the darkness, his features are strangely familiar—comforting, even—but his green eyes lock on mine with an intensity that lays me bare.

My voice rasps out of my parched throat. "What are you..."

With a shift in the moonlight, a shadow lifts from his face. His intoxicating eyes brighten as if verdant flames burn within, the angles of his face sharpening. And his ears... narrow to a point at the tips.

"Fae!" I scramble backward on my butt, my heart pounding. I belatedly realize I should lash out with an incantation, freezing or trapping him somehow. Anything to keep him away.

But he shakes his head with a condescending chuckle and walks off, leaving me... even more confused. And slightly ashamed of my pathetic reaction. So I gather myself up and hobble after him, channeling my tangled emotions into anger as pain underscores my every move.

"You said you don't care about my father," I say, stopping next to him as he kneels, searching through his bag. "Do you even know who he is?"

"Of course I do, Eloise Detura, I just don't care. It has nothing to do with why we're here." He takes a swig from a waterskin, closing his eyes as he swallows.

How is he so casual right now?

"Then... why? What other value do I have?"

Taran sighs, pushing his hands off his knees as he towers above me, my eyes level with his chest. My shoulders tense as I step back.

He could crush me.

"Despite what you may think, I have no qualms with your people," he says. "Twenty-one years ago, our queen—the one who led the war against you—was uncrowned and exiled to your lands. I have reason to think that she has returned and stolen the throne. While she was here, we believe she placed a curse on you, and it's my hope that the reason for that curse makes you"—his brow furrows as if he's struggling to find the proper words—"well-positioned to help me prevent a war between our realms."

He nods, clearly satisfied with his explanation.

I am not.

"What does that even mean? I'm not under a fae curse."

"You are. It has caused you to forget much of the last three weeks."

"That's ridiculous!"

"Didn't they teach you fae can't lie?" he asks, and I shoot him a glare. "I'm told you attended an equinox ball. Try to remember it."

I huff, in no mood to humor his nonsense. I turn to walk away, but a spike of pain in my legs stops me after two steps.

"Fine." He tosses his hands up. "Do what you want. I'm going to collect firewood."

"No need." With three simple incantations, I sprout a small bush, dehydrate it, and engulf it in flames.

Taran scowls at the fire, then at me, the flames reflecting the heat in his eyes. He storms to the opposite side of the blaze, hurling his pack to the ground.

Satisfied with my display, I settle down where I am. But try as I might, his words keep sneaking into my mind. I *did* go to the ball. Alexis and I went together. She met up with Oliver, and I followed her in...

My stomach twists, and my hand shoots to my mouth to cover my reaction. I glance Taran's way—he's too busy beating his pack into the shape of a pillow to have noticed.

I don't *actually* remember entering the ball. In fact, the more I think about it, I don't remember anything until the next morning when I was in class with Reid. I don't even remember walking there.

"Let's say you're right about this queen putting a curse on me."

"I almost certainly am."

Fortune preserve me, this man...

"Why did she?"

Taran doesn't respond immediately. It would seem his limitations on lying make him very deliberate about everything he says, but his expression's unreadable in the darkness.

"I do not believe I could venture a guess without potentially triggering the curse and risking you forgetting this entire conversation. Which I would prefer not to do."

"Because you want me to help you fight this queen and stop her from invading Landore again?"

"I don't expect you to fight her."

The fire pops as I lean closer. "Then how am I of any use? You claim it has nothing to do with my father, but he's the only thing that's special about me. And if you think he won't go to war because you have me as a hostage, I'm afraid you're sorely mistaken."

"I'm not sure why you're questioning my motives. I've explained them to you—I can't lie."

His tone sends my blood boiling. "But you fae like to twist your words around, speaking technical truths that hide your deceptions."

At that, he pushes himself up from his relaxed position, the firelight illuminating the harsh curl of his upper lip.

"What would you know? When was the last time you, or anyone you've ever met, knowingly spoke to a fae? What do your people actually know of us?" His eyes narrow. "Believe the lies you tell yourself all you like. They're the only ones you've heard tonight."

He hits his bag forcefully, causing me to flinch, then takes another gulp from his waterskin before lying with his back to me. "Now go to sleep before I make you sleep."

Considering I have no idea how he forced me to follow him here, I do *not* want to test that threat. My bag full of books is nearly impossible to shape into something comfortable for my head, but I try anyway, then give his back one last glare before I curl myself into a tight ball on the cold, hard ground.

My stomach churns at the thought of what morning will bring. Fae are the enemy, their words riddled with tricks, so I shouldn't believe anything he said. More than that, I don't want to. It would mean that everything I've been taught, everything between humans and fae, the wars... It's all more complicated than I ever imagined.

And for the first time in my life, there's no one to tell me what to do next.

Chapter 21

Reid

"Why are we going to the Academy?" Emmrich hisses as I drag him toward the girls' dormitory, gravel crunching beneath our feet. Even though it's dark out, it'd be too conspicuous to have him bound by incantation. I definitely did not want his arm in my hand.

Wait a minute…

"Your name isn't really Emmrich, is it?" It sounds too normal.

"Ancients, no. It's Emlyn."

Emlyn. That's much nicer.

"But you said—"

"No, I said, 'Call me Emmrich.' Stop trying to catch me in a lie. I'm physically incapable of it."

I sigh. "Whatever. We're going to the Academy to tell Alexis what's going on."

"You can't possibly think that'll go well."

"Her roommate and best friend are about to disappear. She deserves to know."

My arm jerks me back as Emmrich—*Emlyn*—stops walking. "Come on," I urge.

He doesn't budge. "Understand that you're taking me into a very dangerous situation. Everyone in that building is being trained to kill me and mine. I'm putting my life in your hands."

Dammit. He's right. I look from where my hand holds his arm to his honey-colored eyes. Worry leeches out of them, softening my resolve.

"Alright. I promise I'll keep you safe. Is that enough?"

He groans but slowly trudges forward. I haul him the rest of the way until I'm banging on Alexis's door.

"Not so loud," she says when she opens it. "You'll wake the entire building." Her face lights up when she notices Emlyn behind me. "Oh! Are we finally doing this?"

"What? No!" I push past her as my face burns, pulling Emlyn with me so the three of us stand in a triangle in the entryway. "Aren't you with Oliver?"

"Sure, but it's nothing serious yet, and I'm always ready to help a friend." She winks at me, and if I could collapse into a void, I would. "So what's going on?"

After giving her a quick rundown of how Ellie and Caeo have been kidnapped by fae, she frowns. "Why would you possibly think that?"

I gesture to Emlyn. "Because he's fae, and he told me."

The temperature in the room drops about twenty degrees.

"What?" she asks, her voice cold as ice.

Emlyn takes a step behind me.

"He's fae," I repeat.

Alexis's nostrils flare, and I belatedly remember the entire reason I was furious with Emlyn to begin with: because he fucked her.

She lunges at him. "I'll kill you!"

I jump back, knocking into Emlyn, sandwiching him between me and the wall. Alexis claws at him, and I force her hands away.

"Alexis, stop!"

"Water from air, blades of ice—"

An incantation.

She can't do that without a focal, can she?

Icicles as sharp as knives crystalize above Emlyn as she finishes. I release a counter-incantation as they fly toward him, barely melting them in time. Cold water splashes against us.

Emlyn squeezes out from behind me and bolts to the other side of the room. I throw my arms around Alexis as she lunges after him.

"Stop defending him, Reid," she yells as I struggle to restrain her without hurting her.

"I need his help! I can't have you murdering him."

"Did you get some kind of sick pleasure out of it?" She snarls at Emlyn, her face twisted with rage and pain. "Were you laughing at me the entire time?"

"Of course not! You're a person, I don't hold your ignorance against you."

"You murdered my parents!"

"*I* haven't killed anyone from your realm," Emlyn snaps. "*I'm* trying to prevent another war with mortals."

"Yeah, right," she scoffs, still pulling against my grip.

"Fae can't lie, Lexi," I say softly.

"No, but they twist the truth so much, they might as well."

"What's everyone yelling about?" Sophie's door opens, her typical scowl marring her face as she rubs the sleep from her eyes.

"He brought a fae here!" Alexis shouts.

"What?" Sophie's eyes snap open, all drowsiness gone.

My stomach drops.

Alexis gestures wildly at Emlyn. "He's a fae!"

Oh no.

The sleeve of Emlyn's shirt bursts into flames.

"Fuck!" He jumps back.

I instantly extinguish it, but Alexis uses the distraction to break past me and lunge for him. Emlyn barely evades her grasp and clambers onto the settee behind me.

"ENOUGH!"

I blanket the room in a thin layer of ice, startling everyone—including myself, frankly. But nobody moves, and that's all I need.

"Look, I brought him here because Ellie's in trouble, and he's the only one with answers." I look to Alexis. "You have every reason to hate him, but I need you to put that aside for now. For Ellie. Please."

"What exactly happened?" she asks, wrapping her bare arms tightly around herself.

"His friend kidnapped her."

"Oh, come on, Reid. Seriously? And you think you can trust a word he says?"

"He can't lie!"

"Stop it, you two!" Sophie yells. We both shut our mouths. "Get rid of the ice, please." Her eyes move to Emlyn, who I suddenly realize has his hand resting on my back as he hides behind me. "I won't attack. I promise." She looks at Alexis, her teeth chattering from the cold.

"Fine," Alexis sighs. "I'll hear what he has to say."

Keeping a watchful eye on Sophie—I don't trust her one lick—I get to work on the ice. It takes some effort to get it all to dissipate, leaving a decently dry room behind. Alexis tests one of the armchairs for dampness before plopping down on it, crossing her arms and staring expectantly at me.

Where to begin?

I start with introducing the idea of Caeo and Ellie's memory loss. Sure enough, she doesn't believe me.

"That's impossible. How could I not have noticed something like that?"

"Fae magic," Sophie says, still standing next to me and Emlyn.

He nods to her. "Told you."

"Wait, how'd you figure that out?" I turn from Sophie to him. "You said there was something on Caeo that kept anyone from noticing."

"There is."

"I haven't actually met Caeo," Sophie offers. "He's in my classes, but we've never spoken. I doubt he knows who I am. Maybe that's why?"

It's so weird to have a normal conversation with her. Not that this conversation's normal. Not at all.

Emlyn shrugs. "It's possible. I don't know the details."

"Why are there fae spells on Ellie and Caeo?" Alexis demands.

All eyes turn to Emlyn. He sighs.

"Caeo's the half mortal son of the exiled queen of my realm. He wears a charm that prevents anyone from connecting him to anything fae."

The floor slips out from under me. I drop a curse as I collapse onto the settee, and Sophie slowly lowers into the remaining chair.

What has my life turned into? Caeo can't have known this—he'd never have been able to keep it from me. He's a terrible liar.

Oh. That makes sense now.

"You'll need to explain that," Alexis says.

Emlyn paces the room, the only one still standing. "The Border Wars ended twenty-one years ago, yeah? That's when Queen Esyllt was overthrown by her husband. She was exiled to your realm, and Aedys's new king ordered an end to hostilities. That's why you've known peace all these years."

"So Caeo's mom is the one responsible for my parents' deaths?"

Emlyn winces. "Thaaat's oversimplifying a complicated situation."

"Then explain it."

"Sure." Emlyn drops forcefully onto the settee next to me, way closer than necessary. Not that I'm paying attention. "A long time ago, all the realms were fae, until those living in the western realm—Lyndir—betrayed the Land by trying to control Her. The Land abandoned them, and they lost their ability to wield Her gifts freely, including their long lifespans. Those were your ancestors, the Fallen."

The three of us exchange confused glances. I've never heard anything that would even suggest that's true; there must've been some kind of trick in how he worded that.

Alexis opens her mouth, but Emlyn cuts her off.

"Thus began the war between the remaining fae realms and yours. Many saw it as our duty to restore your realm to what it was, but the Land requires balance—our realms must always be the same size as one another. So the southern realm, Ystyr, couldn't claim your land unless we took the same amount. Every time we took ground from you, we ceded some to the east.

"When our new king called off the invasion twenty-one years ago, that angered Ystyr's king. He's been violently encouraging us to reengage with you ever since."

"And we're supposed to thank you for that?" Alexis's voice drips with sarcasm as she sits back in her chair.

Kind of sounds like we should...

"I'm telling you this so you can understand that *I* am not your enemy. About a week ago, our king was assassinated. And our exiled queen—your friend Caeo's mother—has now crossed the border back into our lands with her son in tow. *That's* why you can't find Caeo. He has a half-brother, our prince, who survived the assassination plot. He's the one who took Ellie."

My brow furrows. "Why?"

"If the queen's returned, she'll name Caeo the new Crown Prince when the realm belongs to Taran. And from everything I've seen, Caeo would do anything for Ellie."

While probably true—he's never been as happy with any of his other girlfriends as he is with her—there's one glaring problem.

"If he remembers her," I grumble.

Emlyn waves his hand. "Details."

Uh huh. Even without Ellie, I can't imagine it'd take much to convince Caeo to turn away from his mom. It almost seems like this Taran took Ellie on impulse rather than thinking things through.

"Wait—who cursed Caeo and Ellie to forget each other?" Alexis asks.

Emlyn's shoulder bumps mine as he leans back. "I can't say definitively because I wasn't there when it happened, but I assume it was the queen."

"Caeo's mom? Why would she curse her own son?"

He rolls his head in her direction, his voice exuding impatience. "She's an exiled queen who wants to take back her kingdom and renew the war with the mortals. What reason could she possibly have to curse her son to forget he loves a mortal?"

Sophie stands, staring down Emlyn from across the tea table. "So what's your role in all of this?"

His muscles tense where they press against me. "I'm a spy for Prince Taran. I've been watching the queen and informed him when she disappeared."

"So, you're complicit in this."

"I'm complicit in doing what my prince commands to prevent my people from going to war against yours."

Sophie folds her arms. "A simple 'yes' could've sufficed."

Emlyn's so close he almost smacks me when he throws his hands up. "I can't possibly know everything you're including within the scope of 'this,' so no, I *can't* simply agree with that!" His hand lands on my leg as he turns to me. "Can we go now?"

I blink, trying to get the wheels in my head to catch up with his words, but it's about as effective as blinking to turn wheels.

"Go where?" Alexis demands.

My elbow digs into the armrest as I squeeze my eyes shut, forcing my brain into motion. "After Ellie," I groan. "Then to Caeo, to save him. Then to murder the both of them because they have no appreciation for how difficult they've made my life."

And just in case I didn't know what a wreck it's become, Emlyn reiterates it by taking *my* hand and pulling *me* to the door.

Alexis shoots up, bumping her chair as she follows. "I'm going with you."

I spin around, yanking free of Emlyn and grabbing her shoulders. "Nope, no. You can't. You'll just make everything harder."

"Neither of you should go," Sophie says, eyeing Emlyn as she joins us. "We should tell Headmaster Gleese and let the Order handle it."

I shake my finger at her. "No, we're not doing that. They'll only care about Ellie. Once they find her, they won't give a shit about Caeo."

As far as I know, no human has ever crossed the border to the faelands. If Caeo's already there, Emlyn may be my only shot at getting to him. That won't happen if the Order gets involved.

And I'd probably never see Emlyn again.

Sophie's eyes narrow, but she doesn't argue any further. My stomach contracts, all too aware she'll probably snitch the second I'm gone.

"Let me come," Alexis says, pulling my attention back to her. "I can help."

"I wish you could, but you can barely incant without a focal, and you want to murder the only ally I have. You can help me more by covering for us." I make an exaggerated eye dart toward Sophie.

She tracks my gaze, and her mouth quirks before she nods. Hopefully, she can keep Sophie from talking for at least a couple days.

I wrap her in a tight hug. "I'll bring them back, I promise."

"Mortals and their promises..." Emlyn mumbles under his breath.

Alexis's glare singes the air. "Don't trust him, Reid. He's fae. You can't."

I don't have a response to that. I can't say I won't, because I don't know if that's true. And it would hurt Emlyn; not that I should care—he's an asshole.

Except I do.

"Give me a minute before you go," Alexis says, heading to Ellie's room. She emerges with a bundle of clothing and other personal items. "I imagine she only had a bag of books with her, which won't be terribly useful."

Taking it from her, I shove it into my pack, forcing myself to believe I'll be back soon despite the pit in my stomach warning me otherwise.

Emlyn claps his hands as we leave the building, stepping into the cool night air. "Ready to steal some horses?"

"Steal? No. Besides, there's some things I need to get." I head down the stone path toward the Fire School.

"It's the middle of the night, Reid. The only way we're going anywhere is if we steal horses."

Arandur's foot fungus. I hadn't really thought about how we'd be traveling. "Maybe we should wait till morning."

It isn't long before we arrive at one of the Fire School's side entrances. Not seeing any guards—low-ranking members of the

Order who spend most their days bored out of their minds—I summon some vines inside the lock and expand them until the metal gives, busting it. I force the door open, and we step inside.

Five minutes later, I have a sword. After a quick stop at my dorm to trade my books for necessities, we're on our way back to Haven.

"You just broke into your school to steal a sword, but take issue with stealing horses?" Emlyn asks, the moonlight giving a faint glow to his skin.

"Not so much the stealing part as the riding part."

"Don't tell me you've never ridden a horse before."

"It seems like a bad thing to do for the first time when I can hardly see anything."

Emlyn groans as he runs his hand down his face. "Ancients have mercy. I should leave you behind."

"Don't even think about it."

He kicks up some gravel as he halts and turns, his face inches from mine. "I'd like to hear how you'll stop me."

Not this again.

I push past him. "Fuck you."

"Oh good, that was my first choice."

I freeze mid-stride. *He can't say that unless...*

I spin on my heel, then shove him in the chest. Surprise flashes across his face, but that stupid grin returns almost instantly, as if my anger's nothing more than a source of amusement.

"Back off! In case you haven't noticed, this has been a bad day for me. Not just bad. A *nightmare.* My friends are in trouble, and I'm throwing away everything I've ever worked for by trusting that *you* can help me save them. So can you give me a break and just make one thing easy?"

"I'm easy."

Blood threatens to explode out my ears. "Well, I don't want you to be!"

I storm off, adjusting my bag on my shoulder, then shove my hands in my pockets as curses rampage through my mind.

Breathe. Shit. Breathe.

The boiling slowly eases to a simmer. *Breathe.* I stop walking, tilt my head up, and stare at the sky. It takes a second for the stars to come into focus—dim specks of light in a vast nothingness.

Will they look the same in the fae realm?

Emlyn's fingers come to rest against my elbow. "We can sleep at my place," he says quietly. "You can have the sofa. I won't leave without you."

I nod, not looking at him. I can't bring myself to. His hand moves to my back, and he nudges me forward. He doesn't say another word until we get there.

Chapter 22

Caeo

"Wake up, my child," a voice says. My mother's. But it's different. Lighter.

My eyes blink open.

Splotches of sunlight break through the leaves outside a large open window, and I'm lying on a bed that's as soft as a cloud. I wipe the sleep from my eyes, then groan as I prop myself up on my elbows.

Wait a second. "Where am I?"

The walls of the oddly shaped room seem to be made of trees, with rich brown trunks of various thicknesses, from the width of my thigh to larger than I could wrap my arms around. Polished wood and globular, open-air windows fill the gaps between them, while vines hang from the domed ceiling. Plush animal furs cover the wooden floor.

"Home," my mother says, sitting on the edge of the bed. She's wearing an elaborate gown in a deep forest green, her dark hair somehow looking... bright?

It isn't just her hair—her eyes sparkle, her cheeks are rosier, and her posture is straighter.

"I must be dreaming." A painful knot twists in my throat, like it does whenever I say something that isn't true.

My stomach drops. *If this isn't a dream, then what's going on?*

An almost creepy smile stretches across her face as she rests her hand on my leg. "You're not. This is real."

I swallow, unnerved by the person before me. "You look… healthy."

"Yes. I've been restored. As have you."

I glance down at my bare chest. A thin blanket covers everything below the waist.

"Where are my clothes?!" I tug the blanket higher to cover myself and pull a heavier one from the foot of the bed over my lap.

"Hush. I'm your mother. I've seen you bare countless times."

"When I was a child!"

She makes a *tsk* sound before crossing the room to a wooden wardrobe, then tosses a pile of clothes onto the bed before moving to the window, her back to me. I scramble to pull on the pants and shirt.

The pants, made of supple leather, hug me tighter than I'm comfortable with. And the shirt—it's unlike anything I've ever felt before. Soft, smooth, and… shiny? Its cut completely ignores the rules of modesty, revealing all of my neck and a decent chunk of my chest.

Making it obvious that my father's charm is gone.

"Where's my necklace?"

Mother turns to face me, the dazzling green of her eyes blazing. "You don't need it anymore."

"You don't get to decide that. It's mine. It was my father's." I grimace as the knot twists painfully again.

It wasn't?

No—that doesn't matter. "You gave it to me. You had no right to take it."

She cocks her head. "It was originally mine. A piece of the Land that I split with you, for our protection. Your father 'would have wanted you to wear it' only because he wouldn't have wanted a half fae child."

My mind goes blank.

"A what now?"

Mother sighs, then opens the drawer of the small bedside table, pulling out a dark, round object. "I do not enjoy repeating myself." She holds it up in front of me.

It's some kind of mirror, darker than most, but my reflection's still clear. I swallow the lump in my throat, then snatch it from her, bringing it closer.

My eyes, no longer gray, reflect back at me in a vibrant blue that almost glows in the darkness. The tips of my ears point slightly, and I reach up to feel them.

Oh fuck.

It isn't a trick.

But it has to be, right?

I bend one back and forth, then the other, too. A sharp sting shoots through me when I pinch it, making it throb. My heart pounds in my ears.

My fae ears.

Because I'm half fae.

"H-how did I not notice before?"

"The necklace. It kept the Fallen from noticing your fae features. Because of your father, that included yourself."

I lower the mirror, focusing on my mother's ears. They also point at the tips, but at a sharper angle than mine.

It's like someone pushed all the air out of my lungs. My legs give out, and I collapse against the edge of the bed.

I bring the mirror back up, scouring my face—nothing else pops out as noticeably different, unlike my mother's, which I can only describe as sharper than I remembered.

"Half fae? I really am half fae?"

"Yes. When I was exiled to the mortal lands, I was alone, without my family. I decided I would make a new one. I found a man of acceptable appearance with proven virility and took him to my bed."

I blink, catching up to what she said. "Proven what?"

"He had already fathered six children. It would have been miserable to bed a Fallen and not receive the child I sought."

"If he had six children... was he married? You seduced someone's husband?"

Mother scoffs as she trails her finger along the wall. "There was no seduction involved. I simply took what I needed."

My stomach pushes into my throat. *She took? Like... by force?*

The room closes in around me.

I don't—I can't...

"I think I'm gonna be sick." I bury my face in my hands.

Not only am I not human, but I only exist this way because she... she...

I can't even touch that right now. To go from knowing nothing about him, to this...

Fuck.

"Temper your thoughts. Get some fresh air. See our kingdom." Mother's voice echoes through the hollows of my mind as she takes my arm and pulls me to my feet. My skin crawls at her touch, but my mind clears as my body drags itself where directed, and I look out the window.

What the...?

We stand high in the canopy of a forest, full of oblong wooden structures built into the branches of the trees. Wooden walkways connect each of them, with people—fae—strolling along. While sunlight breaks through the leaves above in patches, warm orbs of flickering light float along the paths, brightening the shadows.

But the colors. It's as if even the brightest shades in Haven were still half gray, and I never noticed until now. Rich greens and browns breathe into the air, as if the colors themselves are alive. I swear they even have a pulse.

I rush to the window on the opposite side of the room. The trees are less dense on this side, opening into far-off fields, full of wildflowers, and a sky that glows with a blue as radiant as my eyes.

"It's so... bright."

"This is how the world is meant to look," Mother says. "It's unfortunate you haven't been able to see it until now."

My wonderment dims at the edge in her voice. This is just a distraction from what's important.

I turn away from the window. "Why are we here? You said you were exiled? Why were you able to come back?"

Mother pats my arm. I flinch away, and she shakes her head before sitting on the bed with a sigh.

"In the simplest terms, I was Queen of this land—Aedys, the northern realm. Before you were born, my husband, Gethin, turned against me. He took stewardship of the realm and cast me out. I was given a piece of the Land to hide my nature, as well as some water to sustain me in the Forsaken Lands, but I eventually ran out."

My eyes narrow. "Your illness? You became weak when you ran out of water?"

"I lost many of my abilities then, and while it certainly made things worse, the weakness was the cost of the Land's protection, so I wouldn't be discovered in that decaying world."

A decaying world? "Is that what you mean by the Forsaken Lands?"

"Yes. The realm you know as Landore." Her voice hardens, her thin, dark brows pressing sharply down. "They were once faelands, but the Fallen desecrated them in their greed, their lust for power. It is our duty to restore them to their natural state."

I hold back a groan as I lean against the window ledge. Asking questions was supposed to make things clearer, not spin the world even more.

"Is that what the Border Wars were? The fae... restoring the land?"

Mother nods. "With every win, we encroached further, freeing the Land from the abuses She suffered at the Fallen's hands."

Why is she talking about the land as if it's a person?

Because that's the most outrageous thing she's said so far. I'm half fae, and the ground is alive. Makes about as much sense as praying to Fortune.

"What abuses?"

"Clearing forests to build cities and farms. Rerouting rivers to feed their fields. Stealing nutrients from the earth for their crops. Stripping the mountains of their iron and gold. Need I go on?"

"So... farming is evil now?"

Mother stands, her glare ramming into me so hard that my younger self would've fled from the incoming beating. "It is a violation. Upsetting the balance necessary for the prosperity of all."

So basically, our entire way of life is an insult to the fae. Or, humans' entire way of life, because I'm apparently not one. Just half.

Fuck. I could really use some long leaf right about now.

Her voice calms as she joins me at the window. "Everything you see has been given to us freely by the Land. We make our homes from fallen wood and stones crumbled off mountains by wind and rain. Our clothing, from the skins and furs of the animals we tend. We cherish and respect the Land, and in return, She gifts us our magic and long lives. Which She reclaimed from the Fallen after they betrayed Her."

"But humans have magic—incanting."

Mother's face twists with disgust, a harsher expression than I've ever seen. She could be a stranger, anger flushing her rosy skin.

"The Second Betrayal. The Fallen, who coveted our gifts, wrested them from the Land in their ultimate act of violation. *That* is why incanting drains the life from everything nearby. Why the Academy of Incantation sits at the center of a desolate wasteland."

The sheer vitriol dripping from her every word...

"Then why did you choose to live there?" I ask. "Out of everywhere in Landore, why live in the one place that offends you the most?"

Her lips curve inward before she answers, then her face relaxes into slightly less concerning territory. "Opportunity. Living there allowed you to attend the Academy and learn the secrets of incantation. That will be valuable knowledge in the war."

My pulse quickens. "But the war's over."

"Not for long." She runs her fingers along the edge of the window, and the smile forming on her crimson lips sends a shiver down my spine.

I step away on instinct. "But—people will die." Like Reid. He just wanted to incant, not fight. How long will it take for him to get pulled in?

"Our losses are acceptable if it means restoring the Land to Her glory."

Fuck. Pressure builds in my chest, compressing my lungs. What kind of person can be so casual about so much death? How is this person my mother?

What happened to my life?

"But I didn't learn anything valuable," I say, desperately stabbing for holes in her plan. "I failed out. I can't incant to save my life."

"You can't incant because you're fae." She tilts her head. "And yes, I am disappointed with how little effort you put into your studies, but I'm confident at least some useful information permeated that skull of yours."

Panic tightens its grip, sweat dripping down the back of my neck. "But we can't go to war against my home."

Mother's eyes pierce into me. "*This* is your home. *These* are your people—not the Fallen. I am their queen, and you their prince."

...Prince?

My stomach drops. Again. It must've reached the forest floor by now.

"I don't know how much more of this I can take." I feel my way down the wall as I crumble to the ground. At least the rug's soft.

I close my eyes, my lungs struggling, then bring my hand to my face. How long have I been awake? Ten minutes? And she's ripped my entire world away, shoving a new one in its place.

Breathe.

"It's a lot to take in at once, isn't it?" Mother's voice softens as she crouches next to me, mussing my hair like she did when I was young. It used to be comforting.

"Perhaps I should have been more considerate," she says. "Let you settle in to being fae, first."

I don't have the energy to pull away, too busy focusing on my breaths. "Because that's something I can just settle into," I mutter.

"Is it so difficult to accept? You've always possessed fae qualities—you simply didn't realize it."

I drop my hand from my eyes. "Like what?"

"Your ineptitude in lying, for one. Your Fallen half seems to allow it, but your fae blood makes it extremely unpleasant. And the voracious attraction the Fallen have toward you."

My brow shoots up. "*That's* a fae trait? How does that even make sense?"

She shrugs. "They long for what they've lost. They can sense your connection to the Land, even if they don't recognize what it is."

"So that's it? People just like my fae blood?" That stings. I haven't always enjoyed the attention, but getting girls was always the one thing I was good at.

Mother runs her fingers along my hair. "It's no different from being beautiful. It draws the eye, but won't keep someone around if they don't like what's underneath."

"Uh huh."

Despite the weight of everything she's dropped on me, we're back to familiar terrain: cold indifference to my feelings, followed by just enough coddling to lure me back into her graces.

Not this time.

"Remember," she continues. "I am fully fae, unlike you—I can't simply say things because I'm your mother."

Sure. Because *this* is how mothers treat their sons. Now I'm gonna spend the rest of the day questioning everything she's ever said to me.

I force a half-smile, the best I can manage right now, hoping it'll bring this conversation to an end.

It doesn't.

"You are a unique blend of both mortal and fae, and there's bound to be some benefit in that. Once you learn to harness your gifts, I have little doubt you could become a beloved Crown Prince of Aedys."

"What happened to being more considerate of rushing me into things?"

Mother chuckles, patting my shoulder as she stands. "You're right, I apologize. I'm sure you could use a break from your dear mother. Shall I send someone to give you a tour?"

My gaze trails along the furry rug as I brush it with my fingers. I'd rather climb back into bed and try to wake up. "Not now. I need some time alone."

"I understand. I hope to see you at supper."

I nod absently as the door shuts behind her. My head falls back against the wall, and I take a deep breath, hoping it'll release all the pressure inside me.

Nope.

My life may have been awful, but it was mine. And now it's gone, something new stuck in its place.

There has to be a way out of this.

Chapter 23

Ellie

I should've let Taran follow through on his threat of forcing me to sleep.

Everything is awful. Even though Professor Beckwith's intensive training over the last few months transformed my body from skin and bones into lean muscle, the stupid horse still turned my legs into useless appendages of pain. They hurt even worse than they did last night.

And my back... my shoulders... my neck... It's surprising I slept at all. I spent most of the night twisting and turning on the cold, hard ground, relieving the pressure in one spot only for my new position to send spikes of agony shooting through me moments later. But I must have succumbed at some point, since I don't remember the sun rising.

With a groan, I pull my blanket over my head to block the sunlight hitting my face. It smells of smoke, but also musky pine, washing away a lingering clove scent—the remnant of a dream.

Hold on. I didn't have a blanket. I pull the fabric off my face and examine it. It's Taran's coat—the one I burned last night.

"You were shivering." Taran sits hunched over in the same spot across the fire, poking it with a long stick. A pile of several shorter ones sits next to him. "It didn't take long for your fire to go out. I had to collect firewood after all."

I push into a seated position. "Did you sleep?"

"No."

That could be good. If he's overtired, it might make it easier for me to escape... if that's what I decide.

I still have no idea what to do, having fought with myself over Taran's words all night as pain wreaked havoc on my limbs. My tactics lessons on dealing with fae warned me against their tricks, but I struggled to find any holes in what he said.

Pushing his smelly coat off me, I scoot closer to the fire as the morning air's still quite crisp despite the sunny blue sky. The pale-green grass and nearby trees remind me of the gardens visible from my bedroom window back home, and it hits me how nice it is to wake up to color for the first time in months.

Now that it's daytime, I have a better view of my captor. The fae clearly don't care about modesty; he wears a tunic of undyed wool that ties loosely in the front but lacks a collar. My gaze lingers on the lump of his throat as heat pools in my cheeks, but it's an effort to look away, his gravity tugging uncomfortably against it.

This must be what they meant by fae being alluring. I need to be mindful of that and not let his looks lull me into a false sense of security. To ignore those striking eyes, swirling with an ethereal green light.

That's easier said than done—somehow, imagining them as gray and lightless only makes the pull twist tighter. So I wrest my gaze away from his face, following the stylized, leafy vines embroidered down the sides of his tunic to his tight leather riding pants.

I quickly turn back to the fire, swallowing the blaze rising within me. "Are we just sitting here today, or are you going to force me back onto that horse?"

Taran's eyes flick in my direction. "I'm waiting for my friend. He should have joined us last night."

"Your friend is Emmrich?" My stomach sinks. *What does that mean for Reid?*

"Emlyn. He told mortals to call him Emmrich."

My brows knit together as I scoot closer to the fire, warming my hands. "But he's been in Haven for months." That's when I first heard about Alexis and Reid vying for his attention.

Oh no. My stomach rises back up, threatening to spew its contents onto the ground. Alexis hates the fae for killing her parents. If she had known...

Taran continues, oblivious to the nausea overtaking me. "He's been spying on the queen for me."

"And that involves having dishonorable relations with my friends?" I snap.

That gets Taran's attention, his emerald eyes piercing into me as much as the bite in his voice. "I don't always approve of his methods, but he does his job well."

"And that's all that matters?"

He shifts his weight, leaning forward. "This is what you're arguing with me about? I didn't tell him to bed your friends. I told him to watch the queen. He couldn't get close to her without being recognized as fae, so he got as deep into her circle as he could risk."

I scoff. "My *friends* are in your exiled queen's inner circle?"

"Yes," Taran exhales. "Reid has known her for over a decade."

What? I bolt upright as curiosity outpaces my skepticism. "He has? Who is she?"

"Someone you've met but don't remember. Because of your curse."

"Then why take me and not Reid? If he remembers her, he could actually be helpful."

Taran's jaw tightens, his frustration bleeding into his words. "I don't need someone who remembers her."

"Then what is it about me you need?"

Instead of responding, he pushes himself to his feet and storms off. My fingers press into the cold, damp grass as I scramble after him, my aching muscles screaming in protest. I'm in no shape to catch up with him.

So I have to stop him. Preferably in the most intimidating way possible.

With a silent incantation, I trace my hand horizontally through the air, and a wall of fire ignites the ground in front of him, flames rising above his head. He stumbles backward, tripping on the roots I rip up from the earth.

My legs burn as I catch up, then form an icicle, sharp as a blade, down the length of my arm. Taran scrambles back, trying to escape the roots clawing at his limbs. He freezes as I stop the icy tip inches from his neck.

"I'm tired of these games," I say. "You're going to tell me what I want to know."

"Stop incanting. Let me go." His voice echoes through the air. Through my bones.

My mind goes slack as I release my incantations. Ice melts. Flames die out. Roots retreat.

What just happened?

I stare at my wet hand, blinking. Taran pushes to his feet, further away, but I barely register him. I try to form more ice, but can't even visualize the focal. Like a door shut in my mind.

My fingers clench. "What did you do?"

Taran pulls himself upright, running his hand through his hair. "It will wear off, eventually." He meets my eyes. "I don't enjoy doing that. I don't *want* to do that."

My mouth goes dry. Despite that sentiment, this changes everything. I've never heard of this kind of fae magic. How can I possibly escape something like this? I'd have to knock him out or kill him before he has a chance to speak.

Could I even bring myself to do that?

I need to stay calm. If he notices my panic, I'll have lost. I splay my fingers, trying to relax, then curl them tight.

"Explain to me why I'm here."

Taran sighs. "You won't remember if I do."

I shoot him my best glare. "Then you'll have to keep doing whatever it is that you don't enjoy doing to keep me from leaving."

He narrows his eyes. "Fine. I'll try." With a glance at our pitiful campsite, he asks, "Do you have anything to write with?"

What? Wary of his intentions, I rifle through my bag, digging out my sketchbook and a piece of charcoal. I quickly flip past a bunch of sketches of Academy students to a blank page near the middle. I offer it to him as he sits on the grass, facing me.

"No, it's for you. I want you to draw lines as you listen."

Weird.

I make two small lines next to each other.

"Like this?" I ask.

"Yes." He waits for me to continue.

I roll my eyes and begin marking the page. "This better be good." I haven't a clue where he's going with this, but it doesn't appear to be a trap.

"The exiled queen is my mother, Queen Esyllt Evermoor. I am the firstborn prince of Aedys, heir to the throne."

My eyes widen, and my hand freezes. "You're a prince?"

"Yes. Keep drawing." He points at my sketchbook, and I dutifully begin again, no longer looking at the marks as I make them.

"The ability I used to bring you with me—and stop your

attacks—is called willbending. It's unique to the Evermoor bloodline, but has been weak for many generations. When I was five, my mother discovered it had manifested in me with a strength not seen since the early days of our history. She couldn't accept her child being stronger than her, so she tried to kill me."

My heart hiccups. *And I thought my father was cold.*

No, don't sympathize with him. He's the enemy. He kidnapped me.

Taran gestures at my sketchbook.

I swallow my pity, then continue my tally marks. I need to uncover where he's going with this.

He takes a breath, his gaze dropping to the ground. He explains how his father, Gethin, foiled her attempt and exiled her, ruling in Taran's stead after the realm passed to him—his first act as king was to end the Border Wars. It's possible he's telling the truth, since we never knew why the fae stopped attacking.

"And the queen went to Landore?" I ask. "To Haven?"

"Eventually. Where are you with your marks?"

I check my sketchbook. "I've almost filled a page."

"Start a new one. Not long after leaving Aedys, my mother found herself with child again. She gave birth to a half mortal, half fae she named Caeo. My brother."

I glance up from my tallying. I missed what he just said.

He continues before I can ask him to repeat himself. "When Caeo was four, she moved them to Haven. Around the same time, we noticed her growing weaker, likely from running out of water from Aedys."

The twittering of a bird catches my ear—I'm not sure which kind. I blink a few times, realizing I stopped paying attention.

Focus.

"A few months ago, Emlyn reported her health was improving. We ordered him to get closer, to discover more. He couldn't approach my mother because she would know him, so he went through Caeo's friend, Reid, instead. He likely would have gone through Caeo himself, except he was already smitten with someone else."

The fire in Taran's green eyes burns into mine. "You."

It ignites a heat within me, but I bury it down—fae charm. I can't fall for it. "What are you talking about?"

"You don't remember Caeo because of your curse. He went to the Equinox Ball with you. That's why you can't recall it. Emlyn spotted the curse and helped Reid notice it, which allowed the two of you to form some semblance of a real relationship.

"We suspected my mother cursed both of you because she planned to return to Aedys with Caeo and didn't want his love for you to get in the way. That was practically confirmed when my father was assassinated." Taran's gaze drifts away, his lips pressing together. A moment later, his eyes flick back to me. "I fled, meeting Emlyn halfway to Haven, and he informed me that the queen and my brother had disappeared."

"And you decided to abduct me?"

"Yes. My brother loves you, and I'm hoping that will help him see the truth our mother has hidden from him. Otherwise..." His face darkens as he trails off, then he swallows. "Otherwise, if he won't listen, I may be forced to kill him. And my mother."

After a moment of silence, he clears his throat. "What's the last thing I told you?"

I blink, startled by the question.

"Uh... that your father ended the Border Wars, and the queen went to Haven."

Taran squeezes his eyes shut. "How many pages had you filled with marks?"

"One."

He opens his eyes and gestures at my sketchbook. My eyes widen at *two and a half* pages full of marks.

I flip back and forth through the pages. "What? How is that possible?"

Taran sighs, running his hand through his chin-length hair. "You've forgotten the part where I explained everything related to your curse."

No, this has to be some kind of trick. There must be something—

I look up at Taran. He must have used that willbending thing again. He made me forget something.

But there's no satisfaction on his face. No gleam in his otherwise brilliant green eyes. If anything, he looks tired. Exhausted. Maybe a little sick.

An icy dread pools in my stomach, sinking all the way to my toes.

It doesn't make sense for this to be a trick. If he could use willbending to make me forget part of this conversation, or mark my sketchbook without realizing it, then he'd have been better off making me forget he could, so I'd be easier to control. Instead, he explained it to me.

As best I can tell, he's answered every question I've asked, and proven I'm under a fae curse in the process.

Where does that leave me now?

I sniff back the emotion threatening to break my voice. "Can you remove the curse? With your willbending? Force me to remember?"

Sorrow fills Taran's eyes. "Not without breaking your mind. There are others more skilled with curses who may be able to, but not me."

I nod, trying to control my breathing. *Don't cry. Don't cry.*

Tears burn behind my eyes anyway. My father, the Order... They won't be able to free me, either.

My hand slips into my pocket, squeezing the stray button. Lost and alone, like me.

"So you can't tell me why you need me?" I ask. If I can actually help him, then maybe he'll help me find someone capable of breaking it.

Taran exhales, then rubs the bridge of his nose. "You remember the queen?"

"Yes."

"She was living in Haven, but disappeared shortly after an attempt on my life and the assassination of my father." The set of his jaw projects strength, but grief fills his eyes.

A pang of sympathy resonates in my chest. I've only known a world at peace, but I've often imagined what would happen if the war started up again. The risk it posed to my father. Such worries always left my mom sleeping worse when he was away.

I wipe the moisture from my cheeks. "You think they're related?"

"I do."

I search his face, seeking any signs of deception. There's... something about him. Something I should know, like a word on the tip of my tongue that I can't reach. The way his tousled, raven hair hangs near his eyes. As if I've met him before, but I can't recall anyone who looks at all similar.

Whatever it is, my gut wants to trust him. Or is this simply the fae charm everyone warned me about?

Arandur's knickers. This is impossible to navigate. But if I accept that he's been telling the truth and that we can help each other, then maybe I can build more trust by showing some compassion?

I rest my hand on his, like my mom always does when comforting me. "I'm sorry about your father."

Taran's gaze drops to our hands, then he pulls away, scooting out of reach.

So much for that.

He clears his throat. "I believe my mother intends to steal my throne, then force my people into war against yours. There are reasons I expect you'll be useful in stopping her, but we've proven I can't explain them in a way you can remember. You just have to trust me."

His face shows no sign of duplicity. For whatever reason, he believes I can help him, and his eyes bleed a desperate hope that I will. That he's convinced me. That he doesn't need to fight me anymore.

Even if my gut is wrong, helping him *is* my best chance to get free of my curse. And if doing so can also save my people from war, it would be selfish not to. Cowardly, even.

But underneath that, something deeper stirs. As if helping him will somehow fill the hole in my heart, like a missing puzzle piece.

"Alright." My chest tightens, hoping I'm making the correct choice. "I'll trust you."

THE REST OF THE DAY CRAWLS BY, with Taran growing more and more agitated as several bells pass without Emlyn arriving. He keeps insisting we're in the correct location, despite nothing about our campsite or the nearby forest seeming particularly identifiable, claiming Emlyn should've found us by now even if something had delayed him. I can only hope that whatever happened, Reid's safe.

I've finally convinced him I'll stay put while he goes and searches, but hesitation blankets his face as he mounts his horse.

"Don't make me regret trusting you." His emerald eyes bore into me, and something flutters uncomfortably in my throat. I swallow it down, my fingers finding their way back to that button.

"I won't leave. I promise."

Even if I wanted to, it's not like I could get very far. He's leaving a horse I'm unable to ride, and based on last night's travel, we must be at least a dozen miles from the Academy. My legs almost gave out when I walked to the trees to relieve myself.

Taran's lips purse as if debating with himself one final time, then he kicks the horse into a gallop, riding south along the tree line.

He's actually trusting me.

I spend most of the afternoon stretching amid tall blades of itchy grass, massaging my legs, and crystallizing blocks of ice to numb my muscles with—as Taran said, his willbending wore off eventually. More proof that he's trustworthy, I suppose. He left some food—mostly nuts and berries—but I'm famished by the time he returns, about a bell before sunset.

"I didn't find him," he says as he dismounts, and his horse wanders to where the other one stands, munching on grass. "But I got more food." He holds up the rabbit carcass that was hanging off his saddle.

My stomach turns, but I'm hungry enough to have no objections. I simply volunteer to collect more firewood while he skins and cleans his catch.

Our meal's hanging over the fire by the time I return, and I sit on the grass next to him, watching the meat cook. Its gamey scent fills my nostrils, sending a sharp hunger pang through my belly.

Despite the pops and cracks of the fire, the silence between us is maddening.

"So, you don't want war with my people?" I ask, hoping to find some common ground. If we both want peace, that's a good place to start.

Taran looks at me out of the corner of his eye. "No. The Land already punished your people, and the wars cost countless lives. And if we had let you be, the Second Betrayal would likely have never occurred."

I raise an eyebrow. "Pretend I don't understand most of what you just said."

Taran exhales, then leans forward to pull the cooked meat from the fire with his knife. But I swear his mouth curls with a hint of a smile.

He sits back down. "You wouldn't, I suppose." He tears the meat with the jagged blade and hands some to me. "I'm sure mortals teach history quite differently than we do."

That doesn't automatically make your version better.

But picking a fight won't help anything, so I swallow my response. Feeling horribly uncivilized, I rip at the meat with my teeth. It's tough, but tasty, and its juices drip down my chin, making me instantly aware of how messy I am—two days since my last bath, sleeping in the dirt. I attempt to wipe my mouth on my shoulder, as if scratching an itch, and take a whiff of myself. I stink of smoke.

Meanwhile, Taran looks... Well, flawless is an understatement. The setting sun reflects off his sleek, midnight hair, perfectly windswept from his ride. His smooth skin practically glows, with not a single sign of stubble. My eyes trace his jawline, down his neck, to his clothes. While patches of dirt and sweat cover mine, his are pristine in comparison.

"How are you so clean?" I ask. There must be some kind of secret to it.

Taran coughs, choking on his food. "What?"

"Is it a fae thing?" I lean closer, inspecting him. His face reddens, and he avoids my eyes. "I'm a mess, but you—"

He presses his fingers against my lips, shushing me. The flustered expression that briefly transformed his features disappears as he tenses, looking westward.

"Horses are approaching."

I move his hand away from my mouth, the cold air kissing my lips as his warmth disappears. There's only silence.

"How can you tell?"

"I can sense them."

What does that mean?

He pulls his hand free of mine, and I flush at the realization I was still holding it. He goes straight to his horse, pulling his bow from the saddle and sliding an arrow into it.

Moments later, two horses appear in the distance, the sound of their hoofbeats arriving soon after. My shoulders relax as I recognize the riders.

Reid. With Taran's friend, Emlyn.

Chapter 24

Caeo

I stare out my bedroom window at the forest canopy above. Deep greens, with a vibrant blue peeking through the gaps. Compared to Haven, this place is paradise—even though it's colder, the air smells better. Sweet, like honey and flowers. Its beauty is the only thing keeping me from bolting, other than the armed guards.

And the fact that I have no idea where I am or how to get home. And that my glowing eyes and pointy ears would get me lynched within minutes of crossing the border. The only person who might look past that is Reid, but I'd be dead long before I found him.

So yeah... There's a lot of reasons to make the best of this, despite everything.

I don't even remember how I got here. I had returned home from the Academy, and Mother was there. I told her I'd been kicked out. She made me some tea—

Did my own mother drug me?

That shouldn't surprise me. Not after finding out she'd deceived me my entire life. What she'd done to my father. Just taking what she wanted from him.

Drugging me is nothing in comparison.

I swallow the nausea forming in my throat. *Just breathe. Breathe and think about something else.*

I've never wanted some speckled long leaf more in my life.

A light knock interrupts my brooding. A young-looking fae woman stands at the door, her face tight with nerves as she wrings her hands. "Pardon me, Your Highness. Her Majesty has requested your presence."

Wonderful. And if I don't go, I'll just be causing problems for this poor girl. My mother probably knew that when she picked who to send.

The servant leads me through what I'm just calling 'the castle.' While the upper levels appear to use tree branches for structural support, with wooden walls that clearly originated elsewhere, the lower floors are mostly constructed from the trees themselves. Their trunks twist and curve unnaturally, as if someone shaped them into walls and columns. Smooth stones fill in the gaps, cut to make a perfect seal.

It's an impressive display of fae craftsmanship. Then I enter the throne room.

Hundreds of tiny windows speckle the walls of the expansive space. Rays of sunlight pour through, reflecting off curved streaks of polished gold that weave between the slats of white wood making up the floor, with more gold amid the stones and tree trunks of the walls.

A large wooden throne—the only chair I've seen so far—stands on a dais on the far side of the room. Likely sculpted from a tree trunk, it's adorned with golden antlers. The queen, someone I barely recognize as my mother now that she wears her full regalia, sits upon it.

My annoyance swells as I take in the golden crown, made of those same antlers, resting upon her dark hair. She wears a lighter green dress than yesterday—more like the color of a meadow on a sunny day, matching her eyes. Pristine white fur lines her shoulders and neckline, and while her hands rest on the arms of the throne, the flood of green and white cloth surrounding them makes it clear that if she stood, her sleeves would hang to the ground.

"His Royal Highness, Prince Caeo," a guard at the door announces. Like the others, he wears dark green and brown under a cream-colored coat lined with fur.

With a cringe, I follow the serving girl to the throne. She gives a low curtsy, which my mother nods to, before scurrying out of the room.

I don't even tilt my head. "You wanted to see me?"

Mother taps her fingers against the arm of the throne. "I appreciate you need time to adjust, but we must begin preparations for your coronation."

I hate standing here while she speaks down to me, and my hand twitches as I struggle to keep my exasperation from showing. "What if I don't want that?"

She narrows her eyes, then slowly rises. Stepping off the dais, her dress trails behind her.

"Walk with me." Her voice echoes through the chamber, and I find myself begrudgingly falling into step beside her.

She leads me through a passage at the side of the room into the chilly air of an outdoor garden. "You cannot change who you are, Caeo. You are a prince of Aedys, whether you wish it or not. With that comes responsibilities that cannot be ignored."

I close my eyes against the bright sunlight. "I don't want anything to do with that. I want to go home."

"I told you: this is your home now. Accept that." Her words seem to echo again, despite being outside, and they hit like a boulder crushing my chest—I'm stuck here, and there's nothing I can do about it.

It should be fine. I *did* want a fresh start after the Academy, after all. But there's an itch in the back of my mind, something clawing its way out. It flails, then goes still.

"Fine," I sigh. "What kind of responsibilities?"

Mother smiles, then pulls me along the grassy path. Bushes dotted with every flower imaginable line our way, the earth beneath them rolling with small hills to show off each type.

"I will be sending tutors to educate you in our history and our ways," she says.

Perfect. More classes. The one misery I thought I'd escaped.

Wait a second...

"What about magic? Can I learn that?" Since being fae is the reason I failed horribly at incanting, maybe that means I can do whatever it is fae do?

Mother pats my arm. "You should have a better understanding of our relationship with the Land before you attempt to wield Her gifts."

"I guess that makes sense." My brief spark of excitement peters out as I stop, brushing my fingers on the soft petals of a thorny blue rose.

"Unfortunately, there is another item to discuss that may be difficult for you."

I straighten, my ribs cramping in warning. "What's that?"

She folds her hands together. "In order to return, I needed to form an alliance. With King Dryfid of Ystyr, to be precise."

"Ystyr is...?"

"The southern realm. You will need to pay better attention to your studies here than you did among the Fallen."

"I'll try." For once, the pain in my throat almost makes me chuckle.

Mother's face presses into a frown, but in a blink, a smile releases the tension. "In order to seal the alliance, I agreed to your betrothal to his daughter, Princess Owena Briarwood."

An avalanche crashes through my gut. "What?" *I can't have heard that right.*

"I've already begun arrangements for the ceremony. Dryfid and his daughter arrived this morning." She continues walking, as if that settled things.

"No." I hurry after her. "You can't just tell me I'm getting married to someone I've never met and expect me to be fine with it."

She stops so fast I almost collide with her. "I can. This is your responsibility as Prince."

Tension burns through my limbs, down to my fingers, itching to wrap around her neck. "No. I'm not doing it." I glance around the garden. If I ran, could I find my way out of here before the guards caught me? Probably not. I need to actually plan an escape to have any chance.

Mother seems to grow taller with her inhale. "What did I tell you? You need to accept your responsibility."

I squeeze my eyes shut, digging my palms into my skull, as her words echo through my mind. My anger slips away, despite grasping desperately for it.

The burden weighs on me, my shoulders sagging. She rests her hand on my arm, and I shrug her off, but she clamps down firmly.

"Perhaps you'll feel better once you've met her. I'm told she's quite beautiful."

I rub my throbbing temples. "You've never even met her?"

"She was a child the last time I saw her."

Which would make her anywhere from two to fifteen years older than me, probably. Not that it matters for fae. I drag my fingers down my face with a groan.

My voice comes out muffled through my hands. "When do I

meet her?"

"I will take you now if you stop moping."

Seriously? I drop my hands, shooting her a glare. After all the shit she's thrown at me in the last day and a half, she's gonna act like *I'm* the unreasonable one?

Of course she is. That's pretty much been standard throughout my entire life.

I take a slow breath before straightening myself up. My mother fusses with my hair, and I shove her hands away.

She chuckles. "If it makes you feel any better, I doubt she's any happier with the arrangement than you are. Perhaps you can bond over that."

Fantastic. She gestures for me to follow, and I trudge behind, not wanting to go, but what else am I gonna do?

The garden connects to another wing of the castle, built around a separate grove of trees from the larger structure, but they lean together and reconnect several stories up, like a gigantic tree whose trunk split at the roots. The guard at the entrance dresses differently from the others, wearing a brighter green and peach, with a light jacket that's probably left him much colder than the rest.

He bows at our approach, then opens the door.

"Her Majesty, Queen Esyllt," he announces.

We stand in an entryway similar to the rest of the rooms I've passed through, with walls of tree trunks and stone. A simple staircase of smooth wood planks curves along the side to the upper floor. A fae man appears at the top, casually descending toward us.

"Queen Esyllt," he says with a jovial voice. "Have you come to see how we've settled in?"

His light peach tunic, embroidered with white flowers, seems too soft for his imposing presence. Leather pants cling to thick legs beneath a crimson robe, while the crown of small, iridescent pearls sitting atop his reddish hair hardly distracts from his assessing, burgundy eyes.

My mother smiles as he approaches. "King Dryfid."

They each raise a hand, pressing their palms together.

"I've come to introduce my son," she says as their hands drop.

The king looks my way, clearly sizing me up. I could attempt to impress him, but why bother? The best-case scenario is that he decides I'm unworthy of his daughter and cancels our betrothal.

Mother rests her hand on my shoulder. "This is Prince Caeo. Be nice—he's only had a day to settle."

The king laughs. "Well, I see nothing for my dear Owena to complain about. Nice, symmetrical face. Toned, but not too sharp."

My jaw tightens as my face burns. Mother's reduced me to a piece of meat to trade off.

Her grip on my shoulder tightens. "Calm yourself."

The words echo around me, and the fire diminishes. After all, women have always seen me that way. Why should it bother me coming from a king?

But I wish someone would see more.

Dryfid cocks his head, then shrugs. "I suppose I should get Owena down here." He flicks his hand to the side, and a fae woman I hadn't noticed standing there curtsies, then hurries up the stairs.

After a few minutes, during which my mother and King Dryfid make small talk, the sound of footsteps draws my attention. A woman with curly golden hair descends the staircase, so graceful she's practically floating. Thanks to the sleeveless, rose-colored bodice she wears, her neck and shoulders are on full display, with a billowing skirt flowing out from under it. A matching shawl hangs around her arms, but she's pulled it tight in the front, clearly trying to keep herself warm.

"Her Highness, Princess Owena," the guard at the door announces.

Her dark eyes meet mine, and her full, rosy lips twist as she evaluates me.

Dryfid guides her closer with a hand on her back. "My dear Owena, this is Prince Caeo."

I force the smile that's always come naturally when talking to pretty girls. Which she is. More than pretty, if I'm being honest. But I can't get past how awkward this is.

Owena's face warms with a smile. "I'm glad to finally put a face to your name." She holds up her hand the way our parents did when they'd greeted one another.

"Nice to meet you." I press my palm against hers and consider her greeting, knowing she can't lie.

She's not happy to meet me. Sure enough, her hand drops the instant our palms meet.

"Perhaps the two of you should go for a walk," my mother says. "Get acquainted."

I shoot her a glare. Is this why she scared away every girlfriend I've ever had? So she could marry me off to someone convenient for her?

"Take her for a walk," she repeats, her voice echoing like a drum.

Owena's brow quirks up, then her eyes widen as I grab her hand and pull her out of the room, back into the gardens.

"This is not the proper way to escort a lady," she says, smacking my arm until I let go of her.

"Sorry," I mumble. Not sure what came over me.

"Here. Bend your arm like this." Owena demonstrates, bringing her right hand to rest on her chest.

I imitate her, then she slips her fingers into the crook of my elbow. It's an improvement—her hand felt wrong in mine. Too smooth, like ice.

"Good. We'll make a prince out of you yet." She meets my gaze as she pulls her shawl tight. The inky wells of her eyes draw me in, practically absorbing the sunlight. "You can walk now," she says, nodding ahead.

I blink free of her haunting eyes. "You seem cold. Would you like my coat?"

A bitter laugh huffs out of her. "We're not there yet." She nudges me forward, and I start walking. "I'm going to need an entirely new wardrobe. It's far too chilly here."

I lead us along a different path from before, this one stone, to a spot with a stream running through it, lined with orange and pink tulips. Some nearby lavender bushes fill the air with their soothing scent. My steps pause, a strange ache twisting in my chest.

"It's warmer where you're from?" I ask.

"Much." Owena turns her gaze to a hummingbird zipping between blossoms. "I'm told you're from the mortal realm?"

"Until yesterday. This is all very"—I lift my free hand to gesture, then drop it—"new, I suppose? So don't take it personally if I don't seem excited about marrying you. I only found out ten minutes ago."

"I found out a week ago and still hate the idea. Nothing against you. You're actually better-looking than I expected, knowing you're half mortal."

I let out a sharp laugh. "At least we're stuck with people who are nice to look at. Could be worse."

"Especially since consummating the marriage is required on our wedding day."

"Wait, what?" Heat rushes to my face. My brain had not gotten that far into this marriage.

Owena frowns. "Is that not how mortal unions work?"

"It is, but... I didn't think it'd happen right away."

"It's necessary. We wouldn't be properly bound in the eyes of the

Land otherwise."

Fuck. I pull my arm free of her and slap my face into my hands.

"I'll try not to take your obvious dismay as a personal affront," Owena says. "Would this be your first time?"

My head shoots up. "What? No! Of course not." *Why am I blushing?* "And it's nothing against you. You're beautiful. I'm sure it'll be very... nice."

What am I saying? And why is this even bothering me?

She's gorgeous. I should be fine with this.

But I'm not.

Why am I not?

A smile twists across her lips as her brow tilts up in amusement. "Pretend I'm any other girl. What would you be doing to get into my bed?"

I take a deep breath, then gesture vaguely before letting my hand fall. "Just existing, mostly." The truth of that grounds me. Even with all this shit, she *is* just another pretty girl. I can handle this.

The smallest laugh huffs out of her nose. "You think so highly of yourself?"

"Not really. But here you are, trying to get *me* to try to get *you* into bed."

"I'm trying"—she pinches my shoulder, making me flinch—"to get you to stop being so miserable. This is your life. You might as well enjoy what you can."

I sigh. "Fine. Twist my arm. I'll try to enjoy fucking you. I don't know how I'll manage it. But maybe it'll be good enough to—stop that!" I laugh as she repeatedly smacks my shoulder, holding up my hands to defend myself.

"That is not"—*smack*—"appropriate language"—*smack*—"for speaking to"—*smack*—"a lady!"

"Is hitting me appropriate?"

She stops, and despite glaring at me, her mouth curls into a smile. "It is not. But on a serious note, I am going to arrange for some time to teach you proper etiquette."

"Wonderful. History and etiquette lessons." I shove my hands in my pockets as I watch the hummingbird flitter away. *Lucky bastard.*

Owena frowns, then gathers her skirt as she sits on the grass. "History won't do you any good. Our lives are basically for show."

I join her, stretching my legs out on the ridiculously soft turf. "My mother said I couldn't learn any magic until after history."

She gives me a pitying look. "She'll never let you learn magic."

"What? Why would you say that?"

"You're the perfect puppet as you are. Trapped in a world you don't understand, completely reliant on her. Learning to shape would give you power."

Damn. Owena sure doesn't beat around the bush. But she's probably right—Mother was always at her kindest when I made her feel needed.

Wait...

"To shape?" I ask.

"That's what we call the magic that manipulates the elements."

Fae incanting, then? I shake my head. "But you can shape, can't you? If that was enough for me to leave, what's keeping you here? You don't want this marriage, either."

Owena's eyes dart away. "I actually can't shape very well—my family's talents lie elsewhere. My father has other methods of ensuring I do as he wishes."

"What do you mean?"

A smirk tugs at her lips as she fiddles with a blade of grass. "I can't go revealing all our secrets to you just yet."

I cock my head. "We're getting married. Shouldn't we try to be friends?"

"There's a difference between being friends and being stupid. Knowledge is power. I have little enough as it is."

That hits. Knowledge is what shattered my world. The meager amount Owena's shared will already help against whatever other surprises my mother has waiting for me.

But I need to get her on my side. To reveal everything she knows. To trust me—then maybe we can find a way out of this together.

"How about a deal?" I ask, and Owena raises an eyebrow. "If I can get you to kiss me before the wedding, you'll tell me about your family's magic."

The one thing I've never failed at is getting kissed, and nothing builds trust like locking lips and spilling secrets. But my chest tightens uncomfortably at the thought. I take a deep breath, trying to force the feeling away, but it lingers.

She folds her hands in her lap. "That's an interesting proposition. *Friends* typically don't kiss."

I shift closer to her, my hands pressing into the soft grass. "If I'm expected to bed you in a week and a half, then we might as well kiss first."

Owena's eyes narrow, but her cheeks flush pink under the afternoon sun. "I'll take that deal." She leans in, bringing her lips to my ear. "But I believe I'll win," she whispers, her citrus scent washing over me.

"What makes you so sure?"

"Because you. Smell. Terrible." She pulls away with a smug grin stretching across her face.

Heat burns up my neck. "What?" I sniff my armpit. "I bathed this morning!"

Owena shrugs, then gathers her skirt. "I should be going."

No—I can't let her leave with the upper hand like that. I need something to bring her back, some way to get her to lower her defenses.

An idea pops into my mind.

"Wait. Before you go... does speckled long leaf grow here?"

Owena's eyes widen. "Your mother would not approve."

"What else is new?"

She scrunches her face in thought, then speaks slowly. "I may be able to get some."

"I would be eternally grateful." My tension loosens at the glimmer of some form of escape.

And with luck, Owena's lips will, too.

Chapter 25

I hurry to my feet as Reid's and Emlyn's horses slow to a stop before reaching our campfire. Even in the dusk light, it's clear who they are. *Why is Taran acting like they're a threat?*

Emlyn's horse tosses its head as he dismounts, his feet hitting the ground. "Ancients, Taran. Lower your bow."

Taran remains still, his arrow trained on Reid, frozen wide-eyed on his saddle. "You weren't supposed to bring any other mortals."

Emlyn marches directly to him and angles the bow to the ground. "No, but mine is Caeo's best friend, and can actually remember what's going on. He'll be useful."

I rush to Reid's side as he stumbles off his horse, giving him a hand for balance. "I never thought I'd be this happy to see you," I admit, breathless.

"Thanks?" He brushes his hands against his pants. "Are you alright?"

"I am." I glance over at the fae, arguing in hushed tones. "Taran explained everything to me."

Reid winces as we step away, and I quickly catch him up on all that's happened. It's borderline offensive how relieved he is that I know about my curse; he can't get into it without me forgetting what he says, but I get the gist. It was apparently the true source of his misery these last few weeks.

He tells me how he got Emlyn to talk, then told Alexis what happened—hopefully, she'll cover our disappearance. After that, it was well past midnight, so they stayed at Emlyn's, accidentally oversleeping. Then Emlyn had to teach Reid to ride, delaying them even more.

I get the distinct impression he's purposely skipping many of the details. Coupled with his less-than-subtle glances at Emlyn, I can't help but wonder how things stand between them. Does he even know himself?

But all that quickly leaves my mind when he pulls a bundle of my things out of his pack, courtesy of Alexis. Fresh clothes, soap, my hairbrush, and some ties for my hair. I practically leap with joy as I snatch them from his hands, then flee into the woods, incanting some water so I can clean myself up.

It's dark when I return, feeling significantly refreshed, and the three of them have finished squabbling and sit quietly around the crackling fire. Taran's returned to poking it with a stick, with Emlyn sprawled out on the opposite side. The four of us sit awkwardly in its flickering glow—two humans and two fae—until Emlyn finally offers to take the first watch while the rest of us sleep. Which, at least for me, means I pretend to sleep while my mind questions every decision I've made and my body screams against the hard ground. Exhaustion eventually overtakes me.

Deep within the shadows, I wander through a gray fog, broken by specks of blue sky. A voice echoes from somewhere within: *I'll find you.*

Then sunlight peeks through, burning it away.

I rub the sleep from my eyes, the cozy warmth in my chest slipping away as the last vestiges of the dream fade under the morning sun. I once again find Taran already up, tending to the horses—despite not being tied to anything, they haven't wandered off. Reid still sleeps on his side next to me, with Emlyn curled up a few feet away.

I grip the button in my pocket. *This is it. No turning back now.*

Reid's determination to go to the faelands, for reasons he can't explain because of my curse, has reinforced that I was correct in my decision to trust Taran. Unless Reid also fell victim to fae trickery...

No. After an entire day and two nights with Taran, nothing I've seen supports anything I've ever learned about fae, other than how captivating they are. I can't deny that truth—every time my gaze lands on either Taran or Emlyn, it's an effort to pull free. That connection, with Taran in particular, sparks an uneasy flutter in my chest. The way his inky black hair curls near his eyes, despite being longer than feels right.

But I recognize that, so I can manage it.

I pause on my way over, watching as he speaks softly to one of the horses while brushing her golden coat.

He glances my direction. "Sleep well?"

I wince. *How long have I been staring?* I just told myself I could handle his charm, and I'm already failing.

"No one ever woke me to take watch," I say, hoping to move past my awkwardness.

"I thought you could use the sleep."

I frown. "But that's not fair to the rest of you. I can do my share." Even now, there's a red tinge to the white of his eyes. I can't let others suffer just so they can coddle me.

His mouth twitches into a hint of a smile. "Then you can help with the horses."

Eyeing the animal, I bite my lip, uncertain if this was really the best way to assert myself. But retreating now would only confirm that I need pampering, so I step closer.

Taran's hand lands on my shoulder, stopping me. "You need to make sure she can see you." He gently guides me into the horse's line of sight. "You don't want to startle her."

I exhale as he lets go, expecting him to move away. Instead, he gives me the brush and guides my hand in a flicking motion along the growth of the horse's hair.

"Her name is Willow," he says. "You'll be riding her today."

My nerves tighten, recalling my last experience on a horse. But he isn't kidnapping me this time, so hopefully it'll go better.

"Willow," I repeat. "Isn't she your horse?"

Taran releases my hand, leaving me to brush on my own, and the morning chill sinks into his absence. "It will be easier for you to ride her than the others. She trusts me, so she'll carry you if I ask. The rest of them would test your control." He moves to Willow's head to scratch behind her ears, his fingers disappearing under her flowing, ivory mane.

"Where exactly are we headed?"

"If we don't push the horses, it'll take a couple days to reach the border. Ultimately, we're going to the capital, but we'll be sticking to paths less traveled, since I have to assume the queen still wants me dead."

I make a couple more swift brushes. "It must be awful to have a mother who's trying to kill you."

Taran stiffens, his fingers pausing mid-scratch. He slowly looks at me.

Why did I say that? "I'm sorry! That was a stupid thing to say." My cheeks burn as I turn away, staring at a slightly off-color spot on Willow's back.

"You're trying to be friendly. I don't need you to be my friend."

My shoulders slump. "Right. Of course you don't."

He sighs. "Go wake the others. I'll finish getting the horses ready." He holds out his hand, waiting for the brush. I give it to him, then scuttle away to do as he asked.

Not his friend. Despite all his efforts to reach me, to convince me to go with him willingly, I'm ultimately just a tool—something to solve a problem for him.

I'll have to prove I have value beyond that.

I'M HOPING FOR a chance to redeem myself when Taran teaches me to ride his horse, but to my disappointment, he asks Emlyn to show me instead.

Like Taran, he now looks entirely fae, having dropped the glamour he used while in Haven—one more secret they explained that makes it easier to trust them. In Emlyn's case, his golden eyes now catch the light like a fire shimmers within, and the tips of his ears come to sharp points against his long blond hair. A pair of braids on each side keep it out of his face.

"I just spent half a day teaching Reid," he grumbles.

"Which makes it fresh in your mind." Taran whispers something to Willow before handing her off to Emlyn, then returns to the other horses.

Minutes later, I almost fall over attempting to get into the saddle, causing Reid to burst out laughing.

"Quit it," Emlyn snaps, glancing over his shoulder. "You were so bad at this, I thought you must be faking it just to get me to touch you more."

Reid shuts his mouth, then decides he has other places to be.

Other than that mishap, my instruction goes relatively smoothly. Emlyn runs me through the basics, occasionally correcting my posture. It's kind of fun, even though I'm still a bit uneasy with all this outdoorsy stuff. But it brings me a sense of joy, enduring experiences I'd only ever read about in adventure stories.

"We don't really have time to get into much more," Emlyn says after a while. "Taran will ride in front, and Willow will follow his lead. If he goes faster, stand up in your stirrups and let your knees absorb the bounce."

I push myself up as he directs, and he nods with approval.

"Reid, your turn!" he calls, heading to the other horses.

I resist the urge to snicker as he helps Reid mount his, noting he's much more handsy about it than he was with me. But now Taran's approaching, and my pulse quickens as I straighten up.

He pats Willow on the shoulder. "Are you comfortable with what you're doing?"

"I trust Willow will take care of me." I've been brainstorming possible responses all morning.

Taran smiles as he glances my way, sending a tingle through my chest. *I finally said something right.*

But my relief fades beneath a gnawing in my chest. I wish that didn't matter so much, that I didn't have to try so hard to do it. That someone existed who was easy for me to talk to. A void pulls from within, as if I once had that and someone took it away—but even with my mom, I was never that comfortable.

My eyes follow Taran as he mounts the remaining horse. They pass over Reid, briefly meeting his gaze. To my surprise, he frowns.

He can't possibly blame me for Emlyn snapping at him earlier, can he?

Before I can spare more thought on the matter, Taran clicks his tongue and Willow starts forward, forcing me to focus all my attention on staying balanced.

AROUND MIDDAY, the rolling hills that mark central Landore break the monotony of our ride. A hummed tune carries on the breeze behind me, and I awkwardly turn in my saddle to see where it's coming from. Emlyn follows behind Reid, and at that moment, he transitions from humming to lightly singing, his soothing tones wafting through the air. The words are foreign to me, but they sound similar to what Taran said when he spoke to the horses.

"What language is that?" I call up to Taran. I've been trying to keep my gaze off the sway of his hips as they move with his horse, but it's been difficult—he's directly in front of me and there isn't much variety in the landscape. Trees to my right, fields to my left.

"It's the Tongue of the Land. The sacred language we use to speak with Her and Her creatures."

Emlyn breaks the song with some loud words in the Tongue. Taran laughs, then yells something in return.

"It can't be that sacred if they're using it for jokes," Reid grumbles from behind me.

My face scrunches as the two fae holler back and forth until Emlyn eventually returns to humming his song.

I nudge Willow to walk faster, until I'm riding beside Taran. Pitching my voice so hopefully only he can hear me, I mutter, "I didn't take you as the sort to joke about people when they can't understand you."

"We weren't speaking of you," he replies, keeping his gaze ahead. "And he said nothing of your friend that he doesn't already know."

After all the effort he spent trying to reach me... "We're supposed to be building trust. That won't happen if you shut us out like that."

"How about this?" Emlyn shouts. "Fae ears aren't just pointy. I can hear everything you're saying."

I stiffen. "Is that supposed to make me feel better?"

"Maybe? Now you know, at least."

I suppose that's good? Though in reality, it means that while the fae can use that language to keep secrets, it'll be nearly impossible to have a private conversation with Reid.

After a while, we turn east into a valley on the northern side of the forest that we've been alongside most of the day. A creek flows through it, its waters flowing over and among various rocks and cattails, their brown tops swaying in the breeze. Taran stops and dismounts.

"We'll break here to water the horses." He scratches Willow's muzzle before offering his hand. I take it, and my other hand ends up on his chest as he guides me to the ground. His jaw tightens before he lets go of me, then he snatches Willow's reins and leads her to the water.

Emlyn grabs his bow, moving toward the trees. "I'll try to catch something to eat."

"No, I'll do it," Taran says quickly.

Emlyn raises an eyebrow. "Forgive me, Your Highness, but we both know I'm the better hunter."

Taran sighs, then nods his head. He glances at me. "You can collect firewood."

"Why? We won't need one for long, and Reid and I can easily keep one going to cook with."

Taran rubs his eyes with his thumb and fingers while mumbling something in the Tongue. "I spoke of the Second Betrayal to you, yes?"

"You did, but I don't know what that is." I look at Reid, who shrugs.

Taran drops his hand. "It's the second time your people betrayed the Land."

"What was the first time?"

Reid groans. "Emlyn mentioned that. He said humans used to be fae until we started controlling the Land?"

"Wait... what?" My mind shatters, its splinters spiraling into my skull.

We used to be fae?

Why didn't Taran say anything about this until now?

I meet his eyes, unable to form the words to demand an explanation. He sighs, then recounts how we humans fell from the Land's grace because of our farming and mining. Every word stirs a whirlwind in my mind, wreaking havoc as I comb through everything I've ever learned.

The air's pressing in on me, my lungs struggling to expand. "How could we not know that? Nothing in our history even suggests it." As far as I know, our earliest records already have us at war with the fae, defending the land they wished to steal from *us*.

"We don't have a written language," Taran says. "We record our history through Keepers of the Memories: fae who dedicate their lives—their *very* long lives—to memorizing tales of the past. When the Keepers in Lyndir became mortal, your history died with them. By the time your people developed writing, most of the stories were already lost."

A weight forms in my stomach, sinking me to the ground.

This is too much. If I'm to believe this... which, how can I not? There hasn't been a single hole in any of Taran's explanations so far. It even justifies why he speaks the same language as us, something that didn't even occur to me to question before.

Is everything I've ever known wrong? My hand goes to my pocket, seeking the touch of my little button.

Taran crouches in the grass in front of me, tilting his head to meet my eyes. "The Second Betrayal was after the wars with my people began. Many of us believed it was our duty, to restore the Land. And we were winning, because we didn't stay in your realm long enough for our gifts to fade."

And then their progress stopped, because we...

My eyes widen, the truth breaking through like a beacon in a storm. "It was Arandur, wasn't it? Incanting. We're forcing magic out of the Land, against Her will."

Taran nods, his face solemn. Reid plops down next to me as he breathes out a curse.

Tears burn behind my eyes. "All this time... we've been wrong."

How much damage have I done in my life alone? All those countless moments of casual incanting? So many days. Years. I saw what it did to the world, how it drained color and life from everything, and I just accepted it. Why didn't that bother me?

Nausea swells from my stomach up into my throat. The fae aren't the monsters after all.

We are.

Taran reaches forward, resting his hand on mine where it sits on my knee. The fingers in my pocket clench around the button.

"You didn't know," he says, "and the responsibility isn't yours alone. If my people had accepted that the Land had already punished yours, then your ancestors would never have been driven to it. Many of us see that now. That's why we stopped attacking."

I take a deep breath, trying to accept Taran's perspective. If I accept everything else he's said, then shouldn't I also accept he doesn't blame me?

But what am I without incanting?

While I don't know the answer to that, it's clear I can no longer blindly follow my father's path. We need to get to the border before he finds out I'm gone and sends the Order after me. They'll never believe the truth. But if I can help Taran—build an alliance with the fae—then perhaps I'll be able to convince them. We can make this right.

Taran hesitates, then meets my gaze. "You really care about this, don't you?"

His eyes don't look like someone staring down a monster. Only concern swirls in those emerald depths. And his face... something about it steadies me.

My grip on the button loosens, and I take his hand from where it sits on mine, pushing past the awkwardness in an attempt to show my sincerity. "Of course I do. Whatever I can do to fix it, I will."

He squeezes my fingers, and I nod, forcing a smile. I have a plan; I just need to follow through. So I focus on his touch, something to hold on to—a certainty amid the storm—but an unease lingers. My thumb brushes against his, and a nervous heat twists in my chest.

Reid grabs my arm and yanks me to my feet. "Firewood it is, then."

I stumble as Taran drops my hand and moves away. Reid keeps pulling me toward the trees.

"I'm going, I'm going," I say, shoving Reid's hands off me. Before we enter the woods, I glance back at Taran.

He stands slumped, one hand rubbing his brow and the other on his hip, as if bearing the weight of both our people on his shoulders.

It's too much for any one person. I won't let him carry it alone.

Chapter 26

Reid

I wake up well before dawn and can't fall back to sleep thanks to the freezing hard ground and the shitstorm rampaging through my mind.

To be honest, what Emlyn said about our ancestors being fae had completely slipped my mind. It was one of the many details thrown at me that night that turned my world completely upside down. But it wasn't as pressing as the rest, so my brain buried it back where it wouldn't bother me.

Until Taran had to not only bring it up again yesterday, but also reveal that the thing I've dedicated my life to since I was eleven years old isn't, in fact, the pinnacle achievement of humanity. Instead, it's a crime against the living spirit of the earth.

How in Arandur's stinking name do I come back from that?

We'd always known incanting was bad for the environment. That's why they outlawed it for anyone outside of the Order of Incanters and the Academy. If everyone did it, nothing would grow anywhere. That never bothered me before—it was just the way things were. Now, the truth has tied my stomach up in a perpetual knot that makes me dry heave every time it tries to unravel itself.

There's no way I'm getting any more shut-eye with all these thoughts slamming around in my head, so I drag myself to the

271

smoldering remains of our campfire. It's wallowing in the chilly air, and I'm almost tempted to return to Ellie's side just to get her warmth back. Having her curled into me wasn't my ideal sleeping arrangement, but fuck if I'm gonna let her sleep out of arm's reach with two men we barely know around. Caeo would kill me.

A sharp pang pierces my chest. I *do* know Emlyn. I've known him for weeks. But it's no longer clear which parts were real and which were an act. Was he building a tower of chips on a wooden duck's head with me because he actually enjoyed it, or was he just passing time until Caeo showed up?

And now he's fae, and I'm...

Stop it. I can sort out my feelings about Emlyn after *I come to terms with all the shit Ellie and I have done.*

Ellie's face when she realized the truth... Slack-jawed, trembling—she can't be feeling any better about it than I am. Over the course of our lives, in trying to be the best, we've turned into some of the worst offenders. I could never incant again, and I'll still likely have done it more than some full-fledged Order members. But despite spending almost the entirety of my days with Ellie for months, we've never waded into the deeper waters of friendship necessary for heart-to-hearts, and I'm not sure I want to start now. I'm already more involved in her relationship with Caeo than I ever wanted to be.

I rub my eyes, then scan our campsite, not that there's much to see in the dark. A blur of trees and silhouettes of horses. Someone should've been keeping watch, but Taran's nowhere to be found. Which is a relief, as I have little desire to sit around in awkward silence with him. He's barely acknowledged my presence since our arrival; I think Emlyn's jab about me being more useful than Ellie unnerved him.

Speaking of Emlyn... where is he?

"You're up early," his mellow voice whispers, inches from my ear. The heat of his breath sends goosebumps along my skin.

I startle back, almost falling over before my hand catches on the cold ground. "Arandur's festering phallus!"

He chuckles as he sits next to me. "That's a good one. Though, as much as I enjoy you insulting the man, it'd be nice if you could stop mentioning him entirely."

I exhale as my racing heart slows. Barely. While the shock of his sudden appearance is dissipating, I'd be lying if I said my heart ever behaved around Emlyn—his being fae hasn't put the slightest damper on that. If anything, it's even worse now that he's stopped using a glamour and I'm drowning in fae charisma with every glimpse of him.

"Yeah, I'll try." I rub my temple. "It's only a twenty-year habit to break."

"You were cursing when you were one?"

I blink. *He knows my age?*

That's right... He was with me on my birthday.

Despite the darkness, his amber eyes sparkle with an inner, golden light. They used to be duller, but I don't miss that. They're more beautiful now.

Stop thinking about him that way.

"Probably? My first word certainly wasn't 'dada.'" Not that I know what it was since my mom didn't give a damn.

I wrap my arms around myself and glare at the lifeless fire. Yesterday, I would've just, *poof!* Made a new one. Now, the thought of doing so makes my skin crawl.

"Something bothering you?" Emlyn asks.

A bitter huff escapes me. "No, not at all. Everything's great. I've only spent the last decade unknowingly violating the spirit of the earth a hundred times a day."

"The Land. But I don't hold it against you—you didn't know. Now that you do…" He shrugs. "We'll see who you really are, I suppose." The light in his eyes softens, and mine drift down to his lips.

No. Nope. Don't go there. He's fae, remember?

The entirety of my chest sinks with my next exhale. Why is that a problem? *I'm* the problem. Me. The human. We're the ones destroying everything.

I stare down the remains of the firewood Ellie and I collected last night, then pick up a couple of sticks and shove them into the pile of smoky embers in front of me.

"That's not gonna do anything," Emlyn says.

"Well, I don't know how to make a fire without incanting, so it's the best I can do." That's me. A life wasted on incanting, and now I have nothing.

Emlyn's eyes seem to narrow—it's too dark to make anything out, but the glowing disks of his irises compress. He pulls out his waterskin and takes a sip, then leans forward and brings his hand next to the dying embers.

A blaze spurts into the air, igniting all the sticks I just added.

"Wait, what?" I shift closer to the fire, glancing between his face and the flames. "Did you just—"

"That's shaping, not incanting."

"Shaping? You mean fae magic?"

With the firelight frolicking on Emlyn's face, the annoyed scrunch of his brows is visible. "It's the gift of the Land that mortals wrest out of Her to incant. I can't create fire, but I can shape what already exists. In this case, turning a spark into a flame."

Wait a second.

"You said your gifts faded while you were here."

Emlyn leans back, propping himself up as he stretches out.

"You'll never stop trying to catch me in a lie, will you?"

I force my gaze to stay on his face and not travel along the toned length of his body. To not remember the fire between us when he pressed it against me that night in the alley.

Looking at his face isn't any better. Those playful curves along his smooth, flawless skin. A smile tugs at the corner of his mouth, as if he knows it.

I turn back to the fire, adjusting where the hem of my pants catches on my boot. "Then explain yourself, or I'll just believe you can lie and never trust a word you say."

"You shouldn't trust a word I say. I may not be capable of lying, but I can misdirect and omit the truth all I want."

"Great. So all of this—everything you and Taran have said— could just be an elaborate trick after all." I can say that because I'm human, even though I know deep down that every word has been true.

Emlyn sighs, then shifts his position until he's sitting next to me, tilting his head to meet my eyes. "I don't think I could misdirect about that much without slipping up, and Taran certainly couldn't. I haven't intentionally deceived you since I told you what I am."

Either the heat of the fire is finally warming me up, or his proximity is.

I swallow. "But you *did* slip up. You said you didn't have your gifts, but you do."

Emlyn holds up his waterskin. "I told you about the river water, remember? I drank enough every day to maintain a glamour. Not enough to shape. But now that we're going home, I can afford to waste some trying to impress you."

The blaze rushing through me is definitely not from the fire. "Why do you care about impressing me? I'm just a corrupt human."

Emlyn purses his lips, then he shrugs. "Good question."

Not an answer. Is that the spy in him, keeping his secrets? But there's one other question, one that's haunted me for weeks. I have to try.

"Why did you sleep with Alexis?"

Emlyn's mouth slowly opens, then he shuts it, chewing at his lip before finally averting his gaze. His voice comes out soft, lacking its usual luster. "I suppose I thought I was growing too attached."

My heart hammers against my ribs. "To me?"

His eyes flick to mine for a second that somehow holds a weight as vast as the universe. Then he scoots away, brushing his hands on his pants as he gets to his feet. "I'm gonna look for Taran. I'm sure he'll want to leave once it's light out, which should be soon."

The breath I was holding escapes as he meanders toward the trees, my chest tightening as he goes.

Why can't my life go back to being simple?

It isn't much later that Emlyn returns with Taran, and sure enough, it's just as sunlight creeps over the hillside. Thank Arandur Ellie's still asleep—wait, no, I shouldn't thank him, he's the one who set us all down the path of desecration, dammit.

At least she's still sleeping. She's been eyeing Taran far too much.

I get it; I really do. He looks exactly like Caeo, if someone carved him out of marble and gave him an extra four inches of height, chiseled muscles, sharper cheekbones and piercing eyes. While Caeo's too much of a brother to me to ever be attractive, I've caught myself staring at Taran more than a few times. Of course Ellie would. She'd have to be blind or dead inside not to.

Especially when she doesn't remember Caeo—at least not consciously. I know part of her does, because I've seen her sketchbook. It wouldn't surprise me that part's mixing the two of them up.

It only took her... what? Half a pint and a couple bells to be all over him when they first met? She's a shining example of how locking up your children just turns them into sex-crazed maniacs once they finally escape into the world. It's pure luck that she ran into a somewhat decent guy like Caeo.

Or the worst luck in the world, considering where we are now.

Except my luck is even worse, because I'm the one stuck keeping her away from the ridiculously unfair specimen of broody manhood that is Taran. Caeo's definitely gonna owe me after this.

The two fae go directly to the horses, murmuring to each other as they prepare them to ride. I reach back, grabbing Ellie's foot, and give it a shake.

"Hey, time to wake up. We're leaving soon."

Ellie pulls her coat over her head, and my annoyance spikes.

"Come on, my life's difficult enough already. Get up."

"You're not the only one suffering, Reid." She tosses her coat down, uncovering her face. "I've barely slept in days."

"You think I have? It's time to go."

She pushes herself upright, flinging her coat to the side before tugging it on. "Alright. I'm up. Are you happy now?"

"No. How could I possibly be happy? My best friend was kidnapped by his mom, everything I thought I knew is wrong, and now I have to make sure you stay out of trouble."

"I can handle myself, Reid."

"No, you can't. Not when you can't remember what's important." I could elaborate, but it's pointless. She won't understand unless I explain Caeo, at which point she'll forget the entire conversation.

She glares at me, her mouth scrunching before it opens—

"Come on, mortals, time to go," Emlyn calls.

I grab my pack, appreciating the timely interruption, and escape to Emlyn and the horses. As soon as I get there, he swipes it from my hands and starts tying it to a saddle.

I let out a sigh. "I can do that myself, you know." The day has barely started, and I'm already tired of it.

"Can you? Seemed to me you were still struggling with all things horsey yesterday." He finishes his knots, then pats the horse on the shoulder and says something in that language of theirs. The Tongue?

"If I'm struggling, it's your fault. You didn't do a good enough job teaching."

Emlyn's brow pops up. "Excuse me? It has nothing to do with technique. It's your attitude. Your relationship with the horse. They can tell when you're nervous." He leans close, brushing shoulders with me. "Which is most of the time."

My entire body tightens with a warm tension. "I'm not nervous."

A playful smirk pulls at his mouth. "Liar." He holds my gaze for a torturous second before swinging his hip into me and stepping back. "Ready to mount?"

He cups his hands and lowers them to a comfortable level for me to put my foot on, keeping his eyes locked on mine the entire time.

He's trying to get under my skin. Or just under me.

Great. Now I'm thinking like him.

I shake my head and put my foot in the stirrup. The horse shifts right when I push my other foot off the ground, and I'm engulfed in a flood of regret.

Emlyn's hands are on me in an instant, keeping me upright as he barks at the horse in the Tongue. The horse stops moving, and his hands slide along my hips as I swing my leg over and settle into the saddle. My heart's pounding with fast, heavy thuds.

"You need to relax." Emlyn pats my thigh, like that could

possibly help. "The horse will only be comfortable letting you be in charge if you're comfortable with it yourself, so channel some top energy."

I pretend I didn't hear that last comment. "Says the person who can talk to horses. Of course it's easy for you."

"Sure, let's ignore the fact that I've been riding them for twenty years."

Twenty years? That's almost my entire life. An icy dread leaks down to my stomach. As a fae, he could be centuries older than me.

"How old are you?"

Emlyn's brow furrows. "It's spring now? That makes me... twenty-four."

A wave of relief washes through me.

He shrugs. "I suppose four-year-old me had that advantage over you. Try 'E'torel sinta nan.' Give a squeeze with your legs first, so she knows you're talking to her."

E'torel sinta nan. "What does that mean?"

"It's a polite way to ask her to walk. 'E'torel challa nan' would ask her to stop. Just 'challa' if you're in a hurry."

I repeat the phrases, and Emlyn's face twists. "Your accent's terrible, but we can work on that. Gotta teach you to move your tongue properly."

Ignoring the insinuation, I bite down to try to keep myself from flushing. "Why do you even have two languages, anyway? Can't you just speak the Tongue all the time?"

"Imagine you're the Land, having to listen to everyone talk all the time," Emlyn says. "That'd get annoying real quick. And *we* don't need animals eavesdropping on our every word."

I guess that makes sense. And if the Land stopped listening to us after we fucked Her over, there would've been no reason for our ancestors to keep using it. Especially if the animals resented us, too.

His hand, which never left my thigh, pats me again. "Wait to follow Ellie. I'll be behind you."

He moves to one of the remaining horses, and with graceful ease, swings himself into the saddle and grabs hold of the reins. Outside of his pack, there are a couple jugs that he brought with us from Haven hanging from the saddle. It must be the water from the faelands.

A minute later, Taran mounts the last horse. Then they're moving, with Ellie following along behind.

I squeeze my legs.

"E'torel sinta nan."

Chapter 27

Ellie

At the end of our second full day of riding, Taran finds a spot alongside a small river to make camp for the night. Today would've been the first full day of classes Reid and I missed. *Has the faculty realized we're gone? How long will it take for them to organize a search and inform my parents?*

I suppress those questions as I hand Willow off to Taran. It won't do me any good to dwell on them. Even if my roommates revealed everything, the odds of anyone catching up at this point are slim. The only real worry is if we come across one of the Order's outposts or border patrols. It's a little surprising we haven't stumbled upon any—but our path seems deliberate, almost as if Taran knows where they are.

In desperate need of some alone time, I set out in the nearby forest to gather some firewood. I've struggled with keeping my head up after Taran's revelations yesterday. All my sins, slowly flooding my chest. But I need to be strong—this isn't about me. It's about helping Taran, so I can fix things, even if the uncertainty of how I'm supposed to do that is chipping away at my resolve.

My body's quaking from within, emotions pushing against my skin, trying to break free. I sit among the ferns, close my eyes, and try to breathe, but there's no room in my lungs. Tears tremble free.

With no one around to see, they burst out.

My chest jolts and heaves, ragged breaths barely escaping. I can't let myself succumb to this. I can't. I need to push through.

Arms shaking, I pull the little button from my pocket, the mother of pearl reflecting the dappled sunlight. So smooth, save for where my skin catches on its holes. *Why does this bring me so much calm? Shouldn't I be able to find that within myself?*

Regardless, it does, my inhales slowly settling. I wipe my eyes, then tuck it away. I need to focus on what I can do, and right now, that's supposed to be gathering firewood.

It's silly, but every stick found in the leafy shadows builds my confidence as I add it to my collection, calming the tremble in my hands. I *can* live without incanting; I simply need to train myself to stop relying on it.

With a final, deep breath, I return with a pile of sticks so generous they threaten to fall from my arms. Emlyn's nowhere to be seen—he must have gone hunting—and Reid sits by the creek, his boots off and his sleeves rolled up as he splashes water on his face. Possibly shaving?

I head straight for Taran, who's almost done settling the horses. Willow's golden coat reflects the warmth of the setting sun as he packs up his brush.

"I collected firewood," I say, announcing my presence.

Taran bites back a chuckle, his eyes glittering with amusement when he spots the considerable stack I carry. "Yes, you did." His expression softens into an almost wistful smile. "You're really intent on changing your ways, aren't you?"

I press my lips together, fighting back against the reminder of my wrongdoings. "Of course."

He holds my gaze, as if considering me, and my weight shifts as heat rises to my face. One of the smaller sticks slips off the top of the heap, but Taran gracefully catches it before it hits the ground.

"Can you teach me how to start a fire?" I hold my breath as he sets the wayward stick back on the pile.

Taran promptly steps back and glances toward the tree line. "Emlyn can show you when he gets back."

My brow furrows. "Why are you always having Emlyn teach me everything?" It's not as if I'm a difficult student.

"He's better at it."

"Well, he's not here, and you're done with the horses." I move into Taran's line of sight, carefully balancing the sticks as I do. "The sooner we have a fire, the sooner we can eat."

He doesn't look away again, but clenches his jaw, obviously weighing his options. The more time I spend with him, the clearer it's become that the warnings about the deceptive nature of fae don't apply. With Emlyn, maybe—he's difficult to read. But Taran? Something's definitely bothering him.

"Have I done something to upset you?" I ask.

"Why would you think that?"

"It's just... I want to help, but I've never made a fire without incanting."

He shifts his gaze to Willow and scratches behind her ear.

What's the issue? He should be glad I'm so motivated. Unless that somehow interferes with how I'm supposed to help him?

"Please?" I say. "I don't want to rely on that anymore."

With a heavy sigh, he gives Willow a final pat. "Fine, I'll show you." Not the enthusiasm I was hoping for, but maybe he just dislikes teaching. He leads me to a spot that's clear and fairly level, and I drop my stack of firewood, stretching out my arms. "Reid, you should learn, too," Taran calls.

He pulls his boots on and joins us as Taran sorts the sticks. I plop down next to the pile and wait, like the excellent student I am.

About half a bell passes, and Reid has started a fire.

I've been here the entire time, listening to all the same instructions, but for some reason, Taran only actually helped Reid. I sit back with my arms crossed, my irritation steaming beneath my ears.

Reid warms his hands by the fire with a smug look on his face. "I'm sure you'll light the next one."

Taran sits on his other side, silently watching the flames as the flickering light dances across the shadows of his face. In a blink, he perks up, glancing toward the trees.

A few seconds later, Emlyn emerges, holding a couple of hare carcasses. "I got lucky, found two of them." He sits down next to Taran. "And you've already got a fire going. Perfect!"

"Reid did it," I grumble.

Emlyn's eyes widen. "Learning to start fires the normal way? I was hoping to teach you myself." He smacks Taran's shoulder playfully. "How dare you rob me of that."

"Just give me those." Taran takes the hares from Emlyn, then goes over to his pack, probably to get whatever he needs to skin them.

A shudder runs down my spine, and I quickly focus my attention on the others. The sight of blood has always turned my stomach.

Emlyn scoots closer to Reid, questioning him about the technique Taran showed us, so Reid grabs a couple of sticks to show off. Emlyn inches even closer, adjusting Reid's hands to make barely perceptible changes in how he places the sticks, and within seconds they erupt into bickering, resulting in even more small taps and shoves between them.

They just need to kiss already and be done with it.

Dismissing the pang of envy in my chest, I roll my eyes and lie back, taking in the idyllic oranges and purples of the evening sky.

Taran settles down a respectable distance away from me and hangs the meat over the fire. I roll my head in his direction to watch. Something about him... Despite being fae, he puts me at ease, as if I knew him in another life. It's a little frightening.

The more I think about it, the more my heart twists, as if winding a coil beneath my skin. While I can't deny some brief moments of connection between us, falling for a fae would only complicate things. I need to stay focused.

"What kind of knife is that?" I ask, noting the small white blade Taran set down next to him. I've never seen anything like it. "It looks... brutal."

I wince at my description, hoping he won't take offense, but there really isn't a better word for it. It lacks a uniform shape, with rough serrations down one edge.

"It's bone."

My horror must be clear on my face, because he glances in my direction and lights up with a laugh.

"We don't use metal," he explains, offering it to me.

I push myself up, sitting closer, and carefully take it. The smooth sides are well polished, its edges quite sharp. "What kind of bone?"

"I believe this one came from a sheep. Though I'll warn you not to ask about my sword."

I hand his knife back. "I don't see how I couldn't now."

Taran slides it onto his belt, and his face softens with a boyish grin that wraps my heart in the warm feeling of home.

Why is his presence so comforting?

He goes over to his pile of things, and I briefly watch Reid and Emlyn, still sitting on the opposite side of the fire. They're likely discussing hunting, as Emlyn's miming shooting a bow. A moment later, Taran returns with a white blade laid out across his lap.

For a sword, it's definitely on the short side—the sabers I trained with were almost twice as long. Like the knife, its bulky handle is wrapped with leather and lacks a hilt. The blade smoothly transitions from thick near the handle to a sharp tip, and despite one side having a slight edge, it's clearly intended to stab, not slice.

I run my fingers along the intricate carvings of leaves that decorate its side. "It's beautiful."

"It's my grandfather's thigh bone."

My hand recoils in a flash, and I grab his shoulder to keep from falling over.

"Your grandfather?" I sputter. "You—you make weapons from your dead?"

"It's considered a great honor." He lifts the blade and turns it over, showing me the other side. "He died fighting Gareth Arandur. My mother had this made so our family would never forget. It passed to me when she was exiled."

That's... morbid. But strangely captivating.

"May I?" I straighten up as he hands it to me. The weight's awkward, completely unbalanced compared to the swords I trained with. "It doesn't seem very practical."

"It's not—it's mostly ceremonial. A symbol of the throne."

He takes it from me, tracing its carvings absently with his fingers as he sets it in his lap. A gentle smile fills his face as his head tilts toward mine. At some point, I must have leaned into him, his solid presence building a steady heat where my shoulder presses into his.

Panic flares in the green of his eyes. His body tenses, and I barely keep from losing my balance as he scoots away, setting his sword on the grass between us. He grabs at the stick holding the cooking hares.

Shame boils within me. I didn't intend to get so close—it just happened. Again, just like him taking my hand last night. But the fact that it keeps happening must mean something. Perhaps all the unease it brings is simply nerves from my lack of experience? As wrong as it feels, this pull… it's getting harder to ignore.

Taran pulls our dinner away from the flames. "I think the meat's done." He nearly drops everything, shaking his hand as if he burned himself.

Emlyn takes half and splits it between him and Reid, leaving Taran to divide what remains with me. I try not to cringe as Taran carves through it with his sheep-bone knife, then hands me my share.

The meat's tougher than our previous meals, which results in my gnawing at it in a very unladylike fashion. But Reid and Emlyn are still squabbling away, and Taran's looking everywhere except at me. A tension stirs within me—I don't like this. Maybe I should find a way to talk to him about it before things become too awkward.

That won't be uncomfortable at all.

To keep my anxiety at bay, I focus my attention on Reid and Emlyn's spat. *What could they possibly be fighting about now?*

"You didn't split the meat evenly, did you?" Reid asks, his cut sagging between his fingers as he eyes Emlyn.

"Huh?"

"The meat. Yours is bigger."

"How could you possibly know that? You haven't seen it."

"I can see it right now, ass," Reid snaps.

Emlyn looks down at the front of his pants, and Reid flushes bright red, forcing me to hold back a snicker. I'd hate to interrupt Reid being on the receiving end of someone's teasing for once.

"No! Not—you know I'm talking about the rabbit!"

Emlyn's eyebrows pop up. "Do I?"

"You do. And you're avoiding answering, which means you did." Triumph shines out of Reid's eyes.

"Not necessarily. I could just find you adorable when you're flustered."

I blush on Reid's behalf, then sneak a glance at Taran.

He's gone.

Their conversation fades as I peer through the darkness behind me and spot Taran at the edge of the woods.

This could be my chance. Even if this is entirely in my head, confirming that will help me focus on our task. I summon my courage, preparing to follow—

"Ellie, don't. He probably just has things to take care of." Firelight flickers on Reid's surprisingly stern face, but he *does* know men better than I do, so I reluctantly settle back down. I'll finish my meal, and if Taran's still not back, then I'll go looking for him.

A coil slowly winds within me as the three of us quietly eat our food, their squabble having finally come to an end. When I finish, I wash my hands and face in the frigid creek as best I can, then hurry to the fire to dry off.

Taran still hasn't returned.

The others seem unbothered. Reid tosses a couple more sticks onto the flames while Emlyn lounges next to him, staring at the blaze.

"Perhaps I should collect some more firewood," I say.

"We have plenty," Emlyn replies.

I shrug. "I thought you might appreciate some time with just the two of you."

Reid goes stiff as a board. Emlyn eyes me for a moment, then laughs, shaking his head. He gets up, pulling his shirt off as he heads to the creek.

My jaw drops. *What have I done?*

Even in the darkness, Reid's face couldn't be any redder if he'd sat out in the sun all day. "What are you doing?" he asks, his gaze tracking Emlyn.

I tear my eyes away from the toned muscles of Emlyn's arms and chest, then creep to my feet, trying not to make a sound.

"Bathing. It's been like, four days." Emlyn pulls his boots off and tugs at the waist of his pants while I pick up my pace toward the woods.

"You don't have to take all your clothes off!"

"And you don't have to look."

I sprint the rest of the way to the trees.

I REGRET MY CHOICES almost immediately.

As dark as our campsite was, the woods are even worse. A wolf howls in the distance as I slowly slink through the trees, feeling my way around, praying my eyes will adjust soon.

Do fae see better in the dark, too? They must, otherwise I don't know how Taran could be out here for so long.

"Taran?" I call softly, hoping he's somewhere nearby. Avoiding each other won't solve anything. We need to talk.

"Ellie, stop," a voice says. Reid. I turn around to find him bumbling through the dark toward me.

I cross my arms. "What is it?"

"I'm not stupid, Ellie. I know what you're doing—it's obvious how you look at him."

Reid sees it, too? Heat fills my face, and I'm glad for the dark so he can't see me blushing. "I don't know what you're talking about. He's been gone for a while. I'm worried."

"Stay away from him," Reid says. "We're here to stop a war, not to get into bed with fae."

That's not what I'm trying to do. I only want to talk. To understand.

Right?

The tightness in my core suggests otherwise.

My fingers find the button in my pocket, letting me breathe. Why is this so confusing? And why is he judging me so harshly?

"But you're seconds away from pouncing all over Emlyn," I say.

Reid tenses, barely perceptible in the darkness. "That's... Look— that's different, alright?"

"How so?"

"Because I'm not—" He balls his fists and lets out a frustrated groan. "It won't hurt anyone if I fuck him."

"What about Alexis?"

"That's not fair, El. If she knew everything we do, she wouldn't hate him so much. But you—"

"What about me?" I snap, my frustration brewing. This conversation's gone far beyond what I'd even considered, but I don't need his condescension. "Who am I hurting?"

"If I could tell you in a way you'd remember, I would. But we've tried that. You just have to trust me."

The bubbling within me simmers to a boil. A lifetime spent blindly following my father's wishes, now Reid wants me to do that for him, too?

"Stop saying that! I don't want to just be a tool in someone else's plan. I want to help. To make my own decisions."

"I get that," Reid says, his voice laced with exasperation, "but you don't have enough information to make good ones!"

"At least they'll be mine. I can deal with consequences, just like everyone else does." I turn away, my foot catching on a tree root.

"Ellie, please." Reid pulls me back, his voice softening as he takes my hands, and I resist the urge to pull them away. "If you could remember everything, you'd want nothing to do with him."

That doesn't make any sense. "What could I possibly be forgetting that would make me not want to help Taran? I need to make up for all the incanting I've done." But deeper than that, there's this itch—that in helping him, I'll find what's missing in my heart.

"You can do that without tying yourself to him." Reid squeezes my hands. "Please. Just wait until we reach the capital. You'll be able to make a better decision then."

The pleading in his voice calms the maelstrom within, but this is more than fae charm: this pull doesn't exist with Emlyn at all. I need to figure out what it is before it overwhelms me.

How can I make Reid see?

I press his fingers between mine. "I understand what you're telling me, but Taran feels familiar. Safe. With everything falling apart, I just—when he smiles, I feel like it will be alright."

My breath catches, having finally said the words aloud. That feeling... How can something feel both so right and so wrong at the same time?

"Believe me, Ellie, I understand. I really do. But you need to ignore that. You need to stay away from him. Just until the capital. Please."

Why does this mean so much to him?

I bite my lip. As conflicted as I am, I won't have any peace until I sort this out, and that won't happen without talking to Taran.

"I just... I need answers," I say.

Reid drops his head. "I'm not gonna convince you, am I?"

I don't have a response. Not one he wants to hear.

He releases my hands, the cold creeping into my fingers. His voice is heavy when he speaks.

"Fine. Do what you want. Just don't blame me."

A weight sinks through me as he returns to camp, leaving me alone in the woods. I don't know how long I linger, hoping I'll catch Taran when he returns.

He never does.

Chapter 28

Reid

By the time I return to camp, Emlyn has thankfully finished his bath in the creek and gotten dressed. I have zero expectations of Ellie or Taran returning anytime soon, and I've reached my limit on what I can deal with for the day. So I shove everything down—my thoughts, frustrations, and even myself—and settle a comfortable distance from the fire. I shut my eyes and wait for sleep to take me.

Which, of course, it doesn't. Instead, I'm extremely aware of Emlyn sitting down behind me, with maybe a cock's length between us.

Why, brain? Why?

"Are you alright?" he asks.

I shake my head. "Did you hear everything?"

Emlyn chuckles. "No—my hearing isn't *that* much better than yours. But don't tell Ellie that." He exhales. "It's not your fault. You gotta let them make their own choices."

A cool breeze rustles my hair as I roll over and look up at the sky, the fire crackling nearby. Its orange glow makes it difficult to pick out the stars.

"Why did you even tell Taran to bring Ellie, anyway?" I ask. "Even without his memories, I doubt Caeo would need much convincing to leave his mom. She's always been horrible to him."

"I know—that was obvious. But I don't make the decisions. Taran does."

So I was right. This is *his* fault.

Still...

"I can't help feeling like Caeo will blame me for this."

"You did your best. You can't destroy yourself to save them. They shouldn't expect you to."

I close my eyes, then reach in his direction, feeling for his hand. He takes it with a reassuring squeeze.

He hasn't let go by the time I drift to sleep.

ELLIE MUST'VE RETURNED sometime during the night, as I find her sleeping on the opposite side of the smoking remains of the fire when Emlyn wakes me. Apparently, I curled up against his shoulder in my sleep. It's cold and he smells like vanilla, dammit.

Taran shows up a while later, a bell or so after dawn based on where the sun's at. He goes straight to the horses, where Ellie immediately joins him. I try to ignore their conversation, digging through Emlyn's pack for some food while he tugs his boots on next to me, but every word chafes my eardrums.

"You were gone all night," Ellie says. "Is everything alright?"

"I wanted some time to myself," Taran replies.

"Did I do something wrong?"

"Why do you always think you did something?"

"Typical fae tactic to avoid the truth—answer a question with a question," Emlyn whispers to me, his soft hair brushing my shoulder.

Ever since we left Haven, he's been wearing it down, with some braids in the front to keep it out of his face. It's an effort to resist the call to my fingers, begging them to run through those blond locks.

"I just... I wanted to talk," Ellie says.

I swear I could punch her, but Caeo would beat me to death. Or would he, if it keeps her out of his brother's pants?

Taran falls silent as he tightens a strap on the horse.

"This is a tough one," Emlyn whispers again. "He can't claim there's nothing to discuss because he knows there is, but if he asks another question, she'll spell it out for him."

Taran shoots a glare our way.

"I figured that out on my own," I mutter, peeking inside a leather sack to find a variety of nuts. "You don't need to explain."

"Just trying to acclimate you to our ways," he says. "We'll be crossing the border today. I'd hate for my kin to scare you off."

"Today?" I glance back at Emlyn, who nods. "Will we be meeting other fae?"

He clicks his tongue, his gaze drifting to the tree line. "I'm not entirely sure of the plan. I thought Taran would go over it last night, but..." He shrugs. "We'll have to get the two of you some different clothes. Preferably something with a hood, because I can't guarantee people won't see through any glamours we put on you. After that... I'm not sure. We're traveling with two Fallen and a prince with enemies in both the northern and southern realms. This was the easy part."

My stomach tightens. "How dangerous will this be?" When I decided to chase after Ellie, I was a capable incanter. Now, I just have a sword I've never actually used in a fight.

I'm not ready to die for Caeo's sake. Stopping a war is a slightly better cause, but as I meet Emlyn's eyes, I know that's not the reason I'm still here, either.

He squeezes my arm. "Don't worry, I'll protect you."

Heat floods my chest; how does 'truth' work in this scenario? Did he just bind himself to that?

But now he's gone, joining Taran at the horses before I even build the courage to ask. Ellie's no longer with them, but back by the fire, staring at her hands as she fiddles with something small between her fingers.

I guess I missed how their conversation ended.

At least Emlyn isn't being a pain in the ass this morning—yet. It's baffling how he can go from being the most irritating person alive to tender as slow-cooked chicken in the blink of an eye. As if all the moments he's needling me are just his weird way of being respectful. Like he's keeping himself entertained until I'm ready to pick up where we left off, before he slept with Alexis.

Because that's inevitable, right? Who cares that he's fae?

I should, shouldn't I?

Despite everything, it's getting harder and harder to remind myself he's fae when I look at him. Alexis's warning, as well-intended as it was, just feels ignorant now. He's not the manipulative villain we've been warned about our entire lives, and I truly believe he never intended to hurt her. Or me.

With my entire world flipped upside down, he's been the single constant. And yet... despite how my heart sprints around him, despite longing for his touch, I don't think my brain can handle any more changes right now. Not with everything else going to shit. I need to focus on what's important—saving Caeo—since Ellie can't.

I bring our packs to the horses, keeping some dried fruit and nuts in hand while Emlyn attaches them to the saddles. When he finishes, he takes the food he wants from me, then playfully shoves what remains into my mouth.

"Time to go," Taran calls to Ellie.

She trudges over, the fire finally out, meeting him at his horse. I turn away, letting Emlyn help me onto mine. Taran does a good job feigning indifference while assisting Ellie, but ruins it by smiling when she thanks him.

You can't destroy yourself to save them.

I force an exhale, then kick my horse into motion behind Ellie's. "E'torel sinta nan."

WE ARRIVE AT THE BORDER in the early afternoon. This being my first time out of Haven, I've obviously never seen it before. But I've heard tales of it—an impenetrable fog that human eyes can't pierce, filling the air from the ground to the highest reaches of the sky.

After leaving the patch of forest that obscured it from our view, I pull my horse to a stop next to Ellie's. Both our jaws hang open as we lose a staring contest against a cloud.

Stories said it felt angry. That's an understatement; it feels like it wants to pulverize me for even daring to gaze upon it.

Emlyn pulls up beside me. "That bad, huh?"

My voice sticks in my throat. "Is it always so... murderous?"

They don't really expect us to walk through this, do they?

Emlyn looks ahead at Taran, who's dismounting his horse. "Not to us," he says. "Just mortals—the Land's way of keeping you out."

Taran pulls his pack from the saddle. "Everyone dismount. The only horse we're bringing through is Willow."

"Why?" Ellie asks as he helps her down. She clutches his arm, unable to wrest her eyes away from the curtain of hatred.

"We won't be able to use them once we get through—the terrain will be too rough. There's no point in risking them getting lost in the fog, but Willow knows her way home."

Emlyn pats my knee, reminding me to dismount. I find myself frozen in place the second my feet hit the ground.

He takes my pack off the horse and feeds my arms through its straps. "Is it really that bad?" He glances between me and the loathsome veil.

I nod, my mouth agape.

Emlyn turns back to Taran. "Are you sure this won't hurt them?"

Taran's lips press together as he looks from us to the blanket of certain death, then back.

"Taran?" Emlyn presses.

He answers slowly. "Not entirely. I'm not aware of a mortal who's ever made it across."

Does this guy ever think things through?

"Ancients, Taran! Why didn't you say something earlier?"

"We don't have a choice. If they're going to help, they have to try."

Fuck. I didn't think I'd be so blatantly risking my life this soon. Maybe I should just accept that Caeo has a new life and I'll never see him again. Find myself a job in a city far, far, away from this abominable place.

Grabbing Taran's free arm, Emlyn yanks him out of Ellie's grasp. Her hands clench into fists, her face white. They argue furiously in the Tongue, but it ends quickly, with Taran getting the last word.

Emlyn storms toward the horses, spouting more words in the Tongue as he smacks one of their rumps. They take off in the direction we came from, except for Willow, whose reins Taran grabs.

His green eyes focus on us. "You'll need to stay close. Do not let go, no matter what. Understand?"

Ellie and I both nod slowly.

"One more thing—" the light in his eyes blazes like a wildfire. "Do not, under any circumstances, incant while you're in there. In fact, do not incant at all within my realm. I'm telling you this as its monarch, not as a friend. I will not stand for any desecrating of the

Land. Do you understand me?"

Despite my current feelings about incanting, that seems like a horribly unwise thing to agree to. My mouth, however, is having difficulty forming words, so I just nod. Hopefully, my couple of months of sword training will be enough if we run into any trouble. I fumble with the saber on my belt to make sure it's still there.

"Hey, look at me." Emlyn pats my cheek as he moves between me and the odious mantle of pure hostility. "I don't know what'll happen, but I'm not gonna pass through without you. If you don't make it, I'm not making it. Alright?"

His golden eyes look different—the mischief is gone. My heart settles slightly, a warm glow shielding it from the fear. He grabs my hand, entwining his fingers with mine, then takes a step.

My feet are rooted to the ground.

"Try closing your eyes." He takes my other hand in his as I do, and walking backward, he pulls again.

I take a deep breath and force my feet to follow.

Oh fuck.

Eyes closed, it's obvious the instant I enter the storm. A blast of frigid air hits me, heavy and still, but full of pressure, even as the roaring sound of a torrential wind pounds against my eardrums.

My knees buckle under the weight of the Land's hatred. Emlyn grunts as he drops one of my hands and wraps his arm around my chest, holding me up.

"Keep moving," he urges, though his voice is barely discernible amid the deafening howls of nonexistent wind.

I force another step, but it's like walking through raging waist-deep mud. With every breath, I sink deeper and deeper as a seething cold fury riddles my bones.

We trudge our way forward at an excruciating pace, with Emlyn's shoulder digging painfully into my chest as he struggles beneath my weight.

"I did not... expect you... to be... this heavy," he says, his voice straining.

My limbs have turned to ice. I open my eyes to nothing but purple haze—I can't even see Emlyn. The pressure increases exponentially, crushing the air out of me.

Emlyn curses, and I immediately squeeze my eyes shut. The oppressive force barely relents as he shifts beneath me.

"How far?" I gasp.

"We're... halfway."

My ears ring with a sharp, unending squeal, and moisture pools within, slowly dripping out. My heart thunders in my skull, and I lose all sense of direction. I'm falling forward but never hit the ground.

Then... sensation returns.

My mind begins to clear.

Arms wrapped under my armpits drag me several feet before dropping me hard against the ground.

"Reid? Reid? Wake up." It's Emlyn's voice, and someone's tapping my cheek.

I open my eyes. "It's you."

Emlyn's face transforms from worry to relief, then he collapses onto the grass next to me, breathing heavily.

"Ancients. You better like it here because I am not dragging your sorry ass through there ever again."

I let out a laugh between breaths, lazily tossing my arm out to smack him. "You say that almost like you care."

"Fuck off."

We both just lay there, catching our breath, as I stare up at the bluest sky I've ever seen.

Taran's horse emerges from the fog first, with him stumbling out soon after. Ellie's curled up in a ball in his arms, tears streaming down her face. As much as I want to punch him on Caeo's behalf, I can't really blame him. The horse wouldn't have been able to handle the crushing pressure of Ellie riding on its back, and I'm sure if I were light enough to carry like that, Emlyn would've done the same in a heartbeat. As it is, he looks nowhere near as exhausted as Emlyn, who doesn't even bother sitting up to greet them.

"What took you so long?" he asks.

"I couldn't get her to take a single step."

Taran sets Ellie on the grass nearby. He tries to move away, but she clutches the front of his shirt in a death grip, her eyes unfocused as they stare into the distance. He leans close, his lips grazing her hair, and whispers something. A lump forms in my throat, and I look away.

There's nothing I could've done to prevent this.

The fog's wrath continues to blaze behind me. I try to ignore it, along with all the feelings squirming around my head, and focus on the world around me. While there's grass on this side instead of dirt—the scars of all the battles that never healed—it otherwise looks exactly how one would have expected the hilly landscape to have continued from the other side, except more... alive?

Every color is a shade deeper than I ever imagined possible. Rich, as if you combined color with flavor. The vibrancy tingles within me, overwhelming my senses, but in a good way—not the death cloud way.

I run my hand along the soft, luminous grass beneath me. Green like the color never made sense before now—a vivacious hue I hadn't known existed. A barely perceptible, rhythmic pulse courses through my fingers as each blade grazes my skin.

Eventually, I realize Taran stands nearby, having freed himself from Ellie's grasp. He's speaking to Emlyn in the Tongue, and after some back and forth, Taran offers Emlyn his hand and pulls him up. Emlyn groans, then lumbers over to the horse and says something to her.

He meets my eyes. "I'll be back soon." He leads her down the hillside and out of sight.

I look to Taran. "Where's he going?"

"To take Willow someplace safe and find you and Ellie some clothing. We need to get moving. We're too exposed here."

He crouches next to Ellie, who's sitting with her hand in her pocket, taking measured breaths. He takes her free hand and whispers to her. To my relief, he lets go once she's standing, but then nudges her forward with a gentle push against the small of her back. That's almost worse.

Taran takes the lead, his boots crunching on loose rocks as he guides us down the eastern side of the hill toward a lush forest blanketing the valley floor.

Ellie falls into step beside me, her face still pale. "Are you alright?"

"I'm getting there. You?" I help her down a particularly large boulder, since she still looks uneasy on her feet.

She nods. "I can't help wondering how we're ever getting home. I don't think I can stomach going through that again. It's going to haunt my dreams for the rest of my life."

"Just one more life-altering event to add to the pile," I mutter. It's difficult to muster the energy to care anymore—it's not like I have anything to go home to at this point. I doubt my mom even noticed I'm gone.

"Do you hate me for it?" Ellie asks after a moment. "If I'd never gone to the Academy, if we'd never met... you'd still be living the life you wanted right now."

I bite back the scoff my gut wants to throw at her. It won't help anything, and despite all the misery she's brought me, none of it's actually her fault.

So I shrug, focusing on the second half of her question. "I don't really want that anymore. But if we hadn't met, I wouldn't know that. It's hard to say."

We eventually reach the trees. Massive pines tower above us, their bark as rich as molten chocolate, with deep green needles shimmering like emeralds in the sun. Lush ferns and clovers carpet the forest floor, with tiny white flowers that practically glow in the shadows.

Instead of taking us deeper into the woods, Taran only goes about fifty feet before following along the tree line.

"Wouldn't we be more hidden further in?" I ask.

"Most of my people live in trees," he replies. "The further we go, the more likely we are to run into them. Once we change your clothes, it will be safer out in the fields."

I glance at our dirty Academy uniforms. They've certainly taken a beating, but still look nothing like what Taran and Emlyn wear. We'd definitely draw attention, even from a distance.

Eventually, we come to a stop, waiting for Emlyn to return. I have no idea how late it is, other than the sun hasn't yet set. Sitting against the trunk of a tree, I close my eyes and attempt to relax. A faint pulse beats against my back.

It must have lulled me to sleep, because it hardly feels like any time's passed when someone shakes my shoulder.

"Wake up, sleepyhead." Emlyn drops a pile of clothes into my lap. "I had to guess your size, but I think they'll look good on you."

Arandur's sagging crack, what did he get me?

I hold the clothes at arm's length in front of me. Going off what Taran and Emlyn wear, it's clear that fae male fashion consists of tight leather pants and loose, collarless shirts, and the clothes he brought me fit that description perfectly. I'm not so attached to propriety that it seems scandalizing to dress in revealing clothes, but the thought of Emlyn picking these out *for me* makes my insides burn up. Thank Arandur he also included a coat with a hood.

Dammit. Stop thanking that asshole.

Ellie's nowhere to be seen, so she must have gone to change. Taran has his back to us, keeping watch for anyone approaching. It seems childish for me to run off in search of privacy.

I undo the top buttons of my shirt, then glance up. Emlyn sits perched on a log, staring at me.

I raise my eyebrows. "Do you mind?"

"Not at all." He tosses a berry into his mouth. My jaw clenches to hold back the smile tugging at my traitorous lips.

"Can you turn around?"

He tilts his head. "I thought we were past this. I distinctly remember doing that for you."

"You started to, but never finished. Now, turn around."

He sighs. "I suppose we can keep it a mystery for a little longer." But he turns around, so rather than waste time thinking of a retort, I change my clothes as quickly as possible.

The pants... take a minute. They are *quite* snug. I do a quick squat test—no rips—then pull the wool coat on because I feel absolutely ridiculous. Just as I finish, Ellie returns. I don't get a good look at what constitutes female fae fashion as she's also wrapped up in a similar coat.

Taran takes stock of both of us. "Good. Now we just need to do a glamour..."

He lowers Ellie's hood and brings his fingers to rest on her face. My jaw drops as her features sharpen before my eyes, her brown eyes brightening to amber, and points forming at the tips of her ears.

"Your turn." Emlyn taps my chin up, then touches my face the same way. His skin against mine is the only thing I feel, but a few seconds later he pulls his hand away, his lips pursed as he tilts his head.

"You better not have made me look stupid."

"No, I didn't. I just prefer you the other way."

I pull my hood up to hide the heat rising to my face.

Taran tucks his hair behind his ear. "Alright. Our goal now is to gather information and collect our allies before we head to the capital. It's a lot to do, and the longer it takes, the more time the queen has to prepare. She already knows I've returned."

He focuses on Emlyn, leaning against a nearby tree. "We'll need to split up. You can take the western side of Anwen's Tears, and I'll go east. Have everyone meet in White Spring in five days. You know who to visit?"

Emlyn nods, but his brow furrows. "White Spring? It'll still have quite the crowd. What happened to staying out of sight?"

Taran's jaw tightens, then he exhales. "We can blend in among the pilgrims."

Emlyn chews his lip, as if holding back from arguing. It wouldn't surprise me if he's running through a list of doubts in his mind. It's starting to seem like we're trying to replace a war-mongering queen with a short-sighted king.

He gestures at Ellie and me. "What about them?"

"You decide." Taran's eyes dart away, then he runs his hand through his hair. "They can both come with me—I know you work best alone."

I frown. *If he doesn't want to be stuck with just Ellie, why not say so?*

Unless he's afraid to admit he does.

Emlyn's gaze meets mine. He doesn't say anything, but it's clear what he wants on his face.

Dammit. What do I do now?

I peek at Taran. He's taken a few steps away, looking at the ground, biting his knuckle. Ellie's watching him, too.

She turns to me. "Go with Emlyn. I'll be alright."

"Ellie..." I can't just leave her with Taran. Caeo will kill me.

Her face hardens. "Go, Reid. It's what you want. Put yourself first for once."

I close my eyes. Exhale slowly.

You can't destroy yourself to save them.

I go with Emlyn.

Chapter 29

Caeo

As promised, Mother's arranged for some wrinkly old fae to teach me their—*our*—history. A pair of servants leads me to a cozy chamber, like a quiet corner of the Academy library, except without any books, desks, or chairs. So maybe not like that at all. A stone table, slightly off-center, sits atop a plush fur rug, while those same glowing orbs I saw drifting along the walkways outside hover near the ceiling. They bob between hanging vines, filling the room with a warm light that flickers in a steady pulse, as if alive.

They're hypnotizing.

"What are those?" I ask.

"Wisps," the old fae responds, but doesn't elaborate any further.

If he were human, I'd guess he'd be in his seventies? He introduces himself as a Keeper of the Memories, then prattles on about how he's been tasked with teaching me all about Aedys and the Evermoor family, which I'm apparently a member of. We'll be starting with the dawn of the first Keepers, about seven thousand years ago.

He's been talking for five minutes, and I have no idea what he's been saying. While the rug's soft, my back aches from holding myself upright, and my thoughts keep circling around my situation; ignoring my forced betrothal, things haven't been as horrible as I'd feared. The food's better, my clothes are nicer, the bed's softer. I have my own space, and everything's beautiful. There are definitely worse places I could be stuck. And as much as I want to escape my mother and marriage, the reality is, I don't have anywhere I can go. Not without being caught or killed.

Which is why I need to get Owena on my side—she could help me plan an escape. And if not, she's gonna be my wife, so we might as well get along.

But all that will have to wait. For now, I'm stuck listening to this geezer's ramblings.

"Can't I just read about this?" I ask, cutting him off mid-sentence.

His face contorts as if I've insulted his mother. "We do not require books when we have our memories."

My elbow slides along the cold tabletop as I slump forward, chin in hand. If Reid were here, he'd probably be gathering as much information as possible—as Owena said, knowledge is power. But there has to be a less boring option than listening to this droning for bells on end.

I straighten up. "How did my mother end up as queen?"

The Keeper pauses his pacing to glare at me. "You haven't been listening to a word I've been saying, have you?"

"Uh... no?"

He shakes his head, then folds his hands together like a schoolteacher addressing a small child. "The Evermoor family has ruled Aedys since our earliest memories. Your mother inherited the throne over two hundred years ago, when Arandur the Desecrator killed her father in battle. As I was saying—"

"But why the Evermoors? What gives us the right to rule?"

The Keeper's arms tense as his hands clench together. "The Land blessed the royal family of each realm with a unique gift, establishing their divine right. For instance, the Duskblooms of Llynos can—"

"I'm more interested in what my family can do," I say, my pulse quickening. A divine gift sounds *really* useful.

The Keeper's jaw twitches, and his eyes flick to the door. "The gift of the Evermoor line is not important to today's lesson. If you'll allow me to return to my instruction—"

The door swings open just as I'm about to press him further. Princess Owena stands there, looking ravishing in a long-sleeved, pine-green gown, with her golden curls catching the warm light as they tumble past her shoulders.

I'd be happier to see her if her timing wasn't so fucking terrible. Relief washes over the Keeper's face as he sinks into a deep bow. Whatever this Evermoor gift is, my mother must have forbidden him from sharing it with me.

"Your Highness," he mumbles, his head still dipped down.

"I've come to borrow Prince Caeo," Owena says, her gaze landing on me.

I lean against the table, eyeing her. Is her sudden appearance really a coincidence? There's no trace of a hidden motive on her face, no tension in her shoulders, but it's entirely possible she wants me kept in the dark as well. To make me reliant on her instead of my mother.

The Keeper straightens. "Of course, Your Highness." He hurries from the room, shutting the door behind him.

"Why'd you have to interrupt? I was so close to getting something useful out of him."

Owena laughs as she picks at a knob on the wall. "No, you weren't. Your mother would have instructed him not to share anything you could turn to your benefit. If anything, I was saving him from risking her wrath."

Wonderful. So this was a waste of time after all.

Owena sighs, then folds her hands. "You should have stood when I entered."

"Huh?"

She stares at me, eyes widening with expectation. This must be the etiquette lesson she was planning. I'm not really in the mood, but I *do* need her to like me. So I get to my feet and give her my most charming smile.

Owena nods. "Now offer your arm so we can go for a walk."

I begrudgingly oblige, and we end up spending the entire afternoon in the gardens. I learn where to stand in relation to her, when to take her arm, the appropriate number of seconds to maintain eye contact... So many little things that fae care about, at least for their royalty. I can't imagine the plebs give a rat's ass about any of this.

Then she goes even further, explaining how every motion can be altered in the teensiest ways to add deeper meaning to the gestures. While the fae can't lie with their words, they *can* deceive one another through body language. It's a lot to take in, but it does ease some of my worries about her intentions. As best I can tell, she just wants a partner to navigate court with. Someone she can rely on, who won't embarrass her.

Once she's satisfied I did everything correctly, we go through it all again. This time, she asks me what I think she means when she alters her movements slightly. It takes much longer, but by the end, I think I'm getting the hang of it. It feels surprisingly good.

Like, *really* good. I can't remember a time when I actually felt proud of my accomplishments, outside of something stupid like climbing to the top of the clock tower without dying when I was ten.

Maybe there is hope for this life.

If not, at least I have the layout of the gardens down now—all the exits, where guards are posted. Even witnessed a shift change, though that seems like the worst time to attempt an escape since the old ones don't leave until their replacements arrive.

And so life continues, my days blurring together as my wedding draws near. I glue a smile on my face every morning for breakfast with Mother, then wander the gardens until someone drags me to more lessons with the Keeper. Owena ended up being right; he dodges all of my questions, so rather than torture the guy, I concentrate on enough of his droning to repeat a few sentences to my mother at suppertime, which seems to keep her happy.

She's less thrilled with my progress on courtly etiquette. She never comments, but her eyelid twitches every time I stand when I'm supposed to or offer Owena my arm without being reminded. And it's immensely satisfying to feign ignorance when interacting with *her*.

But there're no lessons today. Instead, I'm accompanying Mother to a small party in the gardens to celebrate my engagement. The bright notes of woodwinds and thumping of drums fill the air as I escort her down the now familiar paths. A small gathering of courtiers stands in the splotchy light beneath flowering trees, and the second we come into view, they're already bending into bows and curtsies.

I wait patiently, as Owena instructed, while they line up for introductions. Some poor attendant announces everyone's names over and over, then they each genuflect and throw compliments until Mother waves them away. My gaze wanders to Owena, checking out some flowers with her father, beyond the collection of low, wooden tables brought in for the event.

I still haven't found a single chair outside of Mother's throne.

"Prince Caeo," a courtier says, drawing my attention—a blond woman who looks about my mother's age, but who knows what that means when she's apparently over two hundred. I still haven't wrapped my head around that.

"We've just completed work on your crown," she continues. "The antlers your mother selected from our collection are particularly striking."

I flash a smile. "Thank you for your service. I'm certain it will be magnificent."

Not that I'm looking forward to seeing it, but the glittering gold coiled around Mother's head is undeniably impressive. Now that I know why my throat turns on me whenever I lie, I've been able to find ways around it to keep conversations polite.

The woman accepts the compliment before being shooed away so others can have their chance to brown-nose, until the line finally ends with Dryfid and Owena approaching. We trade partners, and I escort Owena to a nearby table, already set with plates, cups, and trays of food.

She's wearing a coral-pink dress today, made of the same mysterious fabric as all my shirts. It wraps tightly around her torso, showing off her voluptuous curves and leaving everything above her cleavage bare—another perk of the fae realm. The same material winds around her arms all the way down to her wrists, probably to keep her warm, but it's not working. Her body keeps tensing as she resists shivering.

All in all, it's not the best color on her. Maybe if she had brown hair. Then she'd be stunning.

I don't bother offering my coat; it's unacceptable in a public gathering. Luckily, a bunch of poles stand between the tables, each with hanging, bowl-shaped lamps made of clay. Flames burn atop their oils, offering heat while saturating the air with a heavy sandalwood scent.

Owena gets to pick where to sit first, and of course she chooses the side closest to the fire. I quickly step beside her, offering my right hand while hovering my left behind her back. She accepts my help and smoothly lowers herself to the grass, like she doesn't even have knees. Just melts straight down.

"And how will this differ once we are married?" she asks, quizzing me on her lessons.

"Then I would've rested my left hand on your back."

"And if you wished me to believe you were angry with me?"

"I'd raise my right hand higher as you sat down. If *you* wished to convey anger, you would've kept your eyes on the table."

A smirk tugs at the corner of her lips. "I could almost believe you were born for this."

"For helping you sit?" I settle down at a diagonal from her, wanting to stay in range of the lamps' heat. My leather pants are supple enough that the ground's chill seeps through.

"For being a prince. If today's showing is anything to go by, I believe your people will like you."

My chest puffs with an unfamiliar pride that's been showing up more often lately. I glance around at the other guests—no outward hostility, mostly curious looks. Some whispers, though they're hard to parse beneath all the chatter and music.

"Now then," Owena continues. "This is a less formal affair, so we're free to serve ourselves. Which dish do you offer me first?"

"That's a trick question. I offer to fill your cup first. If you decline, I can't fill my own, as that would be offensive enough to keep you out of my bed for weeks."

Her lips twist, holding back the smile that breaks through anyway. "You may fill my cup."

We continue our meal, with me getting every point of etiquette right as I toss in the occasional nugget of flirty banter—I haven't forgotten our deal, after all—but Owena's a formidable opponent, slinging every charming remark back with a tease of her own. When she finally clears her plate, I lift my hand, palm up, silently questioning if I should help her up.

"How do you feel about dancing?" she asks, placing her hand in mine.

I shrug, searching the area. While there's an empty swathe of grass near the musicians, everyone else is either eating or gathered in small groups, talking. My mother and King Dryfid sit at a larger table atop a small hill, lording over us.

"Is that allowed?"

Owena's icy fingers press into me as she stands. "They're waiting for us. It's our engagement, after all."

"I only know one. Not sure what it's called." My mother taught me, and it suddenly clicks—it must be a fae dance. No wonder everyone was always so confused.

I lead her to the grassy dance floor, keeping her hand in mine while sliding my other around her waist. After a few beats, I find the rhythm, leading Owena as we whirl round and around in circles. Her fingers shift against mine, finally warm from being held so long, and a smile lights up her face.

"I didn't expect you to know the Heartstep," she says.

Rather than answer, I spin her out, her skirt twirling around her. She laughs as I draw her back, catching her in a dip.

A light applause patters beneath the music as I meet her dark eyes. Rosy lips, slightly agape. Cheeks flushed under the oranges of the afternoon sun. The warmth of her fingers winding around my neck.

I could kiss her right now. Win our bet, and if all else fails, set myself up for a happy marriage. There's this pull tugging at me. It's easy to imagine the taste of those soft lips pressed against mine.

But something feels wrong. A hollowness at the back of my throat.

So I pull her back up, returning to the swaying steps of the dance. Her smile persists, but more restrained than before. Was she hoping I'd kiss her? Or just realizing how close she came to losing our bet?

Maybe she'll write my blunder off as nerves. That has to be what it is. She's not just any girl—we're getting married in a matter of days. That'd make anyone nervous.

But I wanted to get out of that. It's the whole reason I made this deal. I need to know what she knows, for her to care enough to risk everything for me. I can sort out where that leaves us later. For now, I need to go for the kiss.

"He's much better at this than Taran ever was," someone whispers as we spin past.

Taran? My steps stutter, then I perk up, trying to spot who it was. But aside from our parents, everyone's gathered together, murmuring politely as they watch us. It's impossible to guess who said it.

I tilt my head closer to Owena's ear. "Who's Taran?"

Her fingers tense in my grip.

"Don't repeat that where your mother can hear," she whispers.

That's not a good sign. It takes all my willpower not to snap my head in Mother's direction. Instead, I guide Owena around until she comes into view—still sitting with Dryfid, her regular fake smile plastered on her face. Doesn't seem like she heard.

The song peters out, and with the excuse of wanting a break, I lead Owena as far away from Mother as possible without leaving the area. The music picks up again, and the other guests take their turns dancing as we watch from beneath branches heavy with red and gold flowers.

It's like the air's weighing down on me. I'm tired of secrets, done with this party. I want answers, no matter what I have to do to get them.

"How much longer do we have to stay?" I ask.

Owena presses her lips together. "We've done everything required of us," she says slowly, "but it would be more acceptable if we left together. People would question our commitment otherwise."

"Then let's get out of here. Any suggestions?"

Her fingers trail along my arm to where her other hand rests at my elbow. "I *did* have something for you in my room."

I take a deep breath, steadying myself. "Perfect. Let's go."

The sky darkens as I lead Owena away, the whistles of woodwinds fading behind us.

Chapter 30

Ellie

The fae realm—Aedys—is absolutely incredible.

It's as if I didn't know what color was before I came here. Even my most saturated oil paints would look washed out next to the vibrant hues leaking out of our surroundings. It's like the same light that burns in Taran's eyes radiates out of everything, from the vivid green leaves rustling softly in the breeze to the pink and orange wildflowers releasing their sweet perfume along the hillsides.

Even the dirt is captivating. I could spend an entire day pressing it between my fingers, seeking every shade that glistens with its inner radiance, and my paints wouldn't be able to capture a single one.

Not that I've had the chance to do anything like that. From the moment Reid and Emlyn left, Taran's set a pace I've struggled to match. I can barely keep up as he leads the way out of the forest, back into the hills, and a cramp stabs at my side from the effort. But I refuse to be a burden, so I force myself to review my situation to keep the pain from overwhelming me.

While I'm happy Reid's finally paying more attention to his own life instead of mine, I shouldn't have dismissed his warnings so quickly. Talking to Taran this morning didn't bring me any clarity, only more doubt and confusion.

It's wrong, he said. Two words, then silence.

I wasn't even sure a relationship was what I wanted, but I left the conversation with a battlefield raging in my chest. Shame at being so blatantly rejected—*is it because I'm human?*—confusion at how I'd gotten things so wrong, and a single banner of relief waving in the air. At least I knew where he stood, and that would hopefully make ignoring his pull easier.

But then the border passage happened.

Even thinking about the experience turns my insides to ice. The cold fury crushing down on me, the rage battering against my eardrums... but if I push past the horrors, Taran's warmth seeps through. How he took my hands in his, reaching for my mind trapped under the weight of the fog. His voice cracking as he tried to calm me with words I couldn't comprehend. The comforting weight of his arms as he carried me. How his touch lingered when he set me down.

The relief in his eyes when I finally recognized his face.

There's no doubt in my mind that he feels something for me—something he's trying very hard to ignore. But if that's the case, why'd he let me come along? He could've easily made me go with Emlyn.

But he didn't. Instead, he seems to be doing his best to pretend I'm not here. If that's how it's going to be... fine. I don't need anything more between us. I simply need to focus on doing my part, on being helpful. To prove that humans aren't lesser just because of our ancestors' sins.

I huff and puff as I follow him up a steep, rocky hillside, with no idea how far behind I've fallen. The terrain finally levels out, and I find him waiting, looking out over the valley.

"Can we take a break?" I resent having to ask, but the cramp in my side's spiking with every breath. "I'm starving."

Taran glances at me, and I catch what almost looks like sorrow in his gaze. He nods, setting down his pack.

Just as he's pulling out the food Emlyn gave him, he pushes me down behind a boulder.

"What are you—"

Taran brings his finger to his lips as he ducks down next to me, his face alert. Concentrating. But he isn't looking at anything. A couple minutes pass without either of us moving, his musky scent filling my nostrils while the warmth of his body, so close to mine, burns through me.

"What is it?" I whisper, hardly able to stand it anymore.

He holds his finger up again. Another moment passes, and he lowers it, his body practically wilting as the tension breaks.

He lets out a heavy exhale before speaking. "A small group was passing through the valley." He pulls some nuts and cheese from his pack, offering them to me. "They're gone now."

I take a deep breath, pushing past the discomfort of the moment now that he's further away. "How can you tell?" I ask, then shove a handful into my mouth.

"I can sense their movements through the Land."

He's mentioned that before. "What do you mean?"

Taran settles with his back against the boulder. "All fae have what we call land-sense. I can feel where everything is around me. Like a prickle on my skin, but far away." He sighs, then rubs his brow. "It's difficult to explain."

"No, that makes sense." I think back to our travels so far. "Is that why we never came across any border patrols?"

He nods. "It wasn't as strong in your realm, but still better than mortal eyes."

Those eyes that make me not good enough for you. But before my ire can stew, heat flares up my neck. Last night, when I waited for him in the woods... he probably knew I was there the entire time. And with fae hearing—he may have heard my entire conversation with Reid.

I tear a chunk off the cheese and cram it into my mouth, hoping to bury the blaze before it burns in my face. My eyes widen at its earthy flavor, and I quickly take another bite.

"Wouldn't the fae down there sense us, too?" I ask.

Taran shakes his head. "This is my realm. My land-sense is stronger than anyone else's."

"Even the queen's?"

"Her bond with the Land passed to me when she was exiled. She's been fighting me for it—that's how she knows I've returned. But she's been gone for decades. She shouldn't be able to wrest it from me anytime soon, outside of my death."

"Why did it go to you if your father was king?"

"He wasn't an Evermoor," Taran explains. "I was a child when I inherited the throne, and by fae standards, I'm still young and foolish." The words have a ring to them, as if he's repeating a phrase he's heard many times. "He ruled in my name."

I chew my food while considering this new information. Despite calling himself a prince, he's basically the king, which makes his behavior even more understandable. He's already fighting for the crown; even if I wasn't imagining things, it'd be ludicrous to risk alienating his people by getting involved with a human.

"It's weird to think of you as King," I say, tucking away a long blade of grass the wind has tickling my leg.

Taran freezes, a handful of dried fruit hovering inches from his mouth. "I'm not King." He pauses, lowering his hand. "Not yet."

I shrug. "You basically are. You don't have your crown, but you're fighting the queen for your realm, making plans, ordering everyone around, showing off your power…"

His eyes narrow. "I'm not showing off—I'm keeping us alive."

The heat flares again, drying out my mouth. "I know. I'm… simply seeing a different side of you. That's all."

His jaw tightens, and he packs the remaining food back into his pack. "We've lingered long enough. We have a lot of ground to cover."

The wind picks up as he marches away. I really need to start thinking before I speak, or better yet, just keep quiet and follow Taran's lead before I frustrate him enough that he regrets ever seeking my help. But the thought of doing so carves an emptiness into my chest, which is odd—that was all I did before going to the Academy. When did that stop being enough?

Aside from a few more moments where he stops us to hide from far-off eyes, we keep moving until nightfall. My little button is squeezed between my fingers; I'm not sure when my hand drifted to it. Despite everything, it still feels like helping Taran will somehow lead me to what I'm missing. A wholeness that feels otherwise out of reach, except when holding this button. How can such a small, meaningless thing bring me such comfort?

My foot catches on something in the darkness. I lurch forward, arms flying. Taran catches me around the waist, pulling me back from a very steep, rocky descent into blackness.

A glint in the moonlight tumbles down.

My button.

Gone.

I pull myself free of his arms, my body seizing in panic.

My button.

"Are you alright?" Taran asks.

Tears well in my eyes, and I take a deep breath, trying to settle my pounding heart. It's just a button. Small. Meaningless.

So why do I feel like I lost a part of myself?

"We can't keep going like this!" I say, my voice pitching up. "I can't see a thing!"

Taran looks around, apparently having no trouble at all seeing in the dark. "We need to get out of the wind."

He takes my hand, his own rough and warm against mine, then pulls me along, pointing out the obstacles in our way. Eventually, he leads me behind a large boulder that makes a decent windbreak.

My heart finally settles as I collapse against the freezing hillside that might as well be rock instead of grass and dirt. "You'll have to collect firewood this time."

The cold air shocks my toes as I yank my boots off my aching feet, my stomach panging with how useless I've become. *First, I can't incant anymore. Now, I can't even hold on to a button.*

"No more fires," Taran says. "They draw too much attention."

I stare at him, though he's barely more than a silhouette in the darkness. "We'll freeze." Despite escaping the wind, the chill's already piercing my skin now that I've stopped exerting myself.

"That's a wool coat. Sheep survive nights out here just fine."

"Their coats are a lot thicker!"

I regret my outburst almost immediately, my jumbled emotions clogging my throat. It's not his fault I'm so clumsy. But before I can apologize, he stretches his arm out, pressing his hand against the hillside. A few seconds later, he slumps, shaking his head.

"What are you doing?" I ask.

He sighs. "Nothing. You'd still be cold, and it'd just exhaust me."

My jaw clenches, and something snaps within me. "Stop trying to make me feel bad for being human. I do enough of that on my own."

Taran jerks his head toward me. "I didn't... That wasn't my intention. You're not—" He pauses, his glowing eyes turning to the ground. "I'm sorry. I've put more on you than you deserve, but you're still carrying it. You shouldn't feel bad."

My muscles relax as he rubs his brow, his words slowly sinking in. With a heavy sigh, he removes his coat and sits next to me. My entire body locks up as he pulls me against him and wraps his coat around us. His heat blazes against my back, and his soothing scent of musky pine does nothing to release the tension coiling within me.

What is happening?

"Just go to sleep," he says.

I don't dare speak. I close my eyes and try to focus on my breathing, but my nerves twist tighter with every exhale as his warmth flows through me. My exhaustion eventually overtakes me, and I drift away to the sound of his racing heart.

TARAN WAKES ME just before dawn. He's gentle about it, rustling my shoulder with his fingers. With his warmth blanketing me, it's difficult to pull away, and his hand lingers on my arm until I finally do. We have a quick, silent breakfast and set off right as the sun rises. He seems to have taken my outburst to heart, as he doesn't force as arduous a pace, allowing me more opportunity to appreciate the sights.

The landscape remains similar to Landore's. The hills have turned rockier, but they're mostly rolling and green, with patches of trees here and there. But by rolling... I mean, actually rolling. As if the grass is breathing. There's a subtle movement to it, too rhythmic—like a pulse—to be from the wind. The idea of capturing it with paint seems depressingly impossible; my best efforts would result in something as boring and lifeless as home.

After a brief stop hiding behind a tree on our way downhill, Taran points to a river cutting through the lowlands ahead, its deep blue waters glimmering in the sunlight. I'd guess it's at least fifty yards across.

"That's Anwen's Tears," he says. "We'll need to cross it by midday. Can you swim?"

My chest sinks. "No." But I can't let that bring me down—there has to be another solution. "Are there any bridges?"

"They're out of the way, and too risky." Taran chews on his thumb, seemingly considering our options. "Come on, we need to keep moving."

The hillside slopes smoothly down to the river. Trees speckle the terrain, and he moves us from one to another, connecting them with our path to the water's edge. When we reach it, Taran takes a moment to refill our waterskins, then gestures me over.

He kneels by the water, a smile curling his lips as he glances my way. "Time for you to see some fae magic."

Taran holds his left hand out, but instead of breaking the surface, the water flows *around* him. As if he set an invisible boulder in its path. He holds his right hand out, flicking his fingers for me to approach. I carefully lower myself to the riverbank beside him, and he wraps his arm around me.

"You'll need to stay close, and move with me," he says.

For some reason, those words feel intimately familiar in a way that sends my heart squirming into my throat. I swallow, then he takes an awkward step forward. I do my best to match him without falling over, and right before our feet enter the water, the current bends around us.

My body tenses with every step, going deeper into the river. Sunlight filters through the water, reflecting off the silvery scales of fish flitting by. Our boots sink into the mud, and within a few steps, the river's surface flows high above Taran's head, as if we're standing inside a giant bubble.

Such a feat is impossible with incanting. If he lets go, I'll undoubtedly drown just from the force crashing down on me. The harsh grip of that fear keeps my wonderment at bay.

"You need to breathe," Taran says.

I force out the breath I didn't realize I was holding, then inhale deeply. My chest is so tight I choke on the cold, damp air, but my next inhale releases the tension slightly. I maintain my vise-like grip on his torso.

"Would you like to hear how Anwen's Tears was named?" he asks, his voice calm.

I try to nod. When that fails, I let out a stammered, "S-s-s-sure."

Taran gives me a comforting squeeze. "Long ago, when the Land was young and Lyndir still fae, Anwen was a princess of the Evermoor line. Her father, the king, brought her to a great meeting between the leaders of all the realms and their families, and it was there she met Iorweth, the son of Ystyr's queen. It was love at first sight."

I glance at Taran's face, his gaze focused on the waters ahead.

"But they could not be," he continues. "Aedys and Ystyr refused to unite their realms, each wishing to keep their own power. And Lyndir and Llynos wouldn't allow such an alliance to form between their rivals. So Anwen and her love fled in the night, to the frozen north, where they hoped to live out their days in secret."

The tension in my body melts away, lulled by Taran's steady voice, and my breathing calms.

"Unfortunately, her father's men found them. They killed Iorweth in his sleep, as he lay in Anwen's arms. Her grief was so encompassing that the Land's heart broke for her, cracking the earth across the entire stretch of the north and south. Anwen's anguish swallowed her, and the gash in the Land filled with her tears, becoming the mighty river that would forever connect the north and the south."

My brow crinkles. "Did that really happen?"

"It must have. Or enough believe it, that it's become the truth."

I don't think truth works that way... "What happened to her father? Did he regret what he'd done?"

"The story doesn't say. The Evermoor line continued, so he must have had another child." He nods ahead. "We've made it. I'll hold back the water while you climb the bank."

There's about three feet of mud and rock for me to climb, and he steadies me with his arm as I attempt to do so while getting the least amount of muck on my coat as possible. It squishes between my fingers, cold as ice. By the time I reach the top, mud covers my hands and boots, but the rest of me remains fairly clean.

Taran, surprisingly, has a more difficult time of it, since he can only use one hand. He slips, and I lunge forward, grabbing him with muddy hands. I yank him onto the grass as the water collapses behind him. My back hits against the ground, and Taran lands on top of me, his face inches from mine.

Our eyes meet for an instant before he scrambles up.

"Sorry, I didn't mean to—"

"I'm alright." I sit myself up, holding back a laugh at the embarrassed flush of his cheeks. It's the second time his serious demeanor has dropped, letting a boyish charm peek through that feels so familiar, despite its rarity. "A bit muddier than I'd like, but no harm done." I hold out my hands as evidence.

Taran exhales, then turns back to the river to rinse the mud from his hands. "Clean up quickly so we can go."

"Yes, we're far too exposed out here, I know." I kneel beside him to rinse my hands.

He lets out a sigh that almost sounds like a laugh, then flicks my shoulder as he stands. "Hurry up."

I bite back a chuckle as I dry my hands on the grass, then follow.

After what must be a couple bells later, we arrive at a fae village.

Taran calls it Ashbourne and tells me how it was built from the remains of an older city, Greenfair, that was destroyed in a forest fire less than a decade earlier. While most of the survivors fled to nearby towns, some stayed behind, determined to rebuild. The result is a fairly unique fae settlement, according to Taran, but I have nothing to compare it to.

Unlike the first forest we traveled through in the faelands, with tall, thick trees whose branches blocked out the sun, those here are mostly young. The sunlight easily permeates their leaves, lighting up a forest floor filled with tall grasses and ferns. Scattered among the trees stand somewhere between ten and twenty huts of various sizes made of mismatched pieces of wood. Many are scorched and blackened, in sharp contrast to the pale tones of the trees that somehow bleed a depth of color.

I have so many questions, but Taran's made it very clear this is not the time. So it's up to me to pay attention and find the answers myself.

With both our hoods up, he leads me around the outskirts of the village toward one of the larger huts. A couple fae glance over as we pass, pausing curiously.

"Maybe we should act less suspicious?" I whisper.

His jaw tightens, then he snatches my hand and pulls me along, tension radiating from his body. When we arrive at the door, he bangs on it impatiently.

Once it opens, Taran presses me inside the decently sized room—deer and antler motifs decorate the wooden walls, while fur rugs cover the dirt floor. The man before us sputters in protest as he steps back, then recovers with a rushed bow.

"Your Highness," he says, his voice pitching up as he straightens his shirt. "What are you doing here?"

While he looks to be a man in his early forties, with long blond hair he wears braided down his back, he could be three hundred for all I know. Like Taran and Emlyn, his angular face is completely smooth. Do fae men not grow facial hair?

Taran covers a nearby window with an animal pelt that hangs across it. "Calm yourself, Merfyn. Tell me what you've heard."

"Of course." Merfyn tugs at his shirt again. "Messengers arrived two days ago, announcing the king was dead, and Queen Esyllt returned. They said we no longer need to fear attacks from Ystyr— that the prince will seal an alliance with their princess through marriage."

"What?" I ask sharply. Taran never said anything about being engaged.

Merfyn glances my way, as if noticing me for the first time. My chest tightens as Taran shoots me a glare, then steps between us, towering over Merfyn.

"An alliance with Ystyr?" he asks.

"Y-yes," Merfyn says, rubbing his hand along his pants. "I was invited to the wedding, seven days hence." He looks hesitant. "Were you unaware?"

He's awfully nervous. But after Taran's reaction to my last interruption, it might be best to wait until after we leave to say anything.

Taran sighs, then rubs his brow. "What are you doing, Mother?"

Merfyn subtly tilts to the side, peeking around Taran, his gaze pressing uncomfortably against me. My hand twitches toward my pocket, but my button's no longer there. I bite my lip.

"I'm not marrying anyone," Taran says firmly, drawing Merfyn's attention. "The prince they spoke of isn't me. My mother's attempting to take my throne, and it would appear Ystyr's been helping her."

"I see." Merfyn's face tightens.

"I need to stop her. She would trade war with Ystyr for one with the mortals. Can I count on your support?"

Merfyn cocks his head, frowning. "What do you need?"

Taran puts his hand on Merfyn's shoulder. "Meet me in White Spring in four days. I'll have gathered those I trust, and we'll discuss the plan then."

Merfyn's eyes flick briefly in my direction, then he nods. "I'll be there."

Taran reaches for the door, but Merfyn stops him, eyeing me as he says something in the Tongue.

My stomach sinks. I thought they only spoke that when talking to the Land. *Does this mean he saw through my glamour?* But it shouldn't matter. Taran trusts this man, so I should, too.

But I don't. Something's... off... about him. I should bring it up with Taran as soon as possible. He might be too close to see it.

Taran's jaw clenches before he responds, and Merfyn nods. He gives a slight bow as he steps back, then Taran guides me out the door.

Chapter 31

Owena's bedroom is nearly identical to mine, with an enormous bed covered in forest-green blankets sitting atop a collection of soft fur rugs. The main things setting it apart are all the potted flowers and cream-colored candles on every surface, plus the various knick-knacks she's left lying around. A peachy shawl, a hairbrush, and a collection of small jars on a table holding an obsidian mirror.

The western window lets in the warm light of the setting sun. It catches on Owena's golden hair where she sits at a low table, organizing her things. The party's still going, its music faint on the breeze.

"Your gift is in there," she says, nodding toward a small set of drawers by the bed. "Bottom left."

I give her a curious look before crossing the room. Whatever this is, it should work in my favor. Get a gift, give a kiss, get my answers.

The drawer catches as I slide it open, revealing...

A wooden pipe and some speckled long leaf!

"You found some?" My heart leaps upward. I hastily gather everything and dump it on the table Owena just finished clearing, leaving all rules of propriety behind.

She leans closer. "I had to send one of my handmaidens for it."

I inspect the leaf, inhaling its sharp, grassy scent. My shoulders relax instantly.

"It's only orange," I note.

"*Only* orange? You do red?"

I give her a side-eye. "Don't judge—you know my mother."

"True." She shifts her weight, her posture relaxing slightly.

I grab one of her clay jars, using its edge to grind up the leaf. It does a shit job, but it's not like I have any better options. I pack it all into the pipe and swipe the candle from the center of the table.

The first hit melts everything away.

Fuck, I missed this.

I glance at Owena. Time to see if I can loosen her lips. "Want some?"

She accepts, taking a surprisingly long puff.

"Who knew a fancy princess liked to fade on the leaf?"

She raises an eyebrow. "You didn't grow up with my father."

Laughter falls out of me, and I fall over. I could have stayed sitting, but why bother? It's more comfortable down here.

Ooh... I've been doing too much red lately. I'd forgotten what orange is like. More giggles, less floating away.

I run my fingers along the fluffy fur rug. "Why does everyone wear shoes here? These rugs feel amazing." I tug at my boot. My toes need to feel this.

"Do mortals not have rugs?"

"I didn't. We were too poor."

Owena scoots closer to hand me the pipe, and I drop my shoe to take another inhale.

Too much. Coughs burst out of me.

"The queen was poor?" Owena lies on her back next to me, running her arms through the fluff. "I'd have liked to see that."

"She always wore this stupid widow's mantle. Maybe it was to hide her ears." My brow scrunches as I get lost in the whorls on the ceiling. "I don't actually remember her ears..."

"She has ears."

"No, from before. I don't think I ever saw them. How did I not think that was weird?"

"I don't know. How did you miss your own?"

I squint, trying to recall my mother's explanation, but it's been a while and my brain's all funky. "I don't remember."

"Then perhaps you've had too much of this." Owena reaches for the pipe, but I pull it away. She falls on top of me, grasping at air.

Her lips land right in front of mine.

"Hello." Heat rushes into me as I meet her eyes. They're mesmerizing, like staring into an abyss.

Her cheeks flush, whether from our proximity or the long leaf, I don't know. "Hello."

I bring my hand to her face, tucking her soft hair behind her ear. "Ready for that kiss yet?"

The corners of her eyes crinkle with her smile. "Not at all. You still stink." Her fingers press into my chest as she pushes herself off me, and I sit up, sniffing myself.

"How is that possible?" *I don't smell anything.*

Whatever. I take another hit from the pipe, but Owena snatches it from my hands before I'm done. "Hey!"

I hold myself back from fighting her for it; if she wants to play hard to get, letting her loosen up more could be exactly what I need. She scooches away as she inhales, then relaxes with her back against the wall. I slump next to her, taking it out of her loose grip.

"So where do you want us to live?" I send some smoke rings toward the ceiling. "The south? I assume it's warmer there."

"That would be my preference, yes." Soft curls tickle my cheek as her shoulder sinks into mine.

"I could do that. Get away from my mother."

Owena lets out a sharp laugh. "That's why it's unlikely to happen. She won't let you go."

"She doesn't care about me that much." If she did, she wouldn't be forcing me to marry.

"*Caring* has nothing to do with it. We're both just tools for our parents. We live and die at their whims."

Huh? "What are you talking about?"

The shadows of the room flicker in the candlelight as Owena goes quiet, picking at my fingers. "There's so much you don't understand, Caeo."

"Then explain it to me."

"You're better off not knowing."

"You don't get to decide that." My stomach tightens, and my high wavers as goosebumps tingle a warning down my spine. But I need to push. To know.

"Who's Taran?" I ask.

Owena closes her eyes, taking a breath. "Your brother. The one your mother's in the process of stealing the realm from."

My high is officially gone. I drop her hand.

"What?"

My brain stumbles through my memories, through conversations with Mother. There—when I first woke up here. *I was alone, without my family. I decided I would make a new one.*

Oh shit.

"I thought she took the realm from her husband when he died."

Owena opens her eyes, their darkness full of sympathy. "Gethin wasn't an Evermoor. Taran inherited the throne when your mother was exiled, and Gethin ruled since he was a child. I'm fairly certain my father organized his assassination on your mother's behalf, allowing her to reclaim the throne—I know he was smuggling her water near the end. Our marriage is simply a cover to hide the true reason for peace between our realms."

Fuck. That's probably Taran's bed I'm sleeping in. He must hate me for taking his place.

This is not what I was expecting from loosening Owena's lips. The room's closing in around me, its spacious luxury turning foreign and cramped.

I groan as I rub my face, thinking back to the party guests. They didn't seem troubled by this at all. "Why doesn't this bother anyone?"

"Ignoring that she has my father's support, you'll find most people don't care who rules as long as their lives are comfortable. And she ruled for centuries, while Taran's barely more than a child by our standards."

I drop my hand. "But she wants to start a war."

Owena gathers her hair away from her neck, smoothing it out. "As far as the people know, her return *ended* the conflict with Ystyr—war with the mortals feels more abstract, since they can't attack our villages. It's more palatable than taking up arms against other fae."

"And you didn't think it'd be helpful for me to know any of this? What happened to being friends?"

"How does knowing this help you?" Owena asks, her voice hardening. "By sharing it, I've only made your life more difficult. Which makes *my* life more difficult."

"I could confront her, at least."

She shoots upright, grabbing my arm. "You can't. You don't understand what she can do. She's already cursed you once, and—"

"Curse?" The temperature drops. "What curse? What are you talking about?"

Owena squeezes her eyes shut, pressing her lips tightly together.

She slowly exhales, then looks into my eyes. "You have a curse on you. I can smell it."

My breath hitches. "You can smell curses?"

"My family is particularly skilled with them." She smiles weakly. "Congratulations. You no longer need to kiss me."

I really don't feel like celebrating that right now. I push to my feet, unable to sit still any longer, but there's nowhere to go.

"What kind of curse?"

Owena shrugs, running her finger down the wall from where she still sits on the floor. "A memory one, I'd guess."

A pit opens in my stomach and my entire body sinks into it. "What's she hiding from me? What am I missing?" I scour my memories, but how can I remember something I don't remember?

"I don't know."

I kneel in front of Owena. "Can you break it?"

She bites her lip, twisting her hair for several seconds before letting out a slow breath. "*If* I could... whatever it is you've forgotten, your mother doesn't want you to know. It would be very dangerous for both of us if she discovers you remember."

My heart quickens, pounding in my chest. "Please. I'll keep my mouth shut, do whatever you want, but you have to break it."

Owena searches my face for an agonizing minute. Finally, she nods. "This won't be easy on you."

"I don't care."

She hesitates again, then sighs. "Don't make me regret this."

Owena places her fingers on each of my temples, then closes her eyes. For a moment, nothing happens.

I cry out as a sudden, searing pain slices through my head, weaving between the folds of my brain. Like a scorching hot light, searing every thought I've ever had.

Everything goes black. Then, images. Sounds. Textures. Faint at first, but growing clearer.

Blood rushes through me. My mind reels as memories flash by.

A face.

A beautiful face, with warm, cinnamon eyes, chestnut hair, and a dimple I absolutely adore.

Ellie.

Oh fuck.

I fall away from Owena, retching until my stomach empties onto the rug.

"Caeo!" Owena grabs onto me, keeping me upright. She guides me away from my vomit and leans me against the wall.

"What is it? What do you remember?"

Tears stream down my face. "She took Ellie." I choke on the words. "I couldn't remember her. She couldn't remember me. It was her doing. She took her from me."

I'm breathing deep, heavy breaths, but they aren't doing anything. There's no air.

I need to... I can't...

I close my eyes, the balls of my fists digging into my eye sockets. My chest heaves, a hollow ache throbbing behind my ribs. Then silence, broken only by the distant wails of woodwinds.

"Did you love her?" Owena asks, her voice quiet.

A sharp pain cracks through me. "With all my heart. She's everything." Ellie's face forms in my mind, but the fire it should have ignited is cold as ice.

Owena squeezes my shoulder. "Do you know what happened to her?"

"No." It comes out as a sob, my eyes opening. "I knew my mother wanted to take me away. I told her. She was scared. But we couldn't remember each other when we weren't together—she won't even know I'm gone. That I ever existed."

I curl my knees to my chest as my tears fall. We should've gone to the headmaster. My gut told me it was fae; I should've listened. Should've pushed harder.

Everything hurts, splintering out from my heart. My body wants to collapse into itself, but my mind flails for answers.

Why would Mother do this? All my other girlfriends... She just creeped them out until I wasn't worth it anymore.

Or did she? I wouldn't know if I can't remember.

No—Owena only mentioned one curse.

Unless she had another way of doing it. All fae can curse; I remember that much, at least. But Owena's family is extra good at it. Their royal gift.

I wipe my eyes. "What's the Evermoor family gift?"

Owena blinks as her mouth drops open, then swallows. "Willbending. The ability to force one's will on others. Make them do whatever she wants."

Everything suddenly clicks. So many moments when I wanted nothing to do with my mother, but she'd tell me to do something... to follow, calm down, take Owena for a walk... and I just did.

"Fuck." The back of my head makes a painful thunk as it hits the wall behind me. It's even worse than I thought.

But if it's a family gift...

"Can I willbend?" I rack my brain for any times someone might have done something I asked more easily than I expected. Outside of charming girls, nothing comes to mind.

"With your mortal blood, it's difficult to guess," Owena says, "and it's unlikely your mother would ever teach you how." She takes my hands, pulling them close. "Please, Caeo. You can't confront her. At best, she'll curse you again. At worst, she'll just force you to do whatever she wants. But she'll know it was me who broke it."

I search her face in the dim candlelight, the sun having almost set. Her fear looks real, her lip trembling. *I really did make her life harder, didn't I?* I didn't mean to; I just wanted her help.

My eyes sink shut. *What do I do now?* I thought I understood my situation. That I could manage it.

I was wrong. So wrong.

Owena pulls me into an embrace, and I sob until there's nothing left. Till I can't breathe.

The world goes numb. Nothing but throbbing emptiness.

"I'm sorry, Caeo," Owena whispers. "I should never have said anything. But you need to find a way past this, to pretend nothing's wrong."

"It doesn't matter. She can't take anything else from me. She already took everything."

"And what about me?" Owena tilts my head up till I meet her gaze, her voice soft. "You may be content throwing your life away, but can you throw mine away as well? She'll know it was me."

I take a deep breath. It hurts. A lot. But Owena's only at risk because I pushed her. Manipulated her.

She's the only ally I have—I can't abandon her. But more importantly, she can free Ellie from the curse.

It's something to hold on to. I just need to somehow bury my aching heart before my mother sees me.

Chapter 32

Ellie

After leaving Ashbourne, Taran takes a moment to adjust my glamour—it seems I was right about Merfyn seeing through it. Heat rushes through me as he rests his fingers gently on my face, and I pray my cheeks haven't turned red as he scours my features.

"You're not making me look worse, are you?" I ask, hoping to ease the tension.

His eyes flick to mine, and his hand wavers against my skin. "What? No."

"So, better?"

He breaks eye contact, his cheeks flushing. "Different. More fae."

"Does it suit me?" His gaze shoots back, and I quickly stammer, "I mean, since Merfyn saw through the old one."

"It doesn't," he says, his voice catching. "Which may be why he did." His hand lingers another second before he turns away. "Let's go."

I swallow, but the lump in my throat won't go down, my stomach rising to meet it the more I try. It must be my worries about Merfyn. So I catch up, attempting to dig out information on how Taran knows him. He doesn't share much, outside of Merfyn's family having long served as caretakers of the royal deer. The more I question, the more curt his answers become, until it's clear I need to stop or risk drawing his ire. So I back off, reminding myself that a lifetime of anti-fae propaganda has likely colored my perspective. But the tightness in my throat builds, as if I'm holding back for the sake of his ego.

I don't like it.

He leads us north, out of the forest and into a valley where we continue westward. Sheep cover the surrounding hills, with the pungent smell of manure wafting on every breeze. After a while, it's clear we're headed directly toward one of the herds. Barely visible fae—at least by my human eyes—weave between the grazing sheep.

I hurry to Taran's side. "Why aren't we hiding?" After all the sneaking around we've done, my stomach's twisting from being so conspicuous in our approach.

"Cadoc's an old friend. His people would never betray me." His voice is firm, as if countering my earlier questions.

"Since when are princes *old friends* with shepherds?"

Taran pauses, his brow furrowing. "Are shepherds not respected members of mortal communities?"

My body's about to fold in on itself. "Not really, no." *How is it I always manage to say the wrong thing?*

He frowns. "Our lives depend on those who tend the herds. We use every part of the animals for food, clothing, and other necessities. As leader of this community, Cadoc is one of the most respected people in the region."

My mouth's completely dry. "I'm sorry—I had no idea. I didn't mean to insult him."

Taran's face softens. "You had no way of knowing. Now you do."

This time, he leaves me behind at the edge of the herd while he makes his way to a gathering of small, tent-like structures I assume are the herders' homes. Whether to avoid the risk of Cadoc seeing through my glamour or me questioning his intentions, I don't know. Chewing my lip, I sit on the cool grass and rummage through my bag for my sketchbook. Drawing has always relaxed me, and the sheep are kind of cute—if I ignore the dark stains on their rear ends.

Their bleating fills the air as I flip open my sketchbook and land on a page filled with drawings of a handsome, dark-haired man.

Where did these come from?

I skip a few pages ahead and find more of them.

Did I draw these while daydreaming?

I scrutinize the charcoal drawings. The face... A warm glow builds in my heart as I absorb its features. He looks vaguely familiar...

My stomach clenches as it hits me—he looks like Taran.

I frantically flip further through the book until I reach the pages I'd marked when Taran proved my curse's existence. I haven't drawn anything since.

How did I draw Taran before I knew him?

Inspecting the sketches, it becomes apparent: he isn't *quite* Taran. His features are softer. I rub some lines with my finger, blurring them, each smudge like a bruise in my mind. I pick up my charcoal and make some adjustments—a straighter line here, a sharper angle there. About a minute later, Taran's face is staring back at me.

What does this mean?

"We can go now."

I slam the book shut, blushing furiously. Taran stands a few feet ahead, covering a yawn with his fist. It doesn't seem like he noticed the sketches. The last thing I need is for him to think I've been obsessively drawing him this entire time. So I shove the sketchbook to the bottom of my bag.

As we walk away, I glance back at the sheep. I remember taking my sketchbook out, but then... I must have gotten too lost in thought to draw them. My hands sink into my empty pockets.

OVER THE NEXT TWO DAYS, my tension increases exponentially. Taran spends most of the time keeping his distance, until I trip, slip, or otherwise highlight my humanity. Then he coddles me until his touch lingers for a moment too long, and it's back to frosty indifference.

Despite my best attempts to help—asking about his plans, trying to offer suggestions—I'm basically luggage he's dragging around the countryside. He lets me gather food, but only after he's used fae magic to sprout an unnatural amount of berries on the bushes *he* finds. And when it comes time for his meetings, he simply stashes me away, out of sight, returning with hardly a word. It's hard to hold back the tears in those moments, not knowing if he can hear me.

On the third morning, I startle awake from haunting visions of the border to find his arm around me, his warmth permeating my back as his form follows mine. It'd been another frigid night, so he'd sat against a tree with me tucked into his chest. He must have grown uncomfortable during the night and laid us down.

And for once, I woke up first.

What should I do?

My throat tightens, and I squeeze my eyes shut, willing myself to stay still as my entire body tenses. I don't want to wake him and have this moment end. How pathetic is that?

It's not right to think of him this way—even if he weren't a fae prince and me a lowly human, he's made it clear he doesn't want this. But how could this have happened if he didn't? If only he were willing to look past all that and let me be more than just another burden. A tool. Then my being here would actually matter.

Is it wrong to want that?

No, but I don't know how to do it on my own. Everything I've tried has failed, which makes sense; I've never done anything other than follow expectations.

Maybe that's what I need to figure out. My own path.

Taran shifts behind me. I wipe my eyes and focus on breathing.

In an instant, he shoots away, cold air rushing to fill the void he left behind. I curl tighter into a ball, sniffing back tears.

He clears his throat, and his words come out as if they tripped on a gravel road. "We should get ready to go."

Of course.

I barely manage a nod.

"Ellie?" Concern laces his voice.

I nod again, choking out a response. "I'm alright." With a deep breath, I force myself up, keeping my back to him as I wipe my face again.

"I didn't mean to..." His voice wavers, then he sighs. "I'm sorry."

I swallow, tasting the bitterness of my frustration, then spit out, "For what?"

He doesn't answer, and I'm tired of waiting, so I pull on my pack and start walking. He'll correct my direction when he catches up.

SOMETIME AROUND MID-MORNING, we step through a shadowy forest of gargantuan trees—they must be ancient—until we arrive at an absolutely stunning fae village. Its dwellings sit high among the forest's branches; smooth pieces of wood wrapped around the tree trunks, like lumps of clay someone formed around them. We ascend along a spiraling walkway of flattened wood, passing by some ethereal orbs floating through the air, pulsing with a warm, pinkish light. I reach out to touch one, but Taran stops me, grabbing my hand with a silent shake of his head.

He's been more careful around me this morning, clearly having enough sense to realize I'm upset. Not that he's talked to me about it. Or anything at all, for that matter. But instead of abandoning me at the outskirts, he's brought me along for this last meeting of his. As we approach one of the dwellings, the door opens before he can knock.

"Taran? What are you doing here?"

A fae woman steps aside as she lets us into her home. A tree grows through one corner of the triangular foyer, with archways leading to two other rooms, one on each side.

I can't help but notice the lack of 'Your Highness' or any bowing on her part. She looks similar in age to him, with umber skin and rosy eyes, her auburn curls flowing freely around her face.

Taran runs his hand through his hair, sweeping it out of his eyes. The gesture—warm, like a memory I can't place—sends a hollow pang through my chest.

"I need your help, Aerona."

Her gaze shifts to me. She raises an eyebrow before turning back to Taran. "With the queen?"

"You've heard?"

She glances at me again, her lips pressing into a frown, then answers Taran in the Tongue. When it's his turn to speak, he responds in kind.

I bite my lip to hold back my annoyance. *Can she see through the glamour, too? Is my humanity that obvious?*

So much for being involved. At this rate, it wouldn't surprise me if they hold their entire planning session at White Spring in the Tongue just to exclude me. How can I be an important part of the plan when I have no idea what's going on? Taran trusts me, so why can't they?

Clamping down on my lip, I run my fingers along the wooden wall, as smooth as polished steel, then step toward one of the other rooms to peek inside.

Taran's voice wavers, then my spine seizes as he cries out, the sound ripping through the air as he crumbles, buckling at the knees.

"Taran!"

His face constricts in pain, the veins in his neck bulging as his eyelids squeeze shut. I rush back, catching him in my arms, but he's *heavy*. I struggle beneath his weight until Aerona helps guide him to the floor.

He leans into me, gasping for air. The moment I take his hand, searing pain shoots through me at his vise-like grip, but it's nothing compared to the panic thundering in my chest.

"Taran? What's happening?"

He grits his teeth and squeezes so tight my fingers might break.

"You're hurting me," I gasp.

He drops my hand in an instant, his chest heaving with ragged breaths. I take his face in my hands and meet the depths of his eyes. An emerald fire blazes within, crackling with an otherworldly energy.

These aren't the soulful eyes I know. "What can I do?"

A flicker within their radiant swirls. Focus.

His breathing slows, and the fire diminishes. His eyelids flutter shut, and he collapses against the wall.

I turn to Aerona. "What was that?"

She cocks her head to the side, but keeps quiet.

"It was the Land." Taran's voice rasps out between breaths. He grimaces as he shifts his weight. "She was in pain. So much pain. I've never felt anything like that."

Aerona frowns. "What could it be?"

Taran ignores her, shaking his head. "We should go."

He pushes himself up, but stumbles, and I quickly slide under his arm, keeping him upright. He accepts my help, leaning against me until he gets his footing.

Aerona stands, her eyes narrowing as she watches Taran.

He meets her gaze. "You'll be there?"

She answers in the Tongue, and Taran's face hardens as she speaks.

"I know," he says, his voice firm. "Will you be there or not?"

Aerona glares at him. "I will." Then she opens the door and slams it shut behind us.

I TRY TO GET ANSWERS out of Taran—about what happened, what Aerona said—but he says nothing. After a while, I give up, and we spend the next several bells hiking in silence, my head throbbing from all my bottled-up tension. Taran eventually leads us down the hillside to a well-worn path at its base.

There's not a fae in sight, but this is such a departure from how we've spent the last few days that my nerves spike. "I thought we were staying off the common paths?"

"We're almost to White Spring. I'm hopeful we'll look like any other pilgrims. Try to keep your distance from anyone we come across."

"What kind of pilgrims?"

"You'll see."

A few minutes later, we round the base of the hill into a valley flooded with white.

My hand hitches halfway to my mouth, paralyzed by the sheer beauty. "What is this?"

Countless trees, as far as the eye can see, fill the valley. In place of leaves, delicate white flowers coat their branches.

Taran nudges me forward with a gentle smile. "White Spring is famous for its trees. Their flowers bloom every spring, drawing visitors from across the continent."

"I've never seen anything like it."

His eyes meet mine. "We have some time to wander."

The smile that stretches across my face almost brings me to tears. I pull him after me, running to the nearest trees.

Golden sunlight breaks through the white flowers that float above our heads, contrasted by the striking, crimson bark that I hadn't noticed from a distance. Blood-red limbs twist and curl, presenting their delicate bouquets to the sky, as falling petals waft gently to the forest floor, speckling it like patches of melting snow. The beauty of it all calms the storm that's been brewing within me.

I long for my paints—it's impossible to capture the splendor of this place with charcoal alone. But even my oils wouldn't convey the depth of color, the vitality flowing through with every heartbeat. The best I can do is cherish every sight, preserving the images in my memory.

As we wander, Taran occasionally guides us away from fellow sightseers whose eyes widen when they glimpse him for too long. Sometimes it's a gentle nudge; other times, a brief tug on my hand. We walk until my neck aches from the strain of looking up so much.

I glance at Taran and find his gaze on me, a slight smile tugging at his lips.

"What?" I ask.

He quickly averts his eyes, clearing his throat. "Just, the wonder on your face. Even with all the pilgrims flocking here, I've never seen someone so infatuated with my realm."

His words sound familiar, but I can't place where I'd heard them before. It's a good thing he's looking away and can't see the blush warming my cheeks. "You speak almost as if it's a part of you."

"It is," he says, turning back to me. "That's what it means to be—to rule. She exists within me at an intrinsic level, deeper than anyone else in Aedys."

He almost called himself King, but wavered. *Why does he hesitate so much to claim his title?* Could it be self-doubt? Fear of failing?

I can certainly relate to that, and my arms itch to wrap around him, to tell him not to worry so much—I would've appreciated someone doing that for me. But with how he's responded to my questions in the past, I'll have to tread carefully to get anything deeper out of him. If I succeed, maybe I can help him come to terms with all that.

"Can we sit for a while?" I ask.

His jaw tightens. "You'll have time tomorrow, but we should head to the meeting spot."

"But no one's supposed to arrive today."

He turns toward the hillside, his brow furrowing. "I sense someone already there."

With reluctant feet, I follow him toward the town of White Spring itself, but my spirits lift as we climb the slope and enjoy a wondrous view of the trees from above. The setting sun paints the blossoms in warm yellows and golds beneath the orange sky.

The trees, as majestic as they are, are too fragile to support structures in their branches like other fae villages. Instead, the fae have dug their dwellings into the goat-covered hills that line the valley. Each has a wooden door and a window or two, with a stone chimney poking out of the grass above.

Crowds of fae have gathered along the paths, enchanted by the golden light washing over the trees as their branches dance in the wind. Taran guides me past until he eventually turns to a door in the hillside, stopping to peek through the open window. A warm glow fills the interior, and someone sits in front of the hearth, their back to us.

"I don't recognize this person," Taran says, his voice low. "Stay behind me. Be ready to run if you need to."

My next inhale dries my mouth as I look around. The path nearby is busy with fae, but not so much that I'd have trouble getting away.

Taran slowly opens the door. "Who's here?"

He steps cautiously inside, and I follow, my eyes locked on the stranger.

"Look out!" Taran whirls around, grabbing my arm.

In the next instant, a force plows into me from behind, lurching me into Taran's chest. The fae sitting at the fire flies toward us, slicing at Taran with a long white knife. Taran dodges as I go sprawling to the floor. He pulls out a dagger and swipes at his attacker's side.

Two more fae burst into the room from outside, slamming the door behind them. I scramble away, colliding with the wall behind me. One newcomer goes straight for Taran, interrupting his attack on their friend, but the other grabs me by the front of my coat and smashes me hard against the wall.

"This must be the mortal," he sneers.

One incantation—just one—and I could save myself. It's right there, on the tip of my tongue.

But Taran forbade it. He'd never forgive me if I did.

I grab the fae's arm, but I can't make it budge. I kick and squirm, and he laughs. All the strength I've gained from my months of drills means nothing—I'm going to die, before I ever knew what it was like to live.

He pushes harder against my chest, and I gasp for breath. My lungs are screaming, begging for air.

The curved lines of a focal form in my mind.

His grip on me slackens, and the incantation evaporates before completion.

He coughs up blood. Taran pulls his dagger out of the fae's throat, blood splattering where it pierced a pale tattoo; two twisting paths of curves and sharp angles, reminiscent of antlers.

He falls to the ground, gurgling.

That was too close.

Taran whips around as another fae lunges for him, colliding with a small table as he spins out of the way. The knife finds his leg, and he cries out before throwing his body into his opponent, knocking him to the ground.

He drives his dagger into his enemy's heart.

I scramble over as he falls back, panting heavily.

"You're hurt." My hands shake as I scour his leg, searching for the source of the blood.

This is my fault. If only I'd been able to defend myself.

"I'll be fine," he says. "Try to calm down."

"How can I calm down? They tried to kill us! There are dead bodies everywhere!" And blood. Deep crimson, soaking into the floor. Into my skin. It'll never wash out.

"You're safe now." Taran takes my hands. "I'll take care of it. It's not the first attempt on my life."

He stands, grimacing as he puts his weight on his injured leg. Then he guides me toward the fireplace, past some floating, glowing orbs I didn't notice before, and onto a soft rug away from the blood.

My head shakes uncontrollably. "No, I need to help. You're hurt."

"It's only a cut, Ellie. I'll be fine. Just breathe." He sits beside me, resting his hand on my shoulder.

I try, but my lungs won't fill. Tears stream down my cheeks.

Taran tilts his head until he meets my eyes, the warm light of the fire and orbs illuminating his face. "Are you hurt?"

My mouth tightens as I shake my head. I'm not hurt, but Taran is. Because of me. Because I can't protect myself. Can't do anything. I've done nothing useful this entire journey.

"Is it shock? It's alright, we're safe now." He squeezes my shoulder.

"No." I sniff back the tears and try to ignore the bodies, focusing on Taran's eyes—they're overflowing with worry.

"I was the best." The words sputter out, and the rest tumble after, like an avalanche. "I never wanted to be, but I was. My father made sure of it. So I could follow in his footsteps. Defend our land. But all I was doing was hurting it."

Taran tries to take my hand again, but I push him away, unable to be restrained as everything I've bottled up comes gushing out.

"I'm useless without it." My voice splinters. "All I've been this entire time is a burden. You tell me I'm important, that I can help you, but I have no idea why or how. And whenever it seems like you might actually let me in, you shove me aside like I'm nothing."

I try to meet his eyes, but he looks away.

"You're not nothing, Ellie," he says quietly. "You have a strength, a perseverance that I wish I had. And you push me, without fear— you don't know how rare that is. But if I let you... if I let myself..." He closes his eyes, pressing his lips together.

So he does care about me.

Taran's eyes open, the sorrow within them pouring into mine. "I'd be throwing away the entire reason I brought you here."

"I can find another way to help." I take his hand, and when he doesn't pull away, hope alights within me. "If you let me, I could share your burden."

Taran's shoulders sink. "But if you ever remember... if we ever break your curse... you might never forgive me."

I squeeze his hand tight. "I won't blame you. This is my choice."

His mouth twitches as he swallows. "It should only be a few more days. Then you'll understand what you're asking."

A tangle of emotions twists in my chest. "What if it's not? We almost died, Taran. We don't know what the future holds. But I *know* I can't keep feeling like this. I don't want to die feeling like I never mattered."

Something tugs at the back of my mind. *Why do I need him to feel that way?* But the thought recedes as he tucks a lock of my hair behind my ear, his finger brushing gently against my skin.

My heart holds its breath.

He squeezes his eyes shut, exhaling slowly. "Forgive me," he whispers.

His lips meet mine, and all the knots within me unravel, the world fading away with his kiss.

Part 3

Unraveled

Chapter 33

Reid

"Would you get your hand off my face already?"

"I haven't quite gotten your ears right," Emlyn says. The sunlight slicing through the leaves above splits his forehead in two, just like my own damn headache.

"It hasn't taken this long before," I grumble.

"Well, I messed up this time. We can't have you walking around with mismatched ears."

"Does it matter? I keep my hood up around everyone else anyway."

"But *I* still have to look at you, and it will bother *me*."

I shove his hand off my face. "Fix it later. I'm tired of standing here." The forest's suffocating me, its massive branches weighing heavily overhead.

Emlyn's had to reapply the glamour every day, and each time it seems to take longer and longer. It's uncomfortable having someone else decide what I look like—I still haven't seen it myself.

It's the third morning since I left Ellie with Taran, and I'm still kicking myself about it. I can't help feeling like I let Caeo down. As Emlyn and I clamber up and down the rocky hills, my imagination conjures images of Taran offering Ellie his hand. When Emlyn pulls me close as we hide from potential enemies, I'm swarmed by visions of Taran doing the same to her. And when we settle down to camp in the cold, dark wilderness, my stomach threatens to empty itself into my throat.

On the first day, Emlyn repeated platitudes about how I should stop worrying, that it wasn't my responsibility, how Taran was smart enough to know it was a terrible idea, and so on. But he eventually gave up, and now most of our conversations devolve into bickering. Not that we didn't do that before, but these arguments are different. Strained.

Outside of that, everything's gone smoothly. We've met with a few supposed allies of Taran's, with Emlyn passing along his message. The last one mentioned they'll be attending the prince's wedding in six days, which at least got my mind off Ellie for a while as I fretted over Caeo instead—he'd never willingly go through with that. Emlyn decided we needed more information, so today we're off to a village near the capital, hoping to uncover more. We'll have to hurry if we want to make it to White Spring in time.

After walking for half the day, past hills full of goats and sheep bleating like their lives depend on it, Emlyn calls for a break. We've abandoned the sunny meadows for a shadowy, overgrown forest that makes all the trees I've seen at home seem like babies. Pale, half-dead babies.

"We're almost there." Emlyn hands me his waterskin as I lean against a tree trunk; the water here has a sweet, refreshing flavor, like it's infused with bliss. "There's a market, so we can get some better food."

"Thank Arandur. I've eaten more nuts and dried fruit in the last three days than in my entire life."

Emlyn cringes. "You really need to stop idolizing that man."

"Shit, I didn't mean to." I give him back the waterskin before scratching behind my head. "I'll work on something else."

"Try the Ancients," Emlyn suggests, then takes a swig.

"Who are they?"

"The oldest of the trees. They're much more worthy of your adoration."

"Right, the Ancients," I grumble. "Thank the Ancients." It has a nice ring to it.

Emlyn nods in approval. "Now then—time to fix your ears."

I sigh and pull down my hood, trying to stay relaxed as he rests his hand on my face. Several seconds pass as he stares at my left ear.

"I'm a little concerned people will see through it," he mutters, tilting his head as he steps back to look at me. "Maybe if I got you to smell like me..."

My throat constricts. "H-how would you do that?"

Emlyn's eyes glimmer with mischief. "How do you think?"

My mouth opens, but nothing comes out. I force a swallow. "I don't think there's time for that," I say weakly.

He shrugs as he pulls his pack onto his shoulders. "Your choice. You could always try telling yourself you're fae."

The absurdity of the suggestion snaps me out of my discomfort. "Are you serious?"

"It couldn't hurt."

I let out a heavy sigh as he leads the way to the village.

I'm fae. I'm fae. I'm fae.

EMLYN LEANS CLOSE to my ear. "You need to relax—you're drawing attention."

"I'm trying to," I mumble.

The path through the village is full of fae buying food and other wares from merchants shouting their prices, and my body jerks every time someone glances my way or bumps into me.

Emlyn rolls his eyes, then wraps his arm around my waist, pulling me close.

"What are you doing?" I snap, tugging myself free, but his grip tightens.

"If you can't stop looking uncomfortable, then you need a reason for it. So now we're on a terrible date."

Did he just decide that's true so he could say it?

Emlyn tickles my side as he weaves me through the crowd toward one of the merchant stalls—a simple wood table creaking under the weight of woven baskets of fruit, its owner shouting about his goods.

Heat rises to my ears as I smack Emlyn's hand away. "Stop that."

"You know you like it." He plasters his most annoying smirk across his face. "Now what would you like to eat, flower?"

"Please don't call me that." I don't need any stupid nicknames.

"How about some figs?"

"There are no figs."

"What?" Emlyn widens his eyes, then looks at the merchant, a stout fellow with dusty black hair. "No figs today?"

The merchant looks back and forth along the path, then grunts. "I might have figs tomorrow."

Emlyn clicks his tongue. "I can't wait that long. I'm only passing through."

"Let's just get the pears," I say, but Emlyn pushes his fingers against my mouth.

"Shush." He doesn't even look at me. "Is there anywhere else I might find some figs?"

The merchant rubs his thumb along his chin while I yank Emlyn's fingers off my lips, then gives a sharp huff. "The tavern down the way serves fig wine. They get busy after supper."

"Wonderful! Thank you very much. We'll take some pears."

Emlyn hands the merchant some wooden disks that I assume are money, then fills my arms with fruit.

"We can go now, flower." He pushes me along as I attempt to keep the pears from spilling out of my hands. "Let's find an inn and see if we can turn this date around."

"I hate you so much right now."

"I can work with that." He pinches my side, and my body jerks, causing a pear to spill to the ground where someone immediately kicks it.

"Hmm," he says. "Too bad. Less for you. Now let's go."

He drags me through the crowd to an inn suspended in the forest canopy. The second he closes the door to our room, I throw the remaining pears at his face.

"What the fuck was that all about?"

Emlyn drops the ones he caught onto the bed, which is apparently the only piece of furniture in our tiny room. He draws the animal hide hanging beside the window across it, plunging us into shadow.

"Quiet down. You were acting suspicious. If you're gonna draw attention to yourself, it's better to have an obvious reason for it instead of making everyone curious. And people avoid the overly affectionate."

I guess that makes sense. I grumble to myself as I sit on the edge of the mattress. It's firm, as if stuffed with straw.

"Why is there only one bed?"

Emlyn peeks out the window. "Because Taran doesn't pay me enough to afford two."

I blink in surprise. I was expecting a comment about wanting to bed me. *Could I have pushed him away one too many times?*

My chest sinks. I should say something. But what?

I pinch the bridge of my nose. "Emlyn, I—"

He drops the curtain as he turns to me. "I need to go back out—hear what people are saying. You're gonna stay here." He pauses at the door. "I'll be back later, then we'll get supper at the tavern."

And then he's gone, leaving an empty void behind.

I fall flat onto the bed and cover my stupid face with my hands. With nothing else to do, I eventually fall asleep.

I wake to Emlyn standing in the shadows next to the bed. His eyes glow with a soft, golden light as he caresses my arm.

A tender smile tugs at his lips. "Are you hungry?"

"For...?"

His laugh ignites a spark in my chest. "For food." He pats my shoulder. "But you need to relax—at least pretend you enjoy my company. Or I'll have no choice but to get you drunk."

"I *do* enjoy your company."

I latch onto his honey-colored eyes. They were one of the first things I noticed about him—such a beautiful shade—and now they glow as if the sun shines within them. It'd be so easy to draw him down to me. To engulf him in a fiery kiss.

But I hesitate. *Why do I hesitate?*

"Then come on." Emlyn wraps his fingers around my hand and pulls me out of the room.

The inn spirals around a grove of enormous pine trees, with a precarious wooden ramp leading to the forest floor. There's not a single straight line to be seen, and I can't for the life of me figure out how everything's fused together.

"How do you build without metal tools?" I ask as we circle down.

Emlyn runs his fingers along the tree trunk, still holding my hand with his other. "Shaping. When mortals incant, they steal from the Land to create what they want. Our magic shapes what we've already been given. We can easily mold wood and stone, we just have a limited supply. This village has existed for millennia, slowly growing piece by piece."

The tavern isn't far—a large building on the forest floor, with walls of massive tree trunks shaped to fill as much horizontal space as possible. When we step inside, the rush of familiarity startles me. It *feels* like walking into the Kettle Maker, despite its interior being completely different. Its irregular shape follows the trees' growth, leaving no corners, and fae apparently don't waste wood on chairs, so the tables all sink low. Most are crowded with fae, drinking and laughing between boisterous conversations, just like the people back home.

Emlyn guides us to one of the outer tables that offers a decent view of the room. He sits with his back against the wall, and I move to the opposite side, but he pats the spot next to him and waves me over.

"I can't have you blocking my view," he says, leaning in as I sit next to him. "We're here to eat, but I'm still working."

"But it's too loud to hear what anyone's saying."

Emlyn chuckles. "Maybe for you. But it doesn't matter—I'm meeting an informant. That's what the figs were all about."

He sticks his arm up in the air and waves. A minute later, a woman comes over, and he orders some food and fig wine, handing her a couple of those wooden disks from before.

"Is that money?" I ask after she leaves.

Emlyn fishes another one out of his pocket and hands it to me. "Don't lose that—I don't have much left."

I flip the disk over in my fingers. The smooth wood has intricately braided patterns carved into both sides, with a small, golden sphere set into the middle.

"That's a piece of antler from a type of deer no one outside of the Evermoor family's allowed to raise. The larger the chip, the more valuable it is." Emlyn leans in so his voice is audible over the buzz of the room. "Supposedly, there's a trick to making those patterns that only the crown's shapers know."

The woman returns with a tray of food and a jug filled with thick maroon liquid. Emlyn pours it into two clay cups, the liquid flowing at the speed of molasses, then passes one to me. The sickeningly sweet smell tugs at my gag reflex.

I lower it away from my face. "I don't see how this classifies as wine."

"Just try it." Emlyn takes a sip of his.

I eye him suspiciously, recalling Caeo's reaction to the last—and first—drink Emlyn bought me, then take the smallest sip possible.

The second it touches my tongue, I nearly spit it out. I force myself to swallow and immediately regret it.

"Ancients, that's awful," I sputter, trying to keep it down. "I can feel it dripping down my throat."

"Hey, you said Ancients!"

Emlyn knocks his cup against mine. He takes a bigger gulp of his, and my stomach lurches just imagining that much of the offensive liquid in my mouth. I set my cup down far, far away, and focus on the food.

The tray contains a variety of fresh fruit, some hard-boiled eggs, and a block of cheese. I go straight for the eggs, savoring their warmth after days of eating nothing but cold nuts and fruit. While we eat, Emlyn swipes the rest of my drink and orders me some water.

He relaxes against the wall, sipping more of the disgusting beverage. "Now we wait for my informant to get here." He glances at me, his eyebrows cinching together. "It might actually be best if you head back to the inn."

"Why?"

Emlyn shifts his position. "He has certain... expectations... about how our conversation will go. I'll have to go along with that to get what I need."

"What kind of expectations?" I ask warily.

Emlyn's eyes dart across the room. I follow his gaze to a tall, brown-haired fae heading toward us. He plops down on the other side of Emlyn, diagonally to me.

"Nye," Emlyn says with a nod.

A shit-eating grin stretches across Nye's face. "Emlyn, what an unexpected pleasure. Who's your friend?" My skin crawls as his eyes roam over me.

Emlyn squeezes my leg under the table. "He's not for you."

Wait... What?

Nye's eyebrow curls up. "Oh? Should I be lowering my expectations for the evening?"

"I didn't say that." Emlyn leans toward Nye with an extremely familiar smile.

It's as if I took a giant gulp of fig wine. Before I know it, I've pushed myself from the table, stumbling for the door.

The moment I step outside, I double over, gasping for air. Emlyn appears a few seconds later, pulling me up and away from the entrance.

"I did suggest you go back to the inn," he says.

A blaze roars to life in my chest. "So you could fuck him without me knowing about it?"

His grip on my arm tightens, and he pulls me further away from the tavern. "Quiet down." He takes a breath. "I didn't... Look—he's one of my best sources. I need to find out what he knows."

I yank free of him. "And how far will you go to get that?"

"As far as I have to. I'm sorry, but this is my job."

My heart lurches. "What about me? What about us?"

He throws his hands up. "There's barely an 'us,' Reid! You're too caught up being a martyr, and I can't keep waiting around for someone who's not even willing to try. If you're gonna be mad at anyone, be mad at yourself. Not me."

His words hit like a punch. Thoughts—excuses, accusations—tumble through my mind, but none make it past more than a few words. The truth sinks in like a brick in a bowl of jelly.

He's right.

All this time, I've been using Ellie and Caeo as a barrier to keep him at arm's length. Putting their needs first to keep from looking deeper.

Falling into a relationship with a fae... it would mean throwing the tattered remains of my life away. Everything I ever worked for, my friends, the world I grew up in—I'd be trading it all for him. A man who's flat out told me not to trust him, yet is the only thing anchoring me in the shitstorm my life's become.

I can't meet his eyes.

Emlyn sighs. "Just... go back to the inn."

He turns away. Gone. Back inside.

Back with Nye.

The shambles of my former life are pinpricks compared to the landslide tearing through my heart. I somehow find my way back to the inn, to our room, and curl up on top of the bed, ignoring the blankets. No thoughts form. Just a raw, aching emptiness.

It's several bells before Emlyn returns, the door barely a whisper as it opens and shuts. A moment later, the mattress shifts as he lies down on the bed beside me.

"Reid?" His voice is quiet, tinged with concern.

I pretend to be asleep.

IT'S MID-MORNING WHEN I WAKE, and Emlyn's gone. I sit on the edge of the bed, staring out the window, dreading his return almost as much as I long for it.

I wish last night had never happened. That I could go back in time and get out of my head, pay attention to what was right in front of me. To be brave enough to take the leap with him.

The door creaks open.

"I got some more food." Emlyn's voice sticks as it comes out. "We should get going. We'll be lucky if we make it to White Spring by nightfall."

I barely manage to speak. "I thought we had till tomorrow."

"Nye had useful information. It'd be good to discuss it with Taran before we meet with everyone else."

My heart can't sink any lower. "I see."

The bed shifts as Emlyn sits next to me, but I keep my gaze out the window.

"I didn't sleep with him. I didn't do anything except talk. He was... very upset when he realized I wasn't giving him anything."

My gaze drifts to Emlyn's hand, resting on his thigh. His finger twitches.

"I gave up my best source for you. I hope..." He sighs, then lifts his hand to tuck his braids back. "This is all new to me, and I don't know what I'm doing. I just... I know this is a risk for you. I hope you think I'm worth it." He grabs his pack and stands, leaving my sight.

Relief trickles down my throat. Maybe it's not too late? But I haven't a clue how to fix things—risking his job is one thing, but giving up my whole life is completely different. So I follow, still numb. Out the door, out of the village. We walk through the forest in silence, my eyes on Emlyn's feet as I trail behind.

Of all things, Ellie's words keep looping through my mind. *Put yourself first for once.* As addled as her brain is, maybe she's right. Even when I dedicated myself to incanting, it wasn't because fighting fae was the life I wanted. It just made me feel special. Without any family who gave a damn about me, it was the only thing that did.

But what would make me happiest?

The shackles constraining my ribs erode into nothing. My lungs breathe deep just as I almost collide with Emlyn's back. He reaches out, steadying me with his hand.

I glance up at his face. "What's wrong?"

Emlyn's expression is tight. "We need to change course." He turns to his right, picking up his pace.

His apprehension's palpable, a jolt of nerves filling the emptiness in my rib cage. A quarter bell later, he sharply changes direction again.

He stops a few minutes later.

"Shit."

My heart pounds as I step beside him. "What's going on?"

Emlyn drops his head, hand braced on his hip as he rubs his face. "We're being followed. Nye must have told someone about us."

"Because you didn't fuck him?" I ask, the words bitter on my tongue.

Emlyn glares at me. "Maybe someday you'll understand how disappointing that can be."

"I'm fairly certain I already know."

"You won't really know until you've experienced it."

Heat floods my chest. "Well, maybe we can resolve that *after* we've dealt with whoever's following us."

Did I really just commit to that? A spark flares amid my rising panic.

A hint of a smile tugs at the corner of Emlyn's mouth before he buries it beneath the gravity of the situation. "If we survive."

"What?!" My flicker of excitement sputters and dies as dread engulfs me in ice. "How many are there?"

"Five. And they're almost here." He draws two long white daggers from straps around his legs.

"You better get your sword out."

Chapter 34

Caeo

Owena has forbidden me from leaving her room.

It makes sense—I'm a wreck. There's no doubt my mother would take one look at me and realize what happened. That I remember. That I'll never do anything she wants, ever again.

Except she can just willbend me. Or curse me again, if that's too much effort.

So I'm lying on Owena's bed, trying to ignore her as she sits next to me, giggling to herself. Odd behavior, but I just close my eyes and bury my face under the blankets.

Now, she's tugging them off and straddling my hips.

"What are you doing?" I ask.

"Shush, this will only take a moment."

She bounces up and down while moaning loudly.

"What the fuck?" I grab her hips to pull her off me, but she leans against my chest, bringing her mouth to my ear.

"If your land-sense worked, you'd understand—I can't simply make noises. So either stay quiet or contribute." She straightens back up and cries out as if I've done something to her I most definitely have not.

Yeah... I can't. So I just lie there, staring at the ceiling until she lets out a final yell and climbs off, lying down beside me. I have a vague idea of what's going on in her head, but some clarification would be nice.

"What was that about?"

"Keep your voice down unless I tell you otherwise," she hisses. "I'm getting you the time you need to pull yourself together." She purses her lips, then sits up. "I need your shirt."

"What? Why?"

"Just give it to me."

Whatever. I do, then pull myself back under the covers.

Sometime later, there's a knock at the door. Owena, wearing only my shirt, pokes her head into the hallway while exchanging words with a servant. Soon, someone knocks again, and Owena brings over a tray of food.

She sits on the bed, placing it between us. "You should eat."

My shirt hangs loose around her, and her normally perfect curls cascade in messy, tousled clumps. If I'd seen her like this yesterday, I'd have probably gone hard in seconds. Instead, I'm sick to my stomach.

"I'm not hungry."

Owena narrows her eyes. "Would Ellie want you to give up? Or would she want you to find a way back and break her curse?"

I push myself up on my elbows. "How would I do that?"

She shrugs. "There's likely no one who could unravel it other than myself or my father. Killing your mother would also work. Beyond that, all curses have a loophole, if you can find it."

"How?" Hope ignites in my chest.

"It would be something unlikely to happen but feels like fate if it does—the more fateful, the more powerful the curse. From what you've said, yours was likely tied to you remembering one another when together, but I don't know how."

"That's not helpful." I fall back onto the pillow. "So I either kill someone who can make me do whatever they want or escape from them and drag you across the border to where everyone wants us dead."

"Both are difficult, yes, but not impossible. They *will* be impossible if you can't behave as if everything is normal. So get it together and eat."

I do, though begrudgingly. My wedding's in... what? Four days? If I can come up with a worthwhile escape plan, maybe that'll be enough time to convince Owena to come with me. Break Ellie's curse, and then... who the fuck knows? I can figure that out later.

But I can't bring myself to imitate sex noises the next two times Owena has at it. By the time she finishes, it's probably close to midnight. She crawls into bed next to me and falls asleep.

She wakes me sometime after the sun rises and demands I spit in her hand.

"What?"

"Just do it already. I need to smell like you."

"Wearing my clothes and sleeping next to me wasn't enough?"

"No, and since I doubt you want to spill your seed on me, your spit is the next best thing."

"You're joking, right?"

"Fae have an excellent sense of smell."

When I make no move to spit on her, she spits on her own hand and rubs it all over my neck.

"Stop it! That's disgusting!" I push her off me, but it's too late. My skin crawls at the sticky layer of moisture coating it.

"Your turn."

I hock the biggest pile of spit possible into my hand and slather it on the bare skin of her neck and the shoulder that my too-big-for-her shirt doesn't cover. She gags, her face blanching.

A twinge of guilt creeps through me. "Sorry," I mumble. "I know you're trying to help."

She meets my gaze, then nods. There's something... wistful... in her dark eyes, but she blinks it away.

"Now turn around so I can get dressed."

IN A MOVE SO BOLD I'm questioning her sanity, Owena accompanies me to breakfast with my mother.

"You need to pretend we've just had the best night of your life and you're excited to marry me in three days," she whispers as I escort her through the empty halls to the dining room. Guess it's safe to talk now—clearly, full-blooded fae have better hearing than I do. Or it's that land-sense she mentioned. Either way, I hate having to rely on Owena to know all this.

"The best of my life? Really?"

She elbows me in my side.

I take a deep breath, steeling myself before we enter, and pretend Owena is Ellie.

My heart fractures with every smile I give her, with every affectionate touch I sneak into what etiquette demands. But catching my mother's growing annoyance out of the corner of my eye welds the cracks together with the fire of my resolve.

I will find a way out of this and back to Ellie.

"It would seem you've decided your wedding is too far away," Mother says, her face barely moving with her words.

"Is there any point in waiting?" Owena asks from where she sits at the table next to me. "As long as it happens then, there's no harm in it also happening now."

"I'd rather not discuss what I do in bed with you, Mother," I add.

Her eyes narrow in barely contained fury. "Then perhaps you should work on your discretion."

"What'd you expect?" I reply. "That I wouldn't bed the beautiful woman you forced upon me? Would you rather drag me unwillingly to our wedding?"

She blinks, and her face warms so fast it chills me. It's like I'm seven years old again, and she just beat the shit out of me for breaking a bowl, only to hug me right after.

"Mothers worry about their sons. It can be upsetting to no longer be the only woman in your life."

I force as natural a smile as I can to that creepy sentiment and turn back to Owena. She appears just as inclined as I am to eat quickly and get the fuck out of here.

"I'M SUPPOSED TO BE FIT for my wedding gown this morning," Owena says as we leave the dining room. "I expect you'll have a fitting today as well. It's likely I won't see you until supper."

I lower my face closer to hers. "There's something I need to ask you about first."

"Take the gardens then, to walk me to my room."

I escort her back to where we first got to know each other, helping her sit on the soft grass. The scent of lavender fills the air, biting at my heart. I force an exhale, trying to stop the tears forming behind my eyes.

I join her, and she tucks herself against my side, taking my hands in hers. She brings her face inches from mine as she plays with my fingers. "What is it?"

My nerves tighten at her proximity. "This is still an act, right?" After the way she looked at me earlier, and during our dance last night... I can't let her get the wrong idea.

"Of course it is. Was that your question?"

All business, then. "No." I take a deep breath. "What happens if we don't consummate our marriage?"

"It's not something we can fake. It seals our bond. The Land Herself responds to it, typically with flowers blooming. Everyone will know if we don't. It would be... very bad, for you and me."

My heart sinks. "I can't do it, Owena. I can't actually sleep with you."

"Sometimes we have to do things we don't want to in order to survive. Your heart still belongs to her. It wouldn't be a betrayal."

I doubt Ellie would see it that way, and I don't know how I'd ever be able to tell her. My chest aches just thinking about it. I have to find a way out before then.

Owena perks up and gently turns my face to hers. "Someone's coming."

I really need to figure out the range of fae senses—any escape attempt will probably fail otherwise. But I'm not sure if asking Owena is smart. She seems content to play the long-game, and I could lose her help entirely if she realizes I plan to be long gone before the wedding. I'll need to ease her into the idea carefully.

I offer my hand to help her up. She takes it, and by the time the servant rounds the tree, we're holding hands while looking at some flowers.

It's time for her fitting.

I make a show of kissing her cheek goodbye, then wander the gardens, trying to catch when the guards notice me.

All of them are already eyeing me the second I spot them.

I'VE NEVER ATTENDED A WEDDING back home, and the only formal events I've ever gone to were the Equinox Balls, which are admittedly on the sluttier side of propriety. As such, I had no idea what to expect from fae wedding attire when I was summoned for my fitting.

Fur, apparently. Lots of fur. It would seem I'm getting married in a blizzard.

The base layer's similar to what I've worn since arriving here—pants and a tunic—both excessively embroidered with white leafy patterns. On top of that, I'm covered with a wool robe in dark blue, like what I've seen King Dryfid wear, but with more embroidery. And despite being comfortably warm by that point, I get a coat of shimmering white fur as well.

Then there's a stole, matching the blue robe to make up for the fact that you can no longer see it. I estimate the entire ensemble weighs a solid twenty pounds.

It's been five minutes and I'm already sweating. "Do I really have to wear all this?"

"The coat is for your coronation," Mother says. Of course she's here, hovering beside me as I take in my reflection in the massive slab of polished obsidian in front of me. "You won't have to wear it for the wedding."

"Can't we skip that? You've already been calling me Prince."

"You're *a* prince, but you are not yet the Crown Prince."

While I want to get this over with so I can get back to planning an escape, I sense an opening. "Why not? What happens if you die before the coronation?"

She brushes a spot of lint from her sleeve. "The realm would not pass to you."

"Who would it go to?"

"It wouldn't go to anyone. Now, if we could stop discussing my future death, there is one more thing for you to try on." She disappears behind me and returns with a glimmering golden crown.

While fancy, it's significantly smaller than hers—more of a

diadem, really—but made of the same gold antlers. She sets it on my head, its sharp tips digging into my scalp.

My stomach churns at my reflection. It isn't who I am. I've grown accustomed to my fae look; the changes to my ears and eyes, the clothes I've been wearing. But this is too much.

I glimpse my mother's eyes, glowing an eerie green in polished, dark stone. She cared about my feelings once, didn't she? Back when she'd kiss my nose after bandaging a scraped knee, telling me I was better than the kids who bullied me for not having a father. When she skipped meals for weeks so she could afford a new toy for my birthday.

So I try, turning to face her. The real her, not her reflection.

"I don't want to be Crown Prince. I don't want to be King someday."

She rests her hand on my shoulder the way she always has when trying to comfort me.

"Don't worry about it," she whispers in my ear. "You won't be."

Chapter 35

Reid

Emlyn and I stand in a forest clearing, weapons drawn, surrounded by five fae. They each wield a pair of white, jagged knives, similar to Emlyn's.

"They're from Ystyr," he whispers.

"Why are they here?"

"I'll figure that out later." He glances at the saber in my hand. "Please tell me you've actually used that before."

I'm sweating so much, the handle's slick against my palm. "Only while practicing forms. And usually incanting fire with it."

"Well, don't do that," Emlyn hisses, then takes a deep breath. "You'll have the advantage in reach. Just keep them off my back and watch your footing. They'll likely shift the earth on us."

"What?!" That does not sound good.

Before he can respond, the ground rolls beneath me. I stumble, my balance thrown. The Ystyr fae closest to me takes the opening, lunging with one of his knives.

Emlyn's there in an instant, parrying the thrust with one dagger before swiping with his other, missing by inches as our enemy jumps back.

"Watch my back," he yells, and I scramble behind him, falling into guard stance as two enemies warily approach. Which leaves three for Emlyn.

We're gonna die.

The closer of the two makes a quick slash forward, and my body automatically responds with a hop back as I extend my blade.

Don't incant!

Professor Beckwith did such a good job drilling the flow of fire into my every movement that it takes conscious effort not to.

My opponent doesn't press his attack. *Was he testing my reach?* His partner crouches, bringing his hand to the ground. A second later, the grassy terrain lurches beneath me.

I dodge to the side, more prepared this time, and sure enough, the other one comes in for a strike. I parry his blade, but he steps closer for a second attempt with his offhand. My sword ricochets back, sweeping his dagger out of the way and slicing straight through his torso as I bring the tip back toward him.

He looks as stunned as I am.

The blade sticks as I tug it out, and he falls to the ground with a grunt, blood oozing from his chest.

I fly forward as someone plows into me from behind.

My saber falls from my grasp, landing in a fern a few feet away. The one who's been shaping the earth jumps for it. A dagger flies at his hand, slicing it, and he pulls back with a yelp of pain.

"Pick up your sword!" Emlyn yells.

I grab it and scramble up, finding myself next to him again, our backs against a tree.

"You took one out?" he asks, breathing heavily.

"Yeah." I'll think about that later. For now, it's four against two, and Emlyn's down a blade.

The three Emlyn's been fighting circle us. The one who's been shifting the ground kicks aside the dagger Emlyn threw. Then he starts to kneel again.

Need to stop him.

I throw myself at him, blade first, as if my body's an arrow. Emlyn blocks a blow from one of the others who tries to intercept me. My target stops mid-crouch, leaping back.

"Trade!" Emlyn shouts.

He pushes ahead of me, chasing after the shifty one, and I whirl around, swinging my sword wildly at the others.

No fire!

My feet glide along the thick grass as I slowly retreat, the three fae spreading around me. A guttural scream cries out from behind. I flinch, praying it wasn't Emlyn.

The fae on my left takes advantage and lunges for me. I jump back, swinging my blade, but miss. The fae on my right slashes across my side.

My body buckles as I howl in pain. I barely register him swinging his other dagger toward me when Emlyn rams into him with his shoulder, knocking him away. He positions himself between me and our enemies as I pull myself up, a searing gash in my chest.

"Two down," he says. "How're you doing?"

I groan through the fire burning in my side. "I think I'll live."

"At least for another few heartbeats." Emlyn's panting and holds only one dagger. Our remaining opponents look in peak condition by comparison.

We're not gonna make it.

My throat clenches. I don't want to incant. Never wanted to, ever again. But between that and dying...

Between Emlyn dying...

"I have to do it, Em."

His jaw tightens, eyes trained on our foes.

He swallows.

He nods.

The words form, heavy in my mind, sinking through me as I release the incantation. Fire bursts to life at their feet, engulfing all three fae. With a roar that tears the air apart, the flames converge into a blazing inferno.

Their screams shudder through me, carrying the stench of hair and flesh burning as a sweltering heat overtakes us. Emlyn drops his dagger, clinging to me as he crumbles to his knees.

"Stop it, Reid!" His voice is strained, full of agony.

The blaze flickers out in seconds, and I collapse to the ground.

Ancients.

My breath dances out of my lungs.

We're alive.

"Reid?" Emlyn rolls me onto my back. His face goes white. "Shit."

He rips off my blood-soaked shirt, then scrambles to his pack, rummaging through it.

"I'm fine, Em," I breathe out. "Just... exhausted."

"Shut up and let me bandage you."

He cleans the wound, which stings like fuck, then breathes a sigh of relief when he confirms it's just a shallow slice against my ribs. As he wraps a bandage around my chest, my gaze snags on these weird, glowing orbs floating amid the branches above, until they drift out of sight. He digs out his extra shirt to replace my bloody one.

His sweet vanilla scent fills my nostrils as I pull it on. "I guess I will smell like you now."

He flicks my nose, then his face turns somber as he takes in the scorched ground before us.

The fire had been roughly ten feet across. Where it burned, an ink-black scar mars the earth. A weight sinks through me as I follow the dark veins spreading at least another ten feet in every direction like a disease, withering the nearby plant life to dust.

"I felt the Land's pain," Emlyn says, his voice thick. "It tore through me. So much pain. So much anger."

My stomach cramps. "I've never seen this happen before. If people saw this every time they incanted... they wouldn't do it. I'm sure of it."

"Even if their lives depended on it?"

My eyes trace the blackness across the earth. I let out a heavy exhale. "I don't know."

But deep down, I do, the shame gnawing at my intestines.

Emlyn rubs my arm, his touch tender. Comforting. "It's not just on you. I gave you permission."

I take his hand. "Neither of us knew it would be this bad."

He squeezes my fingers. "I won't tell Taran," he says, his voice low.

"I wasn't really worried about that."

"You should be. This is his realm. He could kill you for it."

Great. I close my eyes and rub my brow, sighing. Then I push myself to my feet so I can investigate the damage I've done.

Frigid air hits me. Pure, unadulterated rage rises through my feet as I step onto the raw, blackened ground. Not mine—the Land's. It doesn't crush me like it did in the border fog. It simmers, my bones throbbing wherever it spreads.

I kneel at the epicenter of the scar, the charred dirt brittle between my fingers.

"How do I apologize in the Tongue?" I call back to Emlyn.

He grimaces as he steps onto the scarred terrain, clenching his jaw as he kneels beside me. "E'len shillah."

"E'len shillah," I repeat. Again and again, hoping the Land will understand. That maybe it'll ease Her pain.

I freeze as a subtle pulse radiates through my fingers.

"She wants you to prove it," Emlyn says softly.

"How?"

He meets my eyes, biting his lip. Then he takes my hand, forcing it deeper into the dirt, clamping it in place. "This will hurt."

Before I can respond, my insides lurch through my entire body, like they're being sucked through my arm. My fingers contort beneath Emlyn's grip. I gasp for air, but every breath gets instantly lost to the pull.

Emlyn shouts words I can't understand, his voice pleading. Darkness shadows the edge of my vision. Emlyn's voice grows louder, more desperate.

She's killing me.

If that's the price... at least I saved Emlyn.

My heart splinters under the strain of the Land's anger. Images flash through my mind, mostly of him. The moments that could've been. Eyelids... flutter shut.

Then I'm released, a cool wave washing over me.

I slump to the ground, my muscles no longer working now that the tension's broken. Emlyn hauls me up, cradling me in his arms.

"Reid? Are you alright?" His hand's warm against my cheek as his golden eyes scour my face.

I weakly bat it away, trying to end his fussing. "Think so."

I groan as I push myself up, then stop. What had moments before been scorched dirt now has a sprinkling of grass, the delicate blades breaking through the surface.

"She was taking your life to heal Herself," Emlyn says.

"Huh."

Now that the euphoric rush of survival's fading, exhaustion settles in my bones, greater than before. But it's worth it. Everything's coming back to life.

Laughter flutters out of me, cut short by a sharp ache spiking from my wound. "So I just have to nearly die every time I incant and everything'll be fine."

Emlyn grabs my face, his honey eyes swirling with tender panic. His voice comes out raw. "Don't even joke about that."

A frantic heartbeat. One. Two.

It's hard to say which of us closes the gap first. It doesn't matter. All I know is our worlds align when our lips collide. Warm. Wet. Stealing the air from my lungs.

Ever since that night in the alley, part of me always expected he'd kiss me again. I'd dreamed of it—many times. I imagined it'd be much like before—a frenzied rush to devour one another.

This is not that.

His body trembles as he clings to me, gripping me tight, but not from desire. From the fear of almost losing me. As if I'll disappear between breaths.

My fingers get lost tangling through the soft strands of his hair, pulling him closer as our kiss feeds the fire within us. Assuring him I'm still here.

I'm not going anywhere.

Chapter 36

Ellie

Our kiss stretches for an eternity but ends in a moment. It melts away the weight I've been carrying, wrapping me in his tender embrace. And as his lips leave mine, my heart aches as exhaustion sweeps through me. It's not quite the life-altering, void-filling moment I had imagined, ending far too soon, but I couldn't kiss him any longer if I tried. All I want is to curl up in his arms and sleep.

But Taran's still bleeding, there are three dead bodies, and blood soaks the floors. He says he'll take care of it, but he's finally let me in. We're in this together now.

By the light of those strange, flickering orbs hovering near the ceiling, he directs me to some cloth for bandaging his leg. Apparently, this is one of his many homes throughout the realm, but one he only claimed a few years ago, so his mother wouldn't know of it. Or so he hopes. He doesn't recognize our attackers, but doesn't want to discuss what their ambush means. Not yet.

I understand. It's obvious that whoever sent them knew we were coming, which can only mean one of his trusted allies betrayed him. While I didn't meet most of them, those I did both behaved rather suspiciously. Who knows what the others were like? But the last thing I want is to bring Taran any more stress, so I bury my thoughts, hoping he'll be in a better place to discuss things in the morning.

After bandaging his leg, we find extra blankets for the bed. I lay one next to the body of the tattooed fae who tried to strangle me, and together we roll him on top of it. Taran wraps the blanket around the corpse and grabs the side near his head. I take the feet. Together, we drag him outside.

It's well past sunset by this point, with hardly anyone lingering outside. We pull the corpse onto the rougher, sloping terrain beyond the path, where we struggle to keep it from rolling down the hill while Taran shapes the ground around it, as if swallowing the body whole. Then we climb back up and repeat the process twice more, with Taran growing noticeably slower and wobblier in his movements each time.

Next, we have to clean up all the blood. Taran has no magical solution for that, so all we can do is haul buckets of water from a nearby stream and scrub at the stains with whatever we find.

A couple bells later, those glowing orbs have long since disappeared, and we collapse onto the bed with no blankets, having used them to soak up the mess. We fall asleep almost instantly.

A loud bang startles me awake.

Green eyes, framed with black. My chest constricts so fast my lungs seize.

Then a warm, steady hand lands on my shoulder.

Taran.

"It's fine," he says. "It's only Emlyn and Reid."

I blink, my breath coming back as I focus on his face. Those mesmerizing green eyes. *Why did I expect gray?*

He brushes his fingers along my cheek, and a cozy heat blooms within me, washing the lingering panic away. He kisses my forehead, then hauls himself out of bed and stumbles from the room.

There's a thunk, then Emlyn's voice carries through the small home.

"What happened here?"

"We were ambushed," Taran replies.

I begrudgingly push myself up, rubbing my eyes—that was not enough sleep. But it's a new day; an important one, with much to do. Starting with figuring out who attacked us.

"How could anyone sneak up on you?" Emlyn asks, disbelief tinting his words.

"I knew about the one inside, but the others were hiding among the pilgrims." A pause. "It was nearly dawn by the time we got everything cleaned up."

"Where's Ellie?" Reid asks.

"I'm here," I call, then drag myself to the other room. I yawn as I balance against the doorway.

Emlyn rubs at one of the bloodstains with the toe of his boot, Reid leaning against the dirt wall next to him, glamoured to look fae. "You'll wanna put a rug here."

Taran stands before him. His expression hardens, then he responds in the Tongue.

Emlyn goes stiff. "Why would you ask that?"

"It's a yes or no," Taran says firmly.

"It doesn't feel like it is."

"What's going on?" I ask, a sinking feeling in my stomach. I step further into the room, but Taran holds his palm up, halting me.

He glares at Reid. "You incanted, didn't you?"

The color drains from Reid's face. He slowly nods. "I did."

My throat tightens with a flash of that fae's hand, pressing me into the wall, heart racing as if it were the end. Reid didn't want to incant any more than I did.

"What happened?" I ask.

Before Reid can answer, Taran slams his fist into the wall, and my body jolts.

"I told you not to do that," he shouts. "I forbade it. You agreed."

Emlyn's between them in a blink. "We were outnumbered." He braces his hands against Taran's shoulders. "Ystyrian soldiers. There was no chance of winning."

"It doesn't matter."

"You'd rather we were dead?"

"I felt it!" Taran yells. "Like I was burning from the inside. I thought I was going to die."

My hand covers my mouth. *When he collapsed yesterday...*

But that didn't happen when I incanted back home. Is it because we're in the faelands now?

His bond with the Land is stronger than anyone else's.

"He already paid for it," Emlyn says, his knuckles turning white as he holds Taran back.

"He needs to go."

"He already paid for it!"

Taran's voice crashes against my eardrums as he pushes toward Reid. "Get out—"

Emlyn lunges forward, pressing his hand over Taran's mouth, cutting off his words. The door swings as Reid's body jerks, pulling him outside.

My breath catches. That was a willbending.

This is bad. I have to do something, but my limbs won't move. Lungs won't breathe. Taran's face—veins bulging, twisting with fury—he shouldn't be able to look so terrifying.

He shoves Emlyn away. Forcing myself to move, I rush over, taking his hand before he opens his mouth again.

"Taran, stop! You need to calm down." I turn his face to me. "Listen to them, please. Let them explain."

His eyes meet mine. After a sharp inhale, his shoulders sag. He nods. I glance at Emlyn, who scowls at us before throwing the door open. Reid's standing there, looking confused.

Emlyn pulls him back inside, slamming the door behind him. Reid's gaze lands on Taran and me, and his expression hardens.

I meet his eyes, chin up. I made my choice, and I won't let him make me feel guilty about it. If anything, he should appreciate that I've managed to calm things down.

But uncertainty peeks through.

"Explain," Taran says, his voice tight.

Reid straightens, still clutching Emlyn's hand. "We would've died. We were losing."

"I gave my permission," Emlyn cuts in. "I'm just as guilty." He pauses as Taran closes his eyes. "He apologized. The Land did something to him. She hurt him to heal Herself."

"He's already paid for it," I whisper. "Let it go. Please." He has to see... we already have one traitor; he can't afford to push away Reid and Emlyn.

Taran's eyes open, exhaustion bleeding out of them. He drops my hand and sinks to the ground, his back sliding down the wall.

I join him, resting my hand on his leg, hoping to show my support. He rubs his thumb against my fingers, and my heartbeat slowly returns to normal. This side of Taran... it's frightening, if I'm being honest with myself. But I know it's not who he is, deep down.

"It was Ystyr?" he asks, not looking at anyone.

Emlyn's eyes narrow. "Yes."

Taran sighs. "The ones here weren't. They can't be connected."

"It wasn't—I upset someone, and they reported me. They didn't know I was coming here."

"Then we still have a traitor to deal with." Taran rubs his face with his free hand. "Someone we invited, who had time to send people. We need to figure out who. Today."

I'm working out the most tactful way to voice my suspicions when Reid speaks up.

"Can't you just ask everyone?" he asks, drawing stares from both Taran and Emlyn. "What? They can't lie, right?"

"I'd like to pretend you didn't just say that," Emlyn mumbles, flipping his hair away from his neck as he turns to Reid. "Have you paid any attention to what I've been telling you?"

"He literally just did the same thing to you, and it worked."

That is true.

Emlyn leans against the wall. "That was a rare instance of me trapping myself thanks to a promise I made you. Most of the time it won't work."

"Why not?"

"Ellie, ask me if I've fucked Reid. Let's see how long it takes you to get a real answer."

My mouth goes slack, my eyes shooting back and forth between the two of them.

"Uh..."

Reid's face burns bright red. "We don't need to do that."

"No, we don't." Taran shifts his position, letting go of my hand.

Emlyn turns back to him. "Just bend them."

Taran stiffens. "I'm not doing that."

"It's the best option."

"No."

Emlyn crosses his arms. "Forgive me, Your Highness, but I'm beginning to question your judgment on what's best." His gaze flicks to me.

"What are you implying?" *Why are him and Reid so incessant on making me feel like I've done something wrong?*

Emlyn purses his lips, as if debating the risk of answering.

Taran shoots him a glare, then pushes to his feet. "Just keep watch for the others." He peeks out the window.

"There are other things we should discuss," Emlyn says, peeling away from the wall. "Information about the wedding—"

"We can talk about it when everyone's here." Taran lowers the curtain and retreats to the bedroom, ending the conversation.

Emlyn curses under his breath, then storms out, the door slamming behind him.

I thought they were supposed to be friends.

I take a deep breath and look up at Reid, who's rubbing his brow again.

"So... has he?" I ask, hoping to lighten the mood. "Like, you and him?"

Reid's hand freezes, then lowers. "Seems like I should ask you that." He gestures toward the bedroom.

My mouth tightens. "That's not your business."

"You're right. It's not." He yanks the door open and follows Emlyn. I flinch as it slams shut.

A groan rumbles out of me as I get to my feet. That couldn't have gone worse. How did everything turn into such a mess?

I can fix this. Taran listened to me—I helped. And I can do it again.

I find him lying face down across the bed in the dark. "Are you sleeping?" I ask.

"No." The mattress muffles his voice.

"Do you want to talk?"

"No."

My stomach twisting, I sit next to his head. "Perhaps you should. You don't have to carry it all by yourself." I brush an unsure finger through his hair, hoping it's the right choice.

Nothing.

I try again. "Why are you so against willbending? You've done it to me. Twice."

Taran grunts, then rolls to his side. "And I hated doing it, but it was the only way. I can't beat you in a fight when you're incanting and I'm outside of my realm."

Despite everything, part of me swells with pride. That's not my life anymore, but I can be just as useful by helping him work through this.

"You could've tried talking."

"There wasn't time. In either scenario."

"We don't have much time now, either." I tentatively take his hand.

Under the dim light, his eyes focus on our hands as he caresses my fingers.

"My father never loved my mother. He told me so, after she tried to kill me for being better at willbending than her. She made him love her. Every day."

Time slows, the implication snapping into focus. My thoughts spiral, horror consuming me the deeper they delve.

"That's..."

I swallow, my throat suddenly dry. 'Awful' isn't enough. Nothing is. I squeeze his hand, hoping to convey what words can't.

His fingers twitch in my grasp. "He knew what she was doing. She wasn't strong enough to keep his mind twisted at all times, but it was enough that he couldn't escape. Until I bent her and he broke free." The corner of his mouth curls. "I don't even remember what I said. It was just a tantrum."

He pushes himself up, sitting on the bed beside me, half turned away.

"I'm not like my mother, Ellie. I *can* keep someone trapped. Force anyone to do anything, with no fear they'd ever break free. Unless I let them. Could even kill them with a single word." He sighs. "So I *can't* just bend people. Not if there's any other option. I don't want to be like her."

There it is. The burden he's been carrying, all by himself. Holding back such power instead of using it to solve all his problems... No wonder he snapped.

I shift closer, wrapping my arms around him as I rest my head on the back of his shoulder. He relaxes, letting me share his weight.

"I understand. We'll find another way."

"So what's the plan?" Aerona crosses her arms as she leans against the wall of earth in the main room.

She and Taran's other allies gathered over the past few bells, and everyone is finally here. I'm standing by the window, next to Reid and Emlyn, behind most of the others. Taran wanted to bring as little attention to us humans as possible.

Which gives me the opportunity to watch everyone for anything suspicious. So far, they've all noticed the spots of blood on the floor, but their reactions have been mostly what you'd expect—curiosity, avoidance, and disgust.

Taran stands in front of the fireplace, all eyes on him. "The plan is to kill the queen. That's the only way I get my throne. Exiling her again would be foolish."

"That's a tall order," Merfyn says, glancing around. His nerves don't seem to have improved since Ashbourne. "I'm certain you're the only one who could do it."

Taran shakes his head. "Anyone could if she didn't sense them coming."

"She's the queen. Her land-sense is too strong," says one of the others—a large man dressed in wool clothes simpler than the rest.

He must be Cadoc, the shepherd.

"The Land is still bound to me," Taran replies. "Her awareness isn't much better than any of yours right now. But the longer we wait, the stronger she'll become. The wedding is our best chance."

"About that." Emlyn stops peeking out the window, glancing at Taran. "She's expecting you to show up—she's doubled the guard. You won't be able to sneak in. Not without bending or killing someone."

"I want to avoid as many casualties as possible," Taran says. "She would sacrifice everyone there to save herself. I won't let that happen."

"So, bending, then."

If Reid weren't between us, I would've smacked Emlyn's shoulder. He's supposed to be Taran's friend. He shouldn't be giving him such a hard time about this.

Taran shoots him a hard look. "*I* can't sneak in at all. While her land-sense is weaker, she *can* sense me. By the time we reach the castle, she'll know exactly where I am."

"You're making this whole endeavor sound rather hopeless," Merfyn says, tugging his shirt straight.

"It's not. Her attention will be focused entirely on me, and that will provide an opening for the rest of you to steal something of great importance to her. When she realizes what's happened, she'll split her focus. That's when we strike."

"What are we taking?" a red-haired fae asks, whose name I can't possibly guess.

Taran's eyes meet mine.

"Prince Caeo."

The weight of his gaze makes my stomach tighten. *Why is he staring at me?*

Aerona pushes off the wall. "You want us to kidnap the groom from his own wedding?"

"It won't be a kidnapping. He'll come willingly if they do it." He tilts his head toward Reid and me.

Reid tenses, glancing at Emlyn, then nods.

My fingers clench, still seeking the comfort of my lost button. Everyone's looking at me, but I don't know why. "What am I doing?"

Taran's eyes soften. "What I brought you here for, Ellie."

Oh. The curse.

I nod. I don't know what I'm agreeing to, but if this is how I'm supposed to help, I'll do it. For Taran, and to save my people—my father—from war.

A weight sinks down my throat. Even if this all goes well, I may never see my parents again. At least they'll be safe.

But only if we figure out who the traitor is.

Taran turns to Aerona. "The queen's probably given him my chambers. You can get them there."

How does she know the way to his room? Could they have been a couple at some point? That could explain her coldness, but would that make her more or less likely to betray him?

"Once you've taken him, the queen will turn her attention to you," he continues. "You'll need backup."

"I'll do it," Emlyn volunteers.

"No. You know the palace better than anyone other than me. I need you on the queen."

Emlyn's face pales. All at once, the other fae become very interested in the floor and ceiling.

My breath catches. *He wants Emlyn to kill the queen?* Somehow, the fact that we're plotting the assassination of a powerful willbender didn't seem real until now.

"Tell me that isn't your plan," Emlyn says, his body so stiff it almost trembles.

Taran nods. "I'll be moving in as well. I *want* to do this myself, but if you get an opening, I need you to take it."

For a tense moment, no one breathes as they stare at each other.

Then Emlyn walks out, the door swinging behind him. Taran's gaze drops to the floor, and he rubs his brow with his hand.

"Will he be coming back?" Merfyn asks.

Taran sighs. "He'll do it. He just needs a moment."

Reid narrows his eyes at Taran, then goes after Emlyn.

"We should discuss how everyone's getting in and where to be," Taran says after the door slams shut.

I sidle over to the window as Taran continues speaking, carefully pulling the curtain back. Emlyn sits outside, several feet from the door, his back to me. Reid wraps his arm around him, whispering words I can't make out. I drop the curtain as Emlyn leans into Reid—I shouldn't be intruding on this.

As I look over at Taran, plotting with the other fae, a knot in my chest twists. *Is Emlyn right? Should we be questioning Taran's judgment?*

I have no way of knowing if this is a good plan—I don't have enough information. But the other fae... While their heads nod in agreement, their taut faces betray their uncertainty. And Emlyn clearly believes his role is tantamount to suicide.

Not to mention, we still haven't found our betrayer.

If I were a traitor, what would I be doing now?

Silently taking everything in? Shaping the plan into something riskier? Or simply waiting until everyone leaves to stab Taran through the heart?

My gaze wanders to the weapons the fae wear. They're all armed, some with bows, but they almost all bear those bone knives of varying lengths. Merfyn's even has intricate carvings on it, like the sword Taran showed me.

Those look familiar...

Taking a careful step toward the fae man, I feign inspecting a scuff on my boots, kneeling to get the blade on his hip closer to eye level.

The pattern on his blade's identical to the tattoo on my dead attacker's neck.

"Those are some interesting carvings on your blade," I say, interrupting the conversation. Everyone looks at me. "Are they supposed to be antlers?"

Merfyn's brow furrows, and he looks around before answering. "Yes. My family has a long history as stewards of the crown's deer."

I meet Taran's eyes. "I've seen this pattern before—tattooed on the man who tried to kill me."

Merfyn's hand flies to his blade, but Taran's faster. He slams Merfyn against the wall, pressing a knife to his throat. My flash of triumph flickers out, swallowed by the icy darkness of dread.

"You betrayed me?" Taran growls.

Merfyn's face contorts in a mix of anger and fear. "You're a fool, Taran. You don't have what it takes to be King—you won't even use your power to keep your kingdom."

Taran's fingers clench around his blade, and he digs his elbow into Merfyn's chest as he pushes him into the wall. Fury ignites in his eyes, twisting his features until he looks like a stranger, sending a chill down my spine. I start to reach for him, to beg him to calm down, but it's too late.

"You will forget you were ever here. That you ever knew me." Taran's willbending hits heavy as Merfyn's face goes slack, eyes blank. "You will return to your home, and you will never speak another word to anyone for the rest of your miserable life."

Merfyn drops to the floor in a heap, then lifts his head, blinking in confusion. His mouth forms empty shapes, not a sound coming out.

"Get him out of here." Taran's voice echoes as he turns away. Everyone scrambles to do it.

Chapter 37

Caeo

Less than three days until my wedding. I don't have it in me to attend supper this evening, so I attempt to get food delivered, like Owena did last night. My throat twists, making me gag as I lie to the servant about feeling sick. But it works in my favor for once, and he returns shortly with a bowl of some kind of brothy soup and fruit. Not the most filling of meals, but worth avoiding my mother for.

I spend a large chunk of time lying in bed while whispering to myself, attempting to willbend, but it's kind of pointless. My words don't *feel* any different, and there's no way of knowing if I've succeeded—I can't willbend myself, and my mother would undoubtedly hear about it if I practiced on other people. Not that I want to do that to anyone, anyway.

The next morning, sunlight smacks me awake through the open window. I drag myself over, eyeing the gardens below. If I can't convince Owena to help me, it seems like the best I'll be able to do is figure out where the largest gap between guards is and hope I can scale the wall faster than they can run.

My stomach tightens. I'm pretty sure I know where that is, but I'll only have one shot. If I fail... I don't want to think about what'll happen. So I need to be sure. Find the best possible spot, and the best possible moment.

Once dressed, I open the door...

... and almost immediately shut it.

Mother's right there. She isn't even mid-knock. Just standing there, waiting for me.

I feign surprise. But not really, because I *am* surprised, my heart thundering against my ribs. I feign *pleasant* surprise.

"What are you doing here?"

"I was told you seemed ill." She looks me up and down. "It would appear you're feeling better this morning."

Could I knock her out faster than she can say 'stop'? I've never punched anyone before, but it seems like she'd see it coming. And if she does, that's it. I'll have blown all other chances.

So I choose my words carefully. "I have more energy now."

Her crimson lips press into a tight smile. "You'll need it—we have a busy day. Come." Her command echoes in my head, and my feet yank me after her as she turns down the hall.

Fuck.

Now that I'm aware of what's happening, it's so obvious. I tense my legs, fighting the forward pull of my feet, but it only makes me stumble. She eyes me, eyebrow raised, as I attempt a nonchalant recovery.

I can't let her see me fighting it.

"Where are we going?" I ask.

"Breakfast. Then rehearsal."

"Will Owena be there?" Seems like an appropriate question for someone who's smitten.

Mother's face tightens. "At the rehearsal, yes. But this will be your last meal with your mother as an unwed man. I am not sharing it."

My brow furrows. "But the wedding's not for two more days..."

"After the rehearsal, the two of you will share a small meal before beginning a fast in isolation until the ceremony."

"What?" I swallow back the panic that threatens to spill out. "Why wasn't I told about this before?"

"There was no reason to. Does this somehow interfere with your plans?"

A chill crawls down my spine. "What plans?"

Mother tilts her head as one side of her mouth curls up.

"What plans indeed?"

THE REHEARSAL TAKES PLACE on some hill in the gardens. It isn't only for the wedding, but my coronation as well—which doesn't involve Owena, so she stands aside with her father, the embodiment of patience and poise, while I go through all the motions of the ceremony.

It was too much to hope that they'd just put a crown on my head and be done with it. I have to say a bunch of words in a language I've never heard before, and no one bothers to tell me what they mean. I could be promising to dance in the blood of my firstborn for all I know. That's starting to seem like a fae thing.

But I lock away my frustration and pretend I'm excited to bind myself to the Land. Mother doesn't seem convinced, and I'm willing to bet the Land can tell, too. If the ground's gonna be sentient, it's good She's not stupid, but I'm starting to regret not putting more effort into understanding Her before now.

On the bright side, if She takes offense at my insincerity and smites me down, at least I won't be getting married. Now that I've rehearsed the ceremony, a swift death would be a blessing.

Fae weddings are *fucked up*.

Everything was going fine until Owena and I were standing

under the wedding arch. There were so many rules about how we got there—when each of us took a step, when we could look at one another—but that's typical for all the fae propriety I've learned in the last week. Then they pulled out the obsidian blade we're supposed to slice one another's arms open with before drinking each other's blood and I almost passed out.

Seriously. What the actual fuck? I don't even want to drink Ellie's blood, let alone Owena's. That shit's supposed to stay inside your body, not oozing down someone's throat. A shudder runs through me just thinking about it.

Owena doesn't seem fazed at all.

"I'm not doing that," I say to everyone present, then turn to her. "Why didn't you tell me that was a thing?"

Owena's brow crinkles in what seems to be genuine confusion. "Is that not part of mortal weddings?"

"No! It most definitely is not!" I'm minutely relieved this wasn't an intentional deception on her part, but my horror overshadows that completely. I choke back bile as my stomach lurches halfway up my throat.

My veins freeze over as my mother's expression hardens. "You will do your part in the ceremony, and you will do it with a smile on your face."

This time, her words don't echo, my mind and body remaining my own, but I recognize the threat.

If I don't, she'll force me to.

And of course, the blood-sucking will be followed by my public ravishment of Owena for everyone to see.

I'm gonna need something a lot stronger than speckled long leaf.

As it is, I would've bolted the second rehearsal ended if it weren't for my mother's willbending. She knows it, too—I can see it in her eyes. She knows I'm aware of what she's doing to me, and an icy dread grips my insides, making it almost impossible to breathe.

How did I ever find comfort in this person? Sure, she had awful moments... most of them were, in fact, but between them were spots of genuine affection. Wiping my tears, tucking me in, laughing at my jokes. And it's not like I wasn't a disappointing kid, never listening and being terrible at everything.

Was it all an act? Did she ever actually love me?

Thinking back, I can't remember a single time she ever said she did. The realization should probably devastate me, except I'm too busy dealing with the absolute panic of how the fuck am I getting out of here?

"I can't do this!" I hiss at Owena the second the dining room door closes for our private meal. No servants, but my mother stands just outside. "I have to get out of here!"

"She can hear us," Owena warns.

My fingers clench as I try to stop from exploding.

Owena nods at the food. "You should eat."

"I'm not hungry."

"We don't get another meal for two days. To ensure we're hungry enough to stomach one another's blood."

Fuuuuuuuck.

"How do you just accept this?" I snatch some roasted vegetables and smash them onto my plate.

"I have little choice. My father has just as tight a hold on me as your mother does on you."

But their gift is curses, not willbending. That must mean...

"Has he—"

Owena shoves her fingers against my lips and makes an exaggerated glance toward the door.

Right. She's listening.

Which effectively makes our time together useless. I channel my anger into my chewing, scarfing down as much food as possible because I do *not* want to end up hungry for blood.

"Don't do anything stupid." That's the last thing Owena says to me. She didn't need to warn me—I don't get a chance. It's impossible to take a single step without my mother's direction as she leads me and a dozen escorts to the site of my isolation. In this instance, that means sitting in a forest clearing that would normally be stunning, with the sun's golden light filtering through the majestic pines, forming rays in the fog. Except I'm surrounded by heavily armed guards.

'For my protection.' Right. Then why are half of them staring at me instead of looking for intruders? I can't even take a shit without them watching.

I'm supposed to be 'communing with the Land,' whatever that means; no one's bothered explaining it and the guards ignore all my questions. So I sit on the grass and ask if She can sprout some mushrooms for me. The good kind.

She doesn't. I blame the language barrier.

Or maybe She's just ignoring me. Why should She give a damn when my own mother doesn't? I rip out a chunk of grass, scattering the blades in the wind, just to spite Her.

The rest of the afternoon crawls by, with me lying on my back, staring at the sky while dread digs through my guts. I try to breathe away my spiraling thoughts, but they keep creeping back, like an army of ants swarming an apple core.

Blood, dripping down Owena's arm. Me, licking it up. Its awful, metallic taste as I swallow it down, turning her into a part of me I never wanted. Either I do it on my own, or my mother forces me. And then...

My guards say nothing, just standing there, eerily still, spears sharp. Until they shift, grass crunching beneath their feet, the tiny sound startling me into thinking someone's approaching. Sparking hope that they'll take me far away from here. Tell me it's all a mistake.

But no one's coming.

My stomach growls just as the sun sets. *Maybe I should sleep?* Seems pointless. Asleep or awake, what's the difference? Hunger pangs won't bother me while unconscious, but sleeping will only bring me closer to the bloody fuck-fest that is my wedding.

That's my fate, whether I want it or not. Something to do with my life, at least. A bloody fucking purpose.

It fits. That's all I was ever good for.

My ribs constrict around my lungs, pushing out needling hiccups. Like my body's mocking me for ever thinking I could be happy here. That escape was possible.

There's no air. Only shallow, agonizing breaths.

Laughter somehow falls out, broken and wrong. *Is it mine? Why am I laughing? This isn't funny.*

It gushes, the spurts and waves crushing my lungs. Tears pour from my eyes. I curl into a spasming ball, every muscle jerking, pain stabbing my gut.

My brain squeezes, forcing a thought.

Is this how I lose my mind?

No. I can't. Not now.

I claw at the grass, the sharp blades pricking my skin as I grasp for it, but it slips through my trembling fingers. This should be easy—are my hands not working?

The trees spin around me, shadows creeping. Twisting, looming. I need something, *anything*, to latch onto before I tumble into the abyss. It's right there, beckoning me. A wide, empty darkness. I don't want to fall, but I can't pull myself away, every kick in my lungs edging my closer.

I had a reason once, didn't I? To keep going? What was it?

Ellie.

Her face forms in my mind. A warm smile, eyes full of love. The lavender scent of her hair. I hug myself tightly, imagining the soft heat of her arms around me.

Her voice when she told me she loved me.

The laughter breaks, sputtering until it peters out. The tears remain, but I can breathe.

I have to push through. For Ellie. I have no idea how, but there has to be a way.

Footsteps rustle through grass. Someone kneels beside me, cold fingers touching my forehead.

"Sleep." My mother's voice echoes through what remains.

Everything fades to darkness.

IT'S DAYTIME WHEN I WAKE. I'm back in my bed. My fae bed, specifically. I haven't woken up from this nightmare. I never thought I'd miss my shitty mattress from home.

My head's pounding. Mouth's a desert. A cup of water sits on the bedside table—I gulp it down so fast I almost throw it back up. The relief is short-lived, nowhere near enough.

It's hard to say how long I slept—if it'd been an entire day, I'd probably be hungrier? I don't know; I've never fasted before. But that would make my wedding tomorrow.

So I have one day to get out of here. And I'm no longer surrounded by armed guards.

Feeling slightly light-headed, I change into clean clothes—something not covered in dirt and grass stains. I open the door...

...and there stands an armed guard.

Of course.

He stiffens as I step forward, tilting his spear toward me.

I pause, my irritation brewing. "Can I go?"

There's a nervous bend to his brow as he clears his throat. "You're still under isolation. My orders are to keep you here."

Nope, no way—I'm getting out, even if I have to punch him in the face.

Or... I can try to willbend him. It's not like I have anything to lose at this point. So I gather up all the fraying threads of my resolve, pressing them into my words.

"Let me pass," I demand, stepping forward.

His spear moves closer, his face hardening. "I can't. Queen's orders."

Fuck. It didn't work.

A searing anger spikes in my chest—all my pent-up rage, ready to burst. My voice warbles with unbridled frustration. "As your prince, I order you to let me pass."

The guard's eyes widen, then he steps aside.

I guess I should've tried that earlier?

I high-tail it out of there before he changes his mind.

A couple servants pass by as I charge down the stairs. They don't stop me, but they'll probably tell someone, so I pick up my pace. When I reach the second level, I poke my head out a window, checking the distance to the ground.

I've climbed taller trees. Not to mention the clock tower—ignoring the time I fell and almost died—and this is just a really big tree, right?

The odds are better than meeting more guards, at least.

After a few precarious minutes struggling with nonexistent footholds, my feet land on the ground. With a rush of hope, I disappear into the gardens, keeping as straight a path as possible away from the castle.

The stone wall's ahead. Looks scalable. Probably.

But there's also a gate. With two guards.

I spin on my heel, following the garden path in another direction, only to find four soldiers barreling toward me.

Shit.

I bolt for the wall.

The round stones make for easy handholds. I throw myself up it.

One of the guards grabs my leg, yanking me down. My hands slip, but I hold tight, the rough stones scraping my palms.

I kick my leg wildly as panic's icy grip sends my heart hammering. The frantic rhythm echoes through my voice.

"Let go of me!"

A second later, my foot's free.

I clamber over the wall.

I hit the ground running.

I'm doing it. I have no idea where I'm going, but I'm out. I'm free. I'm—

A wrathful voice booms from behind me, echoing through my veins.

"STOP."

My feet halt so fast I tumble forward, as if they landed in the strongest glue ever made. I push myself up, only to realize I haven't moved a muscle.

I can't move. At all.

I'm not even breathing.

"You will not speak." Mother's voice echoes above me, bloated with rage. "You can move, but you will not resist."

I gasp for air as two guards hoist me up by my shoulders. My body's jelly. My shouts empty. They drag me back to my room, step by crushing step, my mother leading the way. Pain hits me as I'm dropped to the floor.

I've never seen an expression so wrathful, Mother's green eyes blazing with fury. Her voice echoes with her inflamed willbending.

"Stay there. Silently."

She moves to one of the windows. Placing her hand on the wall, the wood *stretches* until the window ceases to exist.

My heart hammers in my chest.

She does the same thing to the next window. And the next, and the next, until none remain.

Light leaks in through the open door. She turns toward it.

No! The word doesn't come out, just air scraping my throat.

I can't speak. I frantically shove myself off the floor but don't move an inch.

The last thing I see is her face, twisted in rage, before she slams the door. The cracks of light at its edges melt away, plunging me into total darkness.

I struggle for I don't know how long until I finally fall forward. Scrambling to the spot where the door once existed, I feel it with my hands. It's completely smooth.

There's no way out.

Chapter 38

Reid

"It'll look good on you," Emlyn insists, holding a deep green stretch of fabric up to me.

We stand inside a small clothing shop, with tunics of mostly earth tones and undyed wool hanging from pegs and racks sticking off the walls and ceilings. Only a few other customers wander among the wares.

"That can't possibly qualify as a shirt," I say, eyeing the tangle of straps in his hand.

"I never said it did."

"Then I'm not wearing it."

"It's a wedding. What'd you expect to wear?"

"Clothes?" I lean close to his ear, not that it matters with fae hearing. I just have to trust no one cares what I'm saying. "Please tell me fae wear clothes to weddings."

"Of course we do." Emlyn smacks my shoulder with the back of his hand. "It *is* clothing. Just not a shirt."

"Then what is it?"

"Um..." He holds it up, tilting his head as he squints at it. "I'm not honestly sure. But I'd like to see you in it."

I hold back the smile that wants to break my face. "Another time. Right now, I just need something clean."

We arrived in the capital two days after the meeting in White Spring. Just me, Emlyn, Taran, and Ellie, traveling like a flock of chickens and ducks. Everyone else went their separate ways, aiming to meet again at the wedding when Taran's plan goes into motion.

If it had been up to me, Emlyn and I would've traveled separately, too. I can't stand being around Ellie and Taran. They aren't overly affectionate, but the way they look at one another... Ugh. But Emlyn insisted on sticking with them, at least during the day, so I tried to ignore the anger that ravaged my insides every time I laid eyes on them.

It was Ellie's choice. And Taran's—he, at least, should've known better. Emlyn barely defended him, only mumbling how Taran's cracks are finally showing.

But it wasn't my fault.

At least we camped separately. I could have spent that time fretting over the horrible things my absence was providing them the opportunity to do to one another, but Emlyn didn't give those thoughts a chance to enter my mind.

Our nights have been good. So good. My experience with such things is rather limited since there weren't that many men with similar tastes in Haven, but damn—Emlyn knows what he's doing. He spent our first night together exploring every inch of my body with his fingers, lips, and teeth trailing along my skin, testing everything from tender caresses to spine-tingling bites until he knew more about what I liked than I ever did. The whole thing culminated with him gasping my name as I came inside him, after he somehow kept me at the edge of bursting for almost half a fucking bell.

I was a moron for hesitating as long as I did. And as mind-blowing as the sex is, it's got nothing on waking up to his beautiful eyes, still wrapped around each other. He hasn't been out of arm's reach for more than a few minutes during these last few days.

But now the journey's over. One of Taran's allies, a shepherd named Cadoc, moved his entire clan to the outskirts of the capital, and we've joined them. Tomorrow's the wedding, and according to the plan, Ellie and I will attend as Aerona's guests—Ellie as her servant, and me as her escort. Hence the shopping for clothing.

Emlyn came along, claiming it would be good to get some more information. The key word being 'would.' He's made it quite clear he has no intention of working today.

"This *is* clean," he says, still waving the questionable garment. "It's clearly never been worn."

"Because no one could figure out how." An olive-green tunic catches my eye. "How about this?" I hold it up to myself.

Emlyn shrugs. "I suppose it'll work. Try it on." He nods toward the curtain hanging in the corner, then follows as I head over.

"Stop. You're staying here."

"What? Why?"

"Because I'm trying on a shirt, not putting on a show."

I know exactly what'll happen if he follows me back there. While I'm already going hard at the thought, that curtain wouldn't offer even an illusion of privacy. Emlyn doesn't care, but despite his efforts to immerse me in fae culture, I'm not into public copulation just yet.

"Whatever. But I'm getting you this." He brandishes the swash of green threateningly.

Five minutes later, we join the crowd of people swarming Aedallan, the capital city of Aedys, for the royal wedding. Emlyn explained that this is a big event, since fae royals rarely wed; they can live for thousands of years, and typically only marry once in their lifetime. People have traveled from all over to attend, and while the official celebration isn't until tomorrow afternoon, the common folk have been celebrating all week.

It's not as nerve-wracking as the last time I walked through a fae village, despite the teeming crowds. Everyone's so focused on getting from one celebration to the next, with bodies constantly bumping into one another, that no one spares me a second glance. Emlyn holds my hand as he leads the way, weaving through the party-seekers.

Aedallan's built in a forest of ginormous pine trees. The late afternoon sun peeks through their canopy, the shadows lit by those same floating orbs I spotted in the woods after I incanted. As best I can tell, the places for public gatherings—shops, gardens, taverns, and the like—make up the lower levels of the city.

Emlyn swerves off the main path toward a walled-off area with a line of people waiting outside. Pulling me to the front of the queue, he whispers something to the woman at the entrance. She purses her lips, then nods. Emlyn kisses her cheek and guides me past.

I glance back, but she's already out of sight. "Who was that?"

He lets go of my hand and squeezes my shoulders. "An old fling. You don't need to worry about it."

Even if he could lie, I'd believe him. I see how he looks at me. Though it does leave me wondering just how many people he's slept with.

We stand at the start of a twisting path through a maze-like garden, full of people mingling. Most gather at what looks like barrels—if someone smoothly molded them out of solid chunks of wood—standing about a dozen feet apart along the trail.

Emlyn grabs two wooden cups from someone passing by and hands one to me. "We're gonna find a drink we both like or get completely sloshed trying."

My stomach flips over as I recall the fig wine. "Are you sure you wouldn't rather do something else?" I focus intently on his eyes.

"Literally anything else?" After what I've learned the last two nights with him, that's not an offer I make lightly.

"Hmm…" He trails his finger along my jawline, sending a tingle through me. "Tempting, but no. This is important to me."

I'm not proud of the whine in my voice. "Why?"

"I want to have something we can share."

The sentiment would normally have butterflies flitting through my stomach, but I'm too busy gagging at the gooey liquid oozing down the sides of the nearby revelers' cups. Emlyn pulls me toward the first barrel.

I yank him back. "No, we're skipping that one. Nothing thick. Not unless you're into me spewing my guts all over you."

Emlyn clicks his tongue. "Can't say I am."

The next drink at least has a normal consistency for potable fluids, its bright red liquid filling my cup as I dip it into the barrel. As I bring it to my mouth, my stomach heaves in warning at its sickly sweet scent. I glance at Emlyn, who watches me as he takes a sip, then swallow the whole thing in one gulp. Its sweetness smacks my tastebuds, but at least it passed through my mouth fast enough that its taste doesn't linger.

"Thoughts?" Emlyn asks.

"Definitely not that one." I try to wash out what remains with my spit.

"That's unfortunate. But I appreciate the enthusiasm." He leans in to kiss me, slipping his tongue between my lips.

"Nope!" I yelp, pushing him off me. "You do not get to kiss me tasting like that!"

"Fine," he sighs. "Let's find something bitter, then."

The sun has basically given up and set by the time we do. I've never considered myself a lightweight, but I'm well into tipsy before we find something I can take more than one swig of. Emlyn's brow crinkles as he drinks it, but he claims it's bearable. He disappears briefly to ask what it is, and when he returns, we refill our cups and find somewhere out of the way to sit. Laughter fills the air as we watch the crowd continue hunting for their new favorites.

It's no different from the festivals back home. I wish everyone could see this—that despite being splintered and warring for millennia, fae and humans are basically the same. We all just want to enjoy life with our loved ones.

I wrap my arm around Emlyn, then nod at the glowing orbs dancing above our heads. "What are these things, anyway?"

"Wisps." He snuggles into my chest, careful to avoid my injury. "Spirits of the dead."

"Those are dead fae?" My skin prickles, and I squeeze Emlyn tighter. The ones in the forest... they were my doing.

"Their spirits," he continues. "The spark of the Land within us that gets released when we die."

His voice lacks its usual flair. It's... solemn. He's had moments like this ever since White Spring. Not wanting to linger in such darkness, I change the subject.

"You never told me how you became a spy."

Emlyn's fingers fidget against the side of his cup. "My mom was Taran's governess. When the queen was exiled, we moved into the palace. I think I was two at the time? Younger than I can remember, at least. We grew up together."

Just like Caeo and me. "So he's basically your brother?"

Emlyn snorts. "Definitely not—a prince can't be brother to a commoner. Once he outgrew the need for a governess, they gave Ma a nice home in the countryside. I could've gone with her, but I stayed. Taran didn't need a playmate anymore, so I needed a new purpose. He trusted me more than anyone, so being his spy... It made sense."

"And now?" My mind drifts back to Emlyn's reaction to his latest task. "Does it still make sense?"

He lets out a heavy sigh. "It used to be thrilling. Balancing between what I was willing to do and what was necessary. But now..." His eyes pierce through the darkness as they meet mine. "I find I don't really want to take those risks anymore."

Because of me? I offer him my hand, and he takes it, focusing his fiddling on my fingers.

Despite the relaxing heat from all the alcohol, my chest coils tight. I should be eager for tomorrow to come—it's the whole reason I came here. Instead...

"What if we don't show up tomorrow?"

A burst of laughter sounds nearby as Emlyn's eyes flick to mine. "You'd abandon Caeo like that?"

I shrug, as my suggestion was trivial. "Ellie will be there. He'll remember her, and he'll go." Just like Taran originally planned. He never wanted me here anyway.

Emlyn raises an eyebrow. "Do you really trust that'll work out?"

Ancients' sappy hollows... "No," I sigh. Ellie just can't stop making my life difficult.

"Then I'm going." He squeezes my hand. "I don't like Taran's plan, but if he insists on doing this without willbending, I don't have a better one."

"Why won't he? Why put everyone at risk?"

"He's terrified of becoming his mother. Which is probably good, since I can't think of anything more horrifying than Taran willbending as casually as she does. He'll probably end up doing it anyway once everything goes to shit, so hopefully that happens before his plan gets us killed."

"And then what?" My pulse quickens as I peer into Emlyn's eyes. "What will happen after tomorrow?"

"Assuming everything goes right, and we both survive?" He takes a sip of his drink.

"It will. We will."

A wry smile curls his lips. "To be mortal and able to say such things." He exhales. "*If* I were to imagine that's true, and Taran gets his throne, I would hope that he'd let you stay. As you, not hiding behind a glamour all the time." He tugs at my ear. "If you wanted to, that is."

To spend the rest of my life here, among his people? A warm glow swells in my chest as I bring his hand to my lips, kissing his fingers. "I'd like that."

Emlyn smiles again, but it doesn't light his face like it normally does. My heart dims at the realization that threatens to burn a hole in it.

He doesn't think it will happen. He really believes he could die tomorrow, but he's doing it anyway. For Taran. For Caeo.

For me.

I'm seconds away from begging him to forget about it, to get the fuck out of here with me. But before a response forms, he pats my thigh. "I want to show you something."

He leads me out of the bustling part of the city, through the dwindling crowds. We ascend to the canopy by way of wooden walkways spiraling up the trunks, connecting neighboring trees.

The dwellings up here look like warbly eggs—some tall and narrow, others short and squat—impaled by gigantic pines. At the base of each, wood planks starburst out from the trunk, creating a precarious walkway. Emlyn stops at a smaller one and leads me inside.

"This is my home," he announces.

We're in the only spot with space to stand upright, which makes up about half of the lowest level. The tree itself takes up much of the area, its trunk marked with ladder-like grooves to make climbing easier. The second level, at my eyeline, seems dedicated to storage.

"It's... cramped."

My mom's house—which was always uncomfortably tight for her, me, and whoever she was currently leeching off—seems like a palace in comparison.

Emlyn scratches the back of his neck. "I don't spend much time here. Just the rare nights where I'm in town and haven't found someone's bed to warm."

I crouch, peeking around the tree trunk. A small, knotty table sits low on the floor, and shelves full of clay cups, bowls, and jars splatter the walls, the spaces between embedded with an impressive collection of rocks and shells.

The more I take everything in, the cozier it feels, but we'd have to find someplace bigger if I'm sticking around.

When I stick around.

"Where's your bed?"

Emlyn points up, then starts climbing.

When he reaches the highest level, he pulls himself onto the edge of its floor, sitting with his legs hanging over the side as he looks down at me. I follow him up, and he scoots over to make space for me. The ceiling's mere inches above my head.

Plush fur rugs cover the floor, basically turning the entire level into a bed—one that curves around the tree trunk in a way that makes sleeping in any position other than on your side impossible.

"It's a good thing I like to cuddle."

Emlyn chuckles before leaning into me. "It wouldn't work. There's nowhere near enough room for me to do all the things I want to do to you. It'd be torture." He takes a deep breath. "But I'd like it if you'd be willing to stay here tonight, despite that."

I slip my arm around him, a warm glow infusing my veins as I rest my head against his soft hair. "Of course. Whatever you want."

"Whatever *I* want? Now I feel obligated to make you regret saying that."

"You can try," I whisper, pulling him in for a kiss.

As he lays me down, his lips claiming mine, nothing else matters—the cramped space, what tomorrow will bring—nothing.

Only him.

Come morning, I regret nothing.

Chapter 39

Ellie

Amid the pops and crackles of the fire, smoke swirls, softening the scent of manure and lanolin that's been clinging to my skin ever since we arrived at Cadoc's camp earlier today. Beside me, the warm light dances across Taran's face, casting sharp shadows across his features.

An emptiness hung between us after we left White Spring, with him hardly saying a word the rest of that day. Once Emlyn and Reid disappeared to camp by themselves, I tried to get him to open up about what had happened—how he'd bent Merfyn—but he refused. All I could do was be there for him, curled up in his arms, until his gentle caresses lulled me to sleep.

The next day saw an improvement in his mood—I'd even say he was back to normal, except I don't know what normal is now. It *feels* like we've progressed to being in a relationship, but something's off. An uncertainty, cutting deep in my chest. Having never courted anyone before, I have nothing to compare things to, but I assumed that after our first kiss, there'd be more of that. While he's kissed my temples a few times, his every touch has felt hollow, and there's been no attempt at anything more passionate.

And he looks away whenever I meet his eyes. As if my gaze burns him, or he fears what I'll see.

I'm trying my best not to take it personally. His burdens must be weighing on him more than ever, with the betrayal, willbending, and facing his mother tomorrow. Whatever comfort I can give him will have to be enough; we can sort out the details of our relationship *after* I help take his kingdom back from his mother.

Not that I know *how* I'm doing that, and the ambiguity's been eating me alive.

He's tried to clarify my role, but the most we can get me to remember is that Reid knows what I'm supposed to do, so as long as I go to Taran's old room with him and Aerona, I'll understand when the time is right. Our host, Cadoc, will only be attending the wedding as a guest—he can't risk his people with anything more. But six of them, whose loyalty he vouches for, have volunteered to back us up as we make our escape.

Taran refuses to entertain the possibility of total defeat. It's nerve-wracking, if I'm honest with myself. Emlyn's doubts about Taran's judgment keep creeping up from the darkest corners of my mind.

"Ellie? Did you get that?"

The fire flares with an exceptionally loud crack as I turn my attention back to Taran. He's been reviewing the plan, but my curse has made it nearly impossible to stay focused on the discussion. It's as if it and the wedding are intrinsically linked, but all my attempts to figure out why feel like I'm wandering through a heavy haze.

At my confused expression, Taran gives up, announcing we'll review everything with Reid and Aerona in the morning. Then he disappears into the tent Cadoc offered him for the night.

After a few minutes, I follow.

I poke my head inside the tanned leather tent. Taran sits with one of his bone knives, sharpening it against a stone. A couple candles provide a dim glow, lighting the wool blankets laid out as a makeshift bed.

"Taran?"

"Hmm?" He doesn't look up.

I swallow, considering the best way to show my support. "I'm sorry if I was frustrating you."

"It's not your fault."

I sit next to him, resting my hand on his—the one holding the blade—and he pauses his strokes. "Everything will be alright."

Taran exhales. "I wish I could believe that. You may be the only one who does. But if it does go well…" He still hasn't looked at me, but rubs my hand with his thumb.

I cup his cheek in my palm, tilting his face to mine. Sorrow darkens the green in his eyes.

"It will," I say.

He lifts his hand, running hesitant fingers through my hair. Heat swells at his touch, my heart pounding with every breath between us.

His lips part, a breath away, and the world narrows to that single point of gravity pulling us together. He closes his eyes and tugs me close, pressing against me with a sweet, sealing kiss. Gentle at first, until he catches my lower lip with his teeth. I push into him, his taste stirring a hunger deep within me. But it's not enough; there's an emptiness still unsatisfied.

I climb into his lap, gliding my fingers through his soft hair as I kiss him again, breathing in his pine scent. His tongue slips into my mouth, and teasing fingers grip my back, building an ache in my core that yearns for his touch. He slides his hands further down as our kiss deepens, my body burning with desire as they wrap around my backside.

Taran's hard length presses between my thighs, and a coil of raw anticipation tightens within me. Yearning for him. Ready for him.

But my heart stutters. I pull back, freeing my lips from his.

Something's... wrong. He's the first man I've kissed, yet I'm eager to give him everything, as if my body knows exactly what to do, despite being in the middle of a busy camp that stinks of sheep. I always envisioned my first time being more romantic.

Do I fear tomorrow that much?

I bury the thought. My core's throbbing with impatience, my lips hungry for his.

His eyes slip open.

GREEN.

I throw myself off him, my heart slamming against my chest. Taran scrambles up, his feet tangling in the blanket.

"I shouldn't have done that," he says.

My mouth opens, but nothing comes out. "I-I..."

What just happened?

I shake my head. "No, it's fine," I say, then push myself up. "It's... I can do this."

Taran runs his hand through his hair, shifting it away from his eyes. "No. Not tonight." He swallows. "Tomorrow—after. If you still want to. But not tonight."

He's gone before my mind even catches up to what he said, leaving me alone and more confused than ever.

I STEP INTO THE MORNING AIR with renewed determination to make sure Taran succeeds today; it's unclear what will happen after, but we'll have prevented a war, and then maybe I can figure out how to convince everyone at home that incanting's wrong. But for now, I'm wearing the servant's garb Aerona gave me: a simple, hooded dress of undyed wool, with a long belt that matches the dark blue tunic Aerona wears—the perfect shade against her auburn curls.

She breaks away from her conversation with Taran and Emlyn, giving me a sharp nod. Then she directs me to sit near the remains of last night's fire so she can braid my hair.

"Why? Won't I have the hood up?" The dress, while warmer than the shirt and pants I've been wearing, won't stop the icy morning dew from soaking through. I don't need to spend half the day with a wet backside.

"It's tradition, and people will notice. Now, sit." Her rosy eyes bore into me until I comply.

With a grumble, I bunch my skirt beneath me and sit on the damp ground. "Will they really let you wander through the palace with us?" I wince as she tugs my hair much harder than necessary. Clearly, she has a problem with me.

"My father was one of the queen's most trusted generals. There's little reason to suspect any treachery from me."

"Even though you're friends with Taran?" I ask, watching him weave around some sheep on his way to Cadoc.

"We had a very public breakup four years ago and have hardly been seen together since. No one would consider us friends."

I knew it. I bite back the smile trying to break free. The thought of Taran going from someone as beautiful as her to me? It's petty, but it makes me feel good about myself.

She tucks my hair into my hood as she pulls it over my head, then she leans close to my ear. "A word of advice: keep your distance. You can't fix him."

"Fix him?" *Does everyone really think Taran's that broken?*

But she's already gone, joining Emlyn, who's busy fussing with the bandages on Reid's chest. She hugs him like an old friend, laughing at something he says while Reid blushes. She lifts her palm to Reid, and Emlyn directs him to press his against hers. It must be the fae equivalent of a handshake.

A pang of jealousy cuts through me. All I wanted from attending the Academy was to find people I could truly connect with—people who understood me. Several months later, I'm trapped in the faelands with no way of knowing if I'll ever make it home, Reid wants nothing to do with me, and Taran...

There he is, still talking to Cadoc. I have no idea where he slept, and he's avoided me all morning—I waited for ages inside the tent for him to do my glamour, only for Emlyn to pop in and do it himself, grumbling all the while. As irritating as that was, my heart twists at the thought that Taran may very well go off to face his mother without saying a word to me.

Determined not to let that happen, I march toward him.

"Can we talk?" I say, interrupting Cadoc. He stares at me, and my cheeks burn with regret at my zealousness.

Meanwhile, Taran averts his gaze as he rubs the back of his neck. Cadoc excuses himself, my anxiety swelling as he departs.

"Sorry," I mumble. "I should've waited."

Taran finally looks at me. Despite the healthy glow to his skin, his eyelids sink, as if weighed down. "What did you need?"

"I..." Now that I'm here, everything I could say floods my mind, and my nerves spike with indecision—words of anger, fear—but I settle on honesty. "I didn't want last night to be our last moment together. In case... things don't go well today."

Taran's face softens, his shoulders slumping. "I'm sorry, Ellie. I didn't consider that."

With tentative hands, I wrap my arms around him, tightening the embrace when he doesn't pull away. I rest my face against his chest, melting into him.

"Tell me you'll be safe," I whisper, the steady drum of his heart beating in time with mine.

His fingers caress my back, his voice thick. "I can't."

The rhythm hitches as I fight the sting behind my eyes. He folds his arms around me, and I lift my gaze to his.

"You will be." It's a promise. To him, and myself.

Taran searches my eyes. I could stare into his forever, surrendering to their inner light; this won't be the last time I wander their depths. It doesn't matter if I don't understand the plan. I'll do whatever it takes to make sure he survives.

It takes almost an entire bell, I estimate, to get to the palace. From Cadoc's camp in the plains, we head west into a forest of impossibly large pines. I've heard of trees like this in the northern parts of Landore, but I've never seen them. I doubt they're anywhere near as majestic, with some as wide as I am tall.

They must be ancient.

Aerona talks us through our expected behavior as we travel. If she and Reid walk side-by-side, I'm to follow three paces behind, my footsteps matching hers. If Reid leaves for any reason, I'm to stay two paces behind her right shoulder. At all times, I'm to keep my head down and avoid eye contact.

At least my instructions are straightforward. Evidently, the fae are quite particular about etiquette, and she quickly runs Reid through when to offer his arm, how to carry himself, and how he basically needs to wait for her to act before he does anything himself. Color creeps up his neck as he grows more flustered with every mistake, until Aerona ultimately tells him to hold her arm a specific way the entire time.

The first fae we encounter are obviously visitors here for the wedding. We pass their tents of hide and fur and join them along the path to the city proper, our pace slowing as the crowd thickens the closer we come to the capital.

Aerona's jaw tenses. "Most of these people won't even attend the wedding itself."

"Then why are they here?" I ask.

"The parties," Reid replies.

My eyebrows tilt up. *Is that what he and Emlyn were up to yesterday?*

"You can't speak to one another unless we're alone," Aerona hisses.

Right. I'm the lowly servant. I shut my mouth and follow silently behind them.

By Fortune's favor, we don't have to travel through all of Aedallan. A gasp escapes me when we spot the palace—it resembles a massive tree, several stories tall, woven from dozens of towering pines. Moss-covered stone walls surround it, though the grounds must be quite expansive based on their distance from the structure.

While many fae linger nearby, most of the crowd continues on. Aerona whispers to Reid, then nods at a gate in the stone walls.

He stiffens as he leads us toward it. The guards interrupt our approach, with one of them asking Aerona her name. The other meets my eyes, and I quickly lower my gaze to the ground. Hopefully he assumes I'm so awestruck that I forgot my place.

Aerona introduces herself, with Reid as her companion—carefully worded using some random name she thought up—and a moment later she's walking again. I follow, keeping my eyes on her feet.

"We're later than we should've been," Aerona whispers to Reid. "Try to wander casually toward the main entrance."

"Where's that?" he asks.

"That way."

Of course, I don't know which way she directed him. I'm only watching their feet.

This is it—the day I'm finally supposed to be useful.

My eyes sting as frustration threatens to boil over into bitter tears. Taran will be here soon, risking his life to prevent a war while I stare at well-worn boots. How is this something Reid and Aerona can't handle themselves?

Aerona comes to a stop, so I halt three paces behind her. She says some words, then moves again. After a few steps, the light dims, and the ground transitions from trodden grass to polished wood floors.

It seems we have successfully infiltrated the palace 'for a tour.'

Aerona continues speaking to Reid, describing the entryway like a proper guide. I follow her boots up a staircase of wood planks that curves along the wall of the room.

We've reached the third floor when a thunderous rumble draws my attention upward—a group of at least six guards descending from the level above. Aerona gracefully steps out of their way, pulling Reid with her, and I stumble to follow. Most march past without a glance, but the last one stops to address Aerona.

"What are you doing here?" he demands, his voice sharp.

"I'm giving my companion a tour. I have permission."

"That permission has been rescinded. Return to the reception."

Aerona glances down the stairs toward the others. They've already disappeared from our sight.

I startle as she smashes the remaining guard in the face with an upward thrust from her palm. He collapses onto the floor.

Reid takes a step back. "Shit."

"Take his weapons." Aerona pulls a bone knife from the guard's belt and hands it to Reid, who quickly searches the man for any others, shoving all he finds into his own belt. I move closer to help, but he brushes me aside.

"We can't leave him here," Aerona says. "Grab him and follow me."

"Move," Reid says. I press against the wall as he hooks his arms around the man's shoulders, then drags him down the hall behind Aerona.

They don't need me at all. Maybe they never did.

But if the guards are mobilizing, that can only mean one thing: Taran's here. And if everyone's doubts about the plan are valid, if he can't push past his fears of willbending... he could actually be in danger. Whatever it is we're doing won't matter if he dies.

And that pull, the one that told me that by helping Taran, I'd find what I'm missing—it's stronger than ever.

Aerona and Reid don't even notice when I follow the guards back down the stairs.

Chapter 40

Caeo

I lie in bed, staring at the ceiling. At least there's light now.

I have no idea how long I spent in the suffocating darkness; there's nothing but my empty stomach and sticky, withering tongue to track the passage of time. My blind fumbling discovered someone had left me a small cup of water, and I thankfully found it without spilling much. It was a struggle to pace myself—I could've devoured it all in seconds. As it is, I've long since sipped the last drops.

A grim acceptance has settled within me, like a boulder crushing my spleen. I don't see a way out, short of offing myself. But I don't want to die. I want to live. To see Ellie's face again, hear her laugh, and hold her in my arms.

I can make it through one heart-stomping, soul-crushing, horror of a day if it means there's still hope to reunite with her, can't I? I just have to leave my body somehow.

My wedding must be drawing near. Mother returned recently with servants to dress me, bringing lanterns so they could see. She willbent me the instant the door unsealed, to be silent and not resist. I complied fully, not even lifting my limbs while the servants struggled to change my clothes. She eventually revised her command, compelling me to dress myself, furs and all.

Once I finished, I collapsed back onto the bed, and she ordered me not to move until someone came to retrieve me. Probably so I don't burn the place down, since they left the lanterns. Or she couldn't be bothered to seal the door again; I can't tell if she did since I can't move my head. But going by how long it took me to move the last time she told me not to, it won't be long now.

You can do this. Just pretend you're somewhere else. Anywhere else.

As if that was that easy.

My stomach churns. Not from hunger, but dread. If it weren't empty, I'd probably throw up all over myself. Except I can't move, so I'd just drown in my own vomit.

Visions plague me, battering every corner of my mind. What my mother will force me to do to Owena. Taking control of my body. Yanking it around like a puppet on strings. No choice, no way to defend myself. Flesh against flesh, no way to stop. Twisting what's supposed to be an act of love into a violation.

Just like she did to my father, but now it's me. Her own son. And all I can do is wait for it to happen.

My eyes burn, too dried out for tears.

Every beat of my heart slams against my ribs as my mind flails, desperate to escape. I can't keep the thoughts away. They strike relentlessly, a barrage that never ceases, shattering against my skin—rigid, immovable. I want to scream, but I can't get enough air. A sharp pain carves through me like a knife.

An angry voice rumbles at the edge of my senses, but it slips by, a raindrop next to the hurricane raging within. There's a thud, and then a shift in the light.

Reid's face in front of mine.

At least it looks like Reid, if Reid were fae.

Am I hallucinating now?

"Caeo?" His voice is rushed—panicked—but definitely his. He

shakes my shoulder.

"We need to hurry," a woman's voice says from the door.

"Reid?" I squint, focusing on him through the dots in my vision. "You're fae, too?" *What are the odds?*

"It's a glamour. Come on, we need to go." He pulls my arm, and apparently my body can finally move.

Until someone comes to retrieve me. Ha. Suck on that, Mother.

The world spins, succumbing to darkness as I get to my feet and fall straight to the floor.

"Caeo? What's wrong?" Reid catches me, helping me back up.

"He's weak. He won't have eaten anything for two days." The fae woman, with umber skin and reddish-brown hair, stands at the door. She peeks into the hallway, the unconscious body of a guard at her feet.

"Any water?" I ask, my mouth sticking.

"Not on me, no." Reid moves his face in front of mine. "We're getting you out of here."

"I've never been so happy to see you. I could kiss you right now."

"Please don't."

"We need to go," the fae woman warns again.

Reid steps toward her, tugging my arm. My head's dizzy with questions, but they can wait until after we've gotten the fuck out of here. All except one.

"Is Ellie alright?"

Reid freezes, then slowly turns back to me.

"You remember?"

"It was a curse," I explain, then swallow, trying to moisten the cracks in my tongue. My stomach's pushing up my throat. "From my mother. Someone... broke it for me. Please tell me she's alright."

His face tightens, lips pressing together, and what remains of my insides twists into a knot.

"She's here, Caeo, but she still doesn't remember you."

"She's here?" Everything fades away as my heart breaks free, leaping and pulling my feet along with it. "Then we need to get Owena! She can break the curse!"

"Who?"

"You want us to kidnap the Ystyrian princess?" the woman asks, her voice sharp.

Reid groans as he rubs his brow. "Ancients' shriveled acorns."

My steps falter. That was weird, even for Reid.

Not important. "I'm sure she'll come willingly." Energy fires through me as I rush to the door.

"Caeo, wait!"

But I can't.

Ellie's here, and all that stands between us is getting out of here with Owena. I stumble down the hall, blood pounding in my veins, leaving Reid and his fae friend no choice but to follow.

DESPITE MY SURGE OF ENERGY, I'm gasping for air and on the verge of passing out by the time we reach Owena's room. So I don't feel emasculated at all when Reid's friend, who he called Aerona, takes out the two fae guarding the door as I lean against a nearby wall, trying not to be swallowed by dizziness.

My vision blurs as I stumble to Owena's door, just as the last guard thuds against the floor.

Reid grabs my arm, steadying me. "Are you alright?"

"Nope, definitely not. But I will be once we get out of here." My throat constricts. *That's ominous.* Unfortunately, there's no time to figure out what part of that was a lie, so I swallow the jagged lump as I poke my head into Owena's room.

She's right in front of me, waiting.

The horrors my mind conceived in the darkness flash before me, more substantial than ever now that they include Owena's actual attire. It's barely a dress, with only some strips of fabric hanging from her waist in a vaguely skirt-like fashion. Otherwise, the pinkish-peach and pale-green ensemble leaves absolutely nothing to the imagination. She must be freezing. In fact, I know she is, because I can see how hard her nipples are.

My pulse hammers in my skull. I can't fucking breathe.

"Oh, fuck."

I crumble to the ground.

"Not quite the reaction a bride hopes for from her betrothed," Owena says.

"Caeo!" Reid kneels beside me, hoisting me to my feet. "Shit. What's wrong with you?"

"He's had a rough week," Owena offers. "Who are you?"

I manage to lift my head. We've used up a lot of time coming here. I need to pull it together before anyone comes looking for me. "That's Reid." I cough. "He's my friend. He brought Ellie. You have to come and break her curse."

Owena's face softens. She turns away, moving closer to the fireplace. "I'd like to help, but—"

Aerona steps into the room. "We don't have time for this. Is she coming or not?"

I'm trembling, despite the fireplace warming my skin as I grab Owena's hand. "Please. I'll find some way to make it up to you, but I need your help."

Her dark eyes meet mine, and something flickers in those inky wells. That wistfulness I've glimpsed before, and something else. She lets out a slow breath, then nods, her lips pressed tight.

"Alright. I'll go."

"Thank you." Relief washes over me that it didn't take much

persuasion, and I throw my arms around her in a hug.

Owena startles back. Then it hits me that she's practically naked and I fling myself off her.

"Here, wear this." My hands shake as I pull my ridiculous fur coat off and wrap her up in it. It's far too big, but at least she'll be warmer. And clothed.

Now we just need to get out of here. My nerves claw under my skin, screeching to break free.

Aerona leads us back the way we came, the hallways unnervingly empty, before directing us down the staircase to the throne room. On the landing, she pops open a door that I never noticed before—its edges blend smoothly into the surrounding wood. A narrower set of stairs descends into a section of the castle I hadn't realized existed.

"Servants' passage," she whispers. "If we meet anyone, they'll likely turn and run. We shouldn't have to give chase."

Reid helps me down the stairs after the first time I stumble, with Owena taking slow, cautious steps ahead of us. My pulse thunders with the scrapes of our feet against wood—are we going fast enough? Will my mother catch up? What'll happen if she does?

We bottom out in a dark hallway, its dirt walls lit by the faint glow of wisps flickering overhead. We pass several archways leading into small rooms, and the mouthwatering scent of cooked meats mocks us from one—a kitchen. Owena and I pause as my stomach cries out, begging for food.

"Sorry, Cay, we have to hurry."

Reid and Aerona yank us forward, forcing us to continue. It's a struggle to lift my feet. All the energy I had is gone, completely depleted. Owena's slightly better; she probably had access to water, at least.

We stumble along, and at one point, a servant pokes his head into the hall before skittering away toward the throne room. My blood rushes in a panic, but my feet can't keep up.

And then we're outside, hit by the brisk evening air. We burst into a grove of towering pines, their heavy shadows swallowing us whole. A group of fae surrounds us, but based on Aerona and Reid's reactions, they must be friendly. Aerona says something to them, but the words blur together. Darkness creeps in at the edges of my vision.

One of the fae picks Owena up in his arms and carries her away. I stumble after her, colliding with Reid. Someone grabs my arm and pulls it behind their neck, and with a whoosh, I'm off my feet and hanging over their shoulders.

I bounce and sway uncomfortably with their steps, but I've gone completely limp at this point. I drift off, unable to keep myself awake any longer.

But I'm free.

Chapter 41

Ellie

I don't follow the guards back to the first floor of the palace; that doesn't seem like the best idea. As far as I know, that only leads to the throne room and the gardens where the wedding will be held, where Taran's likely hiding in the crowd.

It'll be easier to spot him from higher up, so I creep along the second-floor hall—if you can call it that. It's reminiscent of an interior balcony, occasionally enclosed on both sides, forming a tunnel of smooth wood. I step lightly, praying fae ears won't hear me padding along the floor. Assuming they don't sense me first.

Maybe this was a bad idea.

My heart races as I peek out each window, nothing more than oblong holes in the wall, until I dead-end at another stairway. The only options are up, down, or back the way I came.

I choose up.

Even if they sense me, that'll at least be one more thing distracting them from Taran. Which can still help, right? Though they'll probably kill me on sight.

Don't think about that. Be brave.

The first window on this level looks over a different side of the palace than the previous ones. Fewer fae meander through the garden, three stories below. A group of six guards marches by, armed with bone-tipped spears and bows hanging from their backs. If I make it to the next window, I'll likely see where they're headed.

I jump as a hand grabs my arm, tearing me away from the window, around the corner, and into a small alcove.

"What are you doing here?" Emlyn hisses, his face inches from mine. "Where's Reid?"

"He's fine—he's with Aerona," I whisper, pulling my arm free of his grasp. "They didn't need my help."

Emlyn groans. "So you decided to risk your life, and the entire plan, by wandering around by yourself?"

I open my mouth, but he immediately covers it with his hand and goes still, as if listening to something. *Like Taran does when he's using his land sense.*

Without warning, his lips crash into mine as my back hits the wall.

WHAT?

My hands flail against him as his tongue invades my mouth. He presses his knee between my legs, pinning me in place. My squealing protests come out muffled against his lips.

A gruff voice breaks through my confusion. "What are you doing here?"

Emlyn's body heat disappears in an instant, with him slipping between me and the guard to lean casually against the wall. "You know how weddings are. Can't let the happy couple have all the fun."

It's nearly impossible to breathe with my heart pounding in my throat.

The guard frowns, stepping aside. "Get out of here. Now."

"Going." Emlyn pulls me toward the stairs. Once we're out of earshot, he wipes his mouth on his sleeve. "You better hope we don't run into any more guards."

I wrest my hand free; how dare he act like *I'm* the problem. "That was entirely your choice!"

"How else am I supposed to justify being where we shouldn't?"

"Aerona was knocking them out."

"She would." Emlyn pivots back in the direction we came from, heading up the stairs.

When I don't immediately follow, he lets out a frustrated exhale as he looks up at the ceiling.

"Look—if I leave you by yourself, you're gonna end up captured or killed, and Taran will never forgive me. So you're gonna do exactly what I tell you, understand?"

His condescension keeps my ire simmering, but it'd be foolish to leave. Sticking with Emlyn is my best chance of helping Taran. So I swallow my resentment and nod. "I understand."

Emlyn pulls his bow off his back, quickly stringing it with practiced fingers. "You really don't. Odds are, we'll die, but he can't yell at me if I'm dead. Now be quiet."

He really doubts the plan that much? A knot cinches within me— but this is why I need to help. If Taran really can't do this on his own, then I need to be there for him.

I follow Emlyn back to the level we met on, then we continue to the fourth floor. At the first window we come to, Emlyn peeks out, his back pressed against the tree trunk that serves as the adjoining wall.

"Shit."

He leans a little further, looking down. I poke my head out, following his gaze.

We've moved further along the castle, to where a wooden balcony curves around the outer walls, two levels beneath us. At least a dozen guards fill the space, armed with bows, nocked and ready to let fly. Just where the balcony turns out of view, I glimpse a woman in a regal gown, the deep green of the surrounding pine trees, with a crown of golden antlers resting upon her raven hair.

The queen.

Power radiates from her, sizzling the air as if resisting her command would burn you alive. The same dread that filled me when Taran bent Merfyn wraps its tendrils around my chest. The realization that I'm powerless against her.

Especially without incanting.

I tear my gaze away, scanning in the direction that holds her attention. There's not a wedding guest in sight, but a small hill rises above the surrounding gardens. A wooden arch decorated with hanging flowers stands atop, and Taran hides behind one of its posts.

My heart drops with a sickening lurch.

"They have him," I whisper. "If he moves, they'll let loose."

"Ancients, Taran," Emlyn mutters. "Just bend them already."

But he won't. I know it in my heart. That fear of becoming his mother, combined with facing her for the first time in twenty years...

He's frozen, just as I'd feared.

After a quick look around, Emlyn's grip on his bow tightens, then he steps onto the window ledge.

I shoot a glance at the queen—she hasn't noticed us. "What are you doing?"

"I need a better shot." He carefully moves onto the branch growing beside the window. It sways beneath him, but he slowly inches his way forward.

"This can't be safe," I mutter to myself, then climb onto the ledge, gripping it tight as I brace myself. Close enough to help if I need to, but not enough to be in his way. Not that I'll be able to do much outside of giving him a hand or incanting.

My stomach clenches. Hopefully it doesn't come to that.

Emlyn shifts, sliding his arrow into place. The branch lurches beneath his weight, dipping sharply. My pulse spikes—

A loud crack pierces the air. Emlyn's bow drops from his grasp. I shoot my hand out as he reaches toward me.

The world stills as the queen turns. Her fiery green eyes lock onto us, seething with fury.

Something stirs within me. Recognition, that I have something to protect. Something she wants to hurt, and I need to do everything in my power to stop her.

But she speaks before I can.

"Fall."

Despite the distance, her voice echoes through my mind.

I'm no longer on the window ledge. She told us to fall, and we did.

The ground rushes toward me. Brilliant green veiled in shadow, about to be splattered with the deep, dull red of my blood.

On instinct, I incant a gust of wind, the familiar power flowing through me.

It catches Emlyn first, slowing our descent. We still hit hard, pain shooting through me as I collide with the dark earth.

My relief fractures as screams fill the air. Emlyn convulses next to me, but it's not just him.

It's everyone.

The guards, the queen...

And Taran. He falls from his hiding spot, crumpling as a roar of pure agony rips from his throat.

My blood turns to ice. Rage burns through my fingertips, rising from the black scar stretching across the terrain beneath me.

I did that.

I swallow the horror surging within me—I can't afford to dwell on it. Emlyn and Taran are down, as are the queen and her guards. But some are already pulling themselves up.

My heart pounds frantically as I grab Emlyn's arm, hauling him after me. "We need to move."

He groans, then staggers to his feet.

It's taking too long.

The guards, struggling to stand, nock their arrows and aim their bows at us. Emlyn shoves me ahead as we sprint toward the hill. To Taran.

Halfway there, Emlyn cries out, a sharp sound that rips through my soul. He stumbles forward, an arrowhead protruding near his right shoulder, just below the collarbone.

"Emlyn!"

"Fuck," he gasps, his face tight.

I rush back, slinging his left arm over my shoulder as I brace him with my back. My knees buckle beneath his weight, every step an excruciating strain as I hoist him up the hill. The way is clear—the guards must be keeping their distance to avoid Taran's willbending. Agonized grunts punctuate our every move, grating against my ears. Emlyn tumbles off me as my legs finally give out.

But Taran's there, catching him before he crashes to the ground. There's a drip of relief before I take in his face. He doesn't look any better than Emlyn, both their faces contorted in pain.

Except for the blood. Deep crimson seeps through Emlyn's shirt. He's already turning pale. But it's just his shoulder—he should be fine if we can get him to safety. Treat the wound.

I chance a look back at the castle.

The queen stands with all her guards. Their arrows are ready, her face triumphant.

We have no cover. Nothing to protect us.

Her words don't reach my ears but they don't need to; it's clear what she said.

Arrows whistle through the air. More than a dozen, flying straight at us.

In half a heartbeat, a wall of ice, larger than any I've summoned before, crystallizes in front of me.

The arrows freeze in place.

A soul-shattering scream tears out of Taran's throat. Pitch-blackness surges out from the ice, charring the terrain. Grass crumbles to dust.

"Taran!" I scramble toward him.

His body spasms, veins bulging against his skin like thick cords as his muscles contract.

"I'm sorry, I'm so sorry! I didn't mean to hurt you!" I take his clenched fist in my hands, his knuckles white from the strain.

He doesn't respond.

I scan the area. The ice blocks everyone from view. No guards have shown up yet, but no doubt they're on their way. If the queen gets any closer, the ice won't save us from her voice—hopefully she'll be delayed by having a reaction similar to Taran's. *But for how long?*

I tug his arm, tears streaming down my face. "You need to get up. I can't do this on my own."

A blaze crackles in Taran's eyes as he inhales sharply, teeth clenched. He wrests his arm free of my grip, clawing his way to Emlyn, every movement strained.

Emlyn lies coiled on his side, a tremor running through him as he gasps for air. Where the arrow protrudes from his chest, thick, crimson blood saturates his clothes.

No, no, no, no, no. It was just his shoulder. He should be fine.

I rush to his side. His skin's cold to the touch.

Taran gets underneath him, pushing to his feet with Emlyn's

weight on his shoulder. Somehow, the two of them stagger down the far side of the hill. I hover nearby, terrified that trying to help will only make things worse.

Emlyn cries out when we reach the bottom. He's almost entirely supported by Taran, and we're miles from camp.

"I'm not gonna make it." His words slur through lips tinged blue.

The force of Taran's willbending plows into me. "Yes, you will. You will not die tonight."

Emlyn grimaces, his face racked with pain. His steps steady, accepting some of his weight, but every move draws an agonized whimper. My heart splinters, thoughts turning to Reid. Hopefully he and Aerona succeeded, and he'll forgive me for leaving. That branch cracking, Taran freezing—it hurts too much to imagine what would've happened if I'd stayed.

But Taran... He bends everyone we come across—frightened servant, confused guest, emboldened guard—demanding they leave. They do, scurrying away in the opposite direction, faster than their legs can carry them.

No one risks following.

Chapter 42

Caeo

My eyelids crack open as my swaying limbs settle. I hit the ground painfully, grunting as I look up at the fae who's been carrying me.

"Sorry," he mumbles, rubbing his shoulder.

Yeah right.

I sit up, blinking as my head spins. It's darker than I remember, the surrounding pine trees blocking what little sunlight remains.

"This is only a quick break," Aerona says, somewhere behind me. "Be ready to move."

The fae who carried me sits on the forest floor and pulls out a waterskin. Another fae sets Owena down much more gently than I was deposited, then joins the other in his water break. The rest set themselves up in a perimeter to keep watch.

My throat cracks as I watch them drink, mouth thick with sticky saliva.

"Here." Reid's hand appears in front of my face, holding a waterskin. I tear it from his grasp, pouring the cold, blissful liquid down my throat.

It washes through me like a flood in the desert, too fast. Not enough. My stomach clenches as it hits. I hold the next mouthful, letting it soak into my parched tongue. Letting its cool relief sink in.

I'm about to chug the rest of it when Reid's hand lands on my shoulder.

"Pace yourself, man." He sets a basket of food on the ground in front of me; Aerona approaches Owena with a similar one, further off. "They're really hoping you'll be able to walk on your own once you've eaten." He sits down next to me.

I'm already scarfing down an exceptionally pungent hunk of cheese, its overpowering flavor not enough to keep me from devouring it in under a minute. It's not blood. That's all that matters.

Concern flickers in Reid's eyes as he watches me eat. "We should talk. Catch up."

I swallow a mash of fruit I didn't quite chew properly. "I don't want to talk about it." My gaze snags on the basket, tracking its weave as it goes round and round, in and out.

It takes another gulp to force the painful lump down. Reid hands me a waterskin, and I dump its contents into my mouth. Half drips along my chin, but at least it washes down the food. My head's still spinning, but not as much as before.

"Slow down, or you'll make yourself sick," Reid warns.

I take a deep breath, then try to take smaller bites. It's difficult. I glance at Reid.

"Your face is back to normal."

He frowns, touching his cheek with his fingers. "It must be the distance," he mutters, then focuses on me. "It was only temporary, unlike you, blue-eyes. I guess that charm you wore made them gray?"

It takes my brain a few seconds to make sense of what he said.

Right. 'My father's charm.'

I frown. "How do you know about that?"

Reid sighs. "Remember Emmrich?"

I nod as I take another swig from the waterskin.

"He's fae—his real name's Emlyn. He told me about it."

Reid launches into a story about how Emlyn was spying on my mother for my half-brother, Prince Taran. When the two of us disappeared, Taran abducted Ellie because he thought he'd need her to convince me to turn against my mother. Reid persuaded Emlyn to talk, and they followed.

I blink. "Huh."

Reid tilts his head, eyeing me. "That's all you have to say?"

Well, my brain is saying a million things, mostly half-formed thoughts about Ellie being kidnapped, Reid going through all that for me, and how I don't really need any more motivation to put as much distance as physically possible between myself and my mother, but its connection to my mouth is apparently broken.

I sink my teeth into an apple and focus on chewing.

"So... what's with you and the princess?" Reid asks after a minute.

"I really don't want to talk about it."

I spot Owena sitting nearby, eating a handful of berries. If things had gone the way Mother planned, I could be at my wedding right now, with her pressed beneath me, my body thrusting, out of my control...

"But are you together?"

I blink, dropping the apple as I whirl toward Reid.

"No! She's just a friend! A good friend. As much a prisoner as I was—I wouldn't have survived without her. But she knows I love Ellie. There's nothing else there!"

"Alright, I get it!" Reid raises his hands defensively. "Ancients. Calm down."

He hands me another hunk of cheese. I stare at it in my palm while counting my breaths, trying to bury the images that keep slithering back up.

One... two... three...

I don't know if this sizzling beneath my skin means I'm about to burst, or shatter into nothing.

Reid groans, dropping his head into his hands. His fingers rake down his skin until they tent over his mouth and nose. A few seconds later, he peeks up at me. "No offense, but you seem a slight breeze away from having a complete mental breakdown."

A sharp laugh huffs out of me. "Oh, we're well past that."

Reid inhales, hesitating. "Maybe we shouldn't meet up with the others just yet."

My stomach heaves, almost spewing everything I just ate.

"But Ellie! You said she was here. I have to get to her." My heart hammers against my ribs. *He can't really mean that, can he? Why would he even suggest that?*

Reid pinches the bridge of his nose and closes his eyes. "I don't actually know where she is at the moment."

"WHAT?" I'm on my feet.

Nope. Too fast.

Reid jumps up and catches me, guiding me down as the forest tilts sideways.

"Calm down, man." He moves in front of my face. "She was with us, but she doesn't remember you. She couldn't understand the plan. I think she went to help Taran."

"You *think*?" My head spins with every pound in my ears. My body spasms with the need to do something—*anything*—but Reid's grip on me tightens, holding me still.

"She was there one second and gone the next. But we needed to get to you, so there wasn't time to go after her."

I shove his hands off me. "So you just left her?"

"You weren't really in the best condition to drag around

searching for her," Reid snaps. "And by that point, the guards were actively hunting us."

"We have to go back." My heart leaps in the direction it assumes the castle is, but my mind blares in warning. My stomach sides with my brain. I gag, barely keeping my insides down.

Hands settle on my shoulder. "We can't go back now, Caeo," Owena says, and I flinch at her touch. "We have to hope she found a way out. If she didn't, we can make a plan to retrieve her—but you're in no shape to do anything useful right now."

I'm on the verge of exploding. "She could be captured—killed!" The other fae are all staring now.

Owena kneels in front of me, her dark eyes absorbing my panic. "It would be foolish of your mother to kill her."

My breath wheezes out as I cover my face with my hands, pressing my eyes shut.

She's right—my mother knows Ellie. If she wants me back, the worst thing she could do is kill her. Ellie'd be much more valuable as bait.

The drumming of my heart slowly settles. I swallow, then nod. Owena squeezes my shoulder before letting go.

I glance up, forcing myself to look at her. "Did you get enough to eat?"

Her lips twitch with a wistful smile. "I don't think I could eat anymore without feeling ill."

"Will you be able to walk?"

Bright laughter bubbles out of her. "Oh, they only want you to walk. They have no qualms about carrying me." She shifts the fur coat I'd given her to reveal her cleavage, in case I didn't catch her meaning.

"Lucky you," I mutter, looking away.

"Time to move," Aerona calls, clapping her hands together.

As Owena returns to the two fae who carried us before, Reid grabs my arm, hauling me up. After a wobbly moment, my balance settles, and he pats my back before following Aerona through the darkening woods.

The sooner we get there, the sooner we can make a plan to find Ellie.

WE APPROACH A CAMP in disarray. Fae rush here and there, packing up leather tents, loading them into wooden carts and wagons as sheep bleat loudly in the distance. It's the exact opposite of what you'd expect of a camp after dark.

A fae man keeping watch jogs toward us, stopping to speak with Aerona and the others at the head of our group. The fae carrying Owena gently lowers her before joining them.

Aerona says something that, judging by her posture and tone, is likely a curse, and the rest of the fae dash to the camp, joining the mad scramble. She storms after them, leaving Reid, Owena, and me looking at one another before coming to an unspoken agreement that we should follow.

We find her at a campfire near the only tent that isn't being torn down, gesticulating wildly at a taller version of me.

He isn't just taller—it's as if someone took me and straightened all my normal person lines into a brooding face and angular frame.

That must be my brother. It'd be easy to feel inferior if he didn't look on the outside exactly how I feel on the inside.

"What do you mean the plan failed?" Aerona barks at him.

"The queen lives. We had to flee. You should go. You don't want to risk being found with me."

"But we did our part! We have your brother!" She flings her arm in my direction.

His gaze lands on me. There's no joy, no satisfaction, no relief in his expression. He turns away.

"I appreciate everything you've done, Aerona. I do. But you should leave."

Her jaw tightens, fists clenching as if holding back an explosion. It comes out as a sharp exhale from her nostrils. "Goodbye, Taran." She storms off, disappearing into the chaos of the camp.

He slumps as he watches her leave, then turns to us. His somber expression transforms, his green eyes narrowing. Not at me, but Owena. She tenses against my arm, tightening a coil beneath my skin as Taran marches over. I force myself to breathe.

"What is she doing here?"

I step between them. "Hi, I'm Caeo."

Taran glares at Reid, ignoring me entirely. "Why did you bring her?"

"Because I wouldn't come without her," I say, and Taran finally looks at me. *This is so weird.* "You must be my brother. Taran?"

He takes a step back. "What have they told you about me?"

Shit. I attempt to pierce through the tornado of memories rampaging through my mind for what Owena actually said. A loud crash interrupts my thoughts—someone running their cart into a wagon.

Shaking my head, I try to focus. "That our mother had your father killed and is trying to steal your throne. And that you brought Ellie here to convince me to side with you over her."

Taran's eyes widen. "You remember Ellie?"

"Owena broke the curse on me. She's here to break Ellie's."

Multiple emotions flash across Taran's face, too quickly to track. His eyebrows press together as he settles on anger.

"You realize that by bringing her here, not only will our mother be hunting us, but now Ystyr will, too."

My chest tightens. "I didn't think that far ahead. I was a little preoccupied with getting as far away from our psychotic mother as possible."

"And yet you've increased the odds that she'll steal you back by adding to our pursuers and saddling us with a pampered enemy princess!"

"Please don't speak about me as if I'm not standing right here." Owena steps out from behind me, meeting Taran head-on. Despite only coming up to his shoulders, she holds herself with the air of someone who towers over him.

Taran stares down at her, his upper lip curled with distaste. "I am quite aware of your presence."

"Of course you are. You're using it as an excuse to ignore your own failings."

Taran's nostrils flare, channeling our mother. I resist the urge to step back, but Owena continues on, unfazed.

"If our risk of being followed is great enough for everyone here to run for the hills, why are we standing around arguing? Shouldn't we flee as well?"

"We can't," I say. "We have to find Ellie."

Taran's face softens. "Ellie's fine." He glances away. "She's here."

My heart jolts, skipping a beat. "Where?"

"Wait." Reid grabs Taran's arm, his face paling as he searches the darkness around us. "Where's Emlyn?"

Taran lets out a slow exhale before he meets Reid's eyes. "He's in the tent. He took an arrow to the chest."

Reid darts away, already halfway into the tent before I process what was said.

Then it dawns on me.

I glance from the tent back to Taran. "Are he and Emlyn...?"

Taran nods, looking at the ground. "Their healer's seen him. He lost a lot of blood, but since he made it this long, she thinks he'll recover. If infection doesn't take him."

I turn back to the tent. A deep, aching sadness rolls through me for Reid, leaving emptiness behind. He never said anything, but I always assumed part of the reason he threw himself into incanting was to avoid being a third wheel to me and my endless stream of girlfriends. To have finally found someone, and be at risk of losing them so soon...

"Can he be moved?" Owena asks.

Taran sighs. "We got him here, but it was painful. Cadoc said he could spare us a horse, but he needs rest."

My mouth tightens. "Where's Ellie?"

"In the tent. She was getting him comfortable after we pulled the arrow out."

I bolt in that direction, but Taran grabs my arm, stopping me.

"There's something we need to talk about." He lifts his head to my face but doesn't meet my eyes.

I tug my arm free. "Can it wait?" Ellie's so close that my insides are leaping against my skin. I can connect with my brother later.

"No, it can't. It's about Ellie."

That stops me. "What is it?"

Taran closes his eyes, taking a deep breath.

"Caeo?"

I whirl around at the most wonderful sound in the world.

Ellie's voice.

She stands at the entrance of the tent, frozen in place, with all the color draining from her beautiful face.

Chapter 43

Ellie

No. *No, no, no, no, no, no.*

I should've listened. To Taran. To Reid. Every warning, every plea.

But I didn't.

I thought I was helping. That being with Taran would make me matter. Let me fix things.

How could I have been so stupid?

Caeo's face lights up as he bounds toward me. Before I know it, I'm wrapped in his arms. I can't move, can't hug him back. If it weren't for him holding me, I would crumble to the ground.

My next breath catches in my throat. Dreading what I'll find, my eyes seek Taran as Caeo embraces me. Cadoc's people rush by all around us, shouting as they pack up their camp.

There—looking away, at the ground. Defeated.

A blond fae woman in a heavy fur coat stands by the campfire nearby, watching. Her dark eyes narrow as they meet mine.

She knows. I don't know how, but she does.

Caeo takes my face in his hands, bringing it to his. He doesn't kiss me, but presses his forehead against mine, our noses touching. Tears glisten in his eyes.

His blue eyes, glowing brilliantly in the darkness. Unfamiliar, yet perfectly him.

"I found you," he whispers, like so many times before.

"I... I didn't remember you," I choke out. My body shakes uncontrollably.

"It's alright." His fingers burn as they caress my cheek. "I brought someone who can break the curse. She broke it for me."

The fae in the fur coat.

He pulls me into another embrace. Tears stream down my face. I gulp some air, but my lungs don't want it. Not after what I've done.

"Caeo, stop. Please."

He pulls back, his eyes searching my face. The same eyes I fell in love with, despite the change in color.

"What's wrong?"

My throat twists with the words I need to say.

"I didn't remember you, Caeo. I didn't..."

My eyes drift to Taran, squeezing his brow with his hand.

I did this to him. All I wanted was to help. Support him. But all I did was push him into betraying the brother he hoped to save.

Caeo follows my gaze. His grip loosens.

"No..."

He looks back at me, and when I don't respond, *can't* respond... the light in his eyes fractures, his heart shattering into a million pieces.

"No. No." He stumbles backward, his head shaking.

"I'm sorry—I'm so sorry."

I made him promise not to break my heart. Instead, I broke his.

He turns away, charging at Taran.

"What did you do?" Caeo shouts, shoving him. A passing fae carrying a large sack jumps out of the way, narrowly avoiding collision.

Frozen in place, I flinch, reaching toward Taran as the bitter sting of self-hatred pierces my chest.

He staggers away, staying on his feet but keeping his eyes down. Like he wants Caeo's rage. Like he deserves it.

"You knew! That was the entire reason you brought her here. You knew she loved me, but you did it anyway!"

My feet finally move, and I grab Caeo's arm. "It's not his fault! It's mine. He warned me, but I ignored him. I pushed him."

Caeo yanks his arm free, then storms off. I glance at Taran. His palms dig into his brow, his fingers clenching his hair.

"Taran? What's wrong?" I rush to his side, taking his hand and turning his face to mine. His eyes clamp shut. With a violent tug, he yanks himself free of my grasp.

"Are you fucking serious right now?!"

I turn at the sound. Caeo's there, hunched over, breathing heavily. I bring my hands to my chest, clutching them tight.

I have to keep Caeo in sight.

I back away from both of them, far enough that they'd have to run in opposite directions to escape my field of vision. Cadoc's people are mostly gone, the frantic sounds of evacuation disappearing into the darkness.

The fae woman approaches Caeo as he drops to the ground, resting her hand on his back as she speaks to him in hushed tones. Shame burns within me—I should be the one comforting him, not her.

His face is wet with tears, his body trembling as he pulls his knees to his chest. And Taran… He can't look at Caeo, or me, his knuckles white as his fingers clench into his palms.

There's so much to say. To both of them, but I can't. Not without destroying the other.

I hit the earth as my knees buckle. Hugging myself tightly, I gasp for air, my lungs compressed by the weight of my mistakes.

How can I possibly fix this?

My heart twists tighter and tighter. I press my eyes shut.

My breathing slows.

The ache loosens. Cold air prickles my skin.

What's going on? Why am I crying?

With a deep inhale, I open my eyes to the grass in front of me. *How did I get here? Did I fall?*

I was with Emlyn when Reid came in, and it felt intrusive to stay, so I left. Then Taran was upset, and I reached for him, and now... *What happened?*

Holes in my memory. It must be the curse.

Every other time this has happened, I've been mid-conversation with someone. But nobody's talking to me now.

Part of the reason we came here, other than confronting the queen, was for something related to my curse. With everything from before my eyes were closed missing, maybe whatever that was is triggering it visually now?

"Taran?" I call, covering my eyes with my hands and squeezing them shut. "Taran, are you there?"

A broken voice sobs, but I don't recognize it.

"I'm here, Ellie." Taran's voice is close. Wrecked.

"I can't remember what's happening. Is it the curse?"

"It is."

"What should I do?"

"I... I don't know. I don't know what the right thing to do is." His voice wavers as he speaks.

"We have to break the curse," the other voice says. Male.

An icy gust of wind. I sit up straighter, resisting the urge to uncover my eyes. "We can break it? How?"

"Owena, break it, please." Raw desperation edges the voice. Beneath the pain, it sounds strangely familiar. Homey.

A new voice cuts through—female. "I'm not certain that's the best course of action right now."

"What the fuck? That's the whole reason I brought you here."

"Taran?" I reach out blindly as bits of conversation fade away. Finding his hand, I squeeze it tight. "I'm missing something. What is she talking about?"

His arm jerks back, wresting his hand free. "Princess Owena can break your curse, but she doesn't think she should."

"I fully intend to release her from the curse, but right now, she's functioning. We don't have time to break her down and sort through this mess—we need to leave."

My head nods in time with my racing heart. "That makes sense, right? The queen will send someone after us. We don't have time to waste." Taran and Emlyn are in no shape to fight, and after what happened when I incanted... Dread clutches my insides at the idea of doing it again.

"It's not a waste!" another voice cries. Seconds later, someone pulls my hands from my face, gripping them tight.

"Ellie, open your eyes, please."

"Caeo?"

I open my eyes to Caeo's face. Blue eyes, swollen and red, with the tips of fae ears peeking out of his midnight hair. My heart folds in on itself, forming a lump in my throat.

My words burst out with a sob. "I'm so sorry, Caeo. I didn't mean for any of this to happen."

His thumb rubs against my fingers. "Owena can break the curse. We can figure this out."

I look between him and Taran, unsure what to say. Then the fae woman, Owena, catches my gaze. Her eyes, dark as night, widen as she subtly shakes her head.

I swallow. "I don't—"

Owena interrupts. "Please trust me. We should wait until we're somewhere safe, so Ellie can have the time she needs to process everything."

Is that really what's best? This woman's a stranger to me; why should I trust her?

Caeo drops my hands, standing to face her. "No. You need to break it."

She draws herself up as she meets him head-on, unflinching. Firelight flickers hauntingly across her face.

"Not now. Remember how you reacted when I broke yours? We don't have time for Ellie to go through that."

Caeo clenches his fists, his jaw tightening. His words burst out of him.

"Just do it!"

His voice slams into me. Like when Taran bent Merfyn.

A pit opens in my stomach.

Owena spasms, her body going stiff. Her mouth slowly opens, twitching, as if trying to speak, but nothing comes out.

In less than a heartbeat, Taran's on Caeo, tearing him away by his shirt. His words hit even harder than Caeo's.

"Stop it. Release her. Now."

Owena gasps as she tumbles forward. She catches herself on the grassy earth, panting.

My heart pounds. I don't understand—she didn't follow his command. "What just happened?"

Taran flings Caeo's shirt from his grip. "He tried to bend her."

Caeo scowls at him. "What are you talking about? I can't willbend." Half a second later, he grimaces in pain.

His face goes white.

"Yes, you can," Taran says. "But you don't know what you're doing and her will is too strong. You'll only end up hurting her."

"I... No... I can't be..." Caeo drags his fingers down his face. "Fuck."

A weight creeps slowly down my chest. He's not the same person I fell in love with at the Academy. He's a fae prince now, with all the power that comes with it.

 I lean closer to Owena. "Are you alright?"

She nods shakily. "Well enough."

Caeo drops beside her, his hand quaking as he rests it on her shoulder. "I'm sorry, Owena. I didn't mean to—I didn't know I could bend people."

She meets his eyes, a slight smirk forming on her lips. "You'll need to learn to control that."

He takes a deep, trembling breath. "I'm sorry, but I still need—"

Taran cuts him off, the force of his voice hitting hard. "Quiet, Caeo, before you do it again."

Caeo's lips continue to move, but no sound comes out. Panic floods his face as he brings his hands to his mouth, trying again and again, but there's nothing. His eyes widen in horror.

My spine shudders. "Taran, stop it!"

"He could hurt someone."

"And you're hurting him!"

Caeo crumbles to the ground. I scramble over, helping him up. He leans into me, shivering, his eyes frantic.

Taran bends him again, his voice heavy. "You can make noise, Caeo."

He coughs violently, gasping for air.

I pull him close, hugging his head against my breast as he convulses in my arms. "It's alright, Caeo, it's over. You can speak."

Taran stumbles back a few steps, shaking his head. "I didn't... No one's ever reacted like that before."

This doesn't make any sense. I know what it feels like—Taran's bent me twice. Even Merfyn didn't respond like that.

There's something more going on.

Owena shoots Taran a hard look. "Your mother's been bending him ever since she brought him here."

She rests her hand on Caeo's shoulder as I squeeze him tight. I can't imagine what he's been through. But he held on. For me. Only to find out I'd fallen for the brother he never knew he had.

Taran slumps. "I didn't..." he repeats, his voice trailing off. Turning away, he lets out a guttural roar that rips through the air, then buries his face in his hands.

Silence. Then Caeo pushes himself up, wiping his face on his sleeve. With a heavy breath, he slowly lifts his head to Owena. "Can you give us a minute?"

She bites her lip, then nods. Getting to her feet, she takes a few steps away, keeping her distance from Taran. Cadoc's people have all left, the eerie quiet interrupted only by the pops of the campfire.

Caeo reaches out, running his fingers gently along my braids, leftover from earlier. "You look so different, dressed all fae-like."

My heart hiccups between a laugh and a sob. "You, too."

I slide my fingers through his soft hair, and a flicker of warmth stirs at the memory of the last time I did that. It seems like ages ago—like the memory belongs to someone else.

They come to rest atop the pointed tip of his ear.

He's changed. Not just in appearance, but his spirit. During our weeks apart, something shattered him.

No. Not something. Some*one*.

His mother.

This is all her fault.

We may not have ended her reign, but we rescued Caeo. The most important thing right now is to make sure she never comes anywhere near him ever again.

Which means…

"Owena's right," I say, taking Caeo's hand. "We don't have time to break the curse now. We need to get moving before your mother sends anyone after us."

"So I'm just supposed to step aside and watch you share tender moments with my brother?"

His words stab me in the heart, but I bite down with my resolve. "We'll fix this. Once you're safe."

I don't know how, but we will. For Caeo. For Taran. And for me.

Caeo sighs, running his hand through his hair.

Taran steps closer, looking away as he towers above us. "Ellie can help Reid with Emlyn. I'll… keep my distance."

Caeo glares at Taran as he gets to his feet. "Fuck you." Then he storms away, dropping down next to the fire and burying his face in his arms.

I start after him, but Owena stops me with a hand on my shoulder. I keep my eyes on Caeo.

"I'll talk to him," she says. "But we need to leave—now." She turns to Taran. "Do you have a destination in mind? Somewhere we can take Emlyn that's safe?"

Taran's jaw tightens, but he nods. "I do."

"Then Taran will lead the way." Owena looks back at me. "He'll explain that you need to stay with Emlyn and not look back because of your curse. I'll follow with Caeo."

My gut twists in protest, but I know this is the best course of action. Every second we stay here, the greater the risk we'll be found. I can't let that happen, for both Caeo's and Taran's sake. A confrontation would force Taran to willbend, ruining him, and capture would destroy them both.

Owena releases me, heading over to Caeo. She rests a hesitant hand on his shoulder as she sits next to him.

I force myself to look away, following Taran to the tent. He explains that I need to pack up and help Reid get Emlyn ready to travel. To stay in the tent until he returns with a horse.

He averts his gaze as he speaks to me. "It's important. Your curse—what makes you forget—it's still here. You need to keep your eyes where I tell you."

I nod. "I understand."

My memory's blank from the moment I was on the ground, eyes closed as Taran spoke about my curse. Whatever happened after that has left me completely drained, but a quiet flame burns within. I squeeze Taran's hand, seeking comfort; this was supposed to be over by now.

He flinches at my touch, pain flashing across his face. "No, Ellie. It's not the time." He pulls his hand free, the light in his eyes crackling like a raging inferno. "We need to hurry."

"Alright, I'm going." I hesitate, then lift myself onto my toes, giving him a quick kiss on the cheek. He recoils as soon as my lips touch him.

Why is he spurning me? Is it because I incanted?

Someone curses behind me. I turn, curious, but Taran stops me, anguish distorting his face.

"Just go inside. Help Reid."

I let out a deep exhale. I can do that. Once we get Emlyn to safety, we can figure out what's next. We may have failed to stop the queen, but it's not over yet.

I have too much to protect.

Epilogue

Dryfid

I drag my fingers along the balcony railing as I meander toward Esyllt. The massive wall of ice, summoned by that Fallen girl, practically glows in the darkness. Despite the distance, a dreadful chill emanates from it. A cold fury settling deep in my bones.

It was foolish to think Esyllt could handle her children. The only reason this wasn't a complete catastrophe is because she's scarred them so irreparably, they can barely function.

And she cost me my daughter in the process.

Not that it matters much—surely, I'll have another. With luck, the next one won't be so cunning.

Apprehension spiders along my spine. Esyllt's spawn may be foolish wretches, but Owena could be problematic. The curse that binds her is one of my best, but if she somehow finds a way through its loophole... the fallout could be devastating.

Esyllt looks over at my approach, her face twisted in deep-seated anger.

"What do you want?"

I shrug, keeping a casual demeanor. "It would seem you have quite the mess to clean up."

She scoffs. "Taran's proven his cowardice—he doesn't have what it takes to keep his throne from me. And Caeo's practically useless. They're hardly a threat."

"On with the war, then?"

There's no point in waiting any longer. My armies have been gathering at the border while I attended this miserable wedding. They simply await my orders to strike against the Forsaken Lands—if anything, the wedding's disruption and loss of our heirs at the hands of a Fallen could rally the support of the people.

Esyllt's lips curl into a thin, crimson smile as she nods.

Finally. My gaze turns back to the ice wall. Beneath it, a colossal black scar, seething with rage, blights the entire hillside. The Fallen will suffer the ultimate price for their desecrations.

"Then I'll be heading back to Ystyr. Best of luck wrangling your children."

Esyllt raises her brow. "You won't be joining your troops at the front?"

I laugh. "Of course not. Waging war against the Fallen is dreadfully boring. I'll be enjoying it from the comfort of home."

I can barely stand another moment here; it's far too cold, and with my strength diminished from being out of my realm... If Owena *is* plotting a betrayal, it would be best to have my full power. It stings that Esyllt has put me in a position where I even have to worry about that.

"It should only take me a few days to return home by Anwen's Tears. I'll send word to my generals and have this war begun by week's end."

"Then I'll set out for the front tomorrow."

I tilt my head. "Really? You won't wait and see if your soldiers return with your wayward children?"

She presses her mouth into a narrow line. "I've ordered them to kill them both. It doesn't matter if I'm here or not."

No—there's more to it. Her darting eyes betray her.

She's afraid.

If her soldiers fail to kill Taran, her safest option is to put as many of her people between him and her as possible. He's proven he won't risk their lives.

Alas, it does me no good to point that out. So I bid her farewell and retire to my room. Once morning comes, I'll leave this horrible place and return home. After twenty-one long years, we'll continue our vengeance on the Land's behalf.

Surely, She approves.

Acknowledgments

IT'S BEEN A CRAZY YEAR getting this book out of my head and into existence, and it wouldn't have happened without the help and support of many people. It may be cliché, but the idea for this story came to me in a dream—two students falling in love, but who couldn't remember each other when they were apart. And while it evolved significantly from there, the only reason it did was because a few weeks before, my friend Meredith complimented some writing of mine she'd read years ago. That gave me the confidence to try turning a dream into the story you're now halfway through.

Thank you to Marley for your unwavering support as this story consumed my life during the last year, and to Rae—my first reader, first fan, and biggest cheerleader. Thank you to all my critique partners who helped me learn how to write, but especially Jennifer Polack and Chris Redd for sticking through the entire thing.

I'm eternally grateful to my editor, Lindsey, who helped me fix the issues I was struggling with and spotted new ones I was unaware of.

While I'm thankful for all my beta readers who helped make the book better with their feedback and affirmed that this story was worth all the hard work, I have to call out two in particular whose notes helped turn the story into what I originally imagined: Loni Townsend and Victoria Szalay.

And lastly, a thank you to everyone in my author's group who helped support my journey into self-publishing.